VERONICA

Book one in the twisted fate standalone series

BY BILLIE JADE KERMACK

All characters and events in this publication, other than those clearly in the public domain, are fictitious, and any resemblance to actual persons, living or dead, is purely coincidental.

Contact the author at:

bilbo86@hotmail.co.uk

Special thanks to –

Author Stephenson Holt for being the best Alpha reader a girl could ask for. Laura Trujillo, for being my late-night book buddy, you rock lady.

K.C. McMillian and Caron Pescatore – two amazing authors and now close friends that keep me sane whilst chatting all things bookish – love you ladies. I can't thank you both enough for your support.

Only suitable for 18+ due to the nature of the contents.

TRIGGER WARNINGS

Rape

SA

Abortion

Descriptive sex scenes

Vulgar speech

Drink and drug use

Readers Note

Veronica is a friends-lovers contemporary romance with a NON-traditional HEA. If you are looking for a cutesy romance with an ending that will make you feel all warm and cosy, this is probably not the book for you. If you want a slow-burn romance that is both sweet and spicy, that has the ability to make you laugh and cry in equal measures, then strap in for the rollercoaster ride that is this book.

To family and friends, thank you for your support in my journey so far, but this is your warning, there will be graphic sex and a fuck-tonne of foul language from this point on, so feel free not to read any further if it might make Christmas gatherings awkward for you.

Still on board? Ace, I hope you adore Veronica and Aiden's story as much as I enjoyed bringing it to life.

REVIEWS

Please do consider leaving a review, as it helps authors to know whether to write more. The more interest there is in a series, the more likely an author will continue with it before completing other projects.

VERONICA PLAYLIST

Crazy little thing called love – QUEEN

Misery business – PARAMORE

God is a freak – PEACH PRC

First day of my life – BRIGHT EYES

Better friends – ABBY CATES

Be alright – DEAN LEWIS

Wonderboy – TENACIOUS D

Superman - EMINEM

Drainpipe Jane - SINK

Cry to me – SOLOMON BLAKE

Heartbreak anniversary – GIVEON

In the stars – BENSON BOONE

I'm not in love – BER

Groundhog day - EM BEIHOLD

Sultans of swing – DIRE STRAITS

Over my head - FURSLIDE

Dream on – AEROSMITH

7 Years – LUKAS GRAHAM

Please Notice – CHRISTIAN LEAVE

Oldest – BROOKE ALEXX

You and I – INGRID MICHAELSON

Zero feelings – ZOE CLARK

Numb little bug – EM BEIHOLD

Fingers crossed-LAUREN SMITH

Next time – JESSIA

abcdefu - GAYLE

Roll to me – DEL AMITRI

Hot mess – ZOE CLARK

20th century boy – T. REX

What's up? –4 NON-BLONDES

Mandagsbarn – VERONICA MAGGIO

What a shame – LEYLA BLUE

Diet coke – LEANNA FIRESTONE

Unsteady – X AMBASSADORS

Friends to lovers – MELINA KB

Two fingers- JAKE BUGG

Tear in my heart – TWENTY-ONE PILOTS

*F*** yourself-* LEYLA BLUE

House of my soul – LANGHORNE SLIM

Tiny dancer – ELTON JOHN

Fictional Men – PEGGY

Come together – THE BEATLES

Last Request – PAOLO NUTINI

Fictional Men – PEGGY

Bruno Mars – WHEN I WAS YOUR MAN

Love nwantiti - CKAY

This book is for Jim, my other half, a man who has accepted my craziness and supported it.

You are my one – thanks for the support dipshit, and the laughs,

Always grateful for the laughs.

Humour will forever be my love language.

DECEMBER 8TH 2018

7.45 PM

RONI

'Fuck you, fuck whatever this is, and for sure, fuck that!' I spit, lingering on the word *that* as my lip curls up in disgust. My eyes fix on the woman with her legs draped around my boyfriend's waist. I scan around the flat that I had called *home* for the past two years, but the space suddenly feels foreign to me. The bag of greasy fast-food goodies in my hand falls towards the floor; lettuce and cola exploding out onto my battered *Converse* as I try to comprehend the sight before me.

'He already did,' the woman I'll forever refer to as *that* replies cockily with a slick smile that lasts for all of 1.3 seconds. Realising her mistake, she swallows back her confidence as her grin fades, arranging the bed runner that I had purchased around herself so less of her peachy skin is on show. She shrinks back behind my boyfriend's still heavy breathing form like the coward she is, and I gulp in air to steady myself. Little does she know that if I wanted to, not even this gelatinous excuse for a man could stop me from rearranging her build-a-bear-painted face. Who knew Hashtag Whore Barbie was trending for Christmas? The cheap ruby red lipstick smeared across her Botox-infused lips and up his bearded neck makes me shudder. I attempt to make sense of the ungodly episode of animal kingdom that has been playing out in front of me since I entered the flat. But the grunting and uncoordinated slapping of skin I'd silently witnessed before finding my voice only proves to embed the unwanted visuals further into my brain. Is it too much to hope for spontaneous human combustion?

'We love each other,' the gutless bitch snipes, a poor attempt to fill the uncomfortable silence. Her voice breaks before she can finish the sentence.

'Calm down *"Debbie Does Dalston"*, the grown-ups are talking,' I retort sardonically, my feet still glued to the spot. I want nothing more than to run away, but my need to dominate the situation and not appear weak has me tethered in place. I make a mental note to thank my mother for my tenacity; it's a trait we share.

'Jealous much?' *That* smirks, running her bubble-gum pink manicured fingers down my boyfriend's torso. He wisely moves to push her hand away as bile rises in my throat. The sneaky portion of mozzarella sticks I had wolfed down in the car ride over threatening to make an appearance.

'In order for me to be jealous of you, Morgan, it would require that you have something I want. Right now, you are merely helping me shed some dead weight,' I bite back sarcastically as I fight to centre my wayward emotions that threaten to overwhelm my thoughts. I glance up at the mirrored ceiling above us as though viewing the situation from another angle would make it any less horrific. I shake my head to dispel thoughts of them together; what I'd seen from the door had been enough to make me lose my appetite for good.

Watching her wind her finger around the pole-straight blonde extensions framing her face, I note how different we are. My low-maintenance chocolate waves are thrown into a messy bun; my face is without a lick of makeup; remnants of ketchup stain the oversized hoodie I've worn for two days straight. I'm chalk to her cheese.

What had I done to deserve such a crappy boyfriend and an equally crappy sister? My list of things to accomplish before turning thirty has quickly morphed from an episode of *Happy Days* into a rerun of *Luther.* All I have now is a depressing list of my failures and how royally I've fucked up my life by trusting such utter cockwombles.

'Well, Merry-fucking-Christmas to me,' I say lightly, although the tears in my eyes deceive my resolve. I may not be jealous of Morgan, but I am certainly hurt by her decision to betray me. Out of the two of them, her lack of loyalty cuts me the deepest. 'Who knew you had such sticky fingers, Morgan? I didn't know that sharing my toys was still an issue for you,' I press through gritted teeth, running my glare over the man I thought I would spend my forever with.

'Sharing is caring,' Morgan replies thoughtlessly with a sickly-sweet grin. I tear the engagement ring off my finger and throw it at them. My sister, ever the opportunistic princess, grabs for it and scrutinises the stone with beady eyes.

'It's fake. You'll probably get all of £3.50 from it, not even enough to get those pretty lips touched up,' I note, as she palms the worthless piece of metal anyways, just as I knew she would. Morgan has never cared about such simplicities as allegiance and consideration; she's always been fuelled by money and status. Before this moment, they were traits that made her seem quite innocent and naïve. Although looking at her now, I know without a shadow of a doubt, that this bitch knew exactly what she wanted. She knew how to get it, and she didn't care who she had to stomp on to get herself there.

'Roni, you don't understand,' Marcus states, finally joining the conversation, continuing to stay seated on the edge of the bed rather than approach me. I wouldn't be held responsible for what level of *Rocky Balboa* I'd channel when re-arranging his face if he continued to push me.

'Oh no, you don't understand,' I correct him. Stumbling forward, my feet finally obey my brain's instructions to move, and thankfully, I don't fall. 'One day, you are going to look back on this moment and realise what a mistake you've made. I, however, will look back on it fondly. FREEDOM!' I yell, throwing my fisted hand up into the air, all *John Hughesy,* as I make my way over to the wardrobe. I pull out my gym bag, which is practically brand new, as my intentions to attend the gym only lasted for about a week into the new year. I shove my belongings haphazardly into it, making a point to take both iPhone cables just to piss him off. I zone out their heated whispers and continue to pack, purposefully knocking some breakables onto the floor as I go. The petty satisfaction as Marcus flinches and reacts is the only thing that helps me banish my tears.

With scorn fuelling me, I grab a thick black sharpie from his desk and pop off the lid, eyeing my ex- fiancé menacingly. A small smile curves at the corners of my lips as he waits with bated breath for my next move. Our eyes lock as I move to scribble a large penis on the blank white wall behind me, a wall that we've watched a thousand movies on with his projector. I owe my ability to draw such a large rendition of the male genitalia, without glancing at my canvas once, to my best friend Aiden, one of the many talents he has shown me over the years. Still grasping the marker in my tensed-up fist, I make my way across the room. As I reach the chest of drawers, Marcus's eyes widen with fear. Another thing that Aiden has taught me springs to mind. With a steadying breath, I let the hate filling my body seep out of me like oil dancing across water as I knock the glass trophy signed by *Christiano Ronaldo*, Marcus' most prized possession, to the ground with the tip of the marker. The biting ache of anger-filled waves that swim in my belly dissipate; only calm, soft swirls of smugness remain.

'Oopsie,' I say sweetly as he throws his hands to his head in disbelief. Sheer devastation colours his face a pale green. I extend my arm and animatedly drop the pen like a stand-up comedian would a mic.

Never leave angry. Aiden's words ring in my head. Again I smile, not even bothering to watch the carnage unfold as Marcus falls to his knees, scooping the shards of glass up into his hands, his mouth agape with shock.

It may be spiteful; my behaviour is probably tacky at best, but it's most definitely necessary. In those brief moments of hate-filled destruction of property, I regain my power and am now level-headed enough to leave the flat with an amused smile tickling at the corners of my lips. Going all *Banksy* on his walls, all the rebellion with zero of the talent, I finish my splurge of graffiti madness with the scrawled italicised phrase, *Adios Bitches.* Then I make my way to the front door with my filled bag hauled up over my shoulder and one arm laden with anything of value I could grab in my hurry to leave. With the palm of my free hand, I grasp the handle and turn on my heels to take one last look at the studio apartment where I had spent my last two years, suddenly accepting the swift change in direction my life is taking.

With despair as my only ally, I finally allow myself to accept the quiet modicum of calm that is desperate to shock my heart back to life. I don't initially recognise the sense of peace filling me, the *drip drip* of realisation leading me to understand without question now, that my future has far more to offer me than my past ever did.

They don't deserve any more of my time or attention.

As I knew he would, Aiden accepts me with open arms; a glass of wine in one hand and a plate piled high with ketchup-smothered bacon sandwiches in the other; my best friend knows me well.

MARCH 2nd 2019

6:38 PM

3 MONTHS LATER

RONI

'Loving the dress,' Aiden muses, animatedly fanning his face as he alludes to my hotness in the black, leather-corseted mini dress hugging my curves. It's a bold choice for a Friday night piss-up, but it deserves to finally see the light of day. Marcus never approved of it, and that only makes me stand a little taller. Aiden fills the mirror from behind me, all of his six-foot-three broadness occupying the empty space around my curvy size twelve frame. Those childbearing hips my nanna spoke of are really quite flattering when they're wrapped up in skin-tight bindings.

'How was the tattoo session?' he asks, running his finger over the plastic wrap secured with tape on my wrist.

'A needed burst of adrenaline and endorphins were exactly what the doctor ordered,' I reply, twisting my arm to get a better look at the colourful rose permanently etched into my skin, completing my sleeve of artwork. The various pinup designs with interwoven floral pieces are what any disposable income went to after taxes, bills, and wine. It was money well spent. On some level, getting a tattoo has helped heal the trauma from recent events, like a story in pictures wrapped beautifully up my arm, set as a reminder that I was in control of my life.

With a little wax in his palms, Aiden runs his hands through his messy crop of brown curly hair, trying and failing to convince it to stay in place. Bedhead looks so good on this man. He runs his hands down the legs of his blue denim jeans to get rid of any remaining hair product and then returns his blue-grey stare to my reflection. I tug at the hem of my mini dress, setting it in place as it skims my thighs—fighting against the urge to change into a pair of skinny jeans and an oversized jumper and retreat to my room with a copy of Beaches and a pint of ice-cream. I run my fingers through the coils of perfectly primped chocolate waves that fall over my shoulders, noting that I could easily sweep them up into my signature messy bun in two seconds flat if I needed to. Not even a wayward thought gets past my best friend.

'You're going, and that's final,' Aiden breathes in my ear, moving my hair over my shoulder, so it falls down my back. He reads my thoughts perfectly, a superpower he's always possessed when it comes to me.

'So, you're going to get changed at the bar?' I ask his reflection cheekily, successfully changing the subject. He doesn't need to know that he's right. Although hiding away from life in my room is preferred, it is a now-or-never sort of situation, and if there was ever a perfect time to get back on the horse and return to the world of the living, tonight is it. Rubbing some beard oil into the structured mass of stubble on his cheeks and along his jawline, he glares at me. I bat my big, cornflower-blue eyes at him. His jeans and white polo combo are hardly going-out clothes, but then Aiden's manager has just implemented a new uniform for him, and the gossip between the workers has left Aiden with the sneaking suspicion that this change will not be in his favour.

'I'm on duty until ten tonight,' he states. I snigger, not because he'll miss out on the fun, but because I'd been the one to convince his boss that this particular uniform would do great for drink sales, effectively screwing over my best friend in the best way. I still haven't admitted to my part in it, but that doesn't mean that, on some level, Aiden doesn't suspect my involvement. The female employees working with him at the bar couldn't do more for me once they had heard the news; the free cocktails? Those are just a bonus.

'I know you think you are smart, Roni, and you can deny it all you want, but I know you had a hand in this,' he accuses, wagging his finger at me. I hold up my arms, mock naivety bathing my expression.

'The truth will come out eventually,' he adds shrewdly when I don't defend my honour, searching for any hint of deception on my face.

'Nah- ah,' I retort quietly like a three-year-old holding onto a secret. Denying the truth yet again, a small glossy smile on my face is the only chink in my armour.

'Yeah, I know what you look like when you're lying. Karma will hit you at some point,' he claps back, re-adjusting his collar until it lays flat, his pearly whites almost blinding as he graces me with a roguish grin that makes my heart flutter in my chest.

'So, how was your dad today?' I ask him as I dust a light sweep of rouge across my cheeks. It makes sense to get it out of the way, and then we could enjoy the evening, the inevitability of it ruining him later almost a certainty if it isn't addressed. I regret my question almost instantly, though, as his face falls, his smile gone.

'The sperm donor is a prick. Let's just leave it at that.' His mood darkens at the mere mention of his father, and although I know it's coming, it still saddens me to see the light in his eyes disappear.

This has always been a sore subject for Aiden, and with good reason. His dad left when he was six without a backwards glance. He strolled back into his life a year ago with no explanation or offer of a guilt-ridden apology. The reason for his miraculous return is still unknown, but Aiden has more than a few conspiracy theories, namely the fact that he needs money, and Aiden's mother is a bit of a pushover, she lives in Australia but often visits England to manage the properties she has here.

Unlike her son, Aiden's mother has fallen under his father's charm once again, and she's welcomed him back into her life with open arms; his lack of explanation has not phased her in the least. Whenever Aiden visits his mum, he runs the risk of crossing paths with the douchebag; the fact that I could hear him pounding the boxing bag in the downstairs office for an hour this afternoon means that today that path has indeed been crossed.

With another coat of mascara, a flick of black liquid liner on my eyelids, and a pair of gold hoop earrings now secured in place, I'm as ready as I'm ever going to be.

'Cabs going to be ten minutes,' Aiden states as his mobile pings and the message from the cab office lights up his screen. I totter over to the vintage drink cabinet and slide the glass door open, pulling out a bottle of *Apple Sourz*, and waving it and two shot glasses in the air to Aiden. He nods, silently accepting my proposal. Dropping down onto the brown leather sofa, Aiden taps at the space next to him. I make my way over as my absurdly high heels tattoo across the wooden floor until my feet reach the sea-blue shaggy rug. Aiden pours us each a shot, handing me the glass filled with the green, atomic waste-coloured liquid, and holds his up in return to clink them together.

'Let's get this fucking party started.' He grins enthusiastically as we tip back our heads and down the shots in one.

Three shots each and a fifteen-minute cab ride with the driver blasting *Celine Dion* at full whack later, we walk into the bar. Aiden slaps Paul, the bouncer, on the shoulder as we pass, all six foot eight of him almost filling the double door entrance; his wide stature resembling a *WWE* wrestler who could snap me in two with minimal effort. We sit at the bar and grab a drink before Casey arrives, and Aiden has to get changed and start his shift.

'So, new date tonight? Who is he?' Aiden quips, never one to shy away from questions regarding my love life, or lack thereof. Arranging dates at the bar was the safest way to spend an evening, and it meant that if it didn't work out, I was surrounded by friends and wouldn't have to head home alone. But I hadn't arranged a date for tonight. The date I attended last week was more than enough to keep my mind busy.

'Will I be cooking breakfast for three tomorrow morning?' he adds with a grin as he assesses the new paper food menu on the bar top. Little does Aiden know, sleeping with someone hasn't even rated as a bullet point in concerns of my love life. Since the incident with Morgan and Marcus, I hold little hope in a magical happily-ever-after. Sex, for the foreseeable future, is merely an exchange of services to feel anything other than heartache, a way to bypass all my feelings of abandonment. The alcohol also seems to help.

'He *was* Harry, window fitter,' I emphasise to relate news of Harry's departure in between bites of the tuna, mayo-filled, wholewheat sandwich the barmaid has placed in front of me. I don't generally trust food at the bar; Aiden has told me some horror stories, but Jenny's on shift tonight, and she's a good friend. She's also eternally grateful for my intervention with Aiden's new uniform selection, so it feels safe enough, and something has to soak up the bloody shots.

'And,' he presses, stealing a salted crisp off the side of my plate.

'And nothing, that is literally all I know, ohh he had blue eyes. No, green. Maybe?' He could have had yellow eyes, for all I know. I really wasn't paying much attention. He's a filler, someone to heal my broken heart momentarily, a brief distraction to interrupt the mundane.

'How do you not know when he spent the night in your bed?' Aiden asks without a speck of judgement in his tone.

'You've just hit the nail on the head; it was night-time,' I respond, taking another generous bite of my sandwich.

'Ooh, brown!' I chime, making Aiden chuckle as a clearer image of Harry pops into my head.

'I get it; he has eyes with the ability to change according to his mood or current sexually–charged status. Maybe that's his superpower,' he offers.

'Well, his superpower certainly wasn't his aim.' I shudder visibly.

'Oh, dare I ask?'

'You could have renamed him *Justin*,' I say slowly. 'I can't see how manoeuvring something that small makes his job harder. If I had to hear *"oops"* for a third time as he directed it haphazardly towards my arsehole, I'd have to kill him and then myself,' I add as his eyes widen. '*Just in*, get it?'

'No need to elaborate. I got it. Thanks for the visual reference, though. It's appreciated.' He laughs. I lower the fingers I had held out in front of me. The fact that I only use my thumb and forefinger is evidence enough to prove my point.

'And there's you looking for a Mister Seabiscuit,' he states, pride brimming in his eyes, his joke successfully landing. He pops another stolen crisp from off my plate into his mouth, feigning innocence as he holds his hands up between us; a jab at my earlier performance, I assume.

'Awe, look how well you know me. I mean, a girl can dream.' I giggle.

'So, he made it to the list at the back then?' Aiden asks as the barmaid Jenny plonks a packet of crisps down on the bar top beside him. A sweet gesture so that he might stop grazing off my plate. He smiles at her in his thanks, and you can practically see her knickers getting wet. She is seriously hot for my best friend and just plain terrible at trying to hide the fact. She's gone just as quickly as she'd appeared.

'So, back or front?' he queries, his wide eyes needing an answer to his question. I sidestep the obvious joke I could make here as our conversation is already dirty enough and drop my half-eaten sandwich back onto my plate, helping myself to a few of his crisps to prove a point and replenish my stock. He feigns annoyance, which makes me smile. I love cheeky Aiden.

Aiden's never actually seen my little black book, although he is aware of its existence; whether your name makes it into the front or the back is key.

'Yeah, standing tall with the cheaters, undecided gay guys, snorers, and bad kissers at the back.'

'That sounds like a pretty specific list,' he adds.

'What can I say? Three for one night is hardly bringing in royalty and billionaires; it's slim pickings.'

'They can't all be bad,' he states, his head falling to the side in disbelief.

'They aren't all bad. They just aren't all for me,' I press nonchalantly, happy with the decisions that I've made. If something doesn't work, why force it? I'm happy being single, or at least that was the lie I often told myself.

What you wanted to say is that they aren't all bad, but they aren't all you, Aiden, the little voice in my head chimes in, hitting the nail on the head. Her opinion is unwanted, though. I quiet my thoughts and keep my mouth shut on this point, promptly changing the subject. No good can come from it. Falling for my best friend is merely a reaction to Marcus's betrayal, and pursuing it would only ruin what we have. Although, running my tongue down his neck might settle the debate of just how delicious Aiden is.

Stop it, Roni! I mutely chastise myself, crossing my legs to calm the dull ache throbbing at my core. I can tell by his face that he notices the shift in my thoughts, although thankfully, he doesn't know that this particular fantasy involves him. I gulp a mouthful of my drink as the tender ache subsides and school my features as I dare to wistfully survey every inch of his handsome face.

'You remember Drew? Lovely guy, helped me rearrange my wardrobe and gave me a facial,' I say, trying to divert my thoughts before he can read any further into my uneasy expression. I focus, once again, on my sandwich as Aiden reacts to my statement, almost spitting out his mouthful of beer as he fights to muffle his laugh.

'Not that sort of facial, perv,' I say around a lump of tuna, punching him playfully in the shoulder. I hold out my sandwich, and Aiden takes a large bite.

'So, what was the problem with Drew?' he asks as he chews, wiping his mouth with a napkin from behind the bar.

'I didn't have a cock.' My brazen statement throws him off. 'Even though he hadn't yet come to the realisation of his preference for some male-on-male action, I, and pretty much every other person that met him, knew that he was gay, even if drinking my weight in Rum had momentarily masked the truth from me that first night. I am clearly not a guy; therefore, I don't possess the equipment needed to make that relationship excel to the next stage, and pegging has never really been on my list of possible new kinks.'

'Okay, that one I will allow. But there's been others that weren't that bad?'

'I don't know whether *tolerable* should be a positive word to use when trying to find a mate,' I reply as I can see him searching his brain through the list of men he's come across over a cup of coffee on a Friday morning at our house.

'Geoff?' he proposes.

'Stalker,' I quip.

'Jake?'

'Made lion noises when he ejaculated,' I reply, the memory in my mind accompanied by *the Lion King* theme song.

'Oh God, I remember that. I thought you two were making out to a David Attenborough special!' Aiden chuckles, running his hand through his hair, moving it from his forehead. The audible gasp from Jenny doesn't go unnoticed as she watches Aiden, doe-eyed and practically vibrating beneath his watchful gaze. I beam at her. She returns a small smile and shuffles over to a customer at the other end of the bar, her face flushed with embarrassment. I turn back to Aiden.

'Sadly not. Although he did get an A+ for entertainment, I couldn't stop laughing when my mum got those tickets for the *Lion King* at the Palladium for my birthday. The ushers were quick to remind me it wasn't a comedy.' Although we're mid-sex talk, the memory reminds me to call my mum later. I haven't been the best daughter lately where contacting her is concerned, but every conversation ended with her professing my sister's apologies. Apologies, I suspect my mother has created in an attempt to mend our relationship. I'm not falling for it, and her need to fix the relationship between my sister and me only pushes a bigger wedge between us.

'There has to be one that's stuck,' Aiden says, determination heavy in his voice.

'You, you prick. You're literally the only guy that has stayed in my life long enough for me to find out his second name,' I quip.

'That's different. We haven't slept together!' He laughs, cupping my face in his warm hands.

I want to say that a tumble in the sheets with me can be arranged. Hell, here are my knickers! Take me. I want to say it all very quickly before my brain can stop me again, but I know it isn't the time. I know although I often stick my middle finger up at the rules and the unwanted advice of others, on this occasion, there is a very real possibility that I might push Aiden away. I don't know if my heart can ever take saying goodbye to him.

'Ooh, what about that guy, the one with, you know, the one?' Aiden fires a salute at me, the name of *the one* he is referring to stuck on the tip of his tongue. 'He used to shout Nazi chants before he went down on you,' Aiden offers, excitedly slamming his beer down onto the bar.

'Ah, Uri. Or known in most circles as The General,' I say gruffly. 'The only Jewish man I've ever met that ate bacon,' I add, noting the salacious intrigue alight on Aiden's face.

'What circles are these? No, actually, I don't think I want to know,' he chuckles, tugging at the neck of his shirt.

'I remember Uri fondly. Apart from the seriously disturbing sexual predilection, he was a nice guy,' I state.

'A Jewish guy ejaculating, chanting Nazi obscenities while balls deep in a catholic girl and finishing the date with a greasy bacon sandwich doesn't seem the type to adhere to the rules set for him.' Aiden chortles.

'He's a dentist now,' I add. 'Caleb wasn't that bad,' I offer in the same breath, mentally going through the list of men with whom I had danced between the sheets.

'Was he the sniffer?'

'Sniffer?' I arch an eyebrow as I try to compartmentalise whatever memory it was that went with Caleb's name.

'You know the one, that guy that used to smell everything to the point where he looked like he was about to climax,' Aiden adds, his mental image of Caleb a far cry away from mine.

'Why is this conversation so sexually based?' I ask.

'It's not like you're bringing them home for a good game of boggle, is it? The *"sex part"* is implied,' he snorts. I nod in agreement because he isn't wrong.

'I don't remember him sniffing everything. He's actually in the front of my little black book with all the normals.'

'You need to rectify that list. Watching a grown man sniff the entire length of a cucumber to where he was red in the face definitely gives cause for him to scurry onto that last page.'

'I wouldn't mind, but cucumber doesn't really smell of anything,' I quip, furrowing my brows. It's sad when that is the part of Aiden's point that grabs my attention the most.

'Yeah, well, when he did the same thing to Doris, it really made me question whether we should ever drink at "3 for 1" night again. I like my partners with a little spice, and I know you're partial to some excitement in the bedroom.' He winks cheekily. 'But he was a little too freaky,' Aiden adds, physically shuddering.

'Doris, the cat, Doris?' I ask, trying to make sense of Aiden's revelation.

'Yes, Doris the cat. That man must have inhaled fur,' Aiden chortles, his blue-grey eyes wide.

I snigger at the thought, making a note to stroke Doris when we go home, just in case she has PTSD.

'Definitely a back page candidate, for sure,' I agree.

'What about *your* little book?' I prompt Aiden, more than happy to envisage him ploughing forward into someone. Hoping *someone* is me is a moot point at this stage, but having a good imagination isn't a crime.

'Haven't seen that for a while. Louisa has pretty much stamped out my need for a conquest notebook,' he mumbles, drumming his foot on the wooden slat of the barstool he's on.

I knew it wouldn't be long before her name came up in this conversation, but as it always did, it still took me off guard.

'You're in a relationship. You're not dead. I bet Louisa has a bloody book.' My distaste for his girlfriend is impossible to hide, and Aiden runs his palm around the back of his neck, tugging at the little hairs there, his go-to stress reliever.

'It wouldn't surprise me. She modelled in college.' He gazes off into the distance, pride warming his eyes with flecks of amber. My stomach flips uneasily.

'What did she model for, Vagisil?' I try to bite back, jealousy heavy in my tone.

'Be nice!' he teases with a smirk.

'Is Miss Thing due over tonight?' I ask, not really caring what his answer is.

'No, she has yoga,' he replies, placing another crisp in his mouth.

Delighted much? That familiar little voice hums in my head, although to spare Aiden the stress, I direct most of my happiness inwards.

'Of course, she does Yoga,' I utter under my breath, but he catches it.

'Hey, you'd probably like it if you gave it a go.' He knows me way too well to even think for a second that could be true.

'I wouldn't attend a yoga class if you were paying me,' I say as I reach out, balancing on the back legs of my bar stool to grab a napkin from off the table behind us rather than calling over Jenny to replenish the container on the bar. I greet the patrons sitting at the table with a smile and a thumbs up as a way of thanks.

'Nailed it—who needs yoga?' I chime proudly as the front legs hit the floor, and I resume my position opposite Aiden, wiping away the mayonnaise from around my mouth. Although I know I shouldn't, I lean forward and open my mouth to speak. My eyes concentrate on the crumpled napkin, at first, as I war with a question lingering just beyond my parted lips.

'What do you see in her? I mean, besides the double D's.' The question wasn't the same one I had in my head, and it takes us both by surprise. I guess it slipped through unfiltered because, well, I'm genuinely curious, and the two vodka tonics have given me some courage. His honest answer makes me instantly regret my honest question.

'Yes, she has great boobs. That's a given, but there's more to her than that. She's smart.'

'Knowing every celebrity in the top fifty hot men's list is not an adequate reflection of what constitutes someone as smart.'

'She's kind. She loves animals. She cares about the world,' he adds, but it sounds more like a question, as though he needs me to agree.

'Being vegan is cancelled out by the fact that her father owns an abattoir,' I retort.

'She loves me,' he responds without hesitation.

'I hope that's true. You deserve to be happy.' Sincerity smacks me in the face. My ability to speak kindly of his girlfriend is an extremely arduous task that I never fully commit to, but wanting Aiden to be happy comes easy to me.

'She's stuck with me through everything. I can't do all of this alone.' His comment hits me hard, but I don't let the hurt reach my face. I know he didn't say it to upset me.

'All of what?' I ask, shaking out my thoughts. My tone is clipped, and I hate that she knows something about my best friend that I don't.

'Nothing, just, you know, life. She isn't scared by what may appear. She's good with uncertain outcomes.'

Let's welcome Mister Vague to the party, shall we?

'*Star Wars* the next chapter is an uncertain outcome; accidentally dropping acid because you thought it was paracetamol is an uncertain outcome. If you'd believe me when I tell you how awesome you are, you'd quickly realise that being with someone because they are good with *"uncertain outcomes"*—I emphasise my point with air quotes—

'doesn't make them a solid, lifelong relationship choice. She talks to you like crap and treats you like her personal assistant.' I take a much-needed breath, my eyes locked on his, fear and knowing etched on my slack-jawed face. So, who has royally fucked up and let her mouth run away with her? Ding, ding, ding! You've got it – me! I've overstepped the mark by about a mile, and my outburst catches Aiden off guard. His face is no longer carefree. The heat of our interaction blooms like a cancer as his body stiffens uncomfortably at my outburst.

'And I've allowed her to do that. I can't change any of it. I have to see her for the good, even if you can't,' he defends the bitch, and all I can muster for a response at this moment is a nod of my head.

'Are you happy?' I ask him tentatively, knowing that, above all else, I wasn't wrong about that. His happiness is what's most important to me.

But if you really did want him to be happy, why did you even bring it up? You knew sharing your opinion wouldn't end well, the little voice in my head snaps. I don't react to the thought and, instead, wait as Aiden prepares to answer my question.

'I think so, as much as any one person can be. Who knows what happy even is?' The indecision in his voice makes my gut thud furiously inside me.

'There shouldn't be an *"I think."* You should know; life's too short for ifs, buts, and maybes. You need to be with someone who knows your true worth.' I don't mention the fact that I'm the one who truly knows his true worth because he doesn't need me confusing him further. Taking a large swig of his beer, Aiden draws a calming breath and turns to face me, his intent on officially changing the subject clear.

'Is Steve popping by?' he asks as he stands from his bar stool, the change in subject the final nail in the coffin of the conversation we were just having. Steve is Aiden's friend from the gym. Once upon a time, Aiden had played cupid and set us up, which still kills me. He'd passed along his mobile number to me, but mooning after my best friend has made the whole exchange awkward. But here I am, going along with it, anything to ignore what I really want most. I haven't met Steve in person yet; the filthy texts he's been sending me don't really propose anything other than a friends-with-benefits sort of scenario, and whilst I'm game to explore whatever this is, I hope the explicit side of Steve I've already experienced is based on the fact that he's nervous. If nervousness isn't the case, then he's definitely heading into the back of my black book to be immortalised for all eternity. There is simply no excuse for using a scarf and a miniature hat as props in a series of dick pics to a woman you've never met.

Is Steve popping by? My brain repeats Aiden's earlier question, getting my thoughts back on track.

'Apparently so,' I retort. My lack of enthusiasm is clear in my tone. My lip curls in disgust at the mental image of Steve's *Sherlock Holmes-inspired* penis attire that's now unfortunately seared into my frontal lobe. You don't want to know how it held that pipe.

'Work, my boy.' Paulie, Aiden's manager, chortles as he slaps a hand on Aiden's back. I wince as it connects, but Aiden simply smiles down at the round man wearing more gold than *Mr T.*

'How you doing, princess?' Paulie lulls sweetly at me in a fatherly tone. His Lancashire accent is strong tonight as he accepts what I assume isn't his first straight whiskey of the evening from Jenny.

'All's good,' I reply, taking a sip of my drink.

'That's what I like to hear.' He gestures for Aiden to follow him and shuffles between the patrons across the chequered dance floor, greeting his customers with a salty smirk as he does.

'Speak soon, baby,' Aiden says childishly, pulling me from my thoughts and raising his pinky finger at me.

'Not soon enough, dipshit,' I chime back, beaming up at him. He chuckles, as he does every single time I choose such a comical term of endearment. I wrap my pinky finger around his and shake.

The small smile he gifts me with as he walks towards the employees' entrance at the back of the bar riles up the butterflies in my belly. Walking through a gaggle of girls on the dance floor, he flips his hips along to the music, making my insides liquify as I swoon, tethered to the spot. Jenny clearly has the same reaction. Sighing deeply, Jenny rests her elbows on the resin bar top and cups her palms over her cheeks, a pink flush of desire heating her skin.

'He has absolutely no idea how amazing he is,' she says quietly, pouting.

'It's part of his charm,' I state as my core uncoils and calms. The distance between Aiden and I grows further, and neither Jenny nor I can take our eyes off him.

I watch as he makes his way through a door marked "Private" next to the DJ booth. I inwardly slump. Jenny is still basking on "Planet Aiden" as she inadvertently stands up straight and places her hand across her chest. It isn't long, and she clocks me, staring at her.

'I need a lobotomy!' she wails.

'Or a less drastic option; a boyfriend, maybe?' She nods, reaching to pour me another drink before pouring herself a shot from a dusty bottle of bourbon on the shelf above her head. I welcome the offering from Jenny with a broad smile when she places a fresh vodka tonic in front of me. I hand her a twenty-pound note. 'That should cover yours too,' I say.

'Paulie owes me overtime; I'd say it's his round.' She slides my twenty-pound note back across the bar to me. Jenny is clearly an absolute rockstar.

Even without Aiden in close proximity, the thought of him half-naked at breakfast this morning hits me—rippling taut muscles, bronzed skin, ruffled hair, and his sweatpants riding low on his hips. I clench my jaw around the short straw between my teeth. That man has no idea what he does to me. I rearrange myself on my stool, an attempt to dull the vibrating throb at the apex of my thighs that has returned at the mere thought of him. Righting myself the best I can and letting out a cough, I notice Jenny beaming at me knowingly.

'Do you think he knows?' she asks, wiping down the spilt liquids on her side of the bar with a dirty rag.

'Knows what?' I query, although my question is redundant; I know what's coming.

'That you've fallen in love with him?' I don't even attempt to feign mock surprise. Jenny could recognise the expression of longing on my face because it was one that she herself has whenever Aiden is in her company. My need to dispel the truth causes me to snort, and my face contorts into a look of confusion that neither of us believes.

'I doubt it,' I concede as my forehead hits the bar with a thud. I lift my head as Jenny pushes a filled shot glass across the bar towards me. 'Men are never really that observant, Jenny,' I say before downing the shot she places in front of me. Moving to chase it with a long sip of my fruity vodka concoction, thankful that I have alcohol to keep me company while my brain berates me for being an absolute loser. A bald guy across the bar whistles loudly, his chubby fingers filling his mouth as he holds up his empty pint glass, waving it at Jenny expectantly.

'See you later, Roni. My audience awaits.' Jenny dances along the galley-way to the rude patron and relieves him of his glass. A sickly sweet grin spreads over his face as Jenny bends down beside the tills to get him a fresh drink, her ample chest peeking out of the collar of her button-up black t-shirt.

As usual, my "ride-or-die" best friend, Casey, is running late, so I'm left alone with my thoughts to people-watch as everyone around me enjoys their night out. An argument that breaks out near the gentleman's toilets beside the pool table quietens everyone. The DJ lowers the music so he and everyone else can hear the details of the commotion. The sick satisfaction from watching a car crash of a relationship implode wasn't new here. The young woman currently at the wheel in said car crash is wearing a bright orange floor-length sundress, her tanned skin unnaturally brown. Berating the young man opposite her, wagging her little finger at him to show their audience exactly what she thinks of his cock, the crowd behaves as expected, a rush of muffled *oooh's* filling the room. Whatever it is that he responds with, I can't hear, but I do catch the tail end of the slaps she peppers over his face as anger consumes her. Cowering in a blue button-down shirt and jeans with his black hair lank and falling across his face, he takes the hits, but everyone has their breaking point. He jumps to his feet and doesn't hesitate as he smashes his beer bottle against the corner of the pool table, shattering the green glass, so just a jagged stump is visible in his hand. With his other hand, he grabs for the woman's throat, his eyes alight with fury, and his fingers tightly squeeze around the woman's neck until her face turns red.

I'm up and off my stool, ready to run towards them, but stop dead when I see Paul, the bouncer, kitted out in a black swat vest with the word SECURITY emblazed in reflective yellow across the back, move to lift the man up and away from the woman as though he weighs little more than a wooden chair. I'm lost in the moment; the room around me is silent as my memories threaten to attack.

'Roni, you okay, hun?' Jenny asks, pulling me from my wayward thoughts. The music returns to normal, and the mood in the bar shifts again to an easy-going vibe as the woman in the sundress continues to drink with her friends, visibly rattled but otherwise okay, as she yells over to the barman closest to her for a bottle of pink fizz.

'All good, thanks,' I reply, but my voice falters. My attempt at nonchalance fails epically, but Jenny doesn't push me and warily makes her way to the other end of the bar to continue working as I offer her a small smile.

I wasn't all good, though. The practised lie I had told Jenny was a response triggered by the fear of those memories of that night. The confrontation had jogged something in me; it was a cruel reminder that I, too, was once held by my throat at the mercy of an evil man. I didn't realise it, but I'm still standing, and my legs are tight from my stance, my calf muscles aching. I had prepared to run and protect the woman in the orange sundress, my body engaging before my brain could offer an opinion. Gulping down a hurried breath, I unsteadily sit back down on my stool and bring my drink to my lips, needing to dampen the fire licking at my throat. Over the years, I've successfully managed to file away my rape and torture at the hands of that creep, storing it alongside all the other fucked up situations I've encountered in my lifetime, locking it away in my memory palace under the title, *"Shit that I wished had never happened".*

Any thoughts of that night, however soaked in Rohypnol they may be, are nestled between the time I had my hair cut and styled into a harsh platinum blonde bob, which made me look like a ten-year-old-boy, and the time Timothy Nickels conned me into giving him a blow job in the corner of a packed club during Mardi Gras. I had accidentally ingested MDMA, so I don't blame myself too harshly for that; apparently, skittles are a completely different shape. Who knew? All my poor choices and scary encounters are locked up in the deepest darkest part of my brain, and having them stowed away allows me to move forward with my life. They may pop up uninvited every once in a while, like a long-distance family member at Christmas, but on the whole, I manage to keep them at bay, momentarily silencing them to keep my head straight. I refuse to give that deviant who stole something from me that was not his to take any more active brain space. He can linger there in the bleakest depths of my memories but forgetting completely is impossible. He deserves nothing more than a slow torturous death, and the only tangible hope I wish for is that Karma is a petty bitch who will gladly let me witness it.

MARCH 2nd 2019

7.29 PM

RONI

I see you, Misses,' Casey sings as I wallow in my daydream, her pert arse occupying the bar stool next to me as she waves excitedly at Jenny. All five-foot-two of one of my oldest friends is as stunning as always. Her soft brown skin is flawless; her pillar-box red hair cut short and choppy on her head, and her nineties-inspired look of wide-leg jeans and a cropped t-shirt is effortlessly chic. Casey can pull off any look, and her confidence has a personality that will grab you all on its own. I shake free of my fears, and as I've expertly practised, I visibly return to the easy-going, happy Roni that I'd been ten minutes before I sank into my dark place. Although, I can no longer hear a word my friend is saying as I try to right myself in the moment. Casey snaps her fingers in my face to get my attention as Jenny tentatively approaches us with a similar slack-jawed expression to match my own, some of the beer in the glass in her hand slipping out onto the floor. But who could blame us? Aiden's exquisite bare chest is now the only thing in my line of vision, and as she glances over her shoulder, even Casey can't help but lick her lips appreciatively.

'Damn!' she utters under her breath, and Jenny and I nod silently in agreement. If ever someone described sexually hungry women in the dictionary, a photo of our faces right now would be found there—the only explanation needed as I wipe the drool from the corner of my mouth with my thumb.

'Well damn, that boy has no business being that fine,' Casey says, seconding my thought as she purses her lips and observes Aiden as he crosses the room, a path of sex-hungry women fawning over him in his wake. Jenny and I once again nod silently in agreement with her statement. Our collective sighs of appreciation take us by surprise, pulling us from the spell he can't possibly even realise he has us under.

'When you're home, why don't you just walk out of the bathroom wearing nothing but a smile and a freshly waxed beaver? That's bound to get his attention,' Casey asks me with a cheeky half-smile that doesn't reach her eyes, as though anyone in the vicinity believed I was that brave. I'll let you in on a little secret. They didn't, and I'm not. Casey knows too well the extent of my feelings for Aiden and, as any good friend would, she keeps my secret close to her chest. She also adores teasing me. Like any good friend would.

'Calling it a "beaver" doesn't make it any cuter, bald or otherwise.' I laugh. I try but fail to shake the image. 'The sweaty red mess I encompass when I get out of the shower is neither sexy nor a turn-on—flushed cheeks with remnants of mascara that my makeup wipes failed to remove caked around my eyes. My hair is limp and soggy, running down my back, and to top it off, my now bare beaver is scared shitless as the cold air slaps at it. You need better advice,' I chortle, my outburst 100% the truth. Casey stifles a laugh, her fingers twiddling with the large gold hoops hanging from her earlobes. Jenny places a tall glass filled with a rum and ginger ale concoction that smells bloody awful on the bar, almost spilling it all over Casey as she falters. Jenny can't seem to keep her wandering stare away from my best friend as he politely fights off the sea of women who have congregated around him.

I know how you feel, sister, my knowing little inner voice seconds.

'You need a better sense of self. You're a stunner! An eight even on your worst day,' Casey chimes in, taking a long sip of her questionable beverage. This is coming from the woman who saw me with a nasty case of food poisoning, where I had diarrhoea and projectile vomiting simultaneously. This is a compliment of epic proportions.

'So, what is your plan?' she asks, edging her stool closer to me. My eyes continue dancing over Aiden's form as he animatedly converses with a table of young women joyously celebrating a hen-do near the bar's entrance. The inflatable willy propped up behind them, and their choice of cock-embellished straws are a dead giveaway as to their festivities. The woman with numerous plastic Mardi-gras beads draped around her neck and a cheap party shop imitation veil on her head would likely be the bride; if she continues to stroke her hands across Aiden's smooth abs, I can't be sure just how primal my reaction might be. Sensing my frustrations, Casey runs her hand along my brightly coloured tattooed forearm that rests on the bar between us, pulling at the fraying edge of the plastic guarding my latest addition, so the tape pinches my skin as it lifts. My knuckles are white as I grip the wooden edge of the bar fiercely. I jolt slightly as she pulls me from my dark thoughts, the crippling jealousy I feel still thrumming at my core.

'I may not know much about men, seeing as I play for team les-B-friends, but I'm still fairly sure Aiden and I have one thing in common: naked women are always firstly appreciated and secondly welcomed. Give the dog a bone... if you know what I mean,' she coos, winking at me, nudging her elbow into my ribs.

'I get your point, however cleverly encrypted it is. Rain Man has nothing on you,' I tease.

'Okay, so, word puzzles aren't my thing,' she bites back, taking another sip of her drink, her face no longer screwed up in disgust as her palate adjusts to the coppery taste.

'I'm intrigued to know what your thing is because compassion clearly also isn't one of them,' I snipe with a laugh.

'Hey, I care. I'm just more of a doer than you are. I like to grab the bull by the horns,' she grunts, mock-grabbing an invisible set of horns, her face pulling shapes I've never seen before.

'Another euphemism?' I ask, chuckling. She smiles broadly, readjusting her crop top to cover the blue lacey bra poking out from the bottom of the distressed white material.

'I am good at three things confidently, Roni, and I'm cool with that,' she replies proudly.

'I dread to ask, but I feel like I need to....'

'Eating, drinking, and...' she interrupts me, pausing briefly as the third point she has in mind causes a slight sneer to play at the corners of her full, glossy red lips.

'And?' I press with a laugh, sure that I already know what she's going to say but playing her game, anyway.

'All things "beaver" related,' she retorts with a wink, beaming as I slap at her hand playfully.

'I can't take you anywhere,' I say, as I use the plastic straw to stir the ice cubes in my teal-coloured cocktail, the clinking as they hit the glass reminiscent of the sounds coming from someone plucking at the strings of an electric guitar. Seven PM to eight PM is "buy one, get one free" on cocktails, and I've never been one to waste money or miss an opportunity. Fortunately for me, I've never had to drink alone, and Casey never needs much convincing where drinking is concerned. Baby Shower – alcohol, wedding – alcohol, her niece's swim meet – surprisingly half a bottle of *Jack Daniels*. Casey is anything but predictable but suffice to say, if a good time is to be had and there is a decent amount of drink involved, she's in.

'If I'm the cause of the dam breaking, and I'll have you know I currently have a one hundred per cent success rate, I'll proudly adopt the "beaver whisperer" name. I take my calling very seriously,' she muses around a sip of my blue lagoon cocktail.

'We have wildly veered off track here,' I note, silently begging her to stop any future desire to use any and all analogies that would allude to "beavers" and just how wet she could make them.

Smiling broadly, that little playful glint alight in her hazel brown eyes, she grabs my hand. Seductively running her tongue over the back of my hand, she continues to empty a line of salt in its wake. Licking my hand for a second time to clear it of the salt path, she follows it up by throwing back the tequila shot sitting in front of her and grasps a wedge of lemon tightly between her clenched teeth. Her eyes close as her jaw tenses, the liquid at war with her gag reflex. It doesn't take long for the sting of sharp citrus to cool the rage of heat the tequila has burned along the soft tissue of her throat; it is something I recognise as her expression softens. She coughs a little, running her ring-clad fingers over the spikes of cherry-red hair slicked into place around her hairline.

'Damn, that's good. Your turn,' she presses, nudging a small orange plastic shot cup towards me. Edging it across the bar as she widens her eyes beneath her fluttering lashes when I don't immediately take hold of it and knock it back. When she is close enough, I grab her hand and repeat the line of salt procedure, running my tongue over her flawless, malty brown skin. I down the offered shot and snatch a lemon wedge from the bowl on the bar between us. My sensitive gag reflex powers forward at the intrusion of the strong liquor, almost forcing me to spit it back out. It has always reminded me more of distilled engine fluid. My mumbling stomach protests at the overpowering offering that's sure to tip me over the edge of tipsy and well on my way to pissing in a bush on the way home. When you are drunk enough and need to wee, anywhere and everywhere is a viable toilet option; a collection of short stories I will save for another time, perhaps.

Our little show hasn't gone unnoticed. The slew of men with their gazes fixed on us from the other end of the bar makes Casey laugh heartily. In response to our audience, Casey trails her henna-decorated, lithe fingers up my bare arm, her long, red-manicured nails painting invisible circles on my skin as though she's playing ring-around-the-roses on my palm—*one-step, two-step, tickly under there*—but she pulls her hand away. As she reaches the crook of my elbow, she chooses to push a curl of my hair over my shoulder. The guy closest to our little show lets out an audible groan that seems to shock him as much as us as he grabs his glass and hops down from his stool. I watch as he retreats sheepishly to the other side of the bar, embarrassment colouring his expression pink.

I note the thrum at my core that her move stirs in me as she dances her fingers over my skin, but it is a one on the turned-on scale compared to what Aiden does to me. I see the pride in Casey's bright face as she reads me a little too well. We both know she's the queen of the Beaver because, as someone firmly placed in team sausage, I can't deny that I've been affected by her powers.

'Welcome to the dark side,' she coos wickedly into my ear, fixing the imaginary crown atop her head as she sits back in her seat. Rolling out my arm and bending forward as though I'm meeting royalty, I move to take another sip of my cocktail, hoping the sweet raspberry liquor will flush the taste of the tequila from my mouth. The sight of my friend motioning to Aiden encourages him to come over to where we're sitting. I swallow hard. With the alcohol, the shot, and the many different drinks beforehand, I'm armed with a sense of bravery that I have no right wielding. My composure is laughable at best.

'Ever heard of the term "loose lips sink chips?"' I fumble my words.

It's Ships, Dickhead! the little voice in my head offers as it fights from beneath the haziness to be heard. Her lack of confidence in my ability to string together a sentence is not a good sign. Casey tips her head at me; an *'are you seriously that smashed?'* expression painted onto her face. I take in a needed glug of air, a poor attempt to clear my mind and keep the drunkenness at bay, as I follow Casey to a tall table flanked by high-backed wooden stools. The bar has grown busier and propping up the counter is no longer wise. Fighting to hear yourself think once the masses descend on the bar is hard enough, let alone trying to keep up with a conversation.

'So, what are we chatting about?' Aiden asks cheerfully as he pulls up a stool to sit between Casey and me. The tubes of tawny-coloured alcoholic shots secured in a band around his taut bare chest clink against the edge of the table as he adjusts his eye-watering tight khaki shorts at the crotch. The unmistakable aroma of sex-deprived pheromones clings to my handsome friend's skin; the mixture of his woody aftershave and the mild addition of a subtle sweat scent makes my hormones dance wildly at my core, eradicating any thoughts of the other women in the bar who have been draped across his steely chest. As I knew it would, that almost mesmerising "v" that defines the base of his waist steals away any composure I've previously been able to salvage. This man reduces me to a gooey mess on an ordinary day. But place him half naked with his boyish grin wide and a sheen of perspiration coating his muscled shoulders, and me being about ten units over the drink-drive limit, I'm sure to say something I shouldn't. The fact that my knickers are damp, and my inability to form a sentence since he's joined our table is close to becoming group knowledge as I squirm in my seat, I fight back the silly girlish words that flitter around in my head. Casey coughs to pull his attention away from me. She knows women and knows only too well the inner workings of my brain. I mouth a silent "thank you" as I regain my composure, crossing my legs to silence the throbbing need for him that pulses at the apex of my thighs and hold my glass with a mock sense of strength.

So, what are we chatting about? was Aiden's question. Trust Casey to demolish all my hard work with her response.

'Chatting about all things *"beavers"* in their natural habitat,' Casey says coolly, trying and failing to mask her mischievous smile as my cheeks flush pink and my composure disintegrates into confetti at my feet.

'Casey!' I chastise. Her answer to his question shocks me enough to drag my stare away from Aiden. She looks at me wide-eyed and unapologetically. Aiden's confused stare dances between us as he waits for the information we're clearly keeping from him.

'Beavers?' he asks, his eyebrows raised; the look of confusion now etched a little stronger into the lines on his forehead.

'Yeah, nature and stuff,' I press through gritted teeth, still glaring at Casey, trying to use my face to silently order her to keep her tequila-riddled mouth closed. Thankfully, my ability to shut her down with one look is still as strong as ever. With my skill to manage awkward situations a step or two behind its usual tenacity, I jump down from my stool and pull Aiden by the wrist, dragging him calmly away from the table when I hear Casey mention *'the world's largest snakes.'* Nothing good could come from this conversation. I know exactly where she is taking it, and I refuse to allow it. She thought *David Attenborough* was a channel five weatherman, which proves just how little knowledge she has of the animal kingdom. She taps her long, red, manicured nails against her glass and chuckles, enjoying the rise she is getting from me a little too much.

'Love you!' she bellows from behind us as we make our way around to the other side of the bar. I can't help but mirror her smile as I manoeuvre around the patrons filling the dance floor, my hand falling from Aiden's wrist as he takes my hand in his. The movement stops me in my tracks as sparks of electricity fly up my arm. Glancing back at Casey—Aiden is now walking ahead of me, pulling me across the dancefloor—I notice that she already has a new friend who's taken my seat at the bar. Even at this distance, I can tell Casey has already secured an evening with the slender young woman with the sharp black bob hairstyle. The invisible cord of mutual affection is ricocheting between their bodies. Black bob fiddles with the gold bangles around Casey's wrist; Casey's deft fingers stroking lightly up the girl's arm as a countermove. I hold eye contact with my friend as she ducks down to take a sip of her whiskey on the rocks, her free hand painting invisible circles on her companion's jean-clad thigh. If the amused grin she is throwing my way is anything to go by Casey will be otherwise engaged for the rest of the evening, which is okay with me now that Aiden has officially finished his night shift. Casey's short sleeve crop top and denim jeans combo is a relaxed choice for a Saturday night, but with her washboard stomach and her voluptuous hips, she's never short of attention. She may have been a beaver fan exclusively since she was seventeen years old, but that doesn't seem to stop her from grabbing the attention of quite a few snakes; pretending on occasion that I'm her wife is one of my favourite pastimes and one that benefited us both regularly. The fact that I'm deeply in love with my roommate, and she heaves every time a guy hits on her, means this little arrangement with Casey has worked out perfectly for us both.

Casey nods towards me with a proud smile, as though what she has done to me and what this woman is now doing to her is an unspoken tactic that could literally light a fire in your belly. The pinch of desire I had for Aiden sparks back to life as I smile over at my friend. She truly is a Queen, and although I can't yet see the future she envisages for Aiden and me, I like to wallow in the dream of it, regardless. Grateful for her input.

MARCH 2nd 2019

10 PM

RONI

Aiden beams down at me as he proceeds to swallow his second tequila shot of the night, ramming a wedge of lemon between his teeth, his smirk still very much present as the burning liquid makes its way down his throat. His gag reflex is at war as it tries to dispel the unwanted offering, his lips pursed as the citrus zing of sensations contorts his features.

'What have I told you? You are not and will never be a tequila man,' I half-heartedly scold him, my hand rising to his chest, instinctively pushing him back playfully. This move would be a natural occurrence except for the fact that he is half naked, and my palm rests there for a little longer than it should. Ever the gentleman, he pretends he hasn't noticed my lingering touch and although I know I shouldn't, I'm not quick to remove it.

'I am literally "THE tequila man,"' he suggests, pointing at his half-naked body that now has a new shot dispenser filled with individual red shot glasses strapped like an army belt across his torso. With a matching black leather belt around his waist that holds three large bottles of the bar's finest tequila, he is certainly dressed to impress, the women at the next table, enthralled by my best friend and his lack of attire, are proof of it, their tongues darting out to wet their lips as they gossip excitedly; four sets of bloodshot eyes ready to tear the scraps of leather from Aiden's stacked frame as they gape at him hungrily. Oblivious to his admirers, Aiden adjusts the strap across his shoulder as the material chafes against his skin. 'While we're on the subject Roni, if I shouldn't drink them, then why the hell are you buying them for me?' he asks, slurring a little as the alcohol takes effect.

'You get off in what? Fifteen minutes? You need to catch up.' I smile brazenly, holding up the three gin and tonics I've acquired from generous, but not suitable, strangers who have approached me, armed with pickup lines about as dodgy as a six-pound note. Free alcohol is usually my favourite kind, but I stopped accepting drinks from strangers a long time ago, so even as I flash my wares at Aiden, I know I won't be drinking them. I can't wait for my wingman to finish work and get our Friday night going. I'm also not completely against him keeping his uniform on once his shift is over, but the likelihood of that happening is slim. Mental images for the wank bank would have to suffice.

'So, Steve is a hard pass then?' Aiden asks as he exchanges a shot for cash with a balding man who only wears one shoe. Steve had made his way to the bar earlier, and for the whole forty-eight minutes that we spoke, he referred to his cock a record number of twenty-six times. I should have trusted my gut.

'Without a doubt. When did it become customary to grab a woman's boob without permission on the first date?' Anger pierces Aiden's normally carefree expression; his eyes filled with a murky darkness as he processes what I've said.

Protective or what? I can't lie; the thought pleases me to no end, but I don't want Aiden getting into trouble on my behalf, so I attempt to placate him.

'I've had worse nights.' I giggle, but it does nothing to settle him.

'I'm going to kill him,' Aiden seethes, his eyes forming slits as he scans the room for Steve and his roaming hands.

'No need. I squeezed his junk to the point that he was crying. He hobbled out of here with his tail between his legs over an hour ago. I doubt you will be seeing him at the gym anymore, and hopefully, he will think first before grabbing at another woman,' I say proudly. 'But thanks for having my corner,' I add, wanting to pull him in for a hug but not trusting myself to keep it PG, so I keep my distance. Intoxicated Roni has far less resolve than sober Roni.

'You are amazing, Roni, do you know that?' he states, all anger now replaced with wonder. He shakes his head, brown curls falling over his forehead as he stifles a small bark of a laugh. His compliment stills my heart from beating briefly; a warmth radiates from it as I gawk up at my best friend, respect brimming from his grey-blue stare. He runs his thumb and forefinger over his bottom lip, and the simple move has my composure slipping a little, the beginnings of an epic swoon threatening to fill the air between us as my eyes inquisitively follow the path of his fingers.

What would those lips of his feel like running down my neck, up my thigh, on my...?

'Roni,' Aiden dips his face towards mine, fighting to be heard over the loud music, looking at me expectantly as though it isn't the first time he has tried to get my attention. I am pulled from my x-rated thoughts, but the redolence of every dirty and depraved thing those lips of his could do to me still lingers between us, as though they are physical wisps of energy that I can reach out and touch if I wanted to. 'Roni.' He chuckles.

I bounce a little on the spot, trying to shake the vibrations that rocket through my belly when my name falls from his full lips for a second time. I smile awkwardly up at Aiden and edge back into my seat. My cool and calm exterior is the complete opposite of the bare-knuckle boxing match going on between my libido and my sense of better judgement that are warring inside my body. My hands fiddle nervously with the straw in my glass as I sit eerily still, my back ruler straight. With my lacy thong damp, a head full of sweat-soaked scenarios and a needy groan threatening to fall from my lips, I cover one knee with the other, the friction between my legs almost unbearable with the move. In a moment of clarity, I watch dopily as my friend continues to talk, and I silently question just how long I can keep this act up. My need to put my hands anywhere but on my best friend is a must if I'm going to contain my urges.

'I see Jonsey has made an appearance,' Aiden says, glancing over my shoulder. Jonsey was a friend, at most. I'd never even thought about sleeping with him if I'm honest; he wasn't really my type, but after the shit show of meeting Steve, my month of celibacy, and the scorching sensation of desire burning at my core for a man that could never be mine, I may just consider it. Reading me perfectly as he always did, Aiden laughs; the gruff melodic sound has me rearranging my legs, my attention now squarely his again.

'He's easy on the eye, has good hygiene, owns his own car, and doesn't live with his mother,' Aiden offers.

'All fantastic selling points, but I don't think so,' I say softly, the words getting stuck in my throat as I find Jonsey's mop of blonde hair in the centre of the dancefloor, a minuscule brunette running her hands up his forearms. I don't miss the stab of hurt in my chest at the idea of Aiden trying to set me up.

'They can't all be that bad?' he muses, an eyebrow raised as I consider his question.

Surely, there is a rule book where it's noted that you should never talk about ex-boyfriends, or in my case, ex-bed-buddies, with a guy you like? The problem is, I'm in that catch-twenty-two, a grey area of the friend zone; sharing the gossip with your best friend trumps holding back the story because you secretly want to shag your best friend, marry him one day, and potentially have all his babies.

'Maybe you're just off with your rating system,' Aiden adds.

'They attend the audition. It's not my fault they never get a call-back,' I reply, knowing there are zero problems with my rating system. If I could patent my system, I would be a multi-millionaire by now.

'So, is Jonsey auditioning tonight?' Aiden asks before he downs another shot. A spark of jealousy dims his blue-grey eyes momentarily, or at least what I think could be jealousy. I shrug away the hope building in my chest, begging my heart to slow its pace, convinced that even over the music blaring around the bar, Aiden can hear it as it thumps wildly against my ribs.

'You never know. It's not like I'm planning on marrying the guy. Where does it say a girl can't have some fun?'

'The bible,' he retorts quickly. Against my earlier advice, he slams back yet another shot. This man is clearly on a mission. 'So, tell me the game plan; feel free to leave out all the saucy stuff,' he presses, his usually confident gaze faltering as though he instantly regrets what he has said.

'Fun, fun, fun. At this point, that's all I have in mind.' Any man I met would always be a filler for the person I wanted but could never have. I limited myself to one guy a month to take home, sure I'd have dates in-between, but they never amounted to anything. I never really went back for seconds and always used protection without fail. I live a life that most probably wouldn't agree with, but then I don't much care what others think, anyway. I have a sister who thought it was okay to sleep with my fiancé, a mother who can never remember my birthday, and a dad who went out for cigarettes one day and never came back. Although I can't really blame my dad for that last one, I don't think getting ploughed into by a ten-tonne truck delivering ladies' menstrual products was on his list of to-dos that day. Life's too short to worry about how people see me.

'Wasn't it you that told me everything leads somewhere, that the people we meet change our life course?' Aiden's tone is mocking as he attempts to mimic my voice, his hands floating around enthusiastically in mid-air, like one of those dancing fabric shapes attached to a wind machine holding up signs for the local car dealership. Or alerting you to the tastiest 99p wings in town that can be found at some dive bar at the next turning.

'Firstly, I don't wave my hands around like that when I'm chatting. Secondly, that was wardrobe talk. I have expressively pointed out to you that what is said in the wardrobe stays in the wardrobe!' My tone is stern, but my playful grin is quick to let me down, as it does every time, without fail. Aiden has a way of demolishing any guards I may try to put in place, and the cheeky sod knows it.

'So, *this* is happening then with Mr Loves himself?' he barks pointedly, emphasising the word *this*, his eyes running up and down my leather-clad body. He pours me a tequila shot and silently orders me to lick my hand as he holds out the saltshaker. I place my drink down, a fresh one

Jenny hadn't long ago deposited in front of me, onto the tall round table between us and do as I'm told, wishing briefly that he had asked me to lick the offering off his hand. I wordlessly berate myself, pushing such thoughts to the back of my mind; it is tiring as hell, and sometimes it makes me feel like I have a split personality disorder when I force myself to keep such a big part of myself a secret from him. Still, a girl has to do what a girl has to do sometimes, and pouring out my feelings would do neither of us any favours.

'If by *this* you mean letting him buy me a drink, some light chit chat, and possibly some over-the-top fondling in the cab ride home, then yes – *this* is most certainly happening.' My use of air quotes to enforce my point has the layer of salt on my hand falling to the floor. Without thinking, I re-lick my hand – the remaining salt still stuck to the spot sets my teeth on edge, sucking all the moisture from my lips. I grab for the shot of tequila in his hand, throw my head back, and down it in one quick motion, slurping on the lemon wedge he holds out in front of my face to conclude the ritual.

'He's got a bigger rack than you, so make sure he knows who's meant to be fondling who, won't you?' Aiden mocks, attempting but failing to straighten his face when he catches sight of my unamused expression.

'They are pecs,' I whine in protest, but on some level, I know he is right. Jonsey has a fondness for tight short sleeve shirts. Not a lot is left to the imagination, and at just the right angle, he could easily pass for a c-cup. But I'm not about to admit that to Aiden. What fun would that be? The irony of Aiden standing here before me half naked, his moulded chest rippled where it should be, polished steel plates to the touch, is a fact that is not lost on me. As though the universe has read my mind and is feeling spunky, it sends a strange woman, well on her way to complete inebriation, past us, her purple-polished fingers rubbing suggestively over Aiden's chest. Her wedding ring catches the strobe lights from above the dance floor just as she blurts an out-of-key purr into his ear, her eyes firmly fixed on the back end of his tight shorts as she stumbles her way over to the bar on unsteady legs.

'Who wears short shorts' I sing, making him smile broadly.

'Well, it certainly isn't Jonsey. Pretty sure he completely missed leg day at the gym. He puts new meaning to the term top heavy.' If I blinked, I would have missed it, but now I am sure I recognise the green tinge of jealousy on his face. 'Just make sure you know where he's been. I wouldn't put anything past him,' Aiden adds before turning and retreating towards a table of rowdy women all wearing feather boas, L plates, and sparkly crowns with mini penises attached to springs protruding from the top, all demanding his tequila-pouring services as they chant *'hot stuff'* in unison. With three bridal parties tonight, he is certainly swimming in tips.

'Hey, you should have taken that advice during that incident with Shelly Moray and that plucked yellow bath duck!' I yell at him across the room at full volume, trying to make the words fly above the deep baseline of the *Fat Boy Slim* track now blaring through the floor-to-ceiling speakers beside me as Aiden strolls away smugly. His bad boy persona, fixed like a mask to his chiselled features, melts away. It is clear he has heard me when he swings around on his army boot-clad heels to face me, his eyes wide, his mouth slack.

That will teach you, I say inwardly, his wardrobe admission now out in the open. The fact that no one has a clue what I am talking about at least keeps it an insider joke. What my triumphant brain is failing to register, though, is that the beat had dropped almost serendipitously to change tracks and everyone filling the bar between us, and quite possibly a few patrons using the downstairs toilets, have heard a muffled *'plucked'* and a very clear *'yellow bath duck',* leaving their intoxicated brains to conclude that the half-naked Aiden in front of them did something very questionable with a poor defenceless rubber ducky. Without realising it, at least four vodkas, two cocktails, an Apple

Sourz, and the subsequent four tequila shots have quite possibly chased away my ability to appropriately gauge a situation like an adult.

'WARDROBE!' he bellows in response, his neck tight, jaw flexed. My natural response is to cackle without hesitation, even when I catch sight of Shelly Moray's glare as it heats my face from a few meters away as she hands a strawberry Daiquiri to a customer. My drunken state had also caused me to forget that Shelly still worked at this bar. Being within spitting distance, she has heard her name and clearly isn't too happy about it. Aiden's boss Paulie, who is drying out pint glasses behind the bar with a rag, can't contain himself, unable to hold back a roaring chuckle, the boom recognisable across the room as all twenty stone of him jiggles. Aiden forgives me immediately as he, too, catches sight of Shelly's exasperated expression as she winds her hands together agitatedly, her beady brown eyes fixed on me. Aiden straightens his mouth, pinching his brows together in an attempt to chastise me further but failing pitifully as the smile slowly creeps back across his full lips. My best friend can't hide anything from me. But God love him; he does try. I should be able to muster a semblance of care over Shelly's restless state, women's solidarity, and all that, but Shelly is a class-A bitch. She treated Aiden like a disposable plaything when they dated briefly, picking him up and dropping him whenever the mood took her, toying with his affections until he gathered enough sense to walk away. She should think herself lucky. The stories I had at my disposal would make her toes curl, but Aiden was right about one thing, our wardrobe was sacred, our little slice of heaven, our happy place—and it had been since the day I had drunkenly gone home with my cowboy.

Aiden's shift has ended, and our plans to move onto another bar are dashed, as they usually were, with the offer of twenty per cent off our tab from Paulie being put into effect; keeping the shot boy in rotation even fully dressed helps to keep the ladies happy and his bar full—win-win. After eight bottles of San Miguel, two yager bombs, a martini, and two shots of sambuca drunk without the use of his hands from the bras of two busty bridesmaids, Aiden is well and truly on his way to being inebriated to the point of no return. His speech slurred as we sing along to *Lonely Day* by *System of the Down*, my rockstar air guitar complementing his voice as he amps up the chorus and matches each note perfectly. Aiden's voice is flawless, but without some liquid courage to back him up, nerves would usually get the better of him. Miming along to the song just so I can hear his mesmerising voice fills me with joy. I know every side of Aiden, his fears, his dreams, and the person he was when he thought no one was looking. Sometimes I knew him better than he knew himself, and on all occasions, whether he noticed it or not, I watched him in awe. He had so much more heart and happiness to give than he knew, and it burst free from him through his beaming smile. He attracts the ladies with ease, his presence; drunk as he is; commanding and hypnotic.

He dances away from the woman; his cobalt-slate eyes, red-rimmed due to the alcohol, are fixed on me. Although glassy, they are no less spellbinding than they always are. He runs the last few paces towards me and sweeps me up into his strong, now baby-blue shirt-covered arms, his taut muscles still obvious as they push against the seams of the fabric, his tattoos creeping out from beneath the rolled-up cuffs around his elbows. Gone is the skinny, shaggy-haired seventeen-year-old boy I had my first kiss with during a game of spin the bottle; his addiction to comic books and his kind nature the only parts of him that hadn't changed. I'm sure if you dug deep enough under his bed, beneath the back issues of playboy and men's fitness weekly, he still has some lurking there. He has done okay for himself in recent years. The new ruffled crop of side swept locks, and well-maintained beard was my input, as it was me dragging him to the barbers every month.

'What do you say to a round of chilli cheese fries and two desperados?' he yells in my ear as we jump around stupidly to the *Kriss Kross* classic blaring from the DJ's mixing table. We have hit junk food time on the evening's roster, and my intoxicated body couldn't be happier, my stomach growling appreciatively at the idea of anything hot and edible.

OCTOBER 31ST 2011

7 YEARS EARLIER

RONI

'Okay, so we're all new to the party; maybe we should go around the circle and introduce ourselves. I know I'm just *dying* to get to know you all.' The word *dying* falling from this young guy's mouth feels almost taboo as he licks his lips lasciviously, the smirk creeping onto his face haunting, almost. I ignore the thud in the pit of my stomach as I watch him cross his dirty jean-clad legs beneath him, his expression alight with excitement as his muddy brown eyes work their way over the bodies of the girls seated around him, admiring them shamefully, dragging his tobacco-stained fingers over his parted lips as he drinks in their unmarred beauty. I couldn't be the only underage girl here; if I had to put money on it, at least half the girls in this room were underage. His eyes meet mine, and he grins wickedly. A shiver dances up my spine, making me shudder in response to the intrusion of his unwanted gaze. I rub my palms up my bare arms, trying to hide my skin from him.

'This isn't school,' a young Asian boy retorts after chugging half his beer bottle, wincing at the taste of it as his throat bobs to accept the alcohol. I am glad for the interruption as the sleaze stops staring at me to glance slowly his way.

'I think we should know something about the person we could lock faces with. Don't you?' The brown-eyed letch responds, licking his lips suggestively as his now darkened gaze locks onto an ample-chested brunette who recoils slightly at the unwanted attention. He is practically salivating, enjoying the effect he has on her. I instinctively edge to my left a little, my pink polka dot skirt sliding easily across the varnished dark wood flooring, and I bump into the person next to me. Turning to apologise, I glance up into the inviting blue-grey pools of the handsome, dark-haired young man sitting beside me, my stare flashing between him and the sight of our knees now touching. His kind face immediately dispels all feelings of apprehension that had previously swamped my body.

'Sorry.' I mutter sheepishly, moving only slightly to break the connection. I would happily sit on his lap if it meant I could be further away from the brown-eyed creep whose stare is now boring into my soul from across the circle. I don't even have to look at him to know his eyes are trained on our interaction, dissecting it hungrily as his gaze runs up my bare legs.

'No need for an apology. I'd want to be as far away from that guy as possible, too, if I were a girl,' he notes quietly, gesturing with a nod of his head across the circle of people, seconding my thought. His eyes are now a warmer shade of blue, flecks of grey and amber catching the light as he looks around to make sure no one has heard his comment.

Running his hand through his shaggy chocolate locks, I gulp down my nervousness as the air between us begins to heat. Each of my breaths is heavy, as my heart beats a little harder with every passing second. He is tall and slender, his muscles defined but yet to reach their full potential; a newbie to the gym scene, I guess, but certainly someone who toys with a weight or two. He smiles at me kindly as he places one hand on my knee and the other around my waist, pulling me closer to him so that, once again, our knees are touching. I beam up at him, appreciating the gentlemanly gesture and the security his proximity instils in me. Without realising it, the circle has already started their introductions. The raven-haired girl to my right, draped top to toe in black, taps me on my leg hesitantly, startling me out of my daydream. Looking around, I see everyone silently waiting with bated breath for me to introduce myself, and I lose my train of thought for a moment.

'Hi, I'm Veronica,' I babble nervously, wincing that I have unintentionally used my full first name for the first time since I was five. I would forever be known as Roni; Veronica reminded me too much of my evil grandmother. I don't know whose bright idea it was to name me after the witch, but it wasn't appreciated. This is the first party I have ever attended, and knowing that half the attendees are of college age does very little to settle my nerves. I am literally a fish out of water and clearly don't yet harness enough social skills to hide my fear.

'And what makes you special, Veronica?' the brown-eyed creep asks from across the circle, his words laden with intent as he pronounces every syllable of my name leisurely, as though it tastes sweet on his tongue. His bony fingers smooth down his cornflower blue shirt that is gaping open, showing his hairless chest. When he shifts on the spot, his adams apple bobbing in his throat, the shine from a chrome medallion pendant hiding behind the fabric comes into view, it's blinding as the overhead bulb reflects off the metal. Clearing his throat, he urges me to answer his question.

'I can recite the alphabet backwards.' As lame as my offering of a useless skill is, it made everyone but the creepy guy chuckle light-heartedly. I'm just grateful no one asked me to prove my statement and share my talent with everyone else in the room. Yes, I could do it, but this pressure cooker situation is currently reducing my bravery to a sloppy mess on the floor. I have two speeds right now and neither one of those is enthusiastic with a side order of this is my life.

'That's cool,' the hot guy next to me whispers into my ear as he leans towards me. I bask in the woodsy scent of a grown man's aftershave, his father's, I presume, and the minty fresh wash of air that laps at my cheek as he sucks on a hard mint.

'Mister *Captain America*, how about you?' the host of our little game pipes up, his distaste for my new friend clear on his contorted face; his grimace is only mildly hidden beneath the surface as all eyes are now fixed on the handsome guy next to me.

'Hi guys, I'm Aiden, and I just recently realised I know all the words to every *NSYNC* song ever created.' I can't stifle my laugh at his revelation. I try, but it's no use. The snort that explodes from my mouth is a shock to both of us, I think. Sheepishly I grin up at him, and he levels me with a wide smile, a sign of kindness rather than mockery. Others around the circle continue to introduce themselves, but I can't seem to drag my eyes away from him. We chat animatedly in our small circle of two, oblivious to anyone else around us until our host coughs loudly to drag us back to the game I still do not want to play. Virgins have no place seated in a circle surrounded by horny college guys, sharing their deepest, darkest secrets.

For thirty minutes or so, the game progresses as you would expect, each of us taking turns spinning the empty green wine bottle around in the centre of the circle to match us with a kissing partner. A soft *awww* resonates from the ladies around the circle as Aiden crawls forward and kisses the back of a girl's hand rather than attempting to lay one on her face. I swoon as he backtracks, returning to his spot next to me. I watch the body language of everyone around me as they each get to their knees confidently without a second thought, some of the girls even putting on a bit of a show as they crawl across the space towards whoever it is that has the neck of the bottle pointing their way. My naivety is showing as the sixteen-year-old part of my innocence prays the neck of that bottle won't land on me, it takes me a moment to realise I'm nervously biting my nails.

You can leave, you can leave, you can leave. My inner voice is small, lacking any commanding tone as I drop my fingers from my mouth and begin fiddling awkwardly with a stray thread on the hem of my skirt.

'Let's make this interesting!' the creepy guy exclaims as he tires of the game, rudely interrupting my inner monologue. Any girl that has had the unfortunate luck of having their spin land on him has apprehensively dotted a feather-light kiss on his waiting lips and hurried back to their space before he can get his hands on them. Creepy guy, otherwise known as Lucas, as I would later discover, isn't bad looking. In fact, if he learned to smile without that rapey glint in his eye, he would be considered pretty damn hot. Something about him just doesn't sit right with me, though. I can't pinpoint the issue, but it has nagged at me from the second I laid my eyes on him. 'How about we get a little tongue action going on?' he suggests making my belly flip, intently ogling me as he speaks, every hair on my body standing to attention in response.

It's immediately clear that the only attendees vehemently against Lucas' idea to ramp up to level *tongue action,* are me, Aiden and a reserved russet-haired girl nervously tugging her long tartan skirt down over her bended knees across from us. The ten or so others around us cheer at the proposal of taking the game up a notch. I have never even really kissed a guy before, and accidently face planting Timmy Dean during a game of don't blink doesn't count. Having my first induction into womanhood surrounded by strangers with an empty alcohol bottle deciding my fate doesn't appeal to me. It is a rite of passage, and I want it to be special.

As each person takes their turn, Lucas is practically dribbling as he watches the show. Rearranging the crotch of his trousers when a size ten blonde and a stacked Tahitian beauty lock lips, each making the trip simultaneously to meet in the centre of the circle. However much I try to fight the nerves, I am very aware it will soon be my turn. I know maths; the odds are against me. Standing up and excusing myself is not an option, I am sixteen, not stupid, and the peer pressure alone holds me firmly in my spot on the floor as I bite nervously at my pink varnished fingernails again. I get onto my knees and reach out for the bottle that has been spun more times than a waltzer ride. Gripping the sides of the fingerprint-dusted green glass, I spin it, praying with every inch of my soul that it will land on anyone but Lucas. I'd even consider the young guy who has taken off his shoe and started picking his toenails a more desirable option and that's saying something. Lucas eyes me as though he can read my mind and distastefully licks his bottom lip, clicking his knuckles on each hand, so the bones creak, a sense of preparation in his movements.

'It looks like we have a winner,' he spits. I didn't realise the bottle had stopped spinning. Each second felt like an hour as I slowly lower my head to see who I have to kiss. The shock on my face is gone, immediately replaced with a beaming smile that stretches from ear to ear. Aiden edges a little closer to me, and my heart begins to pump furiously in my chest.

'Are you sure you want to do this, it's okay if not? I can make an excuse,' Aiden sings softly into my ear as everyone around us waits with bated breath. His words dance across the bare skin of my neck, leaving goosebumps in their wake. Heat spreads throughout my midriff in response, a breath hitching in my throat, the dull ache at the apex of my thighs a relatively new but welcomed feeling. As I lean closer to him, a sudden and unwelcome thought pops into my mind.

Is he trying to get out of it? Maybe he doesn't want to kiss me. I am quickly dragged back into the present and out of my head when his hand rests on mine. His wide blue-grey flecked eyes silently demand my permission to follow through, the rough grazes of his calloused fingertips like honey slipping over yoghurt.

'I'm good.' I say with more confidence than I possess. Before I can indulge another wayward thought, his soft, warm lips are on mine, reserved at first but then more intense as we build up speed. With no experience, my instincts kick in, and I part my lips, desperate for him to take it further, to take what he wants from me. We move in sync, our tongues lapping perfectly against one another, wishing it would never end. I lean into him further. I am about ready to climb onto his lap and wrap my legs around his waist, his thumb running along my jawline, sending a surge of electricity to thrum dully throughout my entire body. I have never felt so alive. Someone clearing their throat from behind me breaks the warm sensation flitting between our bodies, and we instantly snap apart. How long have we been kissing, and why is everyone looking at us like this? It is immediately apparent that we had drifted off into our own little world, oblivious to the others around us for a fleeting moment. They try and fail to hide their smiles as I attempt to regulate my breathing. I beam self-consciously up at Aiden, my fingers running over my throbbing lips, the heat he ignited in me still there, bubbling away under the surface. We exchange shy smiles, our eyes darting every so often over at one another as I fight the urge to fan at my face. The game fizzles out quickly after that; Lucas attempts to up the ante yet again and involve groping, which is a step too far for most of the participants. Everyone disbands and goes on their way to enjoy everything else the party has to offer. I stay there, lost in his gaze for a few more minutes as the room clears of bodies.

'I'll see you later, maybe?' Aiden coos as he shuffles around nervously, his navy-blue *puma* trainers squeaking on the floor. The question that isn't a question hangs in mid-air between us as we try to understand the invisible jolt of electricity that seems to tether us together.

'Okay,' I respond meekly, not knowing what else to say. The feeling he has awoken in me is foreign. I have no idea how to process the emotions that come with my first official kiss. All the teenage magazines and their quizzes are useless now. None of them described how it would feel to have his lips on mine. Left alone contemplating my fantasy, he walks into the next room with a couple of friends, and I exit in the opposite direction. I have some stuff to think about, and being distracted by his face isn't helping me. My fingers instinctively move to my mouth again. My brain is determined to chase the ghost of the memory of Aiden's lips on mine. I may not have expected it, but I was sure that for a game of spin the bottle, that first kiss was the most perfect first kiss anyone could have.

I meet up with a couple of friends from school over the poor excuse for a snack table that consists of stale cheesy crackers and soggy onion rings and spend the next hour sitting around and chatting, glancing around discreetly every so often, looking for Aiden. Not that I would allow myself to believe that I was doing exactly that. *'You're simply scanning the room for familiar faces.'* that little voice in my head assures me. The chuckle my brain offers up, however, exposes the lie I am trying to fool myself with. I turn back to my friends and engross myself in their conversation. The last thing I want to do is appear needy. My sister always says boys hate that, and even though she is younger than me, she would know. Her current reverse harem consists of Chase, Taylor, and Bryce. Thinking about it, can you call it a reverse harem if each guy doesn't know the other one exists?

The grandfather clock in the hallway strikes twelve, and everyone gambolling around the darkened open plan room cheers at the DJ as he flips a switch, the LP on his decks switching out to another as the thumping beat of a garage tune riles up the crowd. Feet pound against the floor as everyone around me jumps to the music; the vibrations have the crème oval coffee table covered in red plastic beer cups, a deck of cards and ashtrays filled to the brim with discarded bubble-gum, ash, and fag butts bouncing. I take another sip of my now warm beer, deciding just to knock it back and finish it, so I can get a refill. I'm desperate to match their energies and enjoy the music like they are, but exhaustion has my limbs feeling heavy and uncooperative. Nervously playing with my father's wedding ring on my middle finger, I loop the metal easily around my finger continuously as unease leaks from my muscles.

This is my last clear memory; I've only had one beer the entire night, and I've gone from lucid to out of my skull in the space of about twenty minutes. To everyone around me, I am just another girl who has drunk far too much at her first college party. The alternative is far more sinister and not something most people want to consider whilst letting their hair down and having a good time. I am the unlucky statistic on this occasion—that unlucky 50% of women who have a horrible nightmare taint a memory that should be filled with joy. When he places his hands around my waist as I stumble to my feet, I happily fall into his body, content to be wrapped up in his broad arms. So although I feel groggy, and everything around me merges into a dark haze of reds and blacks, I feel relatively safe. That woodsy mint scent of his is still present on my skin from earlier, and I happily drink in the familiarity. That is, until I see something that confuses my already frazzled brain. As we make our way through the party, hordes of partygoers losing themselves to the music, wide carefree smiles spread across their faces, I notice someone in the distance, someone that, through all the surrounding haziness, suddenly comes into sharp focus. My heart plummets, my now hollow chest straining to contain the fear pushing against my ribs. My brain's protests to stop my legs from moving are not loud enough to be heard over the panicked howling of blood whooshing in my ears. Tucked away in the corner of the room, he stands there laughing and joking with two other guys, taking another sip of his drink as he slaps the guy next to him on the back jovially.

If Aiden is over there, his arms locked around the shoulder of one of his friends, then who is ushering me through the party?

The panic hits me all at once as the stranger who has staked his claim on me tightens his arm around my waist, my shoes scraping against the floor as he readjusts me in his hold, moving us through the sea of people as though I weigh nothing. Aiden's face disappears as we reach the wide set of carpeted stairs leading up to the second floor, as does any morsel of hope as a darkness overwhelms my senses. My head lulls against the stanger's shoulder and with what little energy I can muster I try to hold onto the memory of Aiden's face for comfort.

It's not him. Aiden isn't with you. You aren't protected. I know I should panic; every speck of my subconscious is screaming at full volume that I should tear myself away from the guy leading me God only knows where, but I'm tired, my limbs lazy—my brain clouded with simple thoughts that shouldn't even pose a problem, my lungs almost forgetting how to take in air.

My voice is non-existent as I fight to construct a plea to the person holding me up. *Who are you? Where are we going?* I have the questions in my mind, but I can't get them out of my mouth. I attempt to fall free of his grasp, to let my body become a dead weight, but he is too strong, his unkempt fingernails now embedded in the skin, holding my arms taught enough that they tug painfully at my shoulders. Uneasiness continues to build in my stomach as we move through the large frat house, each room we enter a little less busy than the last. Until there is no one, I can't even hear the music playing downstairs anymore, but I can't be sure if that is due to our distance from the party or my mind playing tricks on me. I'm not sure of anything right now, which only fuels my impending sense of dread. I try to look up, but the lights above me are blinding. Searing heat burns my retinas as I react idly and screw my eyes shut a little too late in response. We glide through a series of dimly lit hallways and into a small room, a quiet room, an empty room.

'I think, I... think.' *Roni, for God's sake. Speak!* The little voice in my head berates me as I struggle to verbalise my protests. Aware of the terror that has my muscles knotting. Dread is the only emotion now filling my gut as I stumble through my ABCs like a three-year-old new to the alphabet, my brain suddenly unable to match a word with the sound coming out of my mouth. My legs give way, and I fall back into the solid form towering over me. The foul odour of old cigarettes, whisky, and industrial bleach fill my nose as he wraps his arms around my waist from behind, his mouth running down the column of my neck, his tongue leaving a sloppy path of wetness as he tastes me. I want to deny him access to this part of me, but I can't steady myself enough to push him away.

'Aren't you a pretty little thing?' the stranger muses, his callous voice causing me to fight back the bile rising in my throat. He scrapes his fingernail down my face hard enough to mark me, but there is nothing I can do to stop him. Although bearable, the pain is a step behind his movements, as though my brain can't process the action and the reaction simultaneously. In one swift motion, his hand is firmly gripped around my throat, and he swings my limp body around effortlessly like a rag doll, throwing me down onto what I assume is a bed. I fight off the need to close my eyes and fall asleep, although it is obviously what my body is crying out for as my lids grow heavy.

Roni, get the fuck up. You need to move! Even the voice in my head that is screaming at me sounds too far away. I try desperately to follow her instructions, but I still can't move, even with her garbled cries as background noise. I want to scream, but all I can muster are gurgled objections that make no sense. The voice inside my head is now small, defeated, and crying. She knows what is coming. The room is dark, the bedding beneath me rough with an odour of sweat and cigars filling my nose. I hear a door shut and a lock being pushed into place. I want to move; I shriek at my body tirelessly to get up off the bed, my last-ditch attempt to free myself from the horrors unfolding. But I'm still glued to the spot, as though my brain no longer controls my limbs. I feel trapped here, a prisoner in my own body. My mother had told me stories about what happened to drunk young girls at parties. It was this very reason why I limited myself to just one beer. Not that it helped any.

I contemplate my options as I feel my captor skulk around the room to the bedside cabinet. His hazy form comes in and out of focus as he looms over me. The manifestation of aroused heat radiates from him, even in my almost comatose state, his intentions clear. I turn my head languidly, the only movement I can manage. I can't properly make out his face, the pitch-black shadows blanketing the room's walls and my foggy eyesight about as reliable as a prostitutes testimony.

His scrawny hands are on me in a flash as he gropes frantically at the soft flesh of my breasts through my shirt, his inner demon unbridled and on show, and there is absolutely nothing I can do about it.

Close your eyes, Roni. Shut it all out. I'm grateful for the instruction as I fight back tears, but it's pointless. Silent yet palpable sobs wrack my chest as cold tears stream down my face, pooling in my ears and splashing against the covers beneath me. Even the instinct to wipe the tears away is an arduous task my hands cannot comply with. Time passes, but I can't be sure how long I've been lying here.

'You're gonna love it,' he breathes, his tongue running over my earlobe as he collects my salty tears in his mouth. A squeak of sound falls from my shaking lips, *'no'* but there is no conviction in my tone, the one word almost masked by an arduous breath. I pray for the blackness to swallow me whole before he can claim me. Before I can blink, he is jumping off my prone body, the shifting weight allowing me to take in a much-needed breath. As he paces the floor, a part of me hopes he is having second thoughts, but I'm not that naïve. This man has given me no indication that he even has a soul, let alone morals. The evil that swamps his eyes is palpable as he drinks in my prone form, the breeze from an open window somewhere in the room causing the bare skin on my legs to prickle.

~~~~

I come to and see the burning tip of a cigarette in the shadowy room, my captor's face illuminated for a moment by the flame of a match, but my tired brain doesn't recognise him. My screams for help are loud in my head. Yet, the room remains a cold void of silence. The only sound to follow is of the crackling end of the cigarette almost echoing around us as he sucks it between his lips, puffs of white smoke wafting around the shirtless figure sitting motionless in a high-backed chair. The unmistakable rip of a foil packet sends shivers up my spine as I continue to cry. My body is still unresponsive, a dead weight, but I manage to turn my head so all I can see is a bare brick wall inches from my face, painted with scrawls of graffiti I can't quite make out. The bed shifts, and I struggle to breathe again as he lowers himself on top of me. I realise suddenly that I don't need to investigate his face to identify my attacker; I know who it is. As he tears at the buttons of my pink shirt viciously, I feel the burden of a pendant crushing against my chest, the metal cold against my skin.

'Want a kiss?' he sneers, his disgusting voice vibrating against my ear. *Lucas*. Flashes of his preying glare from around the game of spin the bottle hit me, and I know in an instant that he won't pity me in my moment of weakness. He has a plan and is willing to do anything necessary to fulfil it. I accept my fate and choose to succumb to the darkness. I close my eyes, biting back my unheard sobs, and allow myself to fall into the unknown depths of what I assume is a drug-induced slumber. However much the thought saddens me, he can have my body, but he sure as hell can't have my mind. If all I can do at this moment in a bid for self-preservation is protect that, then that is what I am going to do.

I don't know who or what grants my wish, but my world fades to black as I pass out. I wake intermittently as he tortures me relentlessly, the
~~~~

damage to my skin in the wake of his touch making me wince inside. Thankfully, whatever drugs he had slipped me dull the pain the longer he continues his assault. My head is unbearably heavy, only snippets of the room around me registering in my weary brain. A far away *thump, thump, thump* rings out. I muster what energy I can and jerk beneath him, his length no longer in me now. I groan and whine, but the noises are disjointed, fire licking at my dry throat—a throbbing ache bites at me between my blood-splattered legs. Bright white light floods the room, my eyes scrunching closed as the invasion causes my head to throb behind my eyes. My hair is wet with tears, and before I can comprehend the scene playing out in front of me, I am lifted from the bed and scooped up into strong arms into a marital hold, strong arms supporting my back and the underside of my trembling thighs.

Cowering naked in the corner of the room like the animal he is, Lucas is crying out, bright crimson blood covering his face, hands, and chest, shock alight in his eyes as he watches Aiden carry me from the room. His nose is broken as it hangs at an odd angle from his face. This makes me smile, although I note that the muscles in my face don't react as they should, my parted lips set in place as though secured with glue. I may be battered and broken, but now he is the one crying, and I would take my wins where I could get them. I glance up lazily, my head falling back as the slight movement proves too much for my weak body. His beautiful grey-blue eyes are filled with concern as he tries to wrap me up in his coat, protecting my modesty from the other partygoers, who are now reacting in fits of gossip as Lucas' yells travel from the back bedroom. The cold air slaps at my exposed skin, and the sensation is welcomed. To feel anything but Lucas' touch on my body makes me feel instantly safe. Inhaling the familiar scent of Aiden's fresh, woodsy aftershave from his coat as his minty breath fans my face warms me.

'Virgin… don't tell… promise.' I still can't string together a sentence, but thankfully I can express the four most important words I need Aiden to hear before I slip back into nothingness.

'Pinky promise,' he says softly. His head dipped down to my face. His worried smile is small but comforting all the same as he presents me with his pinky finger, his other arm holding me with ease as he keeps his pace moving through the party. I shakily match his gesture and loop my little finger around his—the small movement, a chore, wracking my body with another wave of exhaustion.

'Thank you,' I blurt, my hoarse voice cracking. I sink into his hold, knowing that being suspended in his tight embrace is the safest place for me as tears of gratitude now stain my cheeks. Sleep once again threatens to steal me away as my erratic breathing calms to a steady rhythm. Knowing I am safe I give up the fight, the weight of a heavy heart now a little lighter, thanks to him.

NOVEMBER 1ST 2011

THE MORNING AFTER

RONI

SHIT!' I scream, my hands flying up to cover my eyes. The fullness in my head makes me want to vomit as my brain presses painfully against my skull. My thankfully clothed extremities are tangled in white cotton sheets, but the comfort of my current surroundings do nothing to drown out the assault of hazy memories of Lucas' and what he did to me, the respite of the memories of Aiden saving me are welcomed. The conflicting emotions stir me from the early morning sluggishness that tries to get the better of me. I bolt upright, realising quickly that although I'm comfortable I am still somewhere unfamiliar. Before panic can take hold, I settle as someone walks into the room.

'Hi, you're Veronica, right? How are you feeling?' The smiling blonde-haired girl in her early twenties asks as she offers me a cup of water. I'm thankful as the dryness in my throat is bordering on excruciating. I silently nod my appreciation, unable to find my voice at first, my lips dry and cracked, my body desperate for hydration.

'Stupid question, I guess,' she chuckles, her laugh delightfully whimsical, although it does nothing to conceal the apprehension on her face. She sits on the end of the bed, and although her slight frame doesn't need me to, I swing my legs around to accommodate her. I wince at the sudden movement, rubbing at my temple to ease the sharp, stabbing pain there. 'The headache will wear off eventually. Plenty of water and a couple of painkillers, and the Rohypnol will work its way out of your system. You'll start feeling yourself again in a day or so,' she squeaks softly, an apology that belongs to another lingering on her lips.

'Rohypnol?' I ask, confusion swamping my face, my voice determined but gravelly.

'You were drugged last night,' she says as she gestures to the little antique marble side table. I pick up the folded piece of white paper, and the woman leaves me for a moment to give me some privacy.

Morning, Veronica. I've left paracetamol and one of those fancy coffees with the cream in the kitchen. (Really hope you like coffee.) Sorry, I had to go, but call me when you feel up to it. My sister Paige can drop you home if you want. Feel free not to listen to anything she might say about me. Here if you need to talk. Aiden x

The woman, who I now assume is Aiden's sister Paige, enters the room again with the paracetamol in one hand and the steaming Styrofoam cup filled with caffeine gold in the other. She holds them out, offering them to me, and although I know reaching for them will stir the pain up again, I can't help myself. I am quiet once again, gulping down the coffee, ignoring as it almost burns the delicate skin inside my mouth. I had hoped it was all a horrible dream, but I'm not that lucky. I glance up at Paige; I don't even need to voice the question idly waiting on my lips.

'Aiden didn't know where you lived; he knew you would be okay here. This is his room, he took the sofa of course.' She lulls with a broad smile, flashing me her pristine white teeth as the metal of her lip ring catches the light flooding in through the floor to ceiling windows.

Fear spears me as another memory pops into my head, Lucas roughly trying to remove my top. My hands fly to my chest instinctively, but I am no longer wearing my destroyed shirt. Instead, an oversized black t-shirt with a worn picture of *Jim Morrison* on the front dons my tired frame, its hem reaching my thighs but barely long enough to cover my bum. Paige speaks before I can even form the question in my head. She clearly has a knack for telepathy.

'It belongs to Aiden. He's staying with me while our parents are out of the country. He had to go to work, but he will be back later if you want to wait. He didn't want you to have to wake up in *those* clothes. I've washed what is left, but I don't think they're salvageable.'

'Please throw them away. If it's okay, I'll just borrow this.' I gesture to the t-shirt that swathes me in Aiden's scent. I don't ever want to see those clothes again. I also plan on scrubbing every crevice of my body with bleach when I get home.

'The creep got a good look at your bra, but Aiden said he got there before it went any further,' she says to console me as I fight back the tears. I know I was naked. Aiden knows I was naked, but I appreciate the lie he told his sister. Paige scoots over the mattress and takes a seat next to me, concern heavy in her tone. Before she can utter whatever sentiment laced with pity building behind her lips, I thank her and get to my feet; a little quicker than I should have as I stumble on my unsteady legs, embarrassment swamping my soul as I try to compose myself. The unpleasant pounding between my legs is the only proof I need to know that she is wrong, to know exactly what had happened to me last night. Whether Aiden wanted to believe he had got there in time to save me or hoped I would not remember exactly what went down at the party, I choose not to push this line of conversation with Paige anymore. Aiden trusts her, and she has watched over me, but she is still a stranger to me, and I have shared more than enough of myself in the past twenty-four hours with people I don't know.

'I'm sixteen. I was meant to be at a sleepover, for Christ's sake, or at least that's what I told my mother. She's going to kill me,' I whine, finally showing my true age. 'Could I use your bathroom, please?' I ask her, desperate to be alone where I can cry and wallow in the awful collection of instances that led to my drugging and subsequent rape. I grab my bag from the sofa and thank her profusely, her directions to the bathroom muffled by the pounding in my ears as I run up the stairs and stumble through the first door I come across. Thankfully it is the bathroom because not two seconds later, I am bent over the toilet, expelling my stomach's contents until my body aches with the violent jolts each wretch forces me to endure. I fall back against the wall, climbing uneasily to my feet when the hammering in my chest settles, using the edge of the sink to steady myself. I stare at my reflection in the small rectangular mirror framed with vines of fake ivy on the wall in front of me. Reaching over to turn on the open plan shower attached to the tiled wall to my left, when the spray is at full force, I allow myself to cry harder than I think I ever have before, the sound of the water dampening my sobs. Looking at the remnants of smeared red lipstick on my harassed lips threatens to make me throw up again as my belly flips. Moving to retrieve some toilet paper, I rub roughly at them, dousing the tissue in water from the shower and repeating the action when it doesn't budge. I relish in the new sensation of pain in my lips as, for a moment at least, it distracts me from the monotonous ache between my legs.

How could you be so stupid? I berate myself internally, wishing the ground would open up and swallow me.

With the question comes an onslaught of visuals from last night, disgusting, horrific snapshots of what had happened as my brain fights to fill in the blanks the *roofie* has tried to wipe away.

His hands gripping so tightly onto my hair to manoeuvre my dead weight to where he wanted me, tearing clumps out from the root as my unresponsive body refused to make it easy for him as he assaulted me. The rough denim of his dirty jeans tearing at the flesh of my thighs as he brutally thrust inside of me without care or consideration for the damage he left behind.

I lift the t-shirt I am wearing, pawing at the little red welts on my belly beneath the caked-in blood of the cigarette burns he had inflicted on me mercilessly. Each memory is fighting to free itself from the drug-induced confines of my overworked brain.

'You'll be okay; all of this will be okay,' I say to my reflection, not believing a word of it. I can't even lie to myself. Grief, fury, whatever the emotion is, it is swimming around in my usually bright blue eyes, clouding them with a dank, sorrowful grey. I look away, the small purpling bruises on my throat and around my jaw a reminder that I don't want or need. I pull out the leggings I usually wore for gym class from the bottom of my bag and slip into them, so I don't have to return home wearing only a boy's t-shirt and a pair of black canvas ballet pumps. I turn off the shower and suck in a breath, feigning the composure I need until I can get home and start the process of self-loathing all over again, alone in my bedroom. I push open the door to Aiden's room and grab my coffee from off the short round table.

'Sugar?' Paige interrupts my thoughts, holding a glass jar and motioning towards my coffee cup. I shake my head in response, biting my lip to stifle a sob threatening to burst from behind my clenched teeth.

His voice rings in my head, and there isn't a single thing I can do to stop it.

'You want this, sugar; you want it harder?' I cringe as his voice invades my thoughts, feeling dirty as goosebumps cover my flesh, the sensation of ants crawling unwelcome over my skin making me want to rake my nails over every inch of my body. With the train in motion it's now impossible to get off this fucked up ride, sucked back into the void of last night I remember the silent protests that rang loudly in my head as I lay there beneath him, unable to push him off me, wordlessly howling as he took what he wanted from me without my permission. His lithe body squeezing the life out of me as he pressed me down into the mattress, care, concern and consideration not even piquing an interest on his radar as he savagely stole my innocence.

'I have to go,' I mumble, knowing I am teetering on the verge of a mental breakdown. I have to get out of this house. Before Paige can object and offer me a lift home, I bolt for the door, grabbing my coat off the stand in the hallway as I go.

'Thank you again,' I utter faintly. She simply smiles in response and moves to open the front door. I can tell she is battling the urge to tell me everything is going to be okay. That is what you do in these sorts of situations, right? I'm grateful when she stays quiet.

I sling my bag over my shoulder, stuffing Aiden's note into the inside zip pocket. I promise Paige I will call Aiden, even though I know it is a flat-out lie, and make my way out onto the street. I don't want anyone to hear about what happened to me, and I don't want to rehash it with the godly creature who I had shared my first kiss with. How would he feel if he found out he hadn't saved me in time? What would he think if he knew the bastard had taken my virginity by force? What would he say if I told him I thought it was him guiding me to that bedroom? I can't put him through that. Aiden thought Lucas was putting on a condom in preparation to enter me. That's why he felt he had got there in time. Little did he know I had already been trapped there for over an hour, and the first condom was already coated in my bloody innocence and discarded, the force of his blows tearing it to shreds without a second thought. He just wanted a clean one for round two of my torture.

The cool morning air laps at my face, and with every step I take, the raw sting at my core is reawakened, the clarity of my hazy memories hitting me thick and fast, their presence unwelcome as I sob the entire way home. I don't want to remember anymore; I don't want his cruel face to be there every time I close my eyes. But as the running theme of the past twenty-four hours would suggest, I have no say in the matter.

OCTOBER 31ST 2015

4 YEARS LATER

RONI

Rolling into the biggest party of the year on campus has me debating my mental state. Go to university, they said. Let your hair down, they said. Make new friends, they said. Standing here on the precipice of my young adult existence with an almost perfect GPA and zero experience in social interactions of any kind, I try to remain positive. As I hover in the doorway of the frat party in full swing ahead of me, I chew on my bottom lip, weighing up the importance of being socially accepted when I only have one more term of school left. *I could run away; I could feign an illness.* Before I can follow through and escape to my dorm room, I realise Casey, my roommate and designated fun compass, senses my unease because her small hand tightens around mine looped under her arm, tethering me to her and foiling any escape plan I might have been concocting. I draw in a balanced breath and shake off the trepidation latching itself to my shoulders like a backpack, smoothing my free hand down my floor-length red dress that hugs my midriff like a second skin. Casey is wearing a literal backpack chock full of cigarettes, papers, and weed baggies. Being the local, friendly *distributor* of such things is one reason she opted to dress as *Dora the explorer* for the costume party in the first place. The only downside is her commitment to saying everything with a Spanish twang.

A young guy wearing a gorilla suit meanders through the crowd of chattering students with a cock-sure gait, a tray piled high with shots of yellow liquid balancing on his hairy palm. Casey, never one to be coy, grabs two glasses, nodding at the primate as a way of thanks, and holds one out at me. I push the length of my cheap red wig over my shoulder and huff out a breath, regretting my choice in headwear as I wipe the back of my hand over my sweaty forehead.

'When in Roma,' she beams, her Spanish accent slipping the more alcohol she consumes, now sounding more like a small gruff Italian girl with a nicotine addiction. I take the offered shot, throwing my head back as I down it in one. The liquid burns the lining of my throat as it makes its way down. *Urgh, Tequila.* Casey, being what some might call a hardcore partygoer, doesn't even flinch. Tapping the monkey man on the shoulder so he spins back around, she leans in and ruffles the black fur on his mask, moving to take another two shots from the tray with a salacious smile on her glossy pink lips. She may not have played for the same team as me, her preferred take out being Taco's if you know what I mean, but if the way the guy in the monkey suit shifts the costume around his crotch is anything to go by, she has a way of affecting people regardless of sexual preference. Men, women, and primates, no-one is immune to her charm it would seem. Casey waves the guy off and turns, offering me one of the shot glasses. When I don't immediately take it, again mentally considering my options of escaping, changing into my pyjamas, and climbing into bed to watch *CSI* re-runs, she moves a little closer to me. She eyes me warily, placing the shots down beside us she secures a length of her sleek black bob behind her ear. I tug at the fabric of my costume that is tight enough to cut the circulation off to my arms, the scratchy red material hugging my form anything but comfortable.

'It's an acquired taste, but you'll grow to love it,' she says softly; knowing there is a lot more going on in my head than her choice of liquor, Casey moves to rest her palm on my cheek, waves of comfort rolling from her body as her liquid hazel eyes search mine.

'Everything is going to be okay. Let's have some fun,' she declares, picking up the shots and waving one under my nose.

The internal war I am having with myself shuts down as everyone else around me is happily necking the same shots. I swallow the recurring fear that comes as second nature when taking a drink from someone I don't know, and a weight is lifted from my senses. She is right, as she is most of the time. Holing myself up in the dorm while the world moves on around me is no way to continue my life at university. I swipe both of the miniature shot glasses from her hold and knock them back in quick succession as Casey's eyes widen with surprise at my bolshy move. I refuse to obey my fears and how they threaten to hold me back. This time, the burn in my throat is more bearable, smooth even, and I smile as it warms my belly.

'Whose party is this again?' I ask.

'Smitty, Smithy. I don't know, definitely an S name.' She states while eye fucking a redhead dressed as Poison Ivy, hovering over the lit-up jukebox, hollering out a *James Brown* tune.

'See something you like?' I whisper into Casey's ear, close enough that my warm breath grazes her exposed neck, the hairs of her fake black bob blowing forward into her face.

'I would for sure climb that,' she retorts, tucking her hair behind her ear again, exchanging suggestive smiles with the woman in question, who is running a whip wound with ivy in her gloved hands as she taps at the buttons to select the next song.

'Down, girl. You've got all night to master the art of botany. Let's get me good and drunk before I realise just how much I hate costume parties.' I beam, grabbing her arm and making my way to the makeshift bar with various liquor bottles and stacks upon stacks of the party staple of red plastic beer cups. I opt for the only bottle that hasn't already been opened and remove the metal binding securing the lid. *Better safe than sorry.* I pull out the hip flask secured in my garter belt and fill it with rum until it overflows a little. I lick the spilt liquor off the back of my hand and twist the flask's cap closed, returning it to my belt, jolting as the cold metal makes contact with my balmy skin. That would be my ration for the night. Filling up two red cups with a generous two shots of rum and some diet cola, I hand one to Casey, who is swaying along to Calvin Harris' *How deep is your love* beside me.

The room is draped with orange and black streamers that hang down from the high ceiling, the oversized brown wool rug that is hiding a multitude of sins and stains acting as a makeshift dance floor near the wall-to-wall concertina doors leading out into the garden that is at least an acre in size. People chat animatedly under the nearly bare blossom trees, the glow from the paper pumpkin lanterns above their heads highlighting a cobbled path that snakes down into the forest just beyond the white picket fence. Skeletons holding props are scattered around the room, guitars and cigarettes taped to their hands, and hats glued to their skulls. The vibe in the room is chilled, and it is only as the sun begins to set and the LED fairy lights on the walls shine more vibrantly that the party seems to hit another level. There is a chance that the increasing number of alcohol units flowing through my bloodstream also help jazz up my surroundings, but I'm in no position to split hairs.

~~~~

I am on my eighth rum and cola of the night after refilling my hip flask with a dusty unopened bottle I found in the back of the freezer when I went in search of ice. I welcome the little buzz that makes my shoulders relax and my brain flood with dopamine as I swallow a mouthful of the fruity-tasting liquor. Even with the addition of the thick fake lashes tugging at my eyelids, I see him clearly from across the room, working his way through the crowd, doling out hugs and handshakes when he sees someone he knows. His broad shoulders flex as he lifts another guy into the air, his shirt's red and white check material almost bursting at the seams, his muscles impressive. I allow myself a second to imagine myself trussed up in his tanned, burly arms, pulling off that wide-brimmed hat with the large soft crown from his head so I can run my fingers through his mop of dark hair. My belly cartwheels, dragging me out of my daydream and back to the moment. My heart skips a beat as my gaze trails over the stranger's face. His jaw is angular, his short beard enough to grab onto if the opportunity presents itself. His white-toothed smile is effortless, and his dimples cute. Those blue-grey eyes fall on me momentarily, and I shift uneasily on the spot as though he has caught me doing something I shouldn't be doing. Well, I am staring at him greedily, but that is beside the point. He oozes charm naturally, and once I'm sure he is looking elsewhere, I continue to eye him as though he is a snack sent to satisfy my hunger. I gulp down another mouthful of my drink, willing the alcohol to settle the unfamiliar thrum of excitement that is making my heart beat a little too enthusiastically in my chest.

'See something you like, Roni?' Casey murmurs in my ear, her question slathered with suggestiveness. I cough wildly, dribbling my
~~~~

drink down my chin as she takes me off guard. Spluttering as the drink soaks the front of my dress. I had clearly forgotten the basics of swallowing a drink whilst mesmerised by a guy I didn't even know.

But you do want to know him, the little voice in my head suggests, and I know immediately it is true.

I wipe my mouth with the back of my hand and stand up straight. I not only have the attention of the people around us now but him too. I twist unsteadily on my heels and face Casey with a glare hot enough to rival the Devil himself as she fights to contain her girlish laughter.

'I'm sorry,' she snorts, pulling her lip between her teeth as she tries to mask her smirk.

'Please tell me he isn't looking at me,' I plead with her. She gets onto her tiptoes and glances over my shoulder, her trainers squeaking on the floor as she rests her hands on my shoulders for stability.

'The cowboy has left the building. Adios Guapo,' she quips, stretching out her arm as though he is riding off into the distance.

'Do I want to know what Guapo means?' I ask shrewdly, with my painted lips pursed.

'It either means handsome or horny if my year seven Spanish is correct. Either way, it works,' she jibes.

'Well, in that case, I'm going to go clean myself up or kill myself due to shame. Either way, it works,' I snap as I repeat her words. 'I'll be in the bathroom,' I retort, taking a sip of what is left of my drink and rubbing at the stain already drying at the edges down the front of my red sequined dress.

'Remember to chat,' she says softly, encouragingly. I eye her warily. 'You got this,' she adds with a double thumbs up and a cheesy grin. My brows pinch together in confusion briefly. Deciding her behaviour is more than likely due to an overserving of weed, I turn on my heels and continue to walk towards the toilets marked with a picture of a skeleton peeing into a pumpkin. I dab at my dress with a napkin to soak up the liquid before it has a chance to make my skin sticky. I mumble under my breath as I berate myself. Lost in my little world, I miss my footing and stumble forward into someone's solid back with about as much finesse as a hippo trying to tap dance. I buckle on my heels, sending me crashing to my knees, toppling over and landing face first on the floor with a thud, and everything goes black. My eyes flutter open a moment or two later, my hand moving to grip my forehead as I realise I must have knocked myself out.

'Hey, baby,' his voice is as smooth as melting butter. I have woken up resting between a pair of broad legs, the leather of his chaps cooling my cheeks as the fringe tickles my neck. He dabs at my face with a handkerchief, and I wince at the flush of pain. My long red wig is lying across my stomach, the matted tresses bunched between my fingers. I move to push it to the floor and sit dazed for a moment, my head pounding. I try to get to my feet but sway on the spot as though trying to stand in a paddleboat on choppy waters.

'Now that doesn't seem like a good idea.' The cowboy beams, stroking my forehead and settling me back down into the comfort of his thick thighs. He takes a swig of his half-devoured beer bottle and grins down at me, his full lips glistening. 'Your boobs broke your fall; it could have been a lot worse.' He chuckles, bringing the neck of the bottle to his lips again.

'Words I never thought I would hear,' I retort, wincing as I realise my face has lost the ability to pull any other expressions than brutal and very real pain.

'Sorry, did I say your boobs? I meant your face.' He laughs cockily. I do not. My self-esteem is in tatters as embarrassment floods me.

'Ha, ha, very bloody funny,' I chastise, although I can't mask the humour in my tone as his hearty laugh alone soothes something in me. Playful heartthrob cowboys are my new favourite eye candy.

'Bloody,' he howls, gripping his stomach and handing me some more tissues to mop up the new flow of blood creeping down my face.

'Good to know my pain and discomfort are amusing for you,' I say tartly, although I still can't stifle my smile completely.

'Hey, you make nosediving into the floor look classy,' he adds, running his thumb over my cheek.

'Mr jokes.' I laugh sarcastically, trying to ignore the heat his touch floods me with, as simple and innocent as it is.

'Hey, as I said, it could be worse.'

'How? How in the hell could this be worse?' I ask, flustered and a little annoyed, my face still a little sore and my embarrassment level through the roof as I imagine what a mess I must look like from his vantage point.

'You could have fallen over in front of all these people, obliterated a pair of fake boobs, spilt your drink, and woken up with a bloody nose,' he offers. I don't miss the twinkle in his blue-grey eyes flecked with a deep amber as he watches me intently. A breath hitches in my chest when he takes another sip of his beer. His stubble-dusted neck elongated, his Adam's apple protruding as the liquid runs fluidly down his throat. Thoughts of my lips tracing kisses up and down his neck rile up the previously dormant butterflies that take residence in my belly. My cheeks flush pink, but thankfully, the blood splattering my face masks them.

'That is exactly what happened!' I exclaim, throwing my arms up in the air.

'That's where you are wrong, lady.' He beams, handing me my unsplit cup of rum and cola propped up against his leg on the floor next to us. I can't help but laugh, even though moving my face makes me want to cry. I sit up pawing at my hair and take a much-needed swig of the alcohol, the cool fruitiness immediately calming me. I don't make any effort to move from the floor, though. I would happily spend the rest of the party cocooned in the comforts of his body because, let's face it, there are worse places to be. He pushes a strand of my chocolate brown hair from my face, tucking it behind my ear. My eyes fly up to his, the electricity his touch stirs at my core, causing me to cross my legs, trying and failing to suffocate the familiar sensation building there. I try to blank out the chattering around us as people discuss my fall, giving us a wide berth as we are sprawled out in the middle of the kitchen. I note Casey hasn't moved to help me, the knowing smirk playing on her lips as she watches our interaction explanation enough as to why. I beam up at my protector awkwardly and make my move to get up off the floor finally. The cowboy jumps to his feet and offers me his hand as I rest there for a moment on my knees, not trusting my ankles as the strap of my shoes pinches at my skin. I glance up, and I'm met with those blue-grey eyes again, hooded with fascination, as he stares down at me. Apart from the nosedive incident, I finally feel like I'm holding my own to a certain extent.

Maybe this isn't all bad.

I am, of course, wrong, the air of contentment disappearing like free crack at a Hollywood after-party when I move to speak.

'Woody!' I exclaim, ogling the beautiful young man towering above me as I catch sight of his gold sheriff's badge looped onto his belt, his hand lingering there between us. Now, being at the eye level I am at and shouting *Woody* isn't, and never will be, a memorable first meeting moment. I doubt it has ever been a talking point of anyone's relationship origin story. Still, my brain is running on equal amounts of unease and humiliation, and the epiphany of his costume is out of my mouth before I can contain it. I place my hand in his and move to stand. That bright, white-toothed smile spread wide across his amused face. He chuckles, and as my knees fight to prove me right and betray me, I buckle again and fall forwards into the warm embrace of his solid arms, his broad shoulders making light work of me as he lifts me and seats me on a nearby bar stool at the kitchen island. Now he is the one on his knees as his thick fingers pull at the dainty ribbon straps, keeping my heels on my feet, depositing the offending shoes on the floor beside him with a clunk once he's done.

'I'm sorry, I didn't mean…' I gesture towards his crotch, unable to find any words that would be socially acceptable to say at the moment. His stunning grin is unmoving as his stare flits between my face and my ankle, his long lashes fanning his sun-blushed cheeks. Thank God I am seated. My legs feel like jelly, and my brow is sweaty with the meagre exertion of getting up from the floor. This man does crazy things to my insides, and with the amount of rum I have swimming around in my system, I don't know how well I am hiding this fact. For those of you in the back, POORLY. To anyone with working eyes, it is impossible to miss just how much this man has affected me.

'Jim, the Waco kid,' he affirms assertively with a southern American drawl as he points to his chest with a plastic prop revolver. His deep voice is like molten gold caressing my skin. I shift on the stool in an attempt to dampen the buzz of activity thrumming at my core. I don't know why a child's cartoon character jumped to mind, but I saw the checked shirt, the fringed chaps, and the sheriff's badge, and my brain did the rest, my mouth, as usual, running away with itself before the thought had even been processed for human consumption.

'Jessica rabbit?' he queries with a curious look when I stay silent, pointing his weapon at me—the plastic one usually sheathed in his belt rather than the solid one between his legs that, even soft, leaves an impressive outline in the crotch of his jeans. I giggle at the thought, refusing to glance down again at what he is packing, mainly because I don't need any more excuses to embarrass myself further. It's impossible for him to miss the almost comical paper mâché boob job in my eye-wateringly tight-fitted red fishtail dress that I, at one point before this incredibly disconcerting moment, had considered an idea of comedic genius. Clearly, I was wrong, a soul-destroying error on my part that I wouldn't be forgetting any time soon.

'Mr Jim for tonight. On days without the fetching get-up, people call me O'Shea,' he states and I'm immediately desperate to know more.

'Miss Rabbit on very, *very*, rare occasions because I own a red dress and I have an infinity for craft work, and pretty much Roni all the other times.' I don't miss the waver in my voice as I catch sight the corded muscles flexing in his neck as he swallows down another mouthful of his drink.

He looks at me curiously as what appears to be a moment of long-since-forgotten recognition flutters briefly over his brooding expression. I can't say I mind the way he is intensely observing me. His gaze doesn't feel lecherous or invading as it sometimes did when other guys looked at me this way. Instead, pride fills my chest as I beam up at him politely, fighting off the urge to tell him a dirty joke; usually my go-to move in any awkward situation.

Two hours later, an entire packet of travel tissues for my bloody nose, some more ill-advised alcohol, and a couple of paracetamols, I find myself at his front door, I pull the ring of keys from his jeans pocket and stumble back dropping one of my shoes as I connect with the low brick wall.

Fuck the shoe, there are more pressing matters afoot.

With one eye closed and my tongue hanging out I try to work the wrong key into the lock. My dress is already partially unzipped, exposing my bare back, what's left of my boob job is discarded in the rosebush in the next-door neighbour's front garden, and his check shirt is sprawled on the windshield of someone's mini parked up on the road outside his gate. Once I finally manage to find the right key, I barrel over the threshold taking him with me and kick the door shut with my bare foot as he pulls me up into his arms, my legs instinctively wrapping around his muscled waist and locking at the ankles, my dress splitting at the seams around my thighs. My cowboy doesn't hesitate and with one hand he finishes the job and tears my dress in two, the strips of material falling away, so I'm left in just a bra and my knickers. A hum of satisfaction rumbles from his full lips as he takes a moment to appreciate my half naked form in his hold. The next few minutes are a groping mess of hands, lips, and groans. Smashing into the walls, our bodies devoid of control as I fight to free him from his jeans. The idea of watching Mr O'Shea gloriously naked, wearing just his cowboy boots, has me pulling at his hair. With a mixture of playful laughter and pure, unfiltered passion, my body caves into his embrace.

FEBRUARY 14th 2018

ROUGHLY 3 YEARS LATER

PRE MARCUS BREAKUP

RONI

Lost in thoughts of that first night in this house with Aiden, or Mr. O'Shea as he was otherwise known, I wait for him to return to the kitchen. Muffled chatter from down the hallway beyond the front door makes my heart sink a little as my world flips on its axis. The way it always did when he would introduce me to a new woman in his life. That night that would forever fill me with equal parts happiness for the possibility of something great and heartbreak when I realized it was just out of my reach is never far from my mind. That was the night I met Aiden for the second time. That day after the party, holed up in his wardrobe space, it didn't take long for us to discover why we had felt an air of familiarity with one another. Aiden chose not to delve too deeply into memories of our first meeting the night of my attack, and I was thankful for that. I didn't need pity swamping the light in his blue-grey gaze, so we opted to talk about our childhoods. That was a happier exchange I could get on board with. I left his house that day wearing my heels, once I had retrieved them from the front garden and a grey sweatshirt of Aiden's that was so long it fit me like a mini dress as the hem grazed my bare thighs. My costume in tatters, slung over my arm as I tottered off down the stone walkway to the waiting black cab. The broad smile on my lips refused to settle as I felt him watch me leave. Casey waited patiently on hold on my phone, desperate for me to dissect and share the order of events that occurred after I had left her alone at the party wound around Miss Ivy's long legs.

It only took two weeks after that first night, and I was back at his house, dancing across the threshold early on a Sunday morning with a joint tucked behind my ear courtesy of Casey, a *thanks for letting me live here* gift I thought he'd appreciate. With two cardboard boxes stacked in my arms that contained my entire life and *Del Amitri's Roll to me* blaring through my headphones, I watched as Aiden stood in the kitchen doorway with a bacon sandwich in one hand and a cup of coffee in the other. That was our official beginning, best friends since. Our raunchy night in the walk-in wardrobe was the first and last time Aiden and I were romantically involved. Sweaty, embroiled with lust and intoxication at its most dangerous level playing a key role, was the beginning of our friendship; the foundations, so to speak. Although a brief drunken kiss had been shared over the years, he never allowed it to go any further. I wanted more with him; I always had, but he couldn't see past the secret we shared, the need to protect me squarely forcing me into the little sister zone with none of the friends-with-benefits extras. Witnessing what he had in that bedroom with Lucas the night we met as teenagers broke something in Aiden that I couldn't fix. But I knew without a shadow of a doubt whatever this man offered me, I would accept it with open arms, even if it would forever be purely platonic.

'So, what do you think? She's nice, right?' Aiden asks excitedly, practically bouncing on the spot as he interrupts my train of thought. Leaning across the kitchen island, I flip the switch on the coffee pot. My scepticism about the young woman who had just left our kitchen is clear on my face as I run through the lacklustre offerings my head presented to best answer him without sounding curt. A simple but to-the-point *fuck no* felt a little too harsh.

With all that said, I am acutely aware that I have zero authority when it comes to what Aiden does with his free time or who he chooses to spend it with. Although Marcus and I are currently on a break, taking some time to enjoy our freedoms before we commit to getting married—his idea, not mine—I am technically still tied to him. Or am I?

I wonder what he's doing right now? the snarky little voice in my head snaps, but I ignore it. I've been staying at Aiden's for a few weeks now while Marcus does whatever he needs to do to get us back on track.

'She's nice,' I confirm, but my statement is forced. The small smile tugging at my lips is about as convincing as pineapple on pizza being voted the number one topping choice in some random online poll.

Thanks, brain.

The fact that I can't think of anything else to say other than she's *nice* and that my response sounds more like a question than an affirmation makes Aiden raise his eyebrows quizzically.

You can't lie to him, the little voice in my head barks.

Yes, yes, I can, I yell back, the muted little conversation I'm having with myself only forcing Aiden to become more suspicious. On most occasions, he can read my mind with just a sideward glance, which means that in this case, I'd keep quiet, calm my features, and adopt my mother's advice, *if you can't say anything nice, don't say anything at all.*

'Nice?' He repeats, urging me to elaborate. Those usually big azure eyes of his are now accusing slits as he evaluates my expression, his intense stare beating at my façade like a kid attacking a piñata.

'I wouldn't say she was my favourite person,' I add nonchalantly, trying to dodge his queries by concentrating squarely on my fresh mug of coffee, picking at the invisible lint around the rim. After spending the last four hours in her company, all I get is an unsettling feeling from her, and if my gut reactions are anything to go by, I hope she will be a fling at best. Louisa is beautiful, her long bottle-blonde locks iron-straight, not a hair out of place, her sparkling green eyes bright, her makeup perfect, her two-piece candy pink and peach lounge set immaculately pressed. The shame is that her personality is about as endearing as a jonesing junkie at a preschool fete. I can't prove she is a snake in the grass, and I won't go out of my way to prove it. I have to let him see it for himself. I can't imagine it will take long. Aiden follows me into the living room with his coffee mug and phone in hand, determined to continue our conversation. Slumping down into the sofa beside me, Aiden tugs at his bottom lip, trying and failing to mask the boyish grin that pinches at the corners of his mouth as he glances down at his phone screen. The phone buzzes again, alerting him to yet another incoming message. Relaxing back onto the sofa, he continues to tap away at the screen, excitement bursting from his fingertips between chuckles as I fade into the background.

Maybe I am wrong about this one. Maybe she will end up being the best thing that has ever happened to him. The preposterous thought makes me outwardly chuckle, drawing Aiden's attention away from his phone screen for about 1.3 seconds before it buzzes again. Before coming back to his house to *'check out Aiden's surroundings,'* a place she hadn't expected me to know as well as I did, Louisa had spent the entire lunch at Gino's Italian restaurant berating the young server about everything from a dirty fork to the fact that he had clearly got dressed in the dark because his shirt wasn't tucked in and his tie was fastened incorrectly. And when I say berating, I mean full-blown ripping him a new one. I was always taught that you treat the servers as you would the boss. Clearly never one to mince her words, Louisa was more than a little vocal on her thoughts about my presence at the impromptu lunch date. She had come there dolled up, ready to impress Aiden's best friend, to get the nod of approval. Aiden had forgotten to mention that his best friend was a girl. This fact irked *Malibu Barbie,* and she didn't make any attempt to hide her disdain. The live-action roleplay of *Mean Girls* I had inadvertently become a part of was an unfortunate turn of events. *Regina George* had nothing on Louisa. Thankfully, her introduction to Aiden's home, a home I had once lived in, another factor of our friendship she had issues with, had been a brief experiment before she pulled Aiden in for a kiss goodbye. Her excuses of a yoga class or something equally banal had her trotting off out the front door just thirty minutes after she had entered it. I was grateful for small mercies.

'She's an acquired taste,' I say, only realizing a few moments later that I have voiced aloud what should have been an internal thought. I can't hide the slope of my jaw as my mind fills with all things Louisa. Jealousy may be playing a little part in my current mood, but I refuse to dwell on it. The effort alone it would take to unpack Pandora's box of fucked up feelings that linger between Aiden and me is a *Lewis Carrol* alternate world that my sad, messed up in-the-head self has no desire to explore, not just yet, anyway.

You are technically in a relationship, my brain prompts, but I choose to ignore it, knowing but refusing to accept that it is right to remind me. Although I'm not sure how many relationships there are where the couple split for a month before they get hitched to explore some fucked up notion of a skewed sexual bucket list of missed opportunities. How Marcus had described it in the moment had made more sense, but with time comes clarity and the bullshit notion that this would be the best move for us and our relationship doesn't seem to be holding up. I'm yet to be convinced.

'She's an acquired taste?' Aiden repeats my statement to me, and I wince at the sound. 'Lucky you aren't the one dating her then,' he quips, hurt lacing his words. Leaning in towards me, Aiden concentrates on my face, trying to see his best friend hiding behind the envious monster currently taking over my body. I grin at him, sincerity warming my cheeks whilst I shovel yet another coffee-saturated rich tea biscuit into my mouth. I certainly won't be holding my breath when it comes to the questions surrounding the longevity of Louisa and Aiden's relationship.

'I'm guessing she had a few choice words to say about me turning up?' I inquire, knowing it's true, indifference rolling off me in waves. We both know that I couldn't care less what his response will be. But colour me intrigued. If she didn't like me as much as I didn't like her, that would be a-okay with me; that sort of honesty would be the only redeeming feature I had seen in Louisa thus far. Not enough to make us BFFs, but enough to make it a little easier to tolerate her. I can see Aiden silently warring with himself, deciding what to say to me next.

'Don't hold back for my sake, Aiden. What did little Miss *Mario Kart* say about me when I excused myself to the toilet at Gino's?' I laugh, his silence intriguing the darkest part of me.

'*Mario Kart*?' He responds with a raised brow, his eyes flitting between me and his phone screen.

'She's a princess, and she wore peach. Please don't make me explain it. You're losing your touch.' She has messed with his head. That joke was well thought out and presented beautifully.

'She said what you did, word for word,' he states calmly, clearly hating each word of truth that leaves his lips.

'Word for word or along the same lines?' I press, my interest piqued.

'WORD FOR WORD,' he emphasizes like it is the first time I am hearing his answer. 'There were no similar lines or friendly ballpark. You both dislike one another, and neither of you seems shy about letting me know it. But there is always an up-side,' he adds, hope smothering his words.

'Does she have scurvy?' I retort. *A girl could hope, right?*

'No Funny Bollocks,' he replies caustically.

'Is it gonorrhoea?' I smile annoyingly. This is still considered an up-side when discussing a possible friendship with his girlfriend.

'Okay, there's no up-side. Are you happy?' He asserts, frustration furrowing his brow.

'Ecstatic.' I say, my arms raised in celebration, putting an end to the discussion.

'So, what does Valentine's Day look like for you now you're newly single?' Aiden asks. His diversion tactics about as subtle as *RuPaul's* personality.

'It's a break.'

'It's ludicrous, is what it is. I don't know why you are with someone who would happily share you.'

'I messaged Trevor,' I offer, changing the subject, watching as the frustration slips from Aiden's face. Grateful that any talk of Louisa or Marcus is now in our rearview.

'What did you message him?' he asks, taking my fresh cup of coffee out of my hands and sipping it. The malty lining of dipped biscuits on the surface is his favourite.

'Nothing too strong. I was acting casual,' I reply, pulling the crocheted blanket from the end of the sofa over my bare legs and holding out my hands, silently requesting that Aiden return the stolen coffee.

Trevor is a new guy at work. He is cute, funny, and always up for a laugh. I'm not usually that sort of girl to mix business with pleasure, but with Marcus off on a mission, I think it's about time I follow suit. At least it would be a welcomed distraction. Trevor is a die-hard traveller at heart. He never stays in one place for too long. The itch to see the world a calling of sorts that drags him from one place to another. With his long blonde hair, almond-shaped hazel eyes, healthy glowing tan, big weather-worn hands, and his wrists donning multiple woven leather bracelets, Trevor is certainly a great candidate for possible filler sex. He is positively yummy. The free spirits, those like Trevor, are the best kinds of relationships to explore. They are the easiest to manoeuvre because they don't stick around for long. The washboard abs and the rumour he is packing at least eight inches in his boxer shorts also sweeten the pot. Marcus is many things, hung is not one of them.

'Casual like hey, or casual like I want your babies?' Aiden blurts, interrupting my fantasies. The strawberry flush creeping across my cheeks is the only sign of where my saucy thoughts are heading.

'Surely there is a vast difference and a broad spectrum of message possibilities between those two,' I say, knowing that when it came to me, those were literally my only two speeds.

'You'd like to think so, but no, you and I both know your love language has a point A and a point B. Your flirting abilities weren't made for technology, Roni.' He beams, seconding my earlier thought. *God, how well does this man know me*? 'So, I'll ask you again,' he continues. 'What did you send?'

Aiden waits patiently, fighting the urge to laugh at my expense, my brain working overtime as I decide whether to tell him the truth. Fear hits me like a punch to the gut.

Have I fucked up? Did I underestimate this whole thing? He hadn't even messaged me back, and everyone knows that's a guy's way of letting you down gently. Right?

'I sent him *fancy grabbing something to eat?'* I mumble, my attempt at feigning coolness missing the mark by about twenty feet.

'And?' Aiden presses, expertly reading my expression with a slick know-it-all grin while rolling his wrist, urging me to continue. Even though I know the message had been innocent enough, Aiden is now convincing me that something was wrong with it without knowing exactly what I had written. So I hold back, deciding that maybe on this occasion, denial is the best way to go. But who am I kidding? Aiden has always seen through my lies, or most of them, anyway.

'And the eggplant emoji,' I say almost inaudibly, my jaw tight. I don't know what I have done wrong, but if his blown pupils and slack mouth are an indication of anything, I have royally screwed up here.

'You're fucked. You've been out of the dating game too long,' he chortles, his eyes doubling in size.

'What, why?' I groan. The fact that I knew this response was coming fails to settle me.

'The eggplant emoji?' he says softly, his full lips pouting as he dips his head to one side, pitty for me forming in waves on his face. 'Everyone and their mother knows the eggplant emoji is *I want your dick in me ASAP*. You have insinuated that you *want to eat his cock,'* he sniggers. His use of air quotes makes me want to die inside.

'That is not a thing. He's a vegetarian. I was simply extending an invitation to eat at *Easy Eggplants*. The way to a guy is through his stomach right?'

'And the award for the most poorly named vegan Thai restaurant goes to.' He laughs, drumming his hands on the coffee table theatrically.

'Maybe he didn't get the memo.' I am inwardly praying that this is the case, but my best friend, who cannot keep a straight face right now, jumps to his feet and hops energetically on the spot, and that alone worries me that my naivety has won this battle.

'We all got that memo. That memo was designed in big neon lights by the emoticon-creating legend that designed the eggplant emoji.' He belly laughs, doubling over and burying his face into the couch cushion to stifle his howls of amusement.

I'm fucked.

'How come I didn't know then?' I whine, resisting the urge to throw my phone across the room. If it hit Aiden mid-flight, I wouldn't be sorry. My best friend is relishing in my downfall a little too much. Aiden had met Trevor at my Christmas work party and described him as a *depressing Steve Irwin clone with a God complex and a strange fascination with sea creatures.* Twenty-three minutes on why prawns were the leaders of the sea was more than Aiden had bargained for. Let's just say he isn't Trevor's biggest fan.

'Stop laughing, dipshit—why didn't I know this emoji dick secret?'

'I was asking myself that very question, but there is a more pressing question. What did he write back to your little sex text?' Aiden queries from behind his fingers as he holds his lips together, stifling the smile that attempts to break free at my expense.

'It was NOT a sex text,' I protest and stamp my feet. Even now, when he is teasing me, I can't help but beam up at him. Amusement lighting his grey-blue eyes with a playful intensity.

'I beg to differ, baby. Now let me have it. What did Trevor say?'

'He didn't respond,' I say flatly. My eyes screwed shut as I brace myself for Aiden's retort.

'I mean, I'm not surprised. Maybe he just couldn't believe his luck. Or he couldn't stop laughing?'

'Hey,' I whine, punching at his solid frame.

'Hey, nothing. That is comedy gold for a man. At this point, you're like an STI warning poster,' Aiden offers unhelpfully.

'Eloquently put, thanks.' I am losing my shit; I have to see Trevor at work tomorrow, and I may be many things in that office, but dick emoji connoisseur is not one of them. The rumours of me being the office bike hurt less than this. At least with that, I had plausible deniability, although it wasn't exactly untrue, there was little to no proof. This was in a message, noted in black and white, and he could show it to anyone and everyone if he wanted to.

'Guys want available girls who hide the fact that they are interested. But girls that appear overtly available somehow fall into the desperate category,' Aiden offers, his skewed sense of wisdom muffled as he tilts his head and drops a couple of grapes into his mouth.

Fuck my life.

'That's crazy double standard bullshit,' I bark. Even though I know, I don't have a leg to stand on. Before Marcus my love life's moto was *fuck first, ask questions later*. I tended to chew men up and spit them out again. Let's just say I've had more than my fair share of twists on that gumball machine.

I'm officially delusional.

'Of course it's double standards. I didn't state otherwise, but if I know anything, it's how guys think Roni.'

'How do I fix it?' I grumble like a petulant five-year-old, my window of opportunity to correct my mistake edging closer and closer to oblivion with every passing minute.

'Can you turn back time?' he asks deadpan, his eyes wide.

'Clearly not rain man.' I don't appreciate his mocking tone and by the contorted expression on my face, I'm sure he knows it.

'Then you are screwed. Firing up the *DeLorean* was your best bet,' he says, swerving out of the way as I throw another punch in his direction.

'A fictional time-travelling hunk of machinery. If that was the only way I was getting out of this, I'd say my odds were never really good, Aiden.' He tries not to react to my pout, but I can see his inbuilt sense of solidarity sway him.

'With the eggplant alone, you could have maybe got away with the ditsy vote; *my finger slipped* excuse or the audacious and mostly unbelievable response—which I have received after a drunken four in the morning eggplant text from a girl—where she states that her cat, dog or other pet-like creature has sat on the touchscreen sending the embarrassing emoji.'

I mentally slap myself as I realise just how clueless I am about technology. I am either going to have to get on board and learn the lingo, become a nun, or keep a pet for excuse-text purposes. Between you and me, that middle option was more than likely the most improbable. But I could find a pet online in three seconds flat if I needed to.

'But you knew they were lying? The girls searching for a 4 am cock buddy who sent you their animal regret texts.' I press—my willingness to learn, urging me to scoot over a little closer to Aiden.

'Yes, I did, but they opted out, and if I'm honest, I started enjoying the imagination put into the excuses. Oddly, iguana has been played a few times.'

Iguana works—noted.

'We all make mistakes when we're drunk, although you are texting him in the middle of the day, and that is a red flag for any excuse you might come up with. Unless you feel like telling him you're a raging alcoholic addicted to bottomless champagne brunches.' He sniggers. I both hate and love how much he is enjoying this right now.

'What do I do? This is the part where one friend, *you*'—I throw my hand out wildly at him—'helps the other friend, *me*,' I finish, placing my palm on my chest.

'Okay, how did you end the conversation after the whole gobbling his purple phallic moment?' He laughs again, the gruff sound making my skin prickle in response.

Down girl

'LOL,' I say quietly, my bottom lip pushed out because I know I'm just making this worse for myself. Who needs a shovel when you're currently riding through the remnants of your poor life choices on a *JCB* digger. Any semblance of positivity I may have woken up with this morning is now ripped to shreds like confetti around my feet and not that bright celebration confetti but tattered black sad confetti.

'It's finished. You've managed to embarrass yourself on every level of this backwards pyramid scheme we call dating. If I didn't feel so mortified for you, I'd be congratulating you. It's a very hard thing to achieve what you have here. It's almost unheard of outside of a pathetic teen drama.' Aiden offers, clapping his hands together sardonically.

'Well, at least that's a bonus, then. I'm so glad my drama brings you so much joy.' My mocking grin pinches at my cheeks as I pray for the ground to open up and swallow me whole.

If I didn't shout it loud enough last time, *Fuck my life.*

'Everyone will hear of this, and I mean EVERYONE,' he teases, digging at the soft flesh of my hips and enjoying watching me squirm.

'Hey, best friend code,' I state with my index finger extended in his face, ready and willing to throw him into a headlock. When I say *throw*, I mean jump on his back like a wildcat until he laughs so hard he gives in.

'I uphold all promises I ever made but I know for a fact that unless that guy dropped his phone in a vat of plastic corroding chemicals before he got a chance to read your message, he is sharing it around right now like a plate full of warm special brownies. I also wouldn't be surprised if he embellishes a little.'

'Maybe he will see the funny side?' I say hopefully.

Whatever entity is watching over me, please let him see the funny side.

'Nope,' Aiden replies, pulling me from my prayer.

'Maybe he won't read too much into it?' I panic, less hopeful now.

Spirit guardian, please don't let him read too much into it.

'Nope,' Aiden claps back.

'Maybe he didn't even see it,' I finish, my tone thick with the last smidgen of my optimism.

Dear God, please don't let him have seen it. The fact that I am an Atheist, if anything, spurs me to pray that little bit harder, as though being new to his following would reward me with some bonus perks. As if following a new religion is like joining the latest popular movie streaming site and getting the first two months free.

'Nope. There's no funny side. You can't not read into it, and he soooo read it,' Aiden chortles whilst shoving a cookie into his mouth.

'So, what do I do?' I beg, knowing that at this point, I would accept advice from the Devil himself if it made work easier for me on Monday morning.

'Pray, I only have God to offer you.'

Been there, done that. The little voice in my head teases. I don't appreciate her levity.

'We've had words. He's not on board. The Devil also has questions. Anyway, I'm a Buddhist.' I state coolly, drumming my fingernails against my coffee cup, summing up an eclectic core belief system in four easy sentences. Not bad for someone who up until the age of sixteen thought Jehovah's Witnesses was a football team.

'No, what you are is screwed. At least the Bible vote might have got hope on your side.'

'You are not calming me, Aiden,' I admonish, debating whether hiding out in my bedroom for a week for the dust to settle is an option I am willing to commit to. I don't like my own company that much, and after using the last of my sick days on that impromptu Amsterdam trip with Aiden, I don't think a week off would fly with management. Jobless, penniless, and a whore, aren't exactly the descriptors I had aspired to when I left university.

'When was it decided that it was my job to calm you? I'm the best friend. I offer pain-ridden, no-holds-barred honesty and a warm hug when you con me into watching a rom-com on a Sunday night.' He snickers. But I see that big-brother need to protect me, lingering in his blue-grey gaze. Aiden is all kinds of gorgeous when he is being cheeky. I quickly chastise the growing feeling of need flourishing in the pit of my belly. This is most certainly not the time for thoughts of him shirtless and at my mercy.

Take a breath girl

'I don't know, Aiden; maybe it was decided when I told that girl you no longer lived here? Maybe when I pretended I was a French exchange student so you could score that free Americano at *Costa,* or maybe back when your sister found half a gram of hash in your sock drawer on her last visit, and I convinced her it was dried coriander.' I list my reasons with ease, never faulting a beat. Knowing I had a plethora of answers in my arsenal, ready and waiting for him. Although neither of us believed Paige was that stupid to believe my lies—that we could agree on.

'See, now this is a perfect example of why you set ground rules. Surely the significant time lapse makes those null and void,' he counters.

'Help me, Aiden. I'm slowly losing the will to live.' Shame is no longer a word that exists in my vocabulary. At this point, I would sell my soul to the highest bidder to sort this shit out.

'That's the attitude. Wallow in self-pity until you don't care anymore,' Aiden cajoles, rubbing little condescending circles into my shoulders.

'That is probably the worst advice you have ever given me,' I cry out, still unable to completely banish the small smile playing on my full lips. It doesn't matter what the situation is or how bad things get; Aiden always makes me smile.

'Worst advice? Really? May I remind you of Drake and the chicken fillet debacle of 2016?' he states.

'No, you may not,' I respond curtly. Being reminded of yet more epic relationship fails isn't the way to go, and I'm sure my disinterested scowl makes my thoughts on the matter abundantly clear. It doesn't stop him, though; I knew it wouldn't.

'How was I to know they were meant to be hidden?' he squeals, his face the picture perfect example of innocence as he raises his hands.

'You were pulling them out of my bra and waving them in the air whilst singing *Shakira* along with the DJ at the top of your lungs with half a bottle of rum in your system. It was mortifying not only because Drake and I were on a first date but also because of the other three hundred or so people who watched on in horror. I had to stop shopping at Tesco after that. I was called *chicken little* every time I went to get milk.'

'You know I shouldn't drink rum,' he says as a way of an acceptable explanation.

'I am so close to slapping you right now. Help me or I swear I will add a touch of natural rouge to that cheek.' I point to the left side of his face and roll up my sleeves to solidify my intention.

'Somewhat questionable friend instances aside, I am trying to help you. My advice is that you find a deep dark hole, livable obviously, and get comfy. This is one of those rare cases where a minimum of two months is needed for everything to blow over.'

'To hide? Your advice is to hide. *Oprah,* you are not my friend.' I groan, an awkward harrumph passing my lips.

'You sent an emoji equivalent of a dick pic to a guy who is currently shagging a co-worker of yours. What led you to believe that you could go back to a point before that?' Aiden says calmly.

'It's not a co-worker. He's shagging my boss,' I reply, the familiar pain of regret tugging in my chest as I hear the truth out loud.

'I know. I was trying to make you feel better. Read the room, Roni,' he chastises cheekily, cocking his head and running his thumb down my cheek to comfort me. I stop breathing as he runs his thumb over my bottom lip, freeing it from between my teeth as I chew on it nervously until it's raw. If he notices the change in the air between us, he doesn't let on. He resumes his position on the sofa, the electricity that warms me thanks to his closeness now snuffed out.

'You failed on that one, Aiden. I certainly don't feel better. Shit, do you really think he would show people at work?' I whine, my head falling into my hands.

'Is the pope Catholic?' He jibes, and my head snaps back up to glare at him.

'I'm deciding to air on the side of positivity and believe that it can't be that bad.' I had clearly become skilled in the art of lying to oneself.

'What happened when that computer tech Claude accidentally sent that inappropriate picture message to the company WhatsApp group chat?'

'He moved on to bigger and better things,' I say confidently.

'No, he didn't. He was so traumatized from the onslaught of taunts and Chinese whispers around the office that he quit, moved back in with his mother, and took a job at Cubby's chicken factory.'

'That's not true.' I chuckle, shaking my head in disbelief. *Was it true?* I had heard the rumours, but in the stark light of my current predicament, I hope it was a lie.

'It is 100% factually correct, and I can prove it.' Tapping away at his phone screen, Aiden turns it to me after he's finished with his search. Staring back at me is what I have at this moment convinced myself is a snapshot into my future. —a social media profile picture of a very down-and-out-looking Claude in a muddy brown uniform, a rack adorned with dead featherless chickens hung by their feet above his head.

'Poor guy.' I sigh, for a moment forgetting my plight.

'Technology is not a friend to all.' Aiden's comment only proves to bring my worried thoughts crashing back to me. My phone vibrates, the audible buzz of doom following it, signalling a new message in my inbox.

'Do I want to see this?' I ask Aiden sheepishly, my desire to throw my phone out of the window rather than look at the screen, a choice I am seriously contemplating.

'I don't know about you, but I'm pretty intrigued.'

I decide that throwing it out of the window is my only option and raise my arm above my head. Reading me perfectly, Aiden grabs my arm and relieves me of my phone, tutting at my boldness.

'Let me look for you,' Aiden coos, his hand still clasped around my arm reassuringly. I lessen my grip on my phone and allow him to wrench it from my palm. 'There are two messages from the eggplant guy. Two emojis, a donut, and a hot dog.' Those blue greys of his widen as he pulls his bottom lip between his teeth to contain his smirk.

'So, what does that mean?' I ask cluelessly, grabbing for my phone.

'He's proud to confirm that he knows exactly how well a hot dog fits into a donut. Either that or he's ditched vegetarianism and wants to hit up a local *Wimpy* for dinner and dessert.'

'Nah ah, there is no way he thinks like that.' I eye the message shrewdly and try to weigh what other meanings can be hidden in his reply.

'We all think like that. Men, in general, think like that every three seconds, Roni. In my head, you've been dressed in a floral two-piece, sipping suggestively on the straw of a banana milkshake since you mentioned food.'

'Ewwww.' I fight to react as I should, even though inside my heart leaps with eagerness, butterflies flying aimlessly in wild circles around my stomach at the thought that he would ever view me that way.

'Hey, only sisters, mums, and extended blood family are a no-go. General ladies are simply a given. I don't know the actual numbers, but I reckon we would combust without this.'

'Bullshit,' I state, a broad smile tickling my cheeks.

'Or flattered?' he offers audaciously as I try to hide the surge of need quivering between my legs.

'I should flatten you with a book on women's suffrage. Maybe some of the knowledge would magically rub off,' I tease.

'Hey, I respect women,' he professes, even though we both already know it's true.

'But do you? Are you sure?' I cock my head to the side while I drink in the boyish grin dancing across his lips. Aiden wouldn't know how to disrespect a woman; it is simply not in his nature.

'I hold your coat when we're at a bar when you go to the toilet,' he adds as a means of an epic gesture of chivalry.

'*Gandhi,* everyone, make way,' I tease in a low tone, bowing theatrically, waving my arms up and over my body in a wave of appreciation as though welcoming royalty.

'Well, you're no *Mother Teresa.* I bet she wouldn't have opted straight out for the eggplant.' He laughs, his hand running through his unruly brown hair and settling at the back of his neck.

'I don't think conversing in little colourful images was her thing.' I snort.

'That's religion for you,' he quips as though it's old news.

'I would rather bend towards technology. Not everything is religion's fault,' I say as though I'm not inherently Team Skeptic. Defending Jesus came twice a year only, Christmas and Easter, and even then, the conversation always ended with a black-and-decker nail gun joke.

'We've strayed. Let's just agree that eggplant will never mean the same thing ever again. And while we're at it, let's assume that the phone companies inbuilt the feature that means duck being a replacement word for fuck, even when it's blindingly clear that no one ever chose that word, is an inconvenience to us all,' Aiden says.

He had me there. Fucking autocorrect.

'My Uncle Dave likes ducks,' I blurt out unhelpfully.

'Your Uncle Dave is now your Auntie Doreen, and he, strangely, just so happens to own a duck appreciation sanctuary. I don't think that one-in-a-million situation plays any part here.'

'Did you autocorrect there?' I chuckle, thankful that for a few moments at least I can forget my messaging mishap and just enjoy this exchange with Aiden.

'No, ducks, in this very rare case, mean ducks. Or at least I bloody hope so.' It's in this moment we both share the same daunting mental image, nodding at one another as we allow the thought to grow.

'Yeah, Dick appreciation sanctuary struck me as a pretty good name for a dick farm, too.' He says coolly, mirroring my thought while we each try, without reason or boundaries, to imagine what visiting such a sanctuary would entail.

'Do they make the dicks? Do they worship the dicks? Do they teach you how to use the dicks?' I voice the questions we were both mutely toying with whilst nibbling on a biscuit.

'Sounds like the Government.' Aiden laughs.

'I think I'm reading too much into this. That and now I have *Tony Blair* in my head as a key speaker at *Casa a la Dicks*.' I chortle, making him almost spit out a mouthful of coffee at my remark.

'Ruined! You've completely killed a perfectly good train of thought. Now we will never know the purpose of a dick farm,' Aiden argues, feigning annoyance, but he can't hide that grin; not from me.

DECEMBER 17TH 2018

10 MONTHS LATER

TWO WEEKS POST MARCUS

RONI

I trudge up the cobbled pathway to Aiden's house; well, *our* house now, I guess. Aiden hadn't had to think twice when I left the flat I had shared with Marcus and turned up on his doorstep, welcoming me with open arms. That little *let's have a break and explore ourselves before marriage* really had been the worst idea. Definitely not the finest decision I've ever made. Literally, all he explored was the inside of my sister's vagina, and when we finally did get back together, his little adventures with her continued behind my back until I caught them bumping uglies two weeks ago. When I turned up on Aiden's doorstep, the scents of bacon, coffee, and the familiar aroma of his woodsy aftershave were exactly what I needed to start healing. The memory of him propped up against the kitchen door warms my soul. Unfortunately, it isn't enough to warm my body as I stand here a wet and battered mess from the impromptu rainstorm that decided to come out of nowhere at the exact moment I stepped off the bus. The irony of the now beautiful rays of sunshine that peek out from behind the parting sad grey clouds as I pull my keys out of my pocket only further proves to irk me. Timing is not on my side today; it would seem.

I balance the numerous shopping bags in one hand, the plastic biting into my palm and level the key with the lock. When I've successfully gained entry, frustrated, I kick the door open; it connects with the wall and bounces back at me, nearly hitting me in the face. Stumbling back into the wall, I drop my bags, any breakable containers be damned, and huff tiredly as I slide off my yellow raincoat. The sweat coating my arms makes the cheap laminated pleather material stick to my skin. I throw my bulky ring of keys into the bowl on the side table beneath the oversized gilded mirror that hangs awkwardly at an angle on the wall. Kicking my shoes off and propelling them into our downstairs wardrobe space, I make no attempt to tend to the shopping bags. I shuffle into the living room and throw my coat over the back of the sofa. Sitting across the room without a care in the world, freshly showered, his hair still damp and slicked back, is Aiden wearing nothing but a pair of grey sweatpants and a lopsided smile.

Fuck my resolve as I practically melt on the spot. The heat from the crackling fire warms his muscly chest and colours it with a golden glaze, every inch of him a morsel I would happily tuck into. Aiden relaxes on the brown leather sofa with a magazine in his lap, his bare feet crossed at the ankles and propped up on the low coffee table, looking like a model in some men's weekly magazine, blissfully unaware of what his half-naked form does to me. He beckons me to take a seat next to him with an old school come hither swipe of his fingers and the *Emily Bronte* girl living in my soul, the one who fights for her place in the hierarchy but bends to the romantic whims of a man, folds without question and accepts the freshly made cup of walnut whip topped coffee that this guy is offering her, the open biscuit barrel shaped like *Count Duckula* tucked into his side the cherry on the cake that moves a girl like me to accept the smidgen of hope of *what if*, as an entrée. The dynamics between Aiden and I have shifted since I moved back in two weeks ago, and I appreciate the swift change of direction my life has taken me. Thankfully, I haven't heard anything from Marcus or my sister since the night I found them in bed together, and I am more than okay with that. So essentially, thoughts of Aiden fill my days, and although I don't entertain them, I can't ignore the rumbling of feelings that swell in my chest when he is close by, feelings I thought I had put to bed a long time ago. Moving in with Aiden again is like coming home, a sense of belonging I hadn't realised I had lost. We fell right back into how we had always been, as though no time had passed at all. I slump down beside Aiden and mirror his body, scooting down the couch so that with my considerable height difference, I can lift my feet onto the table next to his, the sodden cuffs of my bell-bottom jeans leaving dirt on the glass top. I grab the biscuit barrel and root around for the chocolate ones Aiden routinely hid at the bottom for me.

'Clothes before cookies,' Aiden commands, swiping the barrel away from me and holding it out of my reach, gesturing at my sodden clothes as I start to shiver, even with the blazing fire it feels like the cold has reached my bones. A squeak of defiance falls out of my mouth before I get to my feet and stride out of the room.

'Bossy much,' I say under my breath as I reach the door.

'I heard that. Now I'm going to eat the last chocolate swirl,' Aiden teases.

'You wouldn't.' I seethe, peering around the wooden door at him, adopting a softer expression when I see the biscuit that I had my eye on in-between his fingers.

'Depends. How quickly can you get changed?' he teases, slowly bringing the biscuit towards his mouth, silently daring me to take my time and watch my treat disappear.

I run from the room, discarding my wet clothes throughout the kitchen as I bundle into the tiny room at the back where the clothes dryer lives. Two orderly loads of clean clothes are stacked high on a shelf beside me, and I grab blindly at my pile, not particularly caring what I've chosen or the mess I'm making of Aiden's meticulous folding. Re-dressing en route, I hightail it back through the kitchen and into the living room in time to see my biscuit resting on Aiden's bottom lip. I jump over the coffee table and slam into the hard steel of Aiden's chest, realizing my error a little too late as I fumble around in his lap, my body rubbing against certain areas of my best friend that I had no right to. Unable to contain his raucous laughter, he continues to hold the chocolatey treat out at arm's length, holding me tethered to his lap as his fingers melt into the bare skin at my waist beneath the jumper I am wearing.

Breathe Roni.

Unable to move, I watch as Aiden runs his tongue over my biscuit, slick satisfaction gleaming in his eyes.

'I licked it, so it's mine,' he teases, his voice gruff, his hand on my waist relaxing. I see my opportunity and cease it, grabbing for the biscuit and promptly shoving the whole thing into my mouth.

'The fact that you thought that would stop me is hilarious,' I mumble as I chew, savouring what I can of the taste—triumphantly flicking any crumbs off my chest with a glossy smile playing on my full lips once I'm done.

'How's my jumper working out for you?'

'It magically makes its way onto my laundry pile.' Bringing the sleeve of the jumper up to my lips I run the tip of my tongue over the fabric. 'I licked it, so it's mine,' I press with an air of finality, using his earlier comment against him. The baggy grey jumper I'm wearing, the same one Aiden had let me wear that first night I had slept over here after the costume party, is easily my favourite of all his clothes, and he knows it. That's why it always miraculously appears in my pile of clean washing.

'So today was the day. You finally met Louisa's parents? On a scale of one to horrendous, how was it?' Although my tone is playful, I unkindly hope that it was awful enough to cause Aiden to reassess his relationship with Louisa, but that is just the bitterness talking. I shuffle in my seat, moving to tuck my legs under myself as I lean with one elbow on the back of the sofa to face him, my coffee cup resting on my knee. The fling with Louisa that I had naively thought back in February would be over in a matter of weeks is still going strong, so not a fling at all. Sadly.

Glancing down, I fiddle nervously at the fraying material of my combat trousers which are torn haphazardly at the knees, my oldest pair. I bet Louisa would never be seen dead in anything even remotely casual; I, however, have two looks: homeless and level seven hot. There is no in-between for me. Sensing but not knowing why it is there, Aiden addresses the unease in my expression by running his thumb over the frown lines carved into my forehead until they disappear.

'It looks better on you than it ever did on me,' he says softly, his thumb lingering on my face for a moment. I look a royal mess, but having his eyes on me in the way that he does has a way of making me feel pretty. Whether or not he is mine, my best friend always makes me feel loved.

'Enough about me. Parents,' I press. He inches away from me and settles back into the sofa, tugging at the hair at the nape of his neck.

'It was pretty painless, to be fair,' he replies, his eye line concentrating on anything but me.

Louisa has an edge that I can't possibly compete with. My only family is a backstabbing sister who wouldn't piss on me if I was on fire; a drink-addled mother whose entire existence is summed up with the saying, *"I didn't want to rock the boat,"* and a father whose current residence is Collingwood Cemetery. The Brady Bunch, we are not.

'Let me guess; her dad's a golf man?' I ask, successfully silencing my wandering mind from exploring the unhappy memories of my childhood.

'Mr. Rinstein owns his own green,' Aiden retorts, a smidgen of wonder tainting his tone.

Of course he fucking does. I am aware that even though I haven't voiced the thought, I still detect a pang of jealousy in the statement. Of course, I shouldn't have assumed anything less; you could probably pull this girl's family out of an episode of *Housewives of Atlanta.*

'Her mum bakes,' he adds, that familiar twinge of awe swimming in his big blue-greys again.

Could this storyline be any more signed, sealed, and delivered? Even Stevie Wonder could have seen this coming, my little inner voice chants annoyingly.

'I didn't think you were into all that.' My voice is small, the statement meant to be a thought but slipping out, regardless. The back catalogue of Aiden's dating life consisted of laid-back brown-haired, blue-eyed girls who wore no makeup and preferred lounge pants. Louisa Rinstein didn't fit that mould.

'I can't play golf to save my life. But my mother told me that if someone asks if you can do something, and you don't know how to, you say yes, and learn to the best of your ability in your spare time,' he replies, gesturing to the gleaming set of golf clubs propped up against the drink's cabinet. From the stories Aiden had told me, although ditsy and a bit of a push-over, his mother's heart is clearly in the right place; she wants the best for Aiden and his sister Paige, that is for sure.

'I think I'd get on with your mum,' I add, dunking yet another biscuit into the mug of coffee Aiden has made me, watching as the heat melts the chocolate coating.

Thank fuck for chocolate.

'Oh, she'd love you. You're pretty much the only reason she sleeps at night.' His remark floors me; my insides suddenly all warm and fluffy. Of course, I laugh because it feels necessary, but I know that the mum vote goes a long way to shaping a young man's decisions in life, and if his mum likes me, I can be sure she wouldn't much like Louisa. The term chalk and cheese springs to mind.

'So how do I help her sleep at night?' I ask, now fully invested in the conversation.

'She's never met you, but she trusts you; she thinks you are what keeps me grounded and sane. For her, that's better than gold,' he states whilst I fight the urge to giddily bounce on the spot.

'It's not such a bad job keeping you on the straight and narrow,' without thinking, I press my palm to his cheek. The connection has tingles warming my blood, the room around me suddenly too hot, but I don't pull away.

'The feeling is mutual,' he states, bringing my hand to his mouth and dotting a kiss on my open palm. My insides liquify. I retract my hand promptly, and if he notices my haste, he doesn't react. He smiles, and I smile. The tension of what *shoulda, woulda, coulda* happened between us had I not moved my hand away, merely a *Beverly Knight* song racing in circles around in my head.

'Mum asked if you wanted to come to Paige's for Christmas?'

Christmas is only a few days away, and he knows that with my mum gallivanting in the Swiss Alp winds with my sister Morgan; in search of husband number five, no doubt, and because of the shitshow that was my breakup with Marcus, I will be alone this year. The idea of being with Aiden after such a significant change in my life feels right, but the very real fear that I could totally screw this all up, if I allow my feelings for him to see the light of day never seems far from my thoughts. While I don't much care for Louisa, I would never act on those feelings. I wouldn't do that to any woman, not even her. Thankfully the crippling fear of Aiden's rejection of me has me tightlipped, I'm not prepared to lose him.

'Is Louisa not going home with you for Christmas?' I press, trying to avoid thoughts of an unachievable future with my best friend. He cocks his head, fighting a laugh at my assumption. We both know that having Louisa and me in the same room for Christmas would be neither festive nor jolly, battle royale *Tekken* style comes to mind, and that's probably not the entertainment Mrs. O'Shea has in mind for the holidays.

'Oh, we're not there yet.' He chuckles as though the thought itself is insane. 'My mother would shoot her dead over the turkey,' he declares, all humor lost from his voice.

'Losing faith in your mother here,' I jibe.

'Oh no, my mum isn't the problem. Louisa has a way of rubbing people up the wrong way. My mother would turn her into a walking, talking shish kebab. The Outback Aussie in her doesn't do well with the prim princess vibes.' I take a second to assess his response as he finishes pouring himself another coffee from the pot.

So, he knows what Louisa is like? I don't understand why the realization surprises me, but it does. I always thought he must have been oblivious to her behavior, but clearly, he saw it all.

Why is he still with her? I think better of voicing my question. I have to respect that he knows what he is doing.

'What is Christmas like in the O'Shea household, then? I should probably bone up if I'm going to be there.' I accept his offer without saying, *"yes, please."* My mind is already racing with what gifts to buy and what dessert to make to decorate the table. I make a mental note to invest in a cookbook; sliced strawberries and brandy cream are hardly going to impress anyone.

'First things first, the Santa rules,' Aiden says, interrupting my thoughts of baked Alaska's and apple pies.

'You and your sister are grownups, right?' I giggle, trying and failing to remember when I last believed in the fat, bearded man that lives at the North Pole.

'Hey, Santa is a state of mind. Getting into the childish spirit is number one on the O'Shea family to-do list.'

'Okay, if Santa *is* real, what about the reindeer?' I press, enjoying his playfulness.

'Everyone but my uncle Myron agreed with the magic of flying reindeer,' he replies solemnly.

'What the hell happened to Uncle Myron?' I take the last biscuit from the cookie jar and break it down the middle, handing half to Aiden.

'He had the tip of his nose bitten off by a reindeer when he was thirteen. Ever since then, he has been anti anything animal related. I tried to make him hold my hamster once. You would have thought World War II had decided to discuss battle strategies over a bowl of pesto pasta,' Aiden fondly relays the story.

'Who won? I'm intrigued to know who officially reigned supreme at battle Santa-gate.'

'No one, the answer is no one won the outrageous commendation attributed to the most left-field battle of all time. I'm not afraid to tell you he was a prick, and your chances of seeing him at Christmas are slim to none.' Aiden rakes his hand through his hair again. It's now almost completely dry, his muddy-brown waves falling over his forehead as he eyes the clock on the wall.

Stunning. I muse, crossing my legs as thoughts of Aiden in his birthday suit roam unguarded around my mind, the movement a must to quieten the throbbing between my thighs. I gulp down the excess saliva in my mouth and watch as his tongue darts out to wet his lips. His long lashes fanning his cheeks, you know, the ones that seem utterly pointless for a man to have when I have to buy a new mascara every two weeks just so they are visible. As they often did, my eyes divert again towards his now slightly parted lips, every word and slight smile inviting my stare more. My heart quickens, each frantic beat audible in my chest, my throat bone dry. I watch him continue to talk, but I can't hear a word that leaves his mouth, my brain too distracted to admire and listen simultaneously. My senses are filled with everything Aiden. My inner voice reminds me that the twenty seconds I have spent admiring his lips, his chiseled jaw, his intoxicating cerulean blue, speckled grey eyes, are twenty seconds too many, my gaze a little more intense than a friendship would usually allow.

'Roni.' The mention of my name drags me out of my daydream, the sense of longing snapping in my abdomen like an elastic band. My preposterous fan girl fantasies ebbing back into the darkness, that mysterious hidey-hole that pulses silently, filled with passion and desire, held back by the solid and unrelenting arms of common sense and a much-needed reality check. I often imagined those arms to be a set of bulky WWE-esque guns ready and willing to pull me back, body slam style, to the ground if my emotions ever attempted to break free past the point of no return. So far, their employment has been much appreciated, the awkward sidestep of full-on embarrassment still just bubbling beneath the surface as it always does. I'm not naïve enough to think that any good could come from exploring my feelings for Aiden. With my rocky relationship with Marcus still lingering in the background, for now, I'll settle for discovering who I am as a single woman. The hot best friend story arc will be a side note up for later investigation.

FEBRUARY 14th, 2019

2 MONTHS LATER

RONI

'You really like Valentine's Day, huh?' I quip before I bite off a piece of beef jerky. The noise of my lips smacking together proving to annoy her as her hackles raise, so I don't stop. Likening Louisa to an animal today wasn't planned but it sure as fuck is welcomed. A feral pettiness pushing me to goad her more. Resting up against the kitchen door, I gesture towards Louisa's attempts at romantic holiday décor with my meaty treat. If glares could kill, Louisa's contorted grimace is prime for a slaying. Always one to take my wins where I can get them. I prove to enrage her further when I blow her a little kiss, her teeth grinding together as she throws a handful of heart confetti in my direction. She eyes my outfit of baggy jeans and a torn band tee as though it is offensive to her, judgment heavy in her murky-green eyes, a smirk creeping onto her preened lips as she smooths her palm down her fitted dress that hugs every inch of her slim frame. 'Do you not think it's a bit... much?' I chime in. Now, by the slight expression of abject horror set in place like a mask over Louisa's features you would think that I had successfully cornered her with a checkmate move, but even my audacity does nothing to dampen the air of superiority radiating from her. Her face unmoving now thanks to grade A Botox injections, and her more than likely using the blood of innocent children as a moisturiser in her morning beauty routine.

'Aiden liked it. How's spinsterhood, Veronica?' Louisa snaps back in a snarl as though her words can hurt me. I hate references to my full name, even more so when it comes from her mouth. The slight *Touché* grin I offer her dispels her glee as she returns to decorating the kitchen table with enough romantic paraphernalia to make Cupid want to shoot himself in the head with one of his arrows. Heart confetti, foil balloons, streamers, banners. If the local shop had it, she bought it. The sea of red blanketing every surface in our kitchen looks more like a scene from some *Wes Craven* flick than a gesture of undying love. 'If you choose to fuck and then discard anything with two legs and a cock, you will remain alone, Veronica,' she offers as though I could give two shits about her opinion of my love life.

'Slightly ableist of you; never underestimate a man in a wheelchair. All that metal gives you something solid to hold on to,' I clap back at her, giggling as her palm flies up to her mouth to stop the gasp falling from her lips, as though she hadn't just said *fuck* and *cock* in the same breath. The prim and proper pretence that Louisa shows the world is highly offended by my crass excuse for an existence, and she doesn't mind reminding me of it whenever she gets the chance. Just to rub salt into the wound, I gyrate my hips crudely in her direction, knowing it will stimulate another wave of disgust to warp what's left of the working nerves in her pretty face. *Just call me Miss Petty.* She moves to speak, her bright red lips partially open as she prepares to let loose yet another derogatory statement at me, even though I know she would love nothing more than to scream *Whore* at me until she's blue in the face. I move across the kitchen towards her, silently willing her to do it, savouring the moment as the need to express herself ticks uncomfortably in her taut jaw.

'You ladies playing nice?' Aiden coos, standing in the doorway sockless, the black and grey tattoos etched into his skin above his peck, that travel up over his shoulder and down his arm doing nothing to calm the horny She-beast currently stirring from her nap inside of me. Beads of water from his shower still trickle down his torso as he rests up against the kitchen door, practically filling the wooden frame entirely with his broad shoulders. He extends his arms up into the air as he yawns, the simple yet effective move stretching every delicious, ripped muscle that dons his form. The V at his waist bulges slightly with the movement. I stifle the groan, ready to fall from my lips in response to the sight of him. The scent of his honey and fig body wash making me want to lean in a little closer. I thankfully resist the urge. Lips parted, Louisa and I watch Aiden appreciatively, his Prince Charming self, oblivious to how women see him, how we see him, how I have always seen him but never had the guts to tell him. He crosses the kitchen, drying his hair with a towel, a larger one wrapped around his waist and covering his modesty. I have never willed a gust of wind to magically materialize as much as I did at this moment. Louisa and I are silent as he grabs a juice carton out of the fridge and heads back out into the hallway. I wobble on my feet as he strolls past me, crossing my legs and wiping away the drool at the corner of my mouth with my thumb. Louisa sees it all and seethes at me, the little hiss of frustration suiting her as her lip twitches with disgust at my boldness to ogle something she considers hers. It doesn't matter that Aiden is a person, to Louisa he has always been her property; one of those in demand blue ones on the *Monopoly* board that everyone wants, but only the filthy rich can afford. Whilst my penniless arse is over here chilling on the brown ones, six spaces shy of prison. The cheaper assets more than likely hiding a brothel or a drug den, I bet she'd love that reality for me.

'Once again, your dirty dishes are everywhere,' Louisa yells, rolling her eyes at me. Calling me a whore now would be dangerous with Aiden in earshot, and she knows it. So picking on my poor cleanliness skills is all she can come up with. This is where the volume of our conversation hit the level of *"shut the fuck up."* We know there is no love lost between us, but if Aiden knew the truth, we would both suffer. Louisa and I could agree on that. We will hate each other in secret, and both vie for Aiden's attention like two healthy, well-put-together 21st-century ladies.

'Veronica, dishes,' Louisa orders like I'm the hired help, even though she knows I would rather suck my eyeballs out with a hoover than follow through on one of her commands. 'They are everywhere,' she adds, in an attempt to get Aiden's attention as she glances into the hallway to track his movements.

'Funny that, considering it's my kitchen,' I bite back. She bares her teeth with disgust, but I don't stop there. 'Louisa, how does it feel knowing another woman is living with your boyfriend?' I snap at her airily. Even though my eyes are trained on admiring my freshly polished nails, I can see the fumes of fury radiating off Louisa in my peripheral vision. I can't say I'm hating the effect my words have on her. At this point, I am simply poking the bear with little regard for my life. I know Louisa isn't against killing me and making it look like an accident if it means getting Aiden to herself, but I just can't find it in myself to give a shit. The heat from her glower blazes against my skin, colouring my cheeks a peony pink as she breathes a little heavier.

'I. Won't. Forget. That,' she hisses, like the snake she is, her ruby-red taloned index finger mere inches from my face as the bitch invades my personal space.

'I've heard that about elephants,' I add, the burning desire to fuck with her a little more just too enticing. She falls for the bait and grabs at her hips, smoothing down the material bunching around her waist.

'I'll have you know I've topped *Heat* magazines slimmer of the month.'

'Oh my God. Your parents must be so proud,' I exclaim, sardonically clapping my hands together and bouncing on the spot like an excited seal.

'It has credentials,' she screams petulantly, stamping her foot like a child.

'So does my eighty-year-old grandmother, who likes to joyride on the weekend while hopped up on *red bull* vodka chasers,' I say as I pass her, heading to the toaster with a crumpet in hand. She moves to close the space between us with her arms stretched towards me. A layman would see this as someone approaching for a hug. However, the flexing of her fists makes me acutely aware that Louisa is about to wrap her tiny princess hands around my throat to strangle me.

Try, bitch. I fucking dare you, my inner voice goads as I purse my lips and eye her intently.

'So, how are my two favourite ladies getting on?' Aiden asks as he enters the kitchen, pulling a black fitted t-shirt over his head and snapping the waistband of his navy-blue boxers as he adjusts himself so they ride a little higher on his hips. The timing this man has, interrupting our stand-off before we can get to the five paces section on today's itinerary. Happiness flourishes in his tone as he stands between us, leaning over me to grab an apple out of the fruit bowl, then lowering to kiss Louisa on the cheek as he passes her. His gesture makes me feel queasy, my displeasure obviously clear on my face because Louisa straightens her back, her salacious grin an immediate result of my sadness.

You can be amicable, Roni, for him, the voice in my head assures me.

'Going great—I couldn't imagine my mornings without seeing the beautiful Veronica here, making coffee. We have our very own *Cinderella*,' she jibes.

'Well, helping the challenged has always been a passion of mine,' I snort.

'What's the plan?' Aiden interjects, rightly sensing danger in the air and trying to deflect to safer ground.

'Well, *Cruella's* little bitch is due a pedicure,' I note as I make my way to the fridge, the butter knife in my hand directed at Louisa as Aiden helps himself to a glass of water, his back turned to us.

'I don't have a dog,' she states, her posh Kensington drawl prominent as she practically spits the words at me, a hint of confusion marring her features.

'My bad, I must have read the message wrong. What time is your nail bar appointment?' I smirk.

Okay, so *amicable* may have been a leap. We spend our shared time snapping and slaying one another in a way that Aiden can construe as friendly banter to alleviate our bitchy girl-on-girl frustrations. Luckily, boy brain doesn't come close to deciphering a problem, let alone reading between the lines and *DaVinci* coding the subtext.

'You can read?' she asks flatly, her head cocked to one side.

'The doctor sent a letter with your recent STI check. I'm sure I managed to read that,' I say sweetly as I butter my crumpet and sink my teeth into it.

'So mini golf—who's up for it?' Aiden asks hopefully, finally noting the tension between Louisa and me. A mildly annoyed Louisa he can handle. An all-out demon bordering psychotic Louisa is a lawsuit waiting to happen. I personally can't think of anything worse to do with my day. A happy family three-way never has and will never be on the cards for us. I think any excursion where we get to wave around metal implements that could potentially be used as weapons is not a safe environment for us to be in together. Although I had often wondered how satisfying it would feel to take an accident-on-purpose swing to her head. Who am I kidding? I needed to ride over her with a tank to really squash all resentment, and I've heard that's illegal.

'I'm out. I have a few Uni things to sort out,' I chirp, taking another bite of my breakfast.

'That sounds like a lie,' Aiden responds, eyeing me to expose the deception he suspects will linger on my face.

'Better than the truth,' I jibe quietly, wide-eyed. It is too damn early for all this. He doesn't need or want to hear my truth. It is ugly, messy, and, in some psychological textbooks, probably considered insane.

'I will help you swing *that* stick any day,' Louisa interjects provocatively, glancing unapologetically down at Aiden's groin. The mental image stirred up by her statement has officially gone so low beyond the bar of socially acceptable behaviour. It takes everything in me not to throw up all over her gold embellished heels. Her suggestiveness makes me cringe, my gag reflex kicking into gear as I swallow the bile rising in my throat. I may be in love with my best friend and have no right to him in the way she does, but imagining this crazy *Alex Forrest wannabe,* even within touching distance of his erect length, makes me want to combust right here in the middle of our kitchen. The idea of him with any woman makes me sad. The idea of him with *her* makes me seriously question the laws of an exorcism—again, a field I haven't trained in, but one I feel could be instrumental in the present situation. I've seen *Ghostbusters. I'm* clearly halfway there already.

'Give me 20 minutes, and I'm ready to go. First, I need to call daddy,' she says sweetly to Aiden, her death stare still trained on me. He nods. His phone rings from the hallway, and he makes his way out of the kitchen to retrieve it.

'Daddy,' I say sweetly under my breath, mocking her.

'At least I have one,' Now, usually this sort of response would warrant a slap, I think in any normal circle bringing up dead relatives in a bitch fight is considered poor taste, but all Louisa has done is reveal yet another layer of her true identity.

'She hasn't fully applied the war paint; she'll probably need at least an hour to prepare and set her disguise.' I yell into the empty space surrounding us. 'Those layers of makeup won't apply themselves,' I add, my voice barely a whisper, lighting a fuse under Louisa. He would never admit it, but even from the back, with his ear filled with the noise coming from his phone, I can sense the smile on Aiden's face at my remark.

'I don't wear that much,' she splutters, all humour at my expense gone from her tone.

'I'm sorry. What did you say? Unfortunately, I couldn't hear you through the entire bottle of *Rimmel* on your face.'

'It's seamless,' she squeals, her tone on par with a dog whistle as she scrambles across the kitchen, scanning her reflection in the floor-to-ceiling mirror attached to the far wall.

'If seamless also means cakey. Remember, more is less. But, for the love of all that's holy, let us get you decent for public viewing.' I laugh as I place my plate in the sink, licking any remaining butter from my fingers.

'I love how you girls help each other out,' Aiden remarks as he holds his phone to his ear, I don't miss the flash of amusement tickling at the corners of his lips.

'I love how you live between the lines. It must be nice,' I say softly to Aiden, but being deep in conversation I'm not sure if he hears me.

'*bitch*' Louisa snarls as she applies another unnecessary coat of lipstick, pinching her cheeks and admiring her reflection before twirling on her heels to face me. This kitchen could be filled to the brim with people and I would still know that '*bitch'* was meant for me.

'I don't know what he sees in you.' Here I go again, my mouth running away from me. It is a thought that I didn't want her opinion on, but stupidly, I just couldn't stop it. She relishes telling me exactly why my best friend is still in a relationship with her, and she enjoys the hurt that each statement leaves me with a little too much. I could go toe-to-toe with Louisa with my witty comebacks all day long, and she knows it. Still, when it comes to the actual feelings that I may have for Aiden, she has mastered the art of twisting in the knife to inflict the most pain. Reigning supreme when it comes to destroying me from the inside out has been Louisa's favourite game to play of late. Credit where it's due. She is great at it.

'You want to know what he sees in me, Veronica?' She hisses with a cloying-sweet smile and darkness swamping her hooded emerald green eyes. 'A tight arse. A perfect face, and I weigh less than 14 stone. It's not rocket science. Maybe you could try keeping your face out of the fridge.' She looks me up and down again for effect with a raised brow. She knows them all, every insecurity that I have about myself. Each of her jabs is painful and perfectly on point, and she knows it. I have never been good enough for him. I didn't do my hair and have impeccably primed nails; I didn't weigh every chocolate bar that passed my lips or beat myself up for the odd fast-food indulgence. I am flawed. My somewhat cushioned exterior is a proud state of proof of my love for food and my equal hate for conformity. I didn't plan on being bigger than the average size, but I also knew I could never walk away from a family-size packet of Maltesers. The hips are officially here to stay.

'Once again, quick with the hate Louisa, grimacing like that is putting lines around your eyes. You want to be careful.'

I'm not proud of it; highlighting someone's insecurity just because they had done so to me, it certainly isn't my finest moment, but she has a way of playing my last nerve like a banjo string, and I just can't resist it. She jumps to check her face in the reflection of the oven door, pulling at the non-existent crow's feet that have been beautifully covered with years of expensive cream application and chemical peels. She resumes her position near the fridge, her spine ruler-straight when Aiden shuffles back into the room.

'You nearly ready, baby?' she clucks at him, knowing what using the pet name he usually reserved for me would do to me.

'Almost. I need to grab my jeans from the dryer and send Paulie a couple of invoices for this week's liquor orders,' he says with a genuine grin as he moves to refill his coffee cup from the pot by the cooker.

'Well, I'm not waiting around here all day. I've got better things to do than to make small talk.' She graces me with a death con-five hate stare that could easily kill me on the spot had I been looking into her hollow, beady eyes for long enough. 'I'll be outside waiting in the BMW.'

Of course she drives a BMW. What a wanker. I wave her farewell for Aiden's sake, and as he leans down to kiss her already pouting lips, she grabs the back of his neck to deepen it; her gaze locks with mine, yet another attempt at provocation. I change my open hand into flipping her off with my middle finger, which only proves to entertain her more as the small showing of a smile creeps up on the part of her lips not covered by Aiden's mouth. I promptly snap my finger down and continue to wave her off as they part.

'Well, that was unexpected,' she coos as though she hadn't planned it.

'I'd say uncalled for,' I mumble under my breath. She hears me, though, and registers the sliver of sadness I'm unable to mask. Her full toothy grin in response is one of victory.

Her black and gold *Prada* kitten heels that cost more than my months' rent *clack* against the already battered teal wood floor of the hallway as she leaves. The soft *clunk* of the front door closing behind her is a beautiful sound. An almost tangible weight lifts from my body as the spawn of Satan goes forth to ruin someone else's day with her presence. I lift myself to sit on the marble island and sip my coffee. Aiden continues to rummage around in the small laundry room in the corner of the kitchen, his rear end poking up in the air as he looks high and low for his jeans.

'I swear I put them in here.'

'What you lost, *Sherlock*?' I ask, already knowing the answer, but quite honestly, the show is just too good from where I'm sitting.

'My jeans. I could have sworn blind I put them in here last night.'

'You did,' I confirm as I tip my coffee cup to my lips.

'So where...?'

Aiden spins slowly on his heels to face me, and I hook the fingers of my free hand into the belt loops of the oversized jeans I am wearing, the very same freshly laundered pair of jeans he has spent the last five minutes looking for.

'Really?' he barks sweetly, running his hand through the thick waves of his damp hair.

'They're comfortable—surely there is something else you can put on,' I whine, putting down my cup and gripping the edge of the side beneath me with both hands.

'Completely my fault. What idiot doesn't prepare what he wants to wear the day before? Oh no, wait, I did,' he states sarcastically, moving towards me slowly like an animal ready to pounce. 'Off!' he orders darkly, his mouth tipping up at the edges. With that one word, I almost lost my knickers and the jeans. His comment has my blood practically boiling as heat radiates beneath my skin throughout my body. His voice alone makes me swoon, my bodily functions momentarily a slave to him as my jaw hangs slack.

'I said off,' he growls, his smile fading, his dominant tone reminiscent of every smutty alpha male from every spicy book I have ever read. He is now right in front of me, close enough that I can feel his warm, minty-fresh breath caress my cheek, the fruity woodsy scent of him filling my nose. His proximity ignites the fuse of the dormant explosion inside of me that makes me yearn to reach out and touch him. To feel those sweet lips brush against the hollow of my neck. With little else but those three words from him, my overactive imagination, and years of friend zone pent-up sexual frustration, I am cornered, horny and damp at my core. He definitely can't have the jeans back now. My lacy thong offers little protection against the pooling wetness between my thighs.

The things this man does to me.

I throw another pair of jeans at him, slung over the back of the high stool behind the counter. He shakes them out, heart-shaped confetti falling to the floor from between the folds.

'How grateful are you that you don't have to do all these dates and flowers romantic shit?' He chuckles.

'I lucked out there.' Now it is my turn to ride the disdain train. I hadn't lucked out there–I had momentarily and monstrously fucked up there. We could be sharing a laugh about my wet knickers and remedying the heavy wanting pang in the pit of my stomach right now if I had bitten the bullet and told him how I felt from day one. But that would have been the big girl thing to do, and I chickened out.

'Can you imagine how differently things might have been the last time I caught you wearing my jeans? You hated all that romantic stuff even back then.' He laughs, his comment offhand like an afterthought, as he uses a wet sponge to remove a stain on the leg of the jeans in his hands. The memory he's referenced pops into my head, and my face falls. I rejected him before he could do it first. The sympathy he reserved for me when he thought about the night we met kept me at arm's length. I often wondered whether he regretted taking me back to his house after the costume party, wished it hadn't happened, or whether asking me to move in was a pity play because of my past. Even through the beer mist, the cocaine haze, and the happy-go-lucky exterior that one year of university fuckboy interactions had taught me, I hadn't expected the good guy to fall into my lap. I was pretty sure his kind didn't exist off the pages of a *Bronte* novel. I had resigned myself to believing that what scraps I got would be on my terms, and they were disposable. I ignored all the good and admirable traits that this man encompassed whilst I prepared myself for the slaughtering brunt of rejection that was surely close to follow. My self-deprecating ways stop me from being happy. The wall I had expertly constructed around my heart when it came to moments like this with Aiden is my only saving grace. I never truly believed him when he said he didn't remember that night we shared after the costume party, mainly because my alcohol-sloshed brain remembered every sordid detail in technicolour fantasy. We hadn't had sex in the textbook sense as we passed out before we could get to the good bit, but surely there was enough interaction to warrant a blip on his sexual encounter radar.

'Oh my God, that night. Two Tequilas down, and I was anyone's. That night was a blur from start to finish.' He had laughed, his statement altering here and there over the years, their subtitle *of 'I don't remember a thing'* always clear and unwavering. When we realised we had met before that night, as we chatted half-dressed on the floor of his wardrobe space, something in Aiden shut down, and it was a bulldozer hit to my soul. His denial kept me quiet from demanding we give it a go. *Was I that forgettable? Had he indeed not remembered what had happened between us?*

I woke up opposite him that morning with a giddy girl fantasy that this could be it, that he could be my one. Trussed up tightly in a sleeping bag wearing the chaps and jeans that were part of his costume from the night before and not much else, I couldn't wipe the smile from my face. We'd passed out around 4am, laughing about early 80's cartoons of all things. While scrambling around for my bra, the early morning sun beaming in through the stained-glass inserts in the front door, something hit me. With my clothes crumpled in my hands, my messy locks cascading down my bare back, I took a moment to admire him, splashes of colour decorating his broad bare chest. His bed hair fell over his face, remnants of my purple eyeshadow present on his neck, his long lashes fanning lightly against his cheeks, soft, deep breaths the only sound in the small room. At that moment, I allowed myself to believe that it was the start of something between us. In the beginning, I attributed the glint in his eye when he relayed the story of what had happened that night as a sign of the truth poking through. His memories of our union may be as clear to him as mine are to me, but he would always stop himself from going into too much detail as though our truth was painful for him. Opting to wear part of his costume rather than my own to sleep in hadn't surprised me. Casey had forced that red sequined dress onto my body before the party, and we're not talking figuratively—she had armed herself with a bottle of olive oil and guided the eye-wateringly tight number down over my hips. Determination making her sweat buckets as she yelled profanities with a Spanish lilt. I smelt like a complimentary snack tray. With each tug of the unforgiving fabric, my body squeaked in defiance, my fake boobs momentarily refusing to be trussed up. Aiden had made light work of ripping it from my body.

I knew within five seconds of meeting Aiden O'Shea—for the second time—that I needed to have him in my life. It hadn't yet occurred to either of us that we had already crossed paths years earlier, that little nugget of information being realised by us both the following day, signalling the beginning of the end of any relationship that could have flourished between us. We didn't reminisce about that night when Lucas assaulted me. The pain of the memory for him was hidden somewhere he had no desire to revisit. I knew if I needed to talk about it, he would listen, but it wasn't an event in my life that I wanted to rehash.

Sucked into the belly of a vortex my mind is ripped from my walk down memory lane when Aiden clears his throat. 'I wonder where that little red number is now?' He smiles wickedly, jumping into his jeans. A breath hitches in my throat at his question. He quickly drags the jeans back down his legs when he notices the gaping hole where the back pocket once was.

'Catalogued between mistakes of 2015 and 2017. It's hard to get rid of stuff, and without first realizing it, my wardrobe is pretty well set up for an era-by-era run-down. The subtitle for that particular outfit is labelled *what the hell were you thinking?*' I leave out that the dress in question, the one I had meticulously sewn back together, is folded on a the stool, continuing to tuck into my breakfast as though I am oblivious to the almost mini orgasm stirring within me. I, of course, am not in the slightest bit oblivious; my damp knickers are proof of that. The torture of this little three-way, that of the non-sweaty, non-fun kind, will always leave me wanting and needing more with him, and even though I know it is something that could never happen for us, I can't seem to shut down the part of my brain that longs for him. Aiden may be ignorant of what is staring him in the face, but her sly smirk alerts me that Louisa knows exactly where my thoughts wander every so often when I am in their presence. I'm sure that a part of her loves watching me squirm, parading her relationship with my best friend in front of me.

You are happy for him! A small voice of reason pipes up. He deserves to have who he wants, and he wants her; however much that breaks my tired heart, it is something I can't deny.

'Thank you, baby,' Louisa whispers loudly into Aiden's ear, her eyes never leaving mine as she plants a chaste kiss on his cheek. Stealing the term of endearment that Aiden commonly saves for me doesn't go unnoticed. Her smirk lets me know her statement has affected me exactly how she intended. I grit my teeth together and try with everything I have to push the anger back down below the surface, my clenched fists loosening as Aiden's broad frame fills my vision.

'I'm going to head up to my room,' I say, making a point to keep my eyes trained on him. His tallness and broad shoulders make me feel impish under his honey-rimmed blue-grey gaze. I shudder at the fire his mere presence stokes in my belly, dousing it to embers as I remind myself he isn't mine.

'I was being silly, Roni; you don't need to leave,' Louisa mutters with feigned concern for my feelings as Aiden stiffens beneath her touch. Her contrived attempt at friendliness is laughable at best. I know I must leave, regardless of her comment. After all, her words are meant more for Aiden's benefit than they are mine. I quietly exit the kitchen, a steaming mug of coffee in one hand and the half-eaten peanut butter sandwich on a plate in the other. I push the bedroom door closed behind me with my foot, plonking my plate and mug onto the desk, and collapse onto my unmade bed. The whole house fills with the nauseating chimes of a *Beethoven* track. I only have two rules for music; no jazz and no classical; Louisa loves them both and has often considered herself a teacher when it came to what she referred to as *a necessary refining of Aiden's musical tastes.* I don't know how far along in her teachings he has got but the fact that he usually plays *Marc Bolan's* entire back catalogue at maximum volume after she leaves for her yoga class—a ploy to retune his rock appreciation—leads me to the conclusion that he isn't the student she had hoped he would be.

JUNE 3RD 2019

2 MONTHS LATER

RONI

I stroll into the kitchen with my dirty washing thrown into the wicker basket under my arm. This is phase one on my task list. I probably won't move the clothes into the washing machine until at least Wednesday, but I have set the task in motion, and that's what matters. If it isn't already blindingly clear, chores aren't exactly my thing. I practically throw the basket into the tiny washroom at the far end of the kitchen and move to take a seat opposite Aiden at the counter. True to form, Aiden slides my little black book across the marble and randomly grabs a pen from the plastic *Subway* cup beside the cooker.

'So, what was wrong with Pete?' Aiden asks, the task of entering my latest fling's name into my little black book, a tradition of sorts for us of late. I watch as he empties two sachets of sweetener into his first cup of coffee of the day—the first of many. He quizzically eyes me as he waits patiently to see if I will jot down Pete's name in the front or back of the book. A little smile, almost non-existent if I weren't paying attention, breaks out on his lips when I flick through to the last page. He lets out a soft *ahhh,* and his eyes meet mine, waiting expectantly for me to elaborate as he finishes half of his coffee in two gulps. I mirror his move with the fresh cup of coffee he has made for me before moving to take a large bite of the peanut butter-smothered toast on the plate in front of him. He doesn't flinch. He always makes three slices, knowing my proclivity to steal food.

'My ladies, that is why Pete will live out his days at the back of my book,' I mumble.

'I'm not surprised. There aren't many women who have porn tattooed up their arms.' He laughs, almost choking on his mouthful of breakfast.

'It's not porn. It's art,' I protest, now a seasoned debater on this particular subject.

'Extremely realistic is what it is,' he adds with a toothy grin.

'I'll pass your thoughts along to my tattooist,' I retort cheekily.

'I mean, look at those boobs,' he chuckles, foiling my attempts at breakfast thievery by grabbing my wrist as I go in for another slice of toast. Laying my arm in his grip on the marble island separating us, he twists it to get a better look at the busty tattoo in question.

'It's an appreciation of women, not porn,' I state again, his stare fixed on the most recent pinup addition, a homage to *Bettie Page* wearing a cheetah print bodysuit. Still considered a relatively fresh tattoo, the flecks of white in her eyes are almost mesmerising. Seconding my thought, Aiden clears his throat. Letting go of my wrist, he straightens his back, not so subtly knocking at his groin beneath his grey sweatpants, quieting little Aiden's opinion on the matter. There is something to be said for a tattooist who can create a picture that, at an angle, almost looks 3D. Worth every penny.

'It doesn't take much to turn a man on, especially someone who looks like Pete. That's just teasing,' he chuckles, motioning to my arm, swooping his other hand around his plate like a convict in prison. His mention of Pete's looks don't go unnoticed. Pete was most definitely the hairiest man to visit my bedroom, but I wouldn't put him below a six.

'Are you trying to convince me that the female characters in Legend of Zelda should have their own hot or not list again?' I can already sense where the conversation is heading.

'I don't think I need to. I've clearly already got my point across.' He remarks.

'It's just a computer game.' With him distracted by my declaration I move stealthily to swipe up his last piece of toast while his guard is down. My attempt is foiled, and he playfully slaps the back of my hand. I can't lie. The connection stirs a flash of electricity to vibrate below the waistband of my sweatpants.

'And *Edward Cullen* is just a glittery glow stick with hair,' he snaps back. My body physically reacts to the gruff tone of his voice, as I'm pulled from thoughts of how best he could alleviate the sensations thrumming between my legs.

'Hey,' I bark, unable to contain my laughter. 'Don't mess with Rob.' I say, my inner teenager rearing her spotty face to fight for her film crush. 'I'd let that man *Diggory* the hell out of me with his magic wand if you know what I mean.' I wink, gyrating my hips forward on my stool. Aiden holds up his hands in mock defeat, his broad smile echoing my own.

'The houseplants know what you mean. Down, girl,' he instructs, tugging at the neck of his white t-shirt and huffing out a breath. Forcing him to endure a *Twilight* marathon was almost the breaking point of our friendship; thankfully, my skills at making hash brownies and our mutual appreciation for *Top Gear* repaired any issues.

'Look, the female form should be celebrated, pixelated or not. I don't think there's a straight man alive that would argue women are by far sexier than men.'

'Except for the sparkly wizard boy?' he offers.

'Two different characters, but I'll allow it.' I beam, popping a grape into my mouth as Aiden still has his arm protectively guarding his breakfast. 'And it's sparkly wizard MAN,' I press wide-eyed.

'Really?' He questions as he wars with the mental image of such a character, his head cocked to one side, his brow raised with amusement.

'You want to do a cartoon character. At least my fantasy is human,' I remark.

'I didn't say I wanted to do *Zelda,* but that female gaming characters could be considered hot.'

'You're not selling your case, dude.'

'But calling them cartoon characters makes it sound so sordid.' He shakes off the fleck of annoyance that my assumptions have stirred in him, the geek in him determined to win on this point at any cost.

'I have two words for you.' I grin wickedly. *'Jessica Rabbit.'* I have him, and we both know it. *By* most people's standards, *Jessica Rabbit* is a hella sexy cartoon character. For Aiden, she was up there with the best on his top ten most shaggable list. Even if he wouldn't admit it outright, he has watched that film at least a hundred times. I also don't miss the paradox of my costume choice that night he brought me home. The universe certainly has a sense of humour. He's quiet for a moment, a wry smile playing across his lips, as memories from the costume party fill his head. Even if poorly constructed, a somewhat alternative to the original character, I remember fondly how he looked at me that night.

'We've swerved majorly off topic,' he says, pulling me from my train of thought while pouring himself his second coffee of the day.

'Cliffs Notes?' I pipe up, following suit and pouring myself another mug of coffee. I place Aiden's empty plate in the sink as I grab the sugar pot.

'Cliffs notes,' he seconds, pulling out the stool next to him as I cross the kitchen, offering me the spot.

'Hairy Pete was more concentrated on the ART tattooed on my arm than on my hand wrapped around his junk,' I press, hanging on the word *ART* to strengthen my earlier remark.

'Oh, Pete, buddy, rookie move. Glances are always key in a situation like that,' Aiden says, a glint of pity filling his eyes in honour of Pete and his roaming leer. He tugs his bottom lip between his fingers as he loses himself while gazing at my tattooed arm. He sucks in a breath, banishing whatever thought is currently stealing away his senses with a flick of his head, and continues. 'So, you kicked him out?'

'No, I let him finish; I'm not a monster.'

'Full on good Samaritan, you are, Roni. *Mother Teresa,* eat your heart out. Solving all the world's struggles one hand job at a time,' he teases.

'God-given gift.' I laugh, flexing my fingers with my palm exposed, loving how his hearty chuckle hits my ear.

'Do you think you make a minor problem into something much bigger as an excuse so you don't have to see these guys again?'

Well fuck me sideways. His question is sobering, knocking all the laughter out of me suddenly. I don't need time to ponder the truth that has a way of eating at my resolve. The men I meet are never invited into my life. The drunken early hours romp between the sheets is all I can give them, and I have yet to find a guy who has complaints about my choices. My dating life can be summed up with one question: *What's your favourite colour?* That is about as in-depth as it gets with my suitors. I never much consider how they might feel. I don't want anything but a meaningless one-night stand, and I have made that clear to everyone who ends up sandwiched between my sheets. My need for a brief companion fix has convinced me I am still living my life and enjoying my youth. I have everything I could need in this kitchen; a fresh pot of coffee, my best friend; and a few hours of uninterrupted hilarity to share in the comfort of our home. Whether or not I want to admit it, this is my happy place—here with Aiden. A part of me wants him sure; hell, who am I kidding? 98% of me wants him; the other 2% is only here in an attempt to hit the situation with at least a fraction of sensibility. Still, that 98% knows the lonely 2% doesn't have a leg to stand on regarding my feelings for this beautiful man.

~~~~

The rest of the afternoon is spent exchanging dating horror stories, each one snapping a dormant memory to life that only makes us laugh harder as we contemplate the powers that be that created the *Tinder* algorithm. Like clockwork, one of us has the brilliant idea to make special brownies; it doesn't matter who instigates the Nobel prize-
~~~~

winning plan because we both agree without contest. The itinerary is this—baking, bullshit, and buddies—the three B's that signal a work-free day. We have no place to be, and as Louisa is away with her girlfriends for some spa retreat, it means zero interruptions. I tug at my long white slouch vest covering the sleep shorts I had changed into when we decided on part one of our plans. Of course, less clothing is necessary when we commit to B days like these.

'Butter,' Aiden stubbornly orders as he channels his inner head chef, directing me to the fridge with a click of his fingers. That move from anyone else would earn them a swift slap to the face. He, however, makes me want to strip down to my underwear and beg him to worship me, to punish me with those fingers.

'Flour,' I reply with a cheeky half-smile, pointing to the cupboard below the marble island, refusing to let my undeniable need for him linger in my expression. We both grab as many ingredients and utensils as we can, as though we are playing a crazy game of *Hungry, Hungry, Hippos*. Then, with our arms laden with stuff the recipe probably doesn't even need, we plop down our wares onto the counter with a huff. I glance at the lean Adonis wearing a white vest and thin grey sleep bottoms, propping himself up against the sideboard as he shakes a little clear bag at me with a salacious grin, its contents reminiscent of crushed dried parsley. Then, licking his full lips, he bounds towards me and slaps the little packet into my palm. I take the offering and mimic his move by hitting the slab of wrapped butter into one of his palms and a wooden spatula in the other.

'Whip it.' I say darkly. My mouth is inches from his as I balance on my tiptoes, enjoying the energy flickering between us, my palms hovering but not making contact with his muscled chest. Aiden lets out a quiet guttural growl that I would have missed if I hadn't been paying attention. But I had been paying attention, and the vibration at the base of my spine is the warning bell that alerts me to my body's reaction to such a seemingly innocent move. Shaking away a thought, Aiden backs away from me, and I settle down onto the soles of my feet, trying desperately to ignore the change in my breathing and the unsteady thump in my chest.

~~~~

With the ingredients all beaten together in the bowl, I wait for Aiden to turn his back when he reaches for the switch to turn on the radio. Then, finally, I see my window of opportunity and go for it as *Otis Redding's Try a Little Tenderness* starts up from overhead. The change in the atmosphere takes me by surprise, and my eyes dart to the speakers, the edge of the chocolate-drizzled spatula secured between my lips. I can feel eyes drilling into me and I don't hesitate to divert my attention to him, all six-foot-three of perfection personified squaring his broad shoulders with his eyes hooded, his jaw taut.

'Now, who said you could do that, baby?' he asks softly, a glint of mischief obscuring his usually bright grey-speckled baby blues. As the song's beat picks up and the chorus begins, he strides towards me, every step slow yet intentional.

'Sharing is caring, Aiden,' I say, biting my bottom lip to stifle the smile forming there as he stops in the centre of the kitchen, his thumb and forefinger gripping his chin as he considers my words. I know what he is thinking even before he does and have anticipated his next move. Before he can take a run at me, I fling the remaining chocolate mixture on the spatula at him, and it hits him in the chest, splattering up one side of his face. His white vest is no longer pristine. Surprise holds us both tethered to the spot—silent for a beat. Then, very calmly, Aiden swipes at the chocolate on his cheek with his forefinger and pushes it into his mouth, tasting the concoction.

'Now that wasn't very nice, was it, Roni?' he says coolly before he runs after me; I am already halfway around the island, dipping back
~~~~

into the chocolate bowl as I move, holding up the freshly coated utensil like a sword. I hit him twice more with the chocolate before I'm hauled up into his strong arms from behind. I squeal as the gooey mixture drips down from his hair and hits my cheek. Immersing his hand into the bowl filled with the chocolate, he grasps a handful, smearing it over my face and neck as I yelp, wriggling to free myself from his tight grip. Unable to stop laughing hysterically as he doesn't let up, I spin in his arms, falling from his embrace. The slickness of chocolate coating our skin makes the task easier than it usually would be. I scoop up the rest of the bowl into my hand and launch it at him with a shriek. Collectively breathing harder, I watch as he moves to grab at me again as he laps at the chocolate on his lips. Slipping on the chocolate-smeared floorboards, we go down hard, me trapped beneath his broad frame, as the slick experience we have created on our kitchen floor makes it impossible for Aiden to get to his feet.

I can't stop my glee as happy tears stream from my eyes. That toothy grin of his wobbles as he falls on me yet again, his hands and knees unable to find the traction they need to lift himself. He rests with a tired huff, his body static as his full weight pushes against me. The laughter dies out when he reaches up and moves a strand of hair from my face. His amber-rimmed pupils dilate, his expression darkening, his hold on my waist tightening. The flash of what I presume is a memory has him drawing his bottom lip between his teeth. Without warning his lips are suddenly on mine, landing me with a bruising kiss. I do nothing but pull him closer, my hands tug at his hair, refusing to let him move away from me as I hold him in place, his thumb is caresseing the curve of my throat as he applies a little pressure there, our tongues melding together as he stokes the fires of desire in my belly. My bare legs wrap around his waist of their own accord, tingles vibrating between my thighs as his groin presses against me. The heat ignited by our joined bodies feels scorching beneath the surface, enough to burn my skin to ash as I feverishly paw at his shoulders, both wanting and fearing the reaction his touch pulls from me. Finally, he breaks the kiss, my lungs and his desperate for air; panting, he drags his tongue up my jawline, collecting the chocolate there, the corded muscles in his neck contracting as he swallows it. I'm suspended in this moment, my fingers gripping onto his arms, my nails leaving indents in his flesh, my limbs weightless as I give in to the blanket of ecstasy his touch wraps me in. I fight the urge to arch my spine, letting my eyes close and my head fall back, too scared to break eye contact, desperate to stay tethered to him as his wide blue-greys asses me.

But as with all dreams, we must wake up at some point. Realisation hits Aiden like a punch to the gut, and that airy sense of need and want scored into his features a moment ago is once again shoved out of view. Banished to a place he won't let me see. Immediately sensing the change in his mood, I watch dumbfounded as he braces himself on one elbow, rising from my body so we're not touching anymore. His expression is filled with confusion as he tries to understand what has just happened. He drags his other hand through his hair to move it from his face, a litany of apologies and excuses waiting to fall from his lips. The magic once alight in his steely gaze is now smothered by the reality that only exists outside of that perfect moment. Feeling exposed I draw my legs together beneath him.

'We should stop. We shouldn't be doing this,' I say sombrely, interpreting his taut expression, saying it first because I don't want to hear the words fall from his lips. My chest is hollow, and my breathing is rapid. I want to cry, but I know I won't. He isn't mine to have. That is the certainty I never want to admit, the reality that has speared my heart one too many times. I don't expect what comes my way next.

'We shouldn't stop. I don't think I can ever stop with you,' he coos tenderly, lowering himself back down so his bulky frame is caging my body. The weight of his impressive body on mine makes my legs part again instinctually. I move my arm to cup his cheek, needing to soften the confusion in his features, and he presses his face into my palm; his eyes are closed as he commits the feel of me beneath him to memory. His admission leaves him with equal parts guilt and hope; not even a face full of chocolate can hide that fact. I move my hand and tug at his chin, coaxing him to look at me. Something will have to change, and soon. I don't know how long Aiden and I can keep this up. He wants me as much as I want him. He has admitted it. He doesn't want to hurt Louisa, and although I don't understand her hold on him, I know it is up to him to decide what he really wants.

Before he can contemplate it anymore, his phone buzzes on the island above us, the vibrations threatening to send it to the kitchen floor. He scrambles to his feet like he's on a *slip 'n' slide* until he's gripping onto the marble to keep himself upright, the muscles in his arms rigid. He turns it over to see the screen. He loses the colour in his chocolate-splattered face as he takes in the name flashing across the screen—an unmistakable pang of shame furrowing his brow again, making his jaw tick. Without a word, he swipes to accept the call and pulls the phone up to his ear. He makes his way carefully out of the kitchen, leaving me a breathless wanton mess on the floor, propped up on my elbows. It doesn't go unnoticed that he subtly has to readjust the material at his crotch as he makes his way out into the hallway. My inner siren practically doubles over with pride at the movement. It has never been my intention to covet another woman's man, and I am acutely aware I am the boy-stealing bitch in this little scenario, but I can't help how I feel about him. I have spent so long denying the feelings I have for him. The fact that Louisa is out here openly parading around with the moral range of a sociopath, ready to step on anyone who has the misfortune of getting in her way, leaves me practically remorse-free. The guilt he carries, however, makes me regret every wayward touch we share; I don't want him to feel this way. I don't want to see his grey-blues lose that sparkle when he gives into his urges with me, I shouldn't be the reason unease eats away at him.

I make my way to the fridge, wading carefully across the floor splattered with the already hardening chocolate mixture. I scoop up the pile of ingredients stacked on the middle shelf, considering the last batch is currently decorating practically every surface in our kitchen. Thankfully, I hadn't added the drugs to the previous batch. It isn't my intention to eavesdrop on the conversation beyond the kitchen door, but my curiosity is piqued and even with my arms full, I can't help but lean up against the doorframe to hear them better.

LIE! my inner voice protests. *Your intentions have never been so crystal clear. Grab a glass, you'll be able to hear them better.* She advises. I don't hesitate to do exactly that, dashing to the sink and grabbing a glass. It doesn't work so instead I gently turn the handle and pull the door open a few inches when I'm sure he's facing away from the kitchen. The car crash appeal of hearing Aiden profess his love to a woman with about as much care and compassion as a flea makes my insides flutter wildly, tugging at what feels like a black, hollow heart in my chest. I can hear her scolding him like he is a small disobedient child as he paces the hallway without her even being on speakerphone.

'It's fine; I'm just hanging out at home with Roni.' I don't need to see his face. I had witnessed this line of questioning from her before, which was never pretty. His eyes would be closed tightly, his jaw taut as he waits for her response. I try to imagine her reaction to him because she has stopped shouting now, and I can only hear his side of the conversation. His revelation of my presence is indeed the cause of her volume dip. But can I blame her? In this instance, she isn't wrong. Things had gone to another level. Before I can reason with a saner part of my brain, I pull open the door a little more so I can see his broad form through the gap.

Fuck it, in for a penny, in for a pound.

Listening intently, I quietly mix the ingredients in the bowl resting in my arm with a wooden spoon, running my tongue over the back of it when the chocolately aroma sends an SOS to my grumbling belly. I'd rather be licking it off Aiden's bare, heaving chest right now but beggers can't be choosers.

'Joggers and a vest,' he whispers into the phone, tugging at his vest drenched in brownie mixture. He neither mentions that he is covered in chocolate thanks to an impromptu food fight that had us entangled on the kitchen floor or that he is soaked in my pheromones, thanks to the delicious roll of his hips against my sweet spot. Those facts would remain our little secret.

'Pyjama bottoms and a jumper,' he says softly after a beat.

Does she want to know what I am wearing?

The fact that I am not wearing pyjama bottoms or a jumper makes me smile, his little white lie somehow comforting. I can only imagine her expression at seeing me in a pair of shorts drenched in need for Aiden and an almost see-through vest heavy with sweet brown sludge, exposing my lacy sports bra and pert nipples. The little bitch inside me squeals with excitement, for the briefest of moments, before the here and now of reality slaps me in the face. I'll never deny that I want him, but the support I have for my friend's choices in life will always have a louder voice, even if I don't particularly agree with his decision to date the bastard child of Beelzebub.

'Film and an early night.' His third lie is a necessary one. Louisa is anti-drug, anti-drink, and anti-fun. Due to the somewhat recognisable smell of my special brownie mix once the main ingredient is added, even unbaked, this particular extra-curricular activity is set aside for days when Louisa won't be visiting, and for good reason. Once I have some heat on that tray, the only thing that helps disguise the sweet piney odour is ramping up the open fires and burning slabs of cinnamon-soaked wood, the preferable scent lingering for days after.

Welcome to the corrupted baked goods sauna.

When I hear his feet padding up the hallway towards me I practically jump, hop and skip to the other side of the marble island, almost dropping the bowl tucked under my arm as I move. Acting aloof doesn't come naturally to me but thankfully when Aiden strolls back into the room, he doesn't even look my way. Choosing silence over conversation as we clean every inch of the kitchen, neither one of us mentions what had occurred between us. As time passes and the tension settles, we sing along to whatever song comes on the radio. After a quick shower, I change into another pair of silky sleep shorts and a red basketball vest of Aiden's, whipping my wet hair up into a messy bun. Walking into the kitchen, the heat from the open fire slaps me in the face, the almost woodsy scent of the tray of brownies permeating the air. I find a clean Aiden wearing another pair of grey sweatpants, the cuffs pulled up just below his knees, and an oversized black vest that allows me a peek at his tattooed muscles beneath it when he moves to grab a couple of beers from the fridge. There is always an upside to having two showers, although I wouldn't protest if he decided he wanted to conserve water. *Veronica Everly, champion for the environment.*

Aiden is barefoot, his curly brown hair still wet as he rakes his hands through it, pushing it from his face as he dips down, wearing flowery oven gloves to pull out the tray of goodies when the timer on the oven beeps. Even overdsized mitts made for Grannies does nothing to quell the pulse of excitement lazily thrumming at the apex of my thighs. The image of Aiden wearing nothing but the patterened oven mitts makes me outwardly mewl, I cough to disguise it but fail epically when the corners of his mouth tip up and tease free those cute dimples of his.

SIX PIECES OF BROWNIE LATER,

THREE BEERS EACH CONSUMED,

ROOM TEMPERATURE – BIBLICAL LEVELS OF SWELTERING.

With the lower part of the house quickly comparable to *Freddy Kruger's* basement inferno, it's a reminder of why the dress code is light and little. We watch *Scooby Doo* cartoons merely for the shits and giggles that come from reminiscing about our childhoods whilst high. Our poor attempt at mimicking their voices makes my belly hurt as we roll around hysterically. Any earlier trepidation has mostly dissipated, and we settle in to enjoy our evening, swathed in a blissful cloud of calm that has every stress from the past week draining from our bodies like steam off a hot bubble bath.

~~~~

The fires are now extinguished, and my cheeks hurt from all the laughing. The room is lit by the dull honey hues of the small lamp beside the television, and wisps of cinnamon-scented air emanate from the now water-doused coal embers in the fireplace. Our collective highs have us quiet and sated as we relax. I am sprawled across the sofa, my legs draped over Aiden's lap, his legs perched on the coffee table as we watch a group of comedians perform on some charity event re-run. When the credits roll, Aiden jumps up from the sofa, edging across the room. Once he's clear of the doorway, I can hear his feet pounding against the stairs as he heads up to the bathroom. Lost in a lazy haze of contentment, my mind is finally clear of conflict. Sadly, the feeling doesn't last long enough as memories of our earlier encounter in the kitchen bubble just beneath the surface, an unwelcome wash of regret settling in my belly. I can't lose my best friend, and whether the urge to rip his clothes off and take him here on the living room floor is what I want, I can't risk ruining what we have.
~~~~

He is happy with Louisa; however hard it hurts to admit it, I will never match up to her. I could offer him bacon sandwiches and cheap beer at best. She is armed with steak and champagne, and without selling a kidney, I don't see that changing anytime soon.

Hearing him descend the stairs, I close my eyes, trying to calm the fluttering of my lashes, burying my face into the cushion and feigning sleep. I can hear his bare feet shuffling across the carpet as he crosses the threshold into the living room, and my heart stills. The light from the television disappears as he switches it off, and he moves to cover me with a blanket, his fingers lingering on my cheek a little longer than they should as he tucks the sheepskin material around me. After a beat, when I am sure he has turned away from me, I ignore my better judgement and partially open my eyes, watching the man I love leave my side, closing the door behind him without a backwards glance. Only then do I allow the gasp of breath I've been holding to leave my lungs. I don't open my eyes again until the next morning; him being the last thing I see before I fall into a deep sleep is all I need to ensure my sluggish brain dreams only of him.

AUGUST 28TH 2019

TWO MONTHS LATER

AIDEN

I have spent the past two months trying to figure out precisely what is happening in my fucked-up head. I know I want Roni way more than I should. But what's that old saying? The heart wants what the heart wants. Deep diving into the laundry list of reasons I should be with Roni is effortless. It is what dreams are made of, and the numerous nights I've spent daydreaming about what future we could have as she lies on the other side of my bedroom wall is killing me. To have her at arm's reach but never knowing if she would even want me to touch her in the way I wanted to. Then there is the one reason I shouldn't make lists about why Roni is the other half of my heart, why being with her, choosing her, would be the best decision I could ever make. That nagging reminder that I have made promises to Louisa, and although she has some flaws, I know she is trying to make it work in her own way. I need to offer her the same courtesy. We have been through something that ties us together, and a part of me will never be able to forget what we have lost. Roni's face flashes in my mind, and I immediately relax, all tension seeping from my limbs as I imagine her dainty arms draped around my neck. For the most part the past two months have glided by, everything going back to how it was before our fumble in the kitchen.

I'm not afforded the moment of reflection for long, though, before that little devil perched on my shoulder argues his views on the matter.

What if what you want is a pipe dream, the remnants of teenage lust sent to fuck with you? What if everything you're feeling right now isn't what Roni wants? What if you've missed your chance? The inner torrent of questions I have no idea how to answer are laughable. I made my choice the moment I returned to her in that kitchen and I didn't whip her up into my arms, kissing her, holding her in the way she deserved. At war with myself, I try to bolster the attention needed to wipe all thoughts of Veronica Everly from my mind. The small smile that forms on my lips as the thought of Roni chastising me for using her full name, even in the confines of my own head, slips past the boundaries I have walled up, and it doesn't go unnoticed. Before I can ponder precisely what I should do for the best, my sense of calm is derailed when Louisa snaps her manicured fingers a little too close to my face, the proximity causing a rush of air to flutter across my cheek. I fight to push down the annoyance rising in my body as she glares at me disapprovingly.

'What is this? Where is it going?' she spits, resuming her earlier rant before thoughts of Roni began to consume me. Her mossy-coloured eyes are wide and tinted with streaks of red as she wrestles with bridling her anger. I immediately miss the serene, clear water blue of

Roni's gaze and the calming effect they always seem to have on me.

'Why can't we just be happy with where we are? Why do you have to label absolutely everything?' I yell back at her, knowing immediately by the curl of her top lip that it isn't the answer she is searching for.

'You're a man-child working in a bar, attending part-time Uni courses, and getting drunk with your whore best friend whenever the mood suits. I don't know what you think you are offering the world right now, Aiden, but it's not substantial. When are you going to grow a pair and adult the fuck up? I think I've been waiting long enough.' I assess her taut expression and realise quickly that her question is rhetorical. She doesn't care about my answer as long as it is an apology stating all the reasons I am wrong and she is right. This isn't our first rodeo, and although my face is screwed up in surprise at her outburst, a surge of adrenaline making my heart beat faster at her reference to Roni, I still can't seem to find my voice. The vile things I want to yell at her refuse to fall from my lips. I know the part she wants me to play. I know that every word directed at me is an attempt to rile me up. I'm many things, but when it comes to Louisa's predilection to battle me on every life choice I make, foolish isn't one of them.

'Is this because I don't want to work with your dad and give up the bar work? Is it because I don't want the big wedding, white picket fence, and the collection of little kids? Is it because I won't allow you to turn me into someone I'm not, into the man you so desperately want?' I ask tentatively, knowing this will bother her more than directly addressing her question. The lack of an apology makes her brows knit together, her hand shaking at her side as she fights the urge to slap me.

'You could have a stable career; you could ask me to marry you, and we could save money to buy a house. We could try again and have a baby. The stuff that every other normal couple does.' Her voice raises a few octaves higher as the little girl in her screams for the happily ever after that every princess deserves. I hate her reference to *normal couples.* The ideals that Louisa wants from me are textbook traits that I don't possess. The nagging thought that I am still with Louisa because of a sense of duty to her is never far from my mind. I don't want to work in her father's office chain, knee-deep in carcases in his abattoirs, or even as a handyman in his cleaning company business. Louisa had tried to sell me on all three at one point or another. I want to learn marketing, the business basics. I want to start up my own bar. I don't want to give up everything that makes me who I am. And the fact that she wants me to do those things makes a part of me resent her.

'If you need to change me so bloody much, why are you with me?' I ask coolly, bracing myself for another switch in her ever-changing moods.

'Well, someone's feeling extra ungrateful today,' she spits venomously.

'I'm not ungrateful; I'm pragmatic,' I retort, jumping into my sweatpants draped over the end of my bed.

'Big word for someone who doles out tequila shots while half-naked.'

'That is what I do because I enjoy it, not because it's who I am.' I bite back.

'There is going to come a day when you have to grow up and take responsibility for your life. This can't be all you have to offer the world,' she laughs.

'Well, it doesn't seem like today is that day, does it?' Now it is my turn for a rhetorical question. Her hands twitch as they ball into fists at my remark, her dainty knuckles white, her teeth bared. A slap wouldn't suffice now. Louisa isn't used to not getting what she wants and it shows.

'You are fucked up in the head if you think I'm just going to sit by your side like a doting mistress while you waste the possible potential we could have,' she yells, pointing her index finger at me, jabbing it into my chest and making me stumble back a step. Now it's my turn to laugh.

'Does my happiness in this relationship even enter your thoughts?' I know it doesn't, but I ask her the question anyway. Call it rebellious curiosity. It's becoming clear that Louisa doesn't think much of me at all, but something in me is enjoying pushing her buttons. All thoughts of right and wrong are officially out of the window.

'Why should it? You don't care what I want.'

'I am here for you. Other than completely changing the person I am, what more can I give you, Louisa? Please enlighten me. I'm dying to know how much more of my soul you need to carve out before you finally have enough.'

'Some space. That is what I need. That is what you can give me. I don't need you holding me back anymore.' Her words don't spear me as she hoped they would, and I'm met with confusion as her lips part in surprise at my lack of response. She stomps around my room, mumbling obscenities as she gathers her stuff. It seems the word *fuck* really does have a million and one uses. I zone out her ranting, catching a slur every so often when she decides my dick is *too fucking small* and my savings account is a *fucking disgrace*. I take a seat on the sandstone sherpa highback armchair under my window, my ankle resting on my knee as I watch her pack up her shit with a smile on my face. Call me childish, but I don't exactly hate how much I am irritating her right now. The fact that I wont retaliate has her red in the face.

'Space works for me,' I snap back, clapping my hands together. I lean over and grab a crimson cashmere jumper from my desk, launching it into the obscenely expensive designer weekend bag open on my bed, helping her move this along. Without knowing it, Louisa has relinquished me of any guilt and decided my fate for me. I couldn't be happier.

'So, you're not even going to talk me out of leaving? You're throwing it all down the drain?' she whines, stunned by my acceptance of the situation.

'Seems that way. Don't let the door hit you on your arse on the way out.' My voice is barely a whisper, my shoulders sagging with relief as the spell she had me under evaporates into the ether. She huffs and stamps her *Louis Vuitton*-clad foot on my rug, her petulant move making zero noise, which only annoys her more. Frustration audibly fumes from her body as she smoothes her palms down her dress, flipping her hair over her shoulder with a head toss that I think is meant to entice me, it doesn't. I extend my arm, pointing at the door just in case all the tension in her has cut off her ability to see it. If anything, I am, at the very least, helpful.

RONI

I have been listening to Louisa and Aiden's argument for about an hour. It started downstairs over coffee and made its way upstairs once Aiden had decided he couldn't listen to her jabs anymore. I am grateful the wall separating our rooms is thin. With a *red bull* in one hand and a bowl of salty popcorn in the other, I sit cross-legged on my bed. I was hungry to know what was happening, and it didn't disappoint. I almost spat a mouthful of drink over myself when he came out with the door line, silently high-fiving mid-air, proud of my best friend as he stood up for himself. I think she hoped Aiden would bow down to her demands without a backward glance, but I am glad to note that today Aiden is determined to take back his power. I don't need to see his face to know my friend has control of the situation. A moment or two later, everything goes silent. I scoot off my bed, grabbing Aiden's jumper off my floor. I tug it over my head and pull at the messy nest of hair I haven't brushed for two days that is arranged haphazardly into a messy bun on top of my head. I open my bedroom door carefully, remembering to lift it slightly to ease the creaking noise as the hinges protest against the movement, reminding me for the third time this week to invest in some *WD40*. Pulling the sleeve of the jumper down over one hand, I pretend to wipe at an invisible mark on the wall next to Aiden's door. My wily-brained scheme to get as close as I can without looking suspicious should anyone catch me. Before I can connect my ear against the wood panelling of the door, it is swung open. My eyes are wide with shock as Louisa stomps into the hallway dragging a bag, barging past me, so her long blonde hair whips across my cheek. Her usually prim and proper face is contorted with rage, her lip raised on one side in disgust as her nostrils flare at the sight of me. I'm familiar with the look.

SEPTEMBER 1ST 2019

3 DAYS LATER

AIDEN

Do it, grow a set and just do it man!' I mumble to myself as my fist hovers inches from the wood of her bedroom door. My little pep talk does nothing to calm the uneasy thump of my heart as the idea of her face has it beating out of control. Even with Louisa officially out of my life, I can't seem to follow through with what my brain is screaming at me to do. I want Roni. I've always wanted her, even when I told myself she could never be mine. But however hard the sentiment hits me, I still can't find the strength to knock on her door. The simple move is arduous as the niggling sense of self-doubt weighs heavy in my chest. Frustration fills me, and before I can bolster up the courage I know is hiding somewhere beneath the surface, my legs have already taken a step back. The air in the hallway is humid. Either that or I'm burning up, my skin prickling with a cold sweat as I overthink what should be a straightforward situation.

I will knock on her door. She will open it and smile and will invite me in. I will worship her body like a slave, intent on granting her every wish whilst I plough forward into her, owning every inch of her heart, body, and soul.

I shake away the intrusive thought that has my cock hardening in my jeans—desire to play out my deepest, darkest fantasies with Roni doing nothing to stop the rush of blood to my crotch. Fear grips me around the throat. A shuddered sigh filled with disappointment falls from my lips—lips that long to trace the lines of her body, to taste her sweet skin as she lays beneath me, my broad body caging in her slight frame until I make her scream my name repeatedly. The daydream is welcomed, but that familiar sense of doubt hits me again, and I retreat into my bedroom. My back presses against the door as I tug at the hair at the nape of my neck. I'm alert to my warring personas as they bicker in my head. The proverbial angel and devil on each shoulder, one intent on using his power for the greater good, the other determined to bathe in debauchery and slick satisfaction. Whether the situation calls for it or not, he's the one currently supplying the visuals that still have my cock rock hard. Day Aiden is laid back, easy-going, suitable for a couple of laughs, and happy to help anyone. Night Aiden, however, is the complete opposite. Night Aiden is a prick, plain and simple. If my earlier analogy is to be believed, this dickhead would be draped in red, downing a bottle of whiskey and smoking a cigar. I have given up trying to make excuses for him. Once things start to wind down of an evening, Night Aiden is on hand with a few choice opinions, my mind free of work, friends, and tv, and all I can hear is the disloyal sound of my own voice ringing in my head. *'Maybe Roni wore those for you? They are inexplicably short, like fanny flashing short. I wonder what it would feel like to remove those with your teeth?'*

'Shut up!' There's the champ that is day Aiden, clocking off shift but not entirely wiped from the playing board. He is the older, more responsible of the two. He is the one who has to consider all the daily life choices that come my way. When the sun sets and darkness falls, he appears, Night Aiden is in charge of alcohol consumption and any form of sexual gratification—he's been overworked since that day with Roni in the kitchen, scantily dressed with chocolate covering her beautiful body. I inadvertently give him yet another visual to play with, and I can't help the memory of her beneath me that clouds my senses, pushing every rational thought from my mind.

'How do you know she wouldn't be into it? She kissed you back right? You're pretty much ready to marry her. Maybe that would interest her to know.' Night Aiden guffaws loudly. I often feel as though I am challenging myself to keep the secret of my true feelings for Roni from spilling from my lips. My grip ever so slightly loosens as night creeps in—my need to have her close to me pushing aside my need to protect our friendship. The times I've been tempted to throw caution to the wind and give in to my urges are too many to count.

'If you never ask her, how will you know if she's into you?' Night Aiden may be a hormonal twat with a questionable moral compass, but he isn't always wrong.

'She doesn't think of me like that. We have moments where I think maybe, but then I can always feel her pull away,' I say silently to my alter ego, not believing a word of my statement. I pull away from Roni, and I do it because going further means everything changes. What if I can't be who she wants me to be? What if I ruin the relationship we have now? Oh, and you know—I've only been single for three days. She'd think I was using her as a rebound; the last thing I want is to hurt

her.

'Please, she has thought about you like that since that first valentine's day. Probably even before then.'

'She gift-wrapped me a piece of dog shit,' I retort, my toothy smile broad as I recall the night she convinced me to tepee my own house with toilet paper after too much whiskey. Our party guests, all in various stages of undress, watched me in the front garden after Roni had decided a game of strip poker was a fitting end to our evening.

'Yes, and look how long you've treasured that,' he quips.

I glance at the mantelpiece in the far corner of my room. Atop the disused black, wrought-iron fireplace where I store my dirty washing is the dried cocoon of shit in question. It was once slightly less rigid than it is currently. Roni had presented it in a small glass box. Her valentine's give to me and her reminder that even though she is usually shockingly shit at buying people gifts, on this occasion, pure shit was the most heartfelt offering she could give me. Roni is the only woman who could give me an ornately boxed piece of animal shit, and I would sincerely thank her for it. Although she has spent years teasing me about the source of the gift, I still like to convince myself that no human could do a poo that small and precise. Although, considering my best friend is always full of surprises, anything is possible.

'So, when are we making our move?' the brusque voice chimes excitedly.

'What move? There is no movement. A move we will not make.' I pretend that the idea alone is ludicrous as I drown in the panic spiking my tone.

'You forget I know what you're thinking. There are only so many times you can imagine her in her underwear, draped across your bed, wet for

you, before the thought takes root and embeds itself in your brain. I did think the stockings were somewhat risqué, though.' He chuckles.

'That was an old Halloween costume from our fresher's week,' I bite back, knowing it is pointless. I'm a moron if I think my brain will disguise the fact that I am madly in love with this woman.

'Yeah, okay, I believe you.' My inner voice sniggers dryly, oozing sarcasm seconding my thought. I try not to imagine her on my bed, in her underwear, wearing those stockings. But every time I scold myself, a new picture forms in my head, her mesmerising cerulean eyes, lashes fanning her full cheeks, those lips; soft, glossy, and slightly parted. Her fingertips dancing across her warm skin as she maps out the route she wants my tongue to follow. Those delicate hands of hers beckoning me towards her, her nails raking up the mesh of the stockings as her thighs part. They inch higher and higher until...

'Boy, you have got it bad,' night Aiden adds, interrupting me. I shake my head vigorously to disperse the thought before he can witness any more. Unfortunately, I have to close the curtains on this particular peep show.

'I feel you have an unfair advantage here,' I grumble.

'I didn't ask to witness Pornhub 3:0 twat edition,' he replies coolly.

'Why am I a twat, exactly?' I bite back, unsure if I want the disembodied voice to answer.

'Because you are crazy about this girl. You have been head over heels in love for years with a girl that sleeps in the room next to yours, and you still refuse to act on it. You, the recently detached bachelor with nothing holding you back.'

I know he is right. Night Aiden, although commonly inappropriate and wildly out of line on pretty much all points, is the voice in my head I secretly know I should listen to. He is careless and insensitive sometimes, but on the whole, I know deep down he represents my fears; he is here to help me overcome them, the voice that assures me everything is going to be okay. I shuffle over to my bed and edge up a little closer to the brick wall separating our rooms, the furniture on her side mirroring my room exactly.

'What do you think she's doing in there?' Night Aiden whispers suggestively as though he is sitting here next to me, the broad grin, although invisible, evident in his tone. It doesn't take much for the pervert in him to bubble to the surface, especially where Roni is concerned. I unbuckle my belt with one hand, freeing the button and zip quickly, pushing the denim down my legs, moving to tug at the hem of each leg and throwing them across the room, trying and failing to get them into the laundry basket piled high in the fireplace. I adjust myself in my boxers and narrowly fail to push the thought of Roni spread-eagled on her bed, wearing nothing but a smile out of my head.

'I saw that. Slightly predictable. That fantasy got a little X-rated quickly there, didn't it?' Night Aiden teases.

'I sometimes wish I could stop you from doing that,' I exclaim as a familiar tingle sparks to life at the base of my spine.

'I am you; you are me. Tough luck, mate.'

Without completely crossing a boundary I could never come back from, I place my palm on the exposed brick wall above my head, sensing her presence even through the concrete as though her body sings to me, mine answering her silent pleas to listen. Only it isn't silence I hear from her side of the wall. Instead, the faint buzzing that penetrates the brick clears my mind of every thought, and my chest is suddenly heavy. I tug at the hair at the nape of my neck as my composure slips, and I consider breaking down the wall to get to her.

'I don't even need the mental image this time. If she groans, I am done,' Night Aiden squeals excitedly.

'Why are you still here?' I press. The fact that he only exists because I allow him to doesn't go unnoticed. But feeling something other than a soul-destroying yearning for my best friend is always welcomed, so his quick comebacks and witty banter help to relieve me of my inner torment if only briefly. I would be a psychiatrist's wet dream.

'I wouldn't wish me away so quickly. I am your driving force, your libido, and your mojo, dude. I'll be here when you reach lift-off. Crowned keeper of the happy juice,' he pronounces as though he's introducing royalty. If he could, he would insert a high five at this point. I just know it.

'Well, isn't that marvellous? I can never unhear that.' I shudder. I get enough performance anxiety during sex without having an audience. I grab my sweatpants on my desk chair and pull them up my legs, snapping the waistband at my waist as I level my ear a little closer to the wall.

'And I can never unsee that,' Night Aiden adds as my eyes are drawn to my cock, pulsing against my sweatpants, the extra layer of clothing doing nothing to mask it. My thoughts are on her bare neck now, her quickened pulse visibly thrumming beneath the thin layer of creamy peach skin covering it as she hums with building pleasure. A pleasure that I am giving to her. I have a good imagination, which is being used to its full potential right now.

'Or unsee that,' the voice adds softly, regarding the picture of Roni bouncing around in my head. My thoughts ebb dangerously close to the prime suspects of what could be making those buzzing sounds. However, I have to challenge myself not to imagine that because Night Aiden will describe it word for word, and this is starting to feel like an unwelcome threesome. I hate the idea of sharing her, crazily even with

my inner voice. I momentarily imagine her whisking up cake batter. That buzzes, right? The notion doesn't stick well enough as my inner voice roars with laughter. Who am I kidding? Roni knows two recipes: bacon sandwiches and Casey's Goat curry. The woman knows what goes best with ketchup and an array of spices, but I don't think she even knows the purpose of a mixer.

The buzzing stops, and I am grateful. I relax as the visions of *Nigella Lawson* with Roni's face superimposed over hers begin to liquefy. With the help of my *Spotify* playlist, I can ignore my thoughts of her in a state of undress or, at the very least, set aside my wandering thoughts for later inspection. I allow myself to store whatever Nigella/Roni mix-up my brain has already concocted because that would never be something I would want to miss.

'I'm telling you now. She is having an Ann Summers party—population of one,' Night Aiden adds, breaking my reverie. Day Aiden has officially packed his bags and left the building.

'That's crazy; why would she do it when I'm home?' I fight the urge to slap myself in the head for being such an idiot, all common sense leaving me with more questions than answers as I try to find any other explanation for the buzzing. I never claimed to be a smart man, but this is ridiculous.

'Maybe she wants help, to order off the menu, so to speak. Or maybe this is her subtle invitation for you to sweep in all Superman style and rock her with your kryptonite.'

I wait a beat because I know there is a punch line coming, I can feel it fermenting in my bones.

'I've got nothing else, all this pent-up sexual tension is messing with my energy,' he mumbles and the dumbass that I am, I laugh out loud. *'She could be waiting for you, jokes aside; and don't doubt I have*

plenty, but have you considered that she may feel the same. How about we conjure up a little Wonder Woman role play, if I've learnt anything, Roni is partial to a costume.'

'I very much doubt it; I'm not that lucky, on both points of your suggestion,' my response leaves me with cricket silence as the *tick tock* of my bedside clock counts down the seconds of time left to take the plunge and go and admit to her how I feel.

A knock at my bedroom door has all the air rushing from my lungs, each aching as I forget how to breathe, every subtle movement sounding like an almighty crash of metal on metal as the pounding of my thumping heart booms in my ears. My vision blurs as I deprive my body of the oxygen it needs as another knock comes, louder and more impatient than the last. I suck in air as my room comes back into focus. Suddenly hoping it is a psychotic stranger waiting for me in the hallway because the alternative is a tad scarier if I'm honest. As I climb up off my bed, I cup my balls and give them a little jiggle to remind myself that I do, in fact, have a pair, pushing aside my moment of abject terror that had me cowering in my covers like a child hiding from the bogeyman. Regaining my six-foot-three status, I remind myself of who I am. A strong man that isn't afraid to openly admit that this woman can reduce me to nothing with little more than a smile. But on the other hand, I'm alpha enough to stand tall, knowing that I could ruin her in the best kind of way if she would let me. Confidence in check I approach the door and reach for the handle but don't immediately open it—an invisible force keeping me from following through as my palm grips the iron lever.

'Hey, roomie, how's it going?' I yell through the closed door, my forehead resting against it as the throbbing in my groin causes the little fellow in my pants to be a little more vertical than I need him to be right now. *Fuck, even the anticipation of hearing her voice has me in knots.*

'As well as can be expected. I'm just...' she says nervously, her voice a higher pitch than it usually is. Consider my interest piqued. An awkward silence hovers between her and the door as she thinks of the perfect word to finish her sentence.

'Shaving, masturbating, stroking, flicking. Dude, I've run out of doing words,' Night Aiden adds unhelpfully in a panic, doing nothing to help me lessen the rush of blood to my cock as I imagine her playing out his suggestions.

'You mean adjectives,' I add silently, rolling my eyes. My college English lit A-level finally proved helpful. What a time to be thankful for education.

'Okay fancy pants, but word selection should be the last thing on your mind. The fact that you have a massive hard-on should be your front and centre priority... Get it, front and centre.' My desire to bring him to life for the pure pleasure of throttling him bumps up on my wish list at this moment.

'Are you okay in there?' Roni asks, the concern evident in her voice as all she is met with is my stupid, heavy breathing. Her knuckles rap against the wood, each knock of her fist against the door painfully slow like a stopwatch sent to warn me of the impending apocalypse, only adding to the discomfort my silence is feeding. I never thought I would regret watching that last episode of *The Walking Dead* but here we are. Swimming in regret, haunted with wishes of do-overs.

Night Aiden motions to my tented pants, highlighting my predicament once again because apparently it hasn't been made perfectly clear to everyone in the room already. At this point if I don't whack one out soon, I will be setting myself up for losing the use of my balls entirely.

'Yes, I get it,' I spit with a tensed jaw at my *Drop-Dead-Fred* alter ego, hoping to quiet him.

'I'm fine, just looking for my underwear,' I yell chipperly to try to stall Roni and her incessant tapping. It doesn't work, and as her worries for my well-being are momentarily abated, the playful sing-song of her off-key humming to a song I can't name fills the room. It is muffled for a moment as I busy myself trying to tuck my length up into the waistband of my boxers, the pinch on the underside when I tug a little too vigorously, making me wince.

'Okay. Do you have any AA batteries?' she hollers with a giggle, the last remnants of her patience waning. The last time I heard impatient Roni this wound up was when it took the staff seven and a half minutes to serve her a bag of chilli cheese bites after a pub crawl for Casey's birthday. You would have thought they had the power to end world hunger. Heads were set to roll.

'I told you it was kinky time at hotel Veronica,' Night Aiden squeals, a reminder of my earlier thoughts making my Johnson anything but slack as it pushes against its stretchy strap bindings.

'She's not running a prostitutes convention,' I hiss.

'Before you shut this down. How do you think that would look? Half-naked and horny would fit our girl like a glove,' he prompts. His ability to guide my thoughts is an improper abuse of power that I am currently in no position to argue with. I shudder at the thought for all the reasons I should as a young straight male intent on fighting for every right a woman holds dear.

'Shut the fuck up! I've got no time and zero tolerance for this shit.' I panic, my hands flying up to grip the hair on my scalp, tugging at it, hoping the pain will scramble my senses. The move does nothing more than make my now almost fully-fledged erection slide out of its restraints. I watch as it tents the material, covering it with no signs of giving up his protest, and I sigh heavily.

'Testy much,' Night Aiden adds, ever the bloody comedian. I inwardly scream obscenities at his lack of concern, arguing silently with my inner voice as I throw random things around my room, trying to convince Roni I am, in fact, looking for some underwear. I may be up shit creek without a paddle, but I know how to commit to a lie. Heads up, though, if ever someone takes this long to find a pair of clean underwear, you probably want to rethink your relationship and their dedication to their hygiene; turning them inside out is and will forever be unacceptable.

'What do you need the batteries for?' I don't know why I yell the question at her, but on some plane of absent-mindedness, one of my personalities seems to think it is a good idea. Maybe keeping her talking will dull my unease, or am I panicking more? Of course, at this point in the game, it is all relative. Any semblance of sanity has officially left the building.

'Hair straighteners.' She answers quickly, as though she is reading from a script. 'Can't you raid one of your GI Joes? Surely one item from your dork shelf takes AA batteries,' she continues, her voice muffled as she practically lip-locks with my bedroom door.

'I never even knew you could get straighteners with a battery compartment.' The innocence of my stupidity is not lost on everyone in my head.

'Yeah, that's not what she needs them for Bro,' Night Aiden retorts sardonically. I ignore him. Glancing up at the wooden shelf that spans the entire length of every wall of my large room above my head, filled with what I summarise as my entire childhood. These aren't just figures. They are memories; they are my comfort.

'Stop gushing on your doll collection, Aiden,' Roni bellows as though she can read my mind in that way only she can, and the seventeen-year-old obsessed teenager who had never seen a pair of boobs in real life shrinks back into his cave. I know Roni won't give up until I answer my door, and the realisation sobers me instantly. I can't let her see me like this. With the thought of me pre-virginity, my Johnson has finally given up the good fight and now rests snugly beneath the cotton casing of my knock-off *Calvin Klint* underwear. I swing the door open, a gush of air from my raised window slat ruffling her wavy chocolate hair.

'What took you so long?' she whines sweetly. Her beautiful red-rimmed blue pools are wide, her pupils blown out, her little side-smile lazy as she licks her lips. I almost combust on the spot. I stupidly allow my eyes to rake down her body, her half-naked form resting against the door frame, her bare legs crossed at the knees. *Dear God, that's hot.* I try to dispel the thought, but I'm weak to the power this woman has over me. Knowing that her radiant face, shapely body, long legs, and dazzling smile have successfully strapped Night Aiden down, we are collectively speechless, which I am thankful for. I don't need a play-by-play commentary in a moment like this.

'Is that my t-shirt?' I ask. I see her toying with her answer to my question as she chews on her bottom lip.

'Possibly,' she coos, tugging at the hem of my worn navy band t-shirt, the material hugging her shape and highlighting every curve as she bunches it in her fists. It looks way better on her. There's no contest. But then, that's hardly surprising. Breasts make everything look better, and hers are magnificent.

'Positively,' I retort with a smirk, trying and failing to hide the need in my stare as I pinch my bottom lip between my fingers, needing to do something with my hands as they yearn to be on her.

'Alright, *Sherlock*.' With those two words and a cheeky grin, she pulls the t-shirt up and over her head, exposing her beautiful body, her long brunet hair draping in thick curls around her black lace bra cups. Each ridge and ripple of her bronzed skin heaves and dips every time she inhales, and I just about lose my mind. I can't help myself as I gape hungrily over her body yet again. I double-take as she throws the t-shirt in my face obstructing my view.

Oh crap, not again. The familiar thrumming beneath my boxers starts up again, signalling the return of my erection. Sensing my inner torment and the ever-changing severity of what is going on in my pants, Night Aiden jumps to the rescue.

'Granny crocheting blankets and making golden syrup cookies,' the little voice in my head spits quickly. I mutely thank the inner voice that effectively helps to bypass the flow of blood heading to my groin with the mention of my grandmother.

'Then Roni pops over in a tank top and a pair of jean shorts, coating her already sweet sun-blushed skin with the oozing syrup, the long spoon resting between her…' he adds just to fuck with me. Helpful for 0.3 seconds. It's officially a record. I feel sorry for my cock. The mixed signals are exhausting, and he has done enough sit-ups in the last ten minutes to make a bodybuilder proud.

'Do you want these back too?' she lulls sweetly, tugging suggestively at the waistband of the boxers that don her body—my *boxers*. I am watching her intently. Every micro-movement she makes hits me with a renewed desire that increases my pulse. I think about my answer as I simultaneously fight with my conscience to remember that this beautiful woman may not be in her right mind. The reality is that, yes, I want those boxers back more than anything. I want to tear them from her body, to remove everything covering her flawless peachy skin, so she stands gloriously naked in front of me. But I know I won't do that because I can't ignore the reality that Roni is drunk. The signs are all there, the swaying, the shouting, and the fact that she would happily strip down to her birthday suit without a second thought when we have memories of the kitchen incident at the forefront of our minds. Her tongue darts out to wet her full lips and she has me transfixed. My body pleading with me to throw that previously mentioned caution to the wind, to ignore my need to do the right thing by her and give in to what she so clearly is asking of me.

'On a scale of 1 to 10, how drunk are you?' I query with my head dipped so I'm in her wandering eyeline. I hoped for a three, but at this point, that felt overly optimistic on my part.

'John F Kennedy,' she fumbles quickly, clapping her hands together animatedly, almost a live wire alight in her red-rimmed baby blue eyes as she celebrates her answer, an answer that isn't even remotely correct.

'Let's, for argument's sake, go with a very moderate 12. And for now, feel free to keep the boxers,' I say, trying to disguise the disappointment in my tone with a small smile. She is way past the three I had hoped for. Now is the time to walk away.

'You're too good to me,' she lulls, her voice breathy as her breasts fight against their black lacy confinements. Ever the gentleman, I divert my gaze and hand her back my t-shirt. I want her desperately. But no woman who considers *John F Kennedy* a sensible response when debating a number option should be standing half naked in front of a man who would like nothing more, than to take her to his bed and ravish her like a fat kid would a banana ice cream sundae. Gobble gobble bitches.

'So, your GI Joe?' she presses as she squirms with impatience, my t-shirt slung over one shoulder. For a moment, I had completely forgotten the reason Roni had knocked on my door in the first place.

I push the door towards her and reach onto my shelf, blindly grabbing the nearest toy that isn't boxed. I hand her the doll, unsure whether it takes the required batteries. I refrain from waving the soldier off, but I do salute my guy wordlessly. Stoic in my homage. Whatever work he or his power source is set to do is for Roni, and I'm okay with that. I watch as she bounds off into her room with GI JOE circa 1998 grasped tightly in her palm, her drunkenness now clearly evident as she stumbles into the wall, barking out a sort of giggle snort when she regains her balance.

With images of her, a bad case of blue balls *and Lewis Capaldi* reminding me lyrically in the background why I'm sad and alone, without fail, I swiftly fall into a deep sleep, trying to distract myself with thoughts of Roni styling her hair at almost 1:45 am. The other part of me, the part that desires her in the most sensual way possible, the part that wonders daily what she would look like naked and straddling me, the irresponsible aspect of my personality that imagines how it would feel to have my cock positioned at full mast firmly inside of her, that part wonders what trouble GI Joe could get into if he isn't packing the batteries she needs.

Go hard soldier

SEPTEMBER 7TH 2019

6 DAYS LATER

RONI

That moment before our lips meet, the churning flutters in my belly are equal parts nervousness and excitement. My brain silently wills him to move closer and give in to the carnal desires flecking his hooded blue-grey eyes with warm amber. His fingers dance up the column of my throat, his light touch leaving prickles on my skin, a gasp escaping from my parted lips in response to his touch. I arch my neck a little, my cheek skimming his. My body willing to argue the laws of science and fold into his touch. I sense the small smile on his full lips, knowing that he is relishing in his sweet torture of my body, fighting the urge to kiss me and finish his exploration of me in my needy state. His warm breath caresses the *sensitive hollow below my ear as a muscular arm wraps around my waist, his fingers digging into my hip as he tugs me against his broad chest. My heart beats furiously in my chest, the thumps loud in my ears. The ache at my core has me gripping onto his shoulders and squeezing my thighs together, a corded muscle in his neck flexing as he realises how his touch affects me. I bite down on my lower lip, needing to feel a pang of pain as pleasure thrums throughout my body, leaving me lightheaded and unsteady. He bends and scoops me into his hold, his arm supporting me under my backside, my legs instinctively wrapping around his hips. Running his thumb across my lip to free it from my teeth, he licks at the self-inflicted red welt forming there, his full lips parting to speak. He could tell me he has just runover and flattened my dog and I would still be mesmerised by everything he has to offer me.*

'Let's play, baby.' Something in me detonates as he gruffly whispers the sentiment into my ear, every syllable powerful enough to stoke back to life the need I have for this man.

~~~~

'Earth to Roni.'

'SHIT!' I bark a little too loudly, grabbing the attention of the patrons closest to us as Casey drags me, practically kicking and screaming from my daydream, a fantasy I want nothing more than to get lost in.

'Where was your mind at, dirty bird?' Casey teases, running her tongue around the tip of the straw suggestively. I wipe the sheen of sweat away from my forehead as I silently scream at my body to quieten the fuck down. Goosebumps prickle my skin as thoughts of a chocolate-covered Aiden hovering above me fills my head.
~~~~

'You need to get laid. I can recognise the signs,' she instructs, as though her statement alone will endeavour to settle the unease ricocheting through my chest, in this little scenario she is a doctor imparting wisdom. Unless avid *Greys anatomy* fan equals a degree, her point isn't hitting the mark. I don't need to get laid, I need to get obliterated by Aiden, and sadly the two things are worlds apart. Right now, I'd settle for boob cuppage and kinky words.

'I wish it were that simple,' I whine back at her, my eyes trained on the six-foot three-man propped up against the DJ booth across the bar out of ear shot. With his broad shoulders, that chiselled jawline, and the sizeable bulge beneath his trousers that has held every one of my thoughts hostage since our fumble in the kitchen, I am officially drowning in lovesick waters. As my eyes roam back up his torso, noting the way his muscles contract with every steady breath he takes, I find those mesmerising blue-grey eyes of his locked on me, hooded and hungry, as though I am a snack he desperately wants to devour. Although he nods away as the guy next to him chats energetically in his ear, fighting to be heard over the music pouring from the speakers, I know Aiden isn't paying attention to him. Instead, he is eye fucking me. Even from across the room, my body reacts obediently, a slave to his deepest desires. My lacy black thong is sopping wet as I shift in my seat to calm the familiar pang of arousal deep in my belly, excitement thrumming at my core at the possibilities of what he could do to me, given half a chance. Crossing my legs, I bite down on my lower lip as my earlier daydream plays on a loop in my head, and I practically melt in my seat. The wolfish grin that spreads across Aiden's face as he realises what has happened to me is dark and brooding as he tugs his bottom lip between his thumb and forefinger.

'You have got it bad,' Casey howls as she places a glass of chardonnay in front of me.

'What do I do?' I cry out, breaking eye contact with Aiden and turning to face my friend, who can't seem to wipe the satisfied smile from her face.

'You get you some Aiden-flavoured cock.' I can't help but laugh out loud at her remark, almost spitting out a mouthful of my drink.

'So eloquently put,' I tease, feigning mock horror.

'Listen, you two are practically vibrating around one another. It's like the build-up in every porn film before swords start flying and women start screaming. And I'm not just talking tonight. When I am around you guys, the air is permeable with desire. As a woman intent on licking her way to snatch land for all eternity, I would give anything at this point for him to bend you over this bar, take you like a beast and finally admit to you, me, and the two hundred other people in here, that you idiots are meant to be together,' she says nonchalantly as though she is merely reading off the bar menu.

I'm silent for the briefest moment, my eyes like saucers as I peek at Aiden's face, his attention still mine as our eyes meet.

'You know I'm right—say it.' She snickers, unable to hide her amusement.

'You're right,' I confess. Lost to the spell that has my gaze trained on only him. 'Except for the audience thing—not really my bag,' I add, turning to face her and downing half of my drink.

'I'll get you another. Looks like you might need it.' Casey chuckles as she rises from her chair, nodding a hi at Aiden as she strolls across to the bar.

Although I allowed myself to dream that this could all be a reality with him, trying and failing to dispel the nagging doubt that maybe he didn't feel the same, that thought hit me full pelt in the chest to where I wanted to sob. Watching Casey chat with Jenny as she pulls pints behind the bar, I take another sip of my wine, the cool liquid momentarily suppressing my nerves. I remind myself that although I had been drunk, I had given Aiden the green light last week, and he hadn't jumped on me like I had hoped he would. Unfortunately, to be that brave, I enlisted Casey's mixing skills and finished an entire bottle of gin to myself. Funny how, as an affirmed mixologist, she is unaware that I could have done with at least a pint of mixer with my alcohol that night. Now when I say you could cut the air in our house with a knife, I wasn't exaggerating. Sexual tension literally dripped from the fixtures. The tournament of emotional hacky sack of who wanted who more was a game we had seemingly enjoyed playing. But games were meant to have an end, every race determining a winner, and if he kept looking at me the way he had been, I was about to reign first place position in the wet sports category, if you know what I mean. I clench my thighs at that thought and turn again to see him still deep in conversation but with a woman now. I can't ignore the stab of jealousy that hollows out my heart. The sensation surprises me with its intensity, and my body moves instinctually to run to him. Thankfully, common sense prevails, and I watch as he moves on to another customer. As though doused with water, the envious flames in my chest fizzle out, and the craving to have his body flush with mine takes over again. He can't possibly see the rosy glow of my cheeks from where he is, but how I am carelessly biting my lower lip has said enough to rouse his interest.

Locking stares with me, Aiden strides across the room towards me as I make my way to the bar. He shares pleasantries with everyone who approaches him, shaking the guys' hands and lightly laying a peck on the cheeks of the ladies who are regulars, his brooding stare never leaving mine for longer than a second—the heat almost a carnal promise that has a direct line to my soul. I grip the bar top behind me, needing to steady myself, my knuckles white as he closes the space between us. He takes long sips from his beer bottle en route, placing the empty bottle on the bar a few feet from me and nodding thanks to Jenny as she scoops it up. He offers his open hand when he reaches me, and I place my palm in his without a second thought. The air around us shifts, and as Aiden dips his head so his mouth is at my ear, a jolt of fervour courses through me, every vein alight with heat as his warm, heavy breaths tickle my neck. My eyes flutter closed as shivers pulse up my spine. I plant my feet into the beer-stained carpet to try to stop the sensation, my elbows hitting the bar as I stumble back, but he has already noticed that I am affected. I can feel the slight smile on his face as he breathes a little heavier against my neck.

'You look tired,' he states airily, his voice nothing more than a gravelly whisper, his tone wickedly playful. Aiden is feeling brave, and I am all here for it. It is now or never; I think if either of us spends another week dancing around the obvious at home as we have been, one or both of us will combust, and unless I am on top of him with his lips locked onto mine when we detonated, I'm not up for trying the odds. I don't know whether it is clear yet, but my dating history doesn't exactly leave much to the imagination in the way of success.

'Exhausted,' I reply mischievously. The hedonistic need to have his hands on me makes him clench his fists. I swallow hard as his eyes darken, an amber haze now clouding them. His lids at half-mast I watch as his attention travels down my neck, across my collarbone and onto my breasts. The quickening pace of my heartbeat is doing little to keep them in place, each breath heavy and fractured as I fight to control the gasp that wants to fall from my lips as he runs his fingers delicately up my tattooed arm.

'On a scale of one to ten, how drunk are you?' I ask, breaking the tension. He laughs heartily, his arm running around my back, his fingers splaying around my hip and digging into the soft skin, pulling my body closer to his.

'John F. Kennedy,' he says coolly, unable to contain his megawatt smile. My hazy memories of that night outside his room are obviously clear in his head. 'I'm at a two Roni,' he adds, that charming toothy grin of his

still fixed in place on his handsome face. Without breaking our contact, Aiden reaches over and hauls up my leather jacket and bag from the bar, pulling me into his side before tipping his head and acknowledging someone behind me. I glance back and find Casey and Jenny both wide-eyed, shock evident on their faces as they watch us stroll across the bar towards the exit. Casey makes a crude gesture with her index finger, and the fingers of her other hand looped into a circle as she bounces excitedly on her stool. I can't contain the bubble of a laugh that falls from my lips as our eyes meet. The sentiment *'it's about fucking time'* pinched at her raised brows. Before we reach the double doors, they both flash me an excited smile and a thumbs up, and I can't help but return the gesture, my grip around Aiden's waist tightening as we barrel through the doors and out into the night.

SEPTEMBER 7TH 2019

LATER THAT NIGHT

RONI

For the longest time, we are silent. Every small interaction or slight touch is enough to convey our thoughts as though we are screaming them at the top of our lungs. I welcome the tranquillity that engulfs us, the steady thumps of his heart beneath my palm, music to my ears as his warm breath caresses my cheek. The light from the lamp on his side table casts a soft tawny blanket of colour across the four walls of Aiden's bedroom, bathing our skin with a golden hue. Aiden tentatively runs his fingers down the front of my navy-blue shirt, his eyes darting between the invisible line left by his touch and my wide eyes as I crane my neck to peer up at him. My body edges towards his, answering his every movement as his fingers glide across my stomach to the waistband of my skinny jeans. He hesitates, skimming over the denim and glancing back at me. I nod, replying without words to his unasked request for approval.

There's no need for words; I don't want another reason for him to second-guess this decision. He runs his fingers tentatively over the button of my jeans, freeing it deftly. The zip is down, and the noise of metal scraping against metal is the only sound filling the surrounding space. They are down and around my ankles in a flash, and before I can move free of them, he bends down, crouching on one knee and taps each ankle lightly, instructing me noiselessly to follow suit. He rewards me as I do as he has ordered with a soft caress of my calf, his splayed palm scorching my skin, making my back arch, my hand flying to his shoulder to steady myself as the world seems to spin beneath me. His mouth hovers dangerously close to my bare thigh, and I can't hold back the needy whimper that barrels out of my mouth. He studies me closely, each glance dancing over my skin, drinking me in, appreciation evident in his fascinated expression. I shudder as a rush of his breath hits my skin as he exhales, but I don't feel cold. His presence, his touch, they warm me. He gets to his feet, his impressively wide torso blocking out the light, a soft glowing halo framing him. Our considerable height difference having me crane my neck again, desperate not to miss a second of the story that is almost alive in the playful darkness brooding on his features. His large hand cups my face, his thumb skimming across my bottom lip tentatively, freeing it from the tight grip of my teeth. Like the good girl I am, I don't hesitate to follow his lead. The fingers of his free hand skim down my spine, gripping my waist forcefully when he reaches the base. The mix of soft and hard touch does nothing to settle the bombardment of sensations currently attacking my brain. He tugs me against him, eliminating the space between us, so I am close enough to feel his booming heartbeat against my chest and the considerable bulge between his legs.

Even before his lips are on mine, I can feel the connection, an almost tangible wisp of cord tethering us together. His warm, minty breath, spiked with tequila, and the haze of yearning swimming in his blue/greys make the tight coils of lust churn on autopilot way down deep in my belly—feelings that before now I had never allowed to materialise like this. Without discussing it, we both recognise that everything has changed and that exploring whatever this is between us will mean that nothing will ever be the same again. He dips his head, his pupils blown, his stare fixed on me, his parted lips mere inches from mine. He teasingly hovers there for a moment, eliciting a stifled groan from me, his fingers securing a stray curl of my hair behind my ear so his palm has better access to my throat. He runs his tongue over my lips, asking for permission to enter, and I respond without a second thought, desperate to taste him.

My legs turn to jelly and threaten to give way as his tongue works with mine, sweet and soft at first, then turning rougher as our kiss becomes more frenzied. Ferocity colours our every move as I tug at his hair, desperate for my hands to explore every inch of him. His grip on my throat tightens, and in response, I buck my hips forward and let out a satisfied whimper I hadn't realised I had been holding back as his thick thigh rubs between my legs, and the friction makes me jolt. The noise shakes his composure and although he doesn't move away, he does pull his lips free, and his body trembles against mine in response to my reaction to his touch. I push against his hold around my neck, urging him to tighten his grip and tuck my face into his neck, inhaling his scent, my tongue darting out to taste his skin. Never one to deny me, Aiden tightens his hold and manoeuvres me around so I have more access to his neck. He doesn't have to tell me twice, and I lay a mixture of nips, licks and kisses across his skin until I'm on my tiptoes, resting for a moment over the hollow below his ear. My calf muscles protest as I linger in this position for too long, but I don't care. His grip eases as his body relaxes under my touch, pleasure stealing away the pressure, but it's only for a moment or two when he tightens his hold on me and pushes my back against the wall with a thud. The audible whimper of excitement in response to him looming over me has a wicked grin stretching across his face. The side of him I have only glimpsed briefly on rare occasions is screaming to break free and play, who am I to deny him of that?

'Who's a dirty girl, then?' he growls in my ear, and my ovaries explode in response. He pulls me up into his arms as though I weigh nothing, his tight hold of me comforting. I wrap my legs around his waist as I grip his shoulders, likely leaving crescent-shaped indents in the skin beneath his top. My staggered, heavy breaths splash against his exposed neck as he bites at my earlobe. I'm lost in his embrace, and he knows it. Aiden roughly splays his large hands across my backside, kneading my flesh and I savour in his sing-song hum of approval as I loop my arms around his neck, winding the curls of hair at his nape around my fingers affectionately. His chest heaves as he silently contemplates his next move. He widens his stance, and I whimper my appreciation at the stretch of my muscles, his body taught in response to the sound. He likes me like this, open and ready for him. Now is the time I take what I want, to finally be with him in the way I need. I wriggle out of his embrace and part from him reluctantly, needing to breathe as I drag his crisp white shirt up and over his head in one swift motion, not caring to unbutton it. My eyes widen at the sight of his sculpted body, a rasping grunt falling from his lips as my hands roam across his tattooed chest, exploring every dip of moulded muscle until I'm following the thin trail of body hair down his centre. With his back to the lamp, his face is now a mask of shadows, his features momentarily hidden from me. I don't miss the toothy grin as he palms the back of my head, though, and I don't need to see his crotch to know his cock is fighting against its denim confines.

'We are still wearing way too many clothes,' he states cheekily as he works his hands down the front of my shirt, unbuttoning it. There is nothing rushed about it, as he takes his time. I resist the impulse to rip off my shirt and jump back up into his arms, loving the beat of excitement that makes my body tingle as he keeps his steady pace. My craving to have him is overshadowed by the desire to enjoy everything this moment can offer—to commit every second to memory. Once he is done, he sweeps his palms up the column of my throat, into the neck of my unbuttoned shirt, running his hands over my shoulders and down my arms. His fingers draw invisible swirls onto my skin as he goes, removing my shirt finally and letting it fall to the ground. I welcome the cold air that nips at my skin now, the exposure tightening my nipples into stiff peaks beneath the cups of my bra.

All it takes to pull me out of my head and propel me headfirst into adoring this man is the light, forceful slap he rains down on my backside. The heady mix of pleasure and pain is another sensation sent to fuck with my body. I fall forward against his chest as the slap lands, the snap of skin connecting with skin echoing as though the room is 40-foot high, but his large frame doesn't budge. Pushing my arse back a little, urging him to strike me again, I am now greedy for the effects of his touch. He reads me perfectly, and his hand rains down on my backside for a second time. I bite my lip again, but this time it is to quiet the rasping squeak of bliss that is currently climbing up my throat. In no time at all, he has deftly removed my bra, and I am standing here before him in just a black lace thong already damp with my arousal.

'Is it wrong that I think you would look just as good in a pair of my boxers?' He chuckles, lazily running his finger under the waistband of my underwear. It's not enough, I need more. I suck in a steadying breath, trying to think of some funny one-liner to throw back at him, but his proximity has me speechless, barring a squeal of elation when his fingers graze my sweet spot.

He takes one of my breasts into his hand, massaging it roughly as his lips nip and suck at my neck. He pulls back to look at me, admiration alight in his expression as a stuttered exhale leaves his full lips. He reaches up, removing the clip securing my hair into a messy bundle of unruly waves on top of my head. My long brown hair cascades around my shoulders, briefly masking my breasts. Aiden softly pushes it back over my shoulders, a cheeky grin playing on his face as his eyes find their way down to my exposed chest. With every moment that passes, the barrier of our friendship falls away. Even though nothing has ever felt more right than the world does at this moment, I am still nervous as my hands reach the waist of the jeans donning his lower half. I look up into those steely blue-grey eyes that I have lost myself in for so many years, although they are darker now, filled with a heat I've longed to drown in. My fingers flick to the zipper of his jeans, and I pop the button free of its enclosure, my eyes never leaving his. A part of me expected him to stop me once I freed the button. I wait tentatively for him to give me the go-ahead. I need to know that he wants this as much as I do.

A small smile tugs at the corner of my mouth as I feel the hard bulge pulsing beneath the denim under my hand. His dark cerulean stare assesses me as he fights to keep his eyes open, the need to take charge making his stubbled jaw tick, his teeth clenched. Unable to fight it any longer, Aiden lifts me into his arms, and I yelp at the swift change of pace. Nothing will be soft or reserved about what he has in store for me. I am sure of that as he strides across the room with me in his arms. Taking a seat on the edge of his desk, he arranges my legs around his waist, my knees bracing on the wood on either side of him. He pulls me closer to him with the arm snaked around my waist. A flurry of sensation darts up my spine in response. His face is mere inches from mine now, and I don't risk closing my eyes even though a deep throb has begun to pulse at my core. I want nothing more than to fall back into nothingness whilst this beautiful man claims me, mind, body, and soul. *What if I close my eyes and he is gone?* Every figment of my being alerts me I am being insane, but the fear is there, heavy on my brain regardless.

I run my hands down his naked, taut torso. My fingers explore the V that heaves heavenly around the waist of his open low-cut jeans. The muscles in his neck tense as he swallows the lump in his throat, my touch doing to him what his does to me. My core pulses as I try to regulate my wayward thoughts. His blue-grey eyes, ringed with amber, dart to my lips, and I tentatively pull my lower lip between my teeth to the point I almost draw blood, that familiar potent mix of all consuming desire and the dull ache of pain only proving to excite me further. He runs his thumb across my lip slowly, freeing it from my teeth's hold, his eyes wide. I realise quickly that the lip thing is a one-way direct line to turning Aiden on, and I just can't seem to help myself. Reading me as he always does, he bucks his hips into me, silencing my thoughts. I let out a strangled breath. The bulge in his trousers hardens in response against my thigh as he grins wickedly down at me.

I part my lips and take his thumb into my mouth, swirling my tongue around it as he throbs below the waist once again. Pride fills me as his body responds so willingly to my touch. Unable to prolong the torture thrumming beneath the surface, his lips crash against mine wildly, his hand gripping the length of my neck to hold me in place, his fingers gently tugging at the soft curls of my chestnut-brown hair. Every touch, however small it is, awakens something in me. Each thrilling pang flies without warning to my stomach's deepest, darkest depths, my core welcoming the wake-up call. I want him next to me, on me, in me, and not necessarily in that order. I want every inch of this man, and however he wants to give it to me suits me just fine. I can't deny what Aiden means to me any longer, and I wouldn't give this moment up for all the gold in Midas' kingdom. I place my hands on either side of his stubbled jaw, needing to feel him beneath my fingers. My tongue battles lavishly against his as we work small groans from one another. I rock my body into his and pull from his lips to look at his perfect face again. My breathing laboured, my lungs working extra hard as they beg for air. Every fierce thump of my heart pushing forcefully against my ribs. I peer down at the man who has my mind, body and soul in a tizzy, squeezing my thighs together against him as I straddle him, enjoying this change in perspective, silently pleading for him to take this to the next level, my body screaming for a release only he can give me. My center is clenched with anticipation. I don't need words with him, and a cheeky thrust up of his hips lets me know he is on board with my plan. A second thrust winds the knot of coils already pulsing at my core, close to near detonation already. In a moment of madness, I speak before I can stop the words from falling from my swollen, abused lips.

'Should we?' My nanosecond of doubt has reared its ugly head. My fear that all this will forever change our friendship is now a genuine reality. The little part of me that knew I would never recover if I lost this man has thrown the question out with little thought.

'We should,' he says pointedly, a small reassuring smile playing on his lips. 'As long as you want to.'

I let out a little giggle. *No need for words*, I remind myself again. My body will convey just how much I want him, and it is as sure as it ever has been in its twenty-four years on this earth that he was made for me. I want this to be our normal. I want only him, and I think he may want only me. Every slight touch, suggestive jab, and second-hand compliment between us has led to this moment, and I couldn't be happier.

He turns me on the spot in one fluid motion, so my back is to his front, pulling my body to rest against his rigid chest as his arm winds around my abdomen, his fingers dancing across my belly. My back arches slightly to gain more traction from his teasingly light touch. Reading me perfectly as I knew he would, Aiden runs his fingers down my lower stomach and over the lace of my knickers. I involuntarily buck my hips in response. My head hits his chest. My eyes shut tightly as consumption takes hold, and I succumb to his will. He holds my waist a little tighter, positioning me where he wants me, and I throw my arm up and around his neck to pull his lips down to my throat as I lose myself to his touch. He nips at the sensitive area below my ear, dotting featherlight kisses after each bite. The part of my brain wholly submersed in all that is Aiden notes that the choice of lace over granny spanks was fortunate. His fingers explore the lace covering my opening, and although he is just skimming my surface, it sends pulses of electricity rocketing through my extremities. He pushes the heel of his hand against my sensitive nub of nerves. Even though I know my friend inside and out, at this moment, we feel like strangers, a new connection being formed. We are discovering a side of each other we haven't explored yet, and it feels wrong in the best kind of way. The giddy nervousness I hadn't expected tinges my cheeks a candy apple pink. My need to be swathed in him is so strong it almost hurts. My mind foggy as jolts of pleasure pulse lazily at my core. Picking up his pace, Aiden moves my thong to one side, teasingly running his fingers over my wet folds. I wrestle with the urge to bend into his touch. His attention to my throat tethering me in his grasp, a silent order to obey, holding me stoic.

'Are you a screamer, Roni?' he growls into my ear, the fingers of his other hand playfully skipping across my throat, his mouth close enough to bite down onto my earlobe if he wanted to.

'No,' I breathe heavily. My gravelly voice is almost unrecognisable.

'Let's rectify that,' he hums, the corner of his mouth tipping up, his hips rocking into me as he thrusts two thick fingers into my centre with abandon, all inhibitions lost. My body suddenly feels like liquid. Too full and not full enough as my body begs for him to do it again. He doesn't deny me as he repeats the delicious move. His grip on my neck tightens, and amongst the wash of pleasure radiating through me beneath his adroit touch, I know it's to hold me in place for whatever he plans to do with me next. That serves to thrill me in the most wonderful way. With the realisation clear in my mind, he releases my throat and I almost stumble forward. In one swift move, he tears my thong from my body, letting the scraps fall to the floor like they are made of tissue paper. He pulls his fingers from inside me and I mewl breathlessly, deprived of his skills, desperate for more of him. I turn my head up at him with wide eyes, ready to plead with him to continue. This pleases him greatly as he draws his fingers coated in my essence between his lips, greedily devouring the sweet spoils of his touch. *Fuck-that's-hot.*

'Mine,' he quietly barks possessively. With that one word whispered into my ear, Aiden answers my prayers, thrusting his fingers back inside my already sopping wet opening without warning, deftly pulling my orgasm front and centre as the contact steals my senses. Before my body can rocket forward in response, his large hand holds me to him, his palm splayed out over my heart, each frantic beat matched perfectly with every thrust of his fingers inside of me. Pressed against his broad chest I feel as though I am suspended in mid-air as my tiptoes graze the carpet. He moves his fingers in and out of me with ease, building his pace as he reads my rearing body like a book, adding a third finger when I'm good and ready. I almost fall apart as the tight knotting low in my belly hums with appreciation. I pant, my throat dry as white spots appear in my vision, my head swimming as arousal threatens to drown me in ecstasy. He stands a little taller, and with his fingers still to the hilt inside me, he flips me around and pushes me back in one fluid motion, so I'm now lying with my back flush with the desk. He splays the palm of his free hand across my stomach and continues his relentless movements inside me, drawing me closer to my release. He works his fingers from my belly up my body as I move to match his thrusts. I grab the edge of the desk with one hand until my knuckles are white, cupping my bare breast with the other. He drags his thumb lazily over my sweet spot while rocketing inside me. I can't fight what he does to me, not anymore. My legs tense as I balance on the verge of falling apart beneath his expert fingers, every nerve in my body alight with wonder, my core throbbing with yearning. The ache is almost unbearable, and my fingers grapple at his forearms as the tell-tale signs of an orgasm pinch at my insides. My need for him is evident as I survey him hungrily, my eyes rolling back each time he rocks his thick fingers into me, each drive more determined than the last as his fingers seem to climb higher inside me. The intensity of the weight at my center only increases further, and there is no going back. I am teetering on a precipice, ready and willing to throw myself over. He gazes down at me, desire filling his almost black–grey eyes as he watches me writhe beneath his touch, his full lips slightly parted. He bends over me, the savage movements of his fingers pistoning into me, never faltering a beat as his warm staggered breaths caress my cheek.

'Come for me, baby,' he orders roughly, those words my undoing.

'Fuck, Aiden!' I cry out his name as I tip over the edge, my bud of nerves pulsing beneath his thumb. Aiden's free hand flies up to my throat again, gripping it as he works the orgasm out of me. I thrash beneath him, ragged breaths puffing out of my mouth as I come apart. My sweaty back arches off the desk as I lose control, giving myself over to the buzzing contentment that is now coursing through my entire body. Cold shakes make me want to curl up into myself as my release hits me again and again. I pull him down onto me, his wet fingers digging into my hips, my body a blissfully happy mess beneath him. I can't hide my smile now; I have been thoroughly fucked, and it feels good. His kiss is fierce. My hands tangle in the hair at the nape of his neck as his tongue slips into my mouth, working to pull free every last remnant of pleasure I have for him.

'Wow,' I mouth the word, unable to find my voice completely around my ragged breaths as he breaks our kiss.

'I've only just started, lady.' At those words, the roguish grin plastered on his face, and his milky blue-grey pools filled with yearning, my core begins to beat lazily once again. His stare alone has the magical ability to reawaken it, and it doesn't need telling twice. The bulge at his crotch is now almost bursting at the seams, and my hands fly down to relieve him from his jeans. Aiden stands so I can impatiently tug the denim down his legs. I take his boxers with them, making light work of freeing his rock-hard length. I hum with appreciation as he takes in a short sharp breath, running my tongue across my swollen lips as I drink in the magnificent sight of him now standing completely naked in front of me. Every inch of me feels heavy as my fingers itch to touch him. My poor lungs struggle to contain every arduous breath as my heart vibrates furiously in my chest. I want him, all of him, and there isn't a single part of me that can deny it at this moment.

'Roni.' My name sounds foreign on his lips as he pulls my attention back to his face. An apprehensive breath hitches in my throat as my need to be even closer to him gnaws at my soul. Everything feels right, a fullness that has my hands shaking, the thrum of sensation travelling up my legs indescribable. A body pulse in Limerick form dances across my bare chest, each phonic hitting me like a brick as I have to remind myself, he really is here, on top of me, about to take me in the most sensual of ways. Our moves are hurried, a beautiful blur of tugging, nipping, and sucking. His need for me is animalistic; my need for him raw. I place my hands on his muscular chest, his heartbeat thumping beneath my palm, and I push him back onto his bed. The idea of a round two with Aiden has me pulling up my big girl boots, my back rod straight, the confidence clear on my face as I glide across the space between us. I want him, and now I get to show him just how much. I straddle him, purposefully positioning myself on his thighs as I run my fingers through his hair, raking them down his face and onto his torso when I know I have his undivided attention. Our eyes are locked as I rest my backside on his knees, and I move to push my hand between my legs to gather up my slickness. I wrap my hand coated in my arousal around his generous offering at its base, mildly amused when I realise how little my hand looks as I struggle to grip it comfortably. Gliding my hand up and down the length of his cock slowly, taking my time, it's my turn to have this man at my mercy dangling over a cliffs edge. His head falls back, and his eyes close as he sucks in air through his clenched teeth at the contact. My core throbs as I lift myself and manoeuvre his cock to my opening. I grind down slowly without a second thought until

I am completely impaled on him. I push my face into the crook of his neck as my body gets used to his thickness. The breath is knocked out of my chest as he fills me.

I need a second to adjust, and Aiden strokes the back of my neck, allowing me the time I need. He lifts my chin with one finger and plants a soft chaste kiss on my lips, his palm moving to settle over my heart as my core grips around him. Moulded to him, I begin to move, picking up my pace as the sting of fullness subsides. Shivers waltz up my spine as I slide up and down, and my body crashes against his. I ignore the bark of refusal to comply from the taut muscles in my thighs, each drive exquisite, every vein in my body shaken as we meld into one another. Every thrust is an acceptance, every spike of my waiting orgasm making me drive down harder, hopeful for and fearing my release in equal measures. I don't want this to ever end. My need for this man is a love story worthy of any Shakespearean play; the longer, the better.

His large palms grip my thighs, squeezing at the flesh beneath his fingers as he assists my movements, pulling me down a little harsher each time. I cry out each time as my swollen sweet spot crashes against his belly when we connect.

'Don't stop,' I beg.

'Never.' He assures me.

In one fluid move, we are up, and I have my back pushed up against the wall, the grind of his hips perfectly timed as I make contact with the exposed brick, the lack of give behind me, heightening the force of his brutal thrusts. Delicious thrums of electricity hit me. His movements are relentless as he pins me in place with ease, his length stretching me to take all of him. All the air is sucked from my lungs as a strangled groan bursts from my lips. Ignoring the burning licking at my throat, I run my hands up and grab at the nape of Aiden's neck, anchoring myself to him and pulling his face to mine. The kiss doesn't last long, though. When his palm connects with my backside once more, I can't help but buck in his hold. I bite down on his shoulder, sinking my teeth into his flesh, eliciting a gruff roar to explode behind Aiden's clenched teeth. He pulls me up higher onto his body, dipping his head down so he can lick and suck at my peaked nipple, his impressive length filling my wet centre at a new angle, my slick folds welcoming him without argument. His eyes are hooded, his pupils blown as he assesses my flushed state, his nails sinking deeper into the soft flesh of my backside as he powers forward again, rocking his taut hips into me without care or concern. Taking everything I have to give like a man possessed.

'Shit, Aiden,' I breathe harshly, suddenly losing my battle to contain the cry of 'yes, yes, yes' that barrels out of my mouth as he hits the spot with a direct link to my impending release. He revels in my screams as his earlier promise is fulfilled, and he has indeed rectified the issue. He swallows the soft whimpers falling from my parted lips as white spots flash again behind my closed lids. My orgasm is teetering on that familiar precipice I'm ready to christen Mount Aiden, as I clench around him, desperate for everything he has to give me. With another ruthless thrust, my head snaps back, my body arching as tingles and liquid heat rush through me. He tightens his grip on me, his mouth latching again onto one of my breasts, toying with it furiously. Yet another sensation my overloaded brain has to try to make sense of. My core thrums with delight as he continues to worship me, slowing his pace but still as forceful with his thrusts. The intensity of my waiting orgasm settles a little. He's teasing me and sparking reverberations of pleasure snap to life as my body pleads with his to never stop, to continue hitting me with everything he has. He tugs at my hair, the stabs of pain on my scalp proving only to send me spiralling further into oblivion. Aiden holds me with one hand under my thigh, the other braced against the brick wall, and I slam myself down again onto him as I use the window seal for leverage. His fingers dig into my pink flesh until it's red and raw, his pace quickening as we both feel our releases approaching. There's no holding him back now.

'You have always been my favourite place, Roni,' his admission tugs at my heartstrings as I recognise immediately the contentment in his baby blue-grey eyes, the calm in a moment so frenzied. There is nothing but love at this moment between us. I rest a palm on his stubbled face, the other gripping onto his shoulder, appreciating the taut corded muscles as they flex with every determined thrust of his hips.

'I—I—I.' I can't even start my sentence, let alone finish it. Each time I try, he drives his hips forward harshly, again and again, the walls inside of me gripping his length.

'Aiden,' I scream his name, my lungs burning as the cusp of my orgasm tears through me, and the world around me fades to black. My body is wrung out; every level of my consciousness overloaded with a thrilling buzz of sensations. Aiden powers forward twice more in response to his name, laden with heat, falling from my lips, losing himself to his release.

'Baby,' he roars. His gruff growl of my pet name as he explodes inside me only intensifies the mini orgasmic aftershocks that pulse through my body, smaller yet just as satisfying as my explosive undoing. Filling me to the hilt, he moves inside me languidly, his tight grip on my hair holding me to him as he tucks his face into my neck and inhales the scent of my skin. My back arches, and the darkest depths of our happy place swallows us whole. His body goes rigid as he writhes against me as the last remnants of the balmy wet heat of his release empties inside me. His pulsing cock calms, but he doesn't attempt to pull out of me, and I still feel deliciously full of him. Our chests rise and fall at an alarmingly fast pace in unison as beads of perspiration dot our hairlines. He hugs my shaking body against his, refusing to allow any space to form between the sticky mess of our joined bodies. A sheen of sweat coats our chests, reflecting the moonlight pouring in through the window, and I suddenly feel dog tired, my arms limp and heavy.

'Fuck baby,' he huskily declares as I pant, trying and failing to regulate my frantic, heavy breathing. I can't help but giggle when he lays another bruising kiss on my lips. Still flickering, embers fill my belly, my core heavy and sensitive, my bud of nerves still pulsing against him as he holds my body close to his. I don't attempt to move from his grip. It feels too right hanging here, stuck to his broad, steady frame. Every nerve in my body stands to attention as I fight to right my fuzzy thoughts. Aiden runs his palm from my backside, still red from his slaps, up the sensitive trail past my tickle spot on my side, then wraps his fingers around the base of my neck, urging my face towards his. This seemingly simple move sends a shot of energy to tug at my limbs, making me jolt, his length pulsing inside me in response. He holds me there, on him, my shaking legs gripping to his sides, his touch soft and sensual, his lips warm and inviting as he kisses me. When he releases me from his lips, I drop my head to his shoulder, kissing the red welts I had caused there, inhaling the scent of his skin. He taps my chin, signalling that he needs to see my face. I glance at the man I love with every inch of my heart, and his dimpled half-smile comforts me. He coaxes me back to him as I banish any second thoughts about what has just happened between us that may still be lingering in the back of my mind. Lavish strokes of his tongue adore mine, stealing an unguarded whimper to fall from my lips. I feel replete, content on a level I have never found with another man. That was making love, I am sure of it, and it doesn't compare to anything else I have ever experienced. Aiden lays me down on his bed and pulls out of me, the lack of his cock inside me stirring a smidgen of sadness to roll through me. I pull him down on top of me and dot featherlight kisses over his face. As he pulls back to rest on his elbows, hovering over my body, I revel in the broad smile plastered on his handsome, stubbled face.

Tracing my fingers over his full brows, around the curve of his ear, across his sharp jawline, I feel a wholeness inside myself that I've never even realised I had been missing. I craved him. I've always known that, but what I'm feeling now is something else entirely. Moving to sit, he scoots back, taking me with him until we hit the headboard. I snuggle into him. With my legs tangled around his body, my fingers trace the lines of the large rose tattoo design on his chest as I watch him avidly, enjoying the view from this new angle. He runs his hand through his dishevelled mop of brown hair, pushing it free of his sweaty brow. Postcoital Aiden is my new favourite. He is sexy, sweet, and easily the most charming man I have ever met. A part of me is green with envy that other women have been able to see my best friend this way, that this is a side of Aiden I have never had the guts to let myself discover. With our eyes locked, his hazy grey pools trained on me, I watch him intently, as though I am seeing the real him for the first time. He moves to tuck a lock of my messy chocolate-brown waves matted with sweat behind my ear, his fingers settling on my skin for a little longer than I expected, as though he is contemplating something. But whatever the thought is, it doesn't linger. His touch, even the light caress of his fingertips, is enough to stir a comforting warmth in my chest. He tugs at the covers, blanketing our entwined bodies, swathing us in cotton. Moving to close the smidgen of space between us, he pulls me over to rest my cheek on his chest. I wrap my arm around his ripped torso, the thrum of his now steadier heartbeat echoing in my ear. He plants the gentlest of kisses on my forehead and lies back on his pillow, his fingers stroking up and down my lower back until he falls asleep. It doesn't take long. The melodic soft purrs of slumber fall from those full lips of his. The heady scent of his aftershave, sweat, sex and lavender comforter-soaked sheets in the air fills my nose. When I am sure he has broken the barrier into a deep sleep, nearing comatose status myself, I glance up at him, careful not to disturb him, as I shift my weight on his chest to climb a little higher up his body. Thankfully, the darkness engulfing the room doesn't hide him from me completely. With our bodies now still and suitably satisfied, I take my time to drink him in, to truly look at the handsome, chiselled lump of perfection beneath me. The man that told me I am his, and he is mine. He has my heart. It's as simple as that.

I love you. I mouth the words I could not say earlier, too afraid now to voice them, even whilst he sleeps. As though he can hear my mind utter the sentiment, his lips tip up at the edges. The faint grin is strong enough to eject any tortured thoughts lurking in the back of my mind of life without Aiden. Content in our moment, the escape of night soothing the broken parts of me. I give in to the exhaustion, my eyelids heavy, my body satiated as I lay encased in his arms and nothing else. The promising light of hope radiating from my best friend tears through the darkness buried in the pit of my soul. I allow myself to bathe in the goodness seeping from his sweat-speckled skin. Banishing any worries of what daybreak may bring, I give in and allow my heavy lids to close, my lashes fanning my cheeks, the smile on my face still refusing to settle.

SEPTEMBER 8TH 2019

THE NEXT DAY

RONI

Hey, beautiful lady, is this one of *those* calls?' Casey murmurs, emphasising the word *those* theatrically as her tinny voice rings out of the phone speaker. A morning-after-the-dirty-deed-rehash isn't a new feature of our friendship, and I love that even with that single word she can convey a multitude of possibilities as to what trouble I might have got myself into. I hear the familiar sound of a paracetamol container being popped open from her end as she waits for the gossip. I instantly know she is nursing an epic hangover. I shift a little on the bed, and as my hand roams across his pillow, the memory of my encounter with Aiden makes my core throb, the dull ache making my thighs rub together. A smile pinches at my cheeks, the crisp pine aftershave and lavender scent of him still lingering on my skin. Casey's alcohol consumption level from last night clearly still has her a little dazed. I wait for a moment to see if she recalls she saw me leave the bar with Aiden, but if she does, she doesn't let on. I hear her thank a barista for a cup of coffee, butchering the *'merci'* with her east London twang, letting me know she had rolled out of bed this morning and could only manage the three-minute walk around the corner to *D'Armor*. I hear Casey sigh heavily. That unbridled groan of pleasure as she takes that first sip of her beverage is almost orgasmic. I wait patiently as she returns to reality, my fingernail tapping against my front teeth as I fight to contain my revelation. When she's collected herself, she clears her throat. 'So, do you need saving?' she utters finally.

'I didn't pull an ugly one, and I don't need an excuse to get out of here,' I chime in response, the broad smile unmoving from my delighted face as snippets from last night flash in my head like instant replay footage; his hands caressing my thighs, his lips exploring the length of my neck, his fingers buried—*there*. I snap back to reality as heat pulses low in my belly, the mere thought of Aiden reawakening the dormant orgasm pulsing between my legs and making me practically giddy. If that is what sex is like, I am all on board. Having Aiden worship my body far surpassed anything my imagination could have dreamt up.

'And where is *here* exactly?' Casey inquires, the caffeine boost adding alertness to her tone. The chatter of other people having conversations around her lets me know this will be anything other than a private conversation.

'At home,' I reply sheepishly, waiting for the penny to drop as I pull the quilt cover over my head, shutting out the world and biting at my nails as I wait for her response.

'You're home?' she queries, confusion evident in her voice.

'Yes, at my home,' I confirm, failing to hide the squeak of excitement.

'I didn't think you were taking men home anymore since the last one turned out to be a few fruit loops short of a cereal bowl.' I can't help but laugh at her statement.

'I didn't bring anyone home,' I state coolly in response, knowing that as I answer her every question with an air of amusement in my tone, it won't be long before she starts screaming down the line. Casey isn't one for people evading her questions.

'I know what you are doing, and you know it's annoying. So either fess up or hang up, lady, because I've got a date with Destiny.'

'Destiny, the predetermined notion of fate, or Destiny, the girl you met at *comic con* with the fascination for motor boating whilst humming *Celine Dion* tunes?' I ask.

'That girl can be the *wind beneath my wings* any day,' she states, confirming my latter assumption. I don't even need to be in her presence to know she is swaying her hips to the track playing out in her head. It only takes her another second or two to realise the proverbial elephant in the room. 'Oh my god, you finally did it. You slept with Aiden?' she bellows, her question not really a question. 'I thought I had dreamt you left the bar with him last night. That is the last time I drink sambuca.' A weight lifts as I speak my truth, and all I can do is shriek excitedly down the line, thumping my feet against the mattress repeatedly as I struggle to contain the thrum of elation bouncing around in my veins. As any great friend would, Casey sits in the middle of the fancy French café, probably wearing a pair of oversized sunglasses, draped in her thick faux fur coat like an uptown woman of leisure and squeals along with me with little regard to who is around her. Fuck everyone else. Casey didn't trouble herself with the opinions of others, and it shows.

'Finally!' she exclaims with a rushed breath. 'Fucking hell, Roni, you took your bloody time!' she howls. After a beat, the line goes quiet. 'You happy?' she asks, a hint of worry marring her tone.

'As a pig knee-deep in shit,' I reply with an air of whimsy, the statement holding more feeling than the undignified string of words would usually allow. Tears of happiness collect in the corners of my eyes. The relief that hits me sharing this news with someone else has my tense muscles relaxing, as though before this moment, being with Aiden had been merely a dream rather than a reality. I leave my hiding place and readjust Aiden's bed sheets around my naked form as I settle into my second favourite place, his arms being my first.

'If I know Aiden, he's making bacon and eggs. Get your arse dressed and downstairs, lady. This is the first day of your forever and always,' she coos authoritatively.

'I love you, girl; you know that, right?' I choke on the sentiment, my chest filling with warmth. Casey is the only positive female presence in my life, and it is moments like these I realise I lucked out the day she stumbled into my life dressed top to toe in cheetah print for some cat sanctuary event. The words *Pussy Power* emblazoned across her chest in red marker. The double entendre of that statement was not lost on me once I got to know her properly. Casey knew how to use her natural gift of sexual suggestiveness. That is clear.

'Forever and always,' she quips, a hidden promise that those three words will never change, making me want to pull her in for a hug.

'Forever and always,' I reply before hanging up the phone and throwing it down on the bed. I fall back onto his pillow and scream into it, still a little shell-shocked at just how perfect last night had been, at just how perfect this man had been for me. I giddily jump to my feet and grab Aiden's discarded, crumpled white shirt from the floor that I had ripped from his body the night before. I revel in his aroma as the cotton material warms my shoulders, the heady mix of sweat, sex and his crisp pine aftershave filling my nose.

My fingers deftly secure the buttons at the top that have too much of my chest on show. Gazing at my thoroughly-fucked reflection in the six-foot-high mirror attached to the back of Aiden's bedroom door, I run my fingers through my mess of curls. My pink-flushed cheeks, the heaviness at my thighs' apex, and the dull ache in my calves are warming reminders of what he had done to me, the sensations he had pulled from my body with his determined touch. The muscles in my neck contract, my chest swells, and my eyes widen as the *drip-drip* of unfiltered need for him fills my belly. I bite my lower lip, closing my eyes as I allow my brain to flick through the mental snapshots of him. I remember stifling my pleas for more as he powers forward, my inner thoughts of *oh fucking God* as those hot lips of his trail feather light kisses down the column of my throat, and his tongue licking at my sweaty, salty skin. My eyes snap open as I sway on the spot. Tugging at the hem of his shirt, I assess the woman reflected in the mirror. I am wet now. The moment I thought of Aiden's lips, it was inevitable. I pick up the tattered material that was once my thong from the carpet, stuff it into my purse, and pull on a pair of Aiden's boxer shorts from the pile of fresh laundry under the window. I have tasted him now, and there is no way I can ever push the image of him holding me in his arms out of my head without the assistance of a questionable psychiatrist and a willing lobotomist.

When I reach the top of the stairs, I can hear an *80's rock number* playing at maximum volume from behind the kitchen door below and Aiden's voice trying and failing to hit those high notes. God love my Adonis for trying. *My Adonis. Mine.* I revel in the thought. I shuffle down one step and stop abruptly, running back down the hall to brush my teeth. I don't need bad morning breath ruining this moment.

SEPTEMBER 8TH 2019

AIDEN

I scramble the eggs minus the yolk, knowing Roni is very particular about her eggs, whatever their form. This egg OCD comes from a woman who would happily eat questionable chicken noodles out of a cart at three AM in the middle of Leicester Square. I chuckle to myself, the thought of her face clear and bright forefront in my mind as she tries to convince me the spit tray heat kills every bacterium known to man in the food that's cooked on it. All this whilst downing a bottle of WKD and complementing Farrah, the vendor, on his choice of a poncho. That's about the limit of her fussiness, though. If Roni were any more laid back, she'd be horizontal. Flashbacks from last night hit me as I ignore the already crispy bacon burning in the frying pan on the stove. Those harassed pink lips sucking on my thumb, the thrum of pleasure making her legs shake with every brutal thrust of my hips, the thwack of my palm as it connects with the soft cherry flesh of her arse cheek. The smoke alarm chiming from above me pulls me from my daydream, and I wave a magazine up towards the ceiling to disperse the smoke. The solid erection currently tenting my superhero-themed pyjama pants is a little harder to get rid of, however. The monotonous whine of the alarm finally stops, and once I tip the bacon onto the metal rack, I launch the singed pan into the already-filled sink. I plan on a game of rock, paper, scissors with Roni later to see whose turn it is to clear it. I try to ignore Day Aiden's note of how much more fun that game would be with no clothes on, and once again, images of Roni naked and needy fill my head. My cock juts up in response, as though it agrees with my inner thought. I move to grab a couple of plates and hum along to the classic 80's rock playlist that reverberates through the speakers of the radio perched on top of the fridge—trying and failing to hit the high notes. I pour steaming hot coffee from the cafetière into two mugs, selecting the *'made to work in porn'* embossed mug for Roni because I know it will make her laugh, and anything I can do to stir a smile on that woman's face is worth the effort.

How have I never pursued these feelings? How have I denied myself the chance to be with her? How have I been so stupid to ignore this thing between us?

A little part of me dies inside as I realise just how foolish I have been, allowing this amazing woman to be in my life but not in my bed. I would give anything to spend a lifetime beneath her and I need her to know it. The clues to my true feelings have always been there. I just hadn't allowed myself to accept the truth. Too scared to venture past our friendship because I feared I would lose everything.

I point the oil-covered spatula in my hand towards the imaginary audience around me that is cheering on what could be the worst *David Bowie* tribute act to have ever existed. A figment of my imagination or not, I can't help but enjoy the buzz. I welcome the feeling, a sense of wholeness filling me at the thought of making love to my best friend, of exploring the body I have wondered about for so many years. It wasn't until I had been with Roni that I realised how unhappy I was with Louisa. Roni accepts my craziness, celebrates my flaws, and appreciates my affections. I am free now to live my life with Roni, explore this thing between us, and love her as she deserves.

The kitchen door swings open behind me. I sway on the spot with the saucepan filled with the egg mixture in one hand and the spatula in the other, stirring it vigorously, so it doesn't burn like the bacon. I don't turn to face her immediately, a roguish grin already tugging at my lips at the mere thought of my gaze meeting hers. I wiggle my hips with vigour, hoping she likes the view.

'Burnt eggs are the new gourmet, right?' I chuckle, emptying the contents of the pan onto two plates and reaching for the bacon cooling on the rack.

'I'm lactose intolerant, so unless you want me suffering from abdominal distension, I'll give it a miss.' I know it isn't Roni behind me. Their voices aren't even remotely similar, but I still hope I am wrong. I silently plead with the universe to take me back, to rewind time to when I was in bed, my limbs intertwined with Roni's. But that sort of fantasy only happens in the movies. I turn on my heels, a splatter of hot fat from the bacon hitting my bare chest as it still sizzles. The shock of her presence means I don't even feel it. I am stoic. All relaxation sucked into oblivion from my body, my muscles taut in preparation to take on whatever abuse this woman is about to throw my way. Before I can ponder her reason for standing in my kitchen at 8 AM, she has closed the distance between us. Louisa leans into my body and whispers something into my ear, but my brain struggles to piece the words together. Her manicured fingers dig into my biceps, and, like with the bacon, my body doesn't register the discomfort. Every sense is confused as to its job as the words take form. Two small words, in fact, that have the ability to throw me off balance as my world implodes at my feet. I sink to the wooden floor and welcome the bite of the cold cupboard door at my back. I tug at my nape, steepling my hands to stop them from shaking.

It can't be true. This can't be it. I glance at Louisa, who has a sly ruby-red smile painted on her pristinely made-up face, noting the *cat that got the cream* twinkle in her mossy green gaze.

She is enjoying this.

Before I can muster up the energy to demand an explanation of Louisa, the *powers that be* fuck me anew. Roni barrels into the kitchen, singing along to the radio, doing a far better job than I had, belting out the chorus of a familiar karaoke tune. She hasn't seen Louisa yet, who is now propping herself against the fridge door as she searches for refreshments. She still can't drop her satisfied smirk as she tips the glass bottle of freshly squeezed orange juice up to her lips.

A nice, cold glass of poison would be great right now, my inner voice chimes, and although I'm the only one that hears him, I nod my agreement.

Wearing my crumpled shirt from last night and a pair of my boxers, Roni swings her hips to the beat. Her eyes close as she really gets into it. Her beautiful mess of chocolate waves fall over her shoulders. When she opens her eyes and finds my still crouched form, her face is suddenly alight with confusion and concern, my face ashen, my jaw tight. She continues to dance across the kitchen towards me playfully, hoping to free my grave expression from the hold of whatever has me on the floor. I jump to my feet before she reaches me, but I can't find my voice. I want to tell her that Louisa is behind her, to tell her what Louisa has just told me, but I am stunned, any attempts to speak stifled by the rock hard lump in my throat. I don't want her to know this truth. In a matter of moments, my future with Roni has been obliterated.

I don't want to witness that beautiful, carefree smile fall from her lips. When she reaches me, she rises on her tiptoes and leans in to kiss me, her small warm palms flat on my bare chest. I don't pull away, even though I should. Each of her movements is determined, her eyes a crystal-clear blue, an element of hopefulness flecking them with an emerald shimmer around each pupil. The sweet aroma of her lilac perfume, her fruity-scented shampoo and an addictive subtle mix of sweat and sex has my cock pushing against her belly through the cotton material of my pyjama bottoms. The spirited gasp that falls from her full lips at my body's reaction to her proximity makes me want to rip the shirt from her body and lay her out on the kitchen island while I worship every inch of her with my mouth. That is until I remind myself Louisa is now sitting at the table behind Roni with a stern expression pulled tight across her face.

I don't move an inch, but Louisa's whimsical cough sufficiently alerts Roni to her presence. Roni jumps back in surprise, turning to face Louisa, who is scowling at her, her lips pursed as she shrewdly assesses the sight playing out before her. Still, I cannot find my voice as Roni's wide eyes dart between the two of us, waiting expectantly for clarification why my now apparently not-so-ex-girlfriend is standing in our kitchen with a triumphant air about her the morning after we had made love. She, of course, has every right to an explanation. I, unfortunately, can't even remember what I was doing five minutes ago, let alone the right thing to say to stop the tears pooling at the corners of her eyes. I want to envelop her in my arms, tell her everything will be okay, assure her that I love her more than I could ever love another human being. But that would be a lie, or at least part of it would be. Nothing from this point on will be okay, and although I will spend the rest of my life loving her, I can't let her know it. The sly sneer on

Louisa's glossed lips tells me she is aware of the realisation I have come to. She knows she has won. She has finally beaten Roni.

'Do you want me to help you with that, Aiden?' Louisa cajoles sardonically, motioning to my semi-erect length, making Roni jump back further. Louisa is practically giddy when she catches the shock, almost a live wire, still etched across Roni's features. 'Seems you've misplaced your *own* clothes again, Veronica,' she spits. Our state of undress is clearly a trigger for her. Louisa has seen Roni and I like this more times than I could count, but today is different, and everyone in attendance knows it. Roni and I are different today. Sexual tension is almost a visible tendril of burning desire heavy in the surrounding air. Never one to fade into the background, Louisa is the first to break the looming silence.

'I turn my back for one minute, and the dogs descend. But I can't blame a bitch for rooting through tasty scraps now, can I?' Louisa barks with slick satisfaction as her comment hits Roni as intended.

The darkness inside me is palpable as the little voice in my head demands I stick up for Roni, but no words leave my mouth. I stand there, disgusted with myself that I cannot stop this. The dread of what is coming stuns me into silence. All I see is her, my beautiful, broken soulmate. Her hazy blue pools, usually filled with humour and admiration, are now muddied with shock and sadness in equal measures. All Roni can see at this moment, however, is my soul-destroying rejection. I am forced to watch the link between us dissolve, a connection I had sworn to her was unbreakable. I can see the torment etched around her furrowed brows as she fights against that deplorable voice in her head that is telling her Louisa has a point. I don't need to be in there to know that self-doubt and blooming anguish are sullying every beautiful moment we shared last night. No reason or reflection will settle her now.

RONI

'How good is my man making me breakfast?' Louisa says sharply from her seat at the kitchen table, the fury bubbling beneath her surface contorting her forced smile. I know she is building up to something here, and I know without a doubt I will not like it. She would have been dragging me across the floor by my hair for touching Aiden by now. That can only mean she has something far more dastardly in mind. I bite back the hurt swimming in my belly as her earlier use of the word *bitch* still resonates. The twitch of annoyance as her tongue darts out to wet her lips means I am successfully hiding the stab of sorrow eating away at my insides, at least for now. One glance at Aiden and I know he can see right through my façade, as though it is a costume made of poorly constructed gossamer ribbons. But I can't deal with him right now.

'I thought you didn't eat eggs?' I say as I watch the scene play out, trepidation heavy in my appearance as I take a tentative step away from her, checking her for concealed weapons as I paw casually at the fruit on the island now separating us, as though this little conference is an everyday occurrence.

Why is she here? Why is Aiden on the floor, and why is he so quiet?

Before I can linger on the questions in my, head, I am dragged back into the moment with a frustrated snap of Louisa's fingers, her silent order for me to concentrate on her face tethering me to the spot.

'I'd eat anything Aiden made so lovingly for me,' she mewls, tooth-achingly sweet, unable to hide the disdain in her voice at my mere presence. I stifle the desire to gag and bless Louisa with the fakest smile to have ever graced my face. *Two can play this game*. I refuse to let her revel in my heartache.

Hey, you, the powers that be. I am about ready for my TV choice award.

Aiden shuffles on the spot, dragging his hands through his hair as I keep my eyes trained on Louisa. It feels like a tense game of *Cluedo* right now as we all push to make sense of the situation, trying to decipher who has the biggest reveal up their sleeve. If I had to take a stab in the dark, Louisa would inevitably wield the knife. She's never exactly been a team player.

'Aiden treats me so well. It's nice having a *boyfriend* intent on making your every whim a reality.'

He isn't hers anymore! Even though the voice barks loudly in my head at her remark, I still can't shake the despair her statement fills me with. I'm reminded that *this* is no game. Although striking her around the head in the library with a candlestick would be my preferable ending to this battle of wits. I don't know how long I have been standing here, mutely weighing up the imaginary wrought iron implement in my hand, but it's long enough that my mouth is dry, the muscles in my legs seizing up as I stand in the same spot for too long. I glance between the two of them as Louisa crosses the room to approach Aiden who is no longer on the floor, they exchange words that refuse to register in my head. I don't need to hear her, though; I can read her lips just fine and catch the tail end of their conversation.

'You are mine,' she spits through gritted teeth.

I want Aiden to correct her, to set the story of *us* straight, but it is as though he isn't even in there. Something clearly happened before I strolled in here. I move to pass Louisa and approach him, but I stop abruptly. The shell of Aiden is now sat on the stool at the island with a tumbler filled with dark liquid. The empty glass bottle poking out of the swing-top bin alerts me it is whisky. I turn on my heels to face her, a soundless question refusing to budge from my mouth. The giddy glint of excitement at the complete destruction of my life flames wildly in her cold green eyes, and it hits me as hard as a punch from her fist would. I move to face Aiden again. Apprehension makes me unsteady on my feet. Any modicum of strength I foolishly thought I had mustered is now gone.

'Missed me?' she asks smarmily, already knowing the answer as I refuse to turn and acknowledge her. 'Whether you like it or not, Roni, I am here, and I'm not here alone. Am I Aiden?' She coos, her breath ruffling my bed hair, directing her question over my shoulder at Aiden. He doesn't say a word, his eyes trained on the marble sideboard as he takes another chug of his drink. *'Not here alone'* her choice of words piques my interest. I turn to face her and glance around the kitchen, finding no one other than her. I grin wickedly at her, but something about her expression quickly wipes the smile from my face.

'So, where's your friend?' I ask, failing to disguise the unease causing my voice to break mid-sentence. A part of me hopes that alone will somehow soften her. It doesn't even make a dent in her steely composure.

'Right here,' she responds with a renewed sense of warmth to her tone. My eyes follow her movement as she rubs her hands over the slight bulge of her stomach, the stretchy emerald-green dress covering the barely there bump, hugging every angle of her thin frame. I stupidly look up at her face, hoping to find the proof of a lie, but it isn't there. I am shell-shocked, muzzled by her admission. My wide-eyed stare flits to Aiden. After meeting my gaze for the briefest of seconds, he dips his head, his shoulders slump, and his fingers resume tugging at the strands of hair at the nape of his neck. I want to cry, but I won't. I'm not getting any information from Aiden, and I desperately want to ignore everything Louisa is telling me. Even with the truth in front of me, the shattered pieces of my psyche refuse to piece themselves together long enough to take in her revelation.

'I'm pregnant,' she exclaims excitedly, determined to twist the knife spearing my chest. She frowns when she doesn't elicit the same enthusiasm from Aiden, but it doesn't bring me any comfort.

'Do you even own your own clothes?' Louisa laughs, her eyes filled with judgement roaming over my dishevelled frame. 'I wonder how long it will take for our baby to fill this,' Louisa spits, pulling Aiden's grey hoodie from the chair beside her, the one she knows I love. She beams over at me impishly, knowing she is beating down the walls of my resolve one brick at a time with her backhanded comments. I know Aiden doesn't miss the jolt of pain she causes me when she mentions the baby.

I already knew the decision my best friend had made the moment Louisa opened her mouth and spilt her truth. Anything other than honouring his responsibilities wouldn't be good enough for Aiden. When it comes to a baby, *his* baby, all bets are off. His truth is far more selfless than Louisa's. As I watch her fondle his jumper, the last of my strength snaps, and I can't hold back the torrent of tears now. I can't possibly fight for my friend whilst I am hurting this much. The only thing clear amongst the tsunami waves of my emotions is the flash of red-hot pain that constricts my heart, invisible hands desperate to pummel it into dust. Each second that passes chips away at my soul.

I need to see his face, I need the comfort I get when I drown in his eyes', but he won't look at me. As though he can hear my desperate thoughts, his head snaps up. All the sweet memories of our union last night are gone. I wipe under my eyes with the sleeve of Aiden's shirt I'm wearing, determined to get through this with, at the very least, an ounce of dignity. Her steel-grey, ringed muddy-green stare is alight with victory—his dark hollow blue stare filled with sorrow. I turn on my heels, bare feet squeaking on the polished wooden floor. The pounding rhythm of my broken heart whooshes in my ears, thankfully offering me a respite as it shuts out the destruction of my world between these four walls as my name falls from his lips. Any other time I would be grateful for the interruption, pleased to hear him speak finally, but too much has happened in such a short time, and the need to be anywhere but here has me picking up my pace and dashing towards the exit.

I barrel out of the kitchen, slamming the door behind me, so it shakes in its frame. I fall against the wall in the hallway, my legs no longer cooperating with my brain's instruction to flee the house, to run away from all the tension in that room, to escape the torment flooding my thoughts as I question everything that has happened in the past twenty-four hours.

'Why did you do that?' I can hear Aiden yell at Louisa behind the battered wooden door.

'What, I can't be happy to share our news?' She feigns surprise. I don't even need to see her to know that an expression of mock horror is donning her perfectly preened face. I pull at my hair, tugging at the scalp, desperate to feel something other than the whirling pool of despair as my brain argues for me to get to my feet.

'She didn't deserve that,' he retorts, finally fighting my corner. I chastise my inner thoughts before they can whisper *too little, too late* in my head.

'She had no right to play with what is mine,' Louisa snaps back petulantly, accentuating the word *mine*. 'Don't think for a second I don't know what you did... with her.'

'You broke up with me!' he exclaims, voicing my earlier thought. The distant crash of pans in the sink makes me jump. 'What was it you wanted, Louisa? Oh, that's right. SPACE.' The roar from Aiden makes my skin prickle, frustration piggybacking every one of his words. After a few beats, the air thick with tension, I can hear Louisa's heels clack against the kitchen floor as she totters from one side to the other.

'Baby,' she says sweetly, her hands undoubtedly on him now. Bile rises in my throat as I wrestle with the need to centre myself. Before I can compose myself and wipe away the tears staining my cheeks, Aiden joins me in the hallway. He pulls the door closed behind him, building a barrier between her and us. He drops to my level on the floor, stroking away the curls falling over my face. His warm touch only proves to add to my agony, though, as I wince in response, edging away from him sharply—the familiar scent of him another thwack to my already bruised heart.

'Roni, I'm sorry. Baby, please,' he croons, sincerity thick in his tone. His sentiment doesn't calm me any. In fact, it has the opposite effect. Anger boils up inside me, and I can't seem to stop myself. I jump to my feet, a move he mirrors, and I get up in his face. All five foot four of me is nothing compared to his broad six foot three, but I am like a dog with a bone, and I refuse to back down.

'Fuck you.' I push my finger into his chest. 'Fuck that.' I laugh with zero humour, motioning to the woman standing in the kitchen behind the closed door. 'And fuck whatever this was.' I gesture between the two of us, unable to stop the onslaught of tears now. The irony of those words and how differently I have used them this time isn't lost on me. I didn't know pain like this existed.

'So, this is it?' he asks, ashen-faced, his tone vacant, emotion bubbling just beneath the surface as tears prick at the corners of his eyes.

'I think it has to be,' I respond, my voice small and broken. His jaw flexes as I fight the urge to look into his beautiful grey-blue eyes, which are now a little softer than they had been. 'I can't watch you take this path, and you can't possibly expect me to. You have been out of reach to me all these years, and then… last night.' My heart can't take much more of this assault, and although I know he doesn't deserve it, I am fighting back the urge to slap him around his face. My hand twitches at my side, my body desperate to rid itself of all the pent-up emotions.

AIDEN

Roni will have to grow to hate me. I know she means every word and watching me become a father with Louisa by my side will tip her over the edge. I ponder for a moment all the things I want to say to this woman but can't. How much I want to tell her my promises of a forever for us will always be my truth. That this thing between us will never go away, we will be together again one day, and all we need is time. But I don't say any of it out loud. I just watch as she berates me, needing her to get angry so I can dampen the guilt gnawing away inside my chest. For the first time in my life, I've hurt the one woman who means the world to me, irreparably tearing a hole in a friendship I thought could never be broken. Fractured slivers of hope are not enough to patch up the gaping holes of despair between us. I wince as I suck in a heavy breath, watching as I take a piece of Roni I have no right to. Grief colours her features a mottled grey as she mutely pleads with me to put her back together again. I want nothing more than to do exactly that, to pull her into my arms and kiss away every fallen tear that splashes against her chest. But I won't be my father; I won't leave my child. I can't be a part-time parent, and Louisa has made it abundantly clear that if she can't have me, I will never see my child. I know Louisa will stop at nothing to have the life she wants, and if I don't comply, she won't hesitate to ruin me. I don't like this cowardly version of myself, but right now, it is the only tangible reality I have to hold on to. I sling shots for a living. I'm still studying part-time at university. Louisa's family has wealth that can make anything happen, and if daddy's little princess wants me, there isn't anything that man wouldn't do to make it happen. The fact that I stupidly considered us officially over when she left the other day shows how blind I've been.

In two minutes of rushed thoughts, I realise I have already accepted my fate, silently mourning that I will never again get to hold Roni in my arms how I want to. To promise her the world, to grant every wish she might have. I bow my head in shame, unable to look at her face anymore. She is filled with an overflowing of sorrow that cripples me. My insides are in knots, knowing I am to blame for her misery, unwittingly, of course, but that doesn't make it any easier to swallow. However impossible it may seem now, I won't stop trying to salvage whatever friendship she may one day allow me to have with her, all the while wishing for more.

Images from last night play out in my head as I watch the woman I love slide down the wall and cry in a crumpled mess on the Moroccan inspired rug, the woman that is usually stronger than any other person I know. I kneel beside her, knowing there is nothing I can say to help heal her. This has broken her. *I* have broken her. That little inner voice screams at me to put her back together, to make this okay, but I can't share my truth with her. It will do far more damage to Roni than any lie could. My truth is that I want *her* to have my babies. I want to wake up to *her* face every morning; the rest of my life filled with *her* laugh, my days alight with *her* smile.

I feel powerless as I reach out to her, and she recoils like a frightened puppy. I will do my duty to Louisa, I know I will love my baby, and although my future is unknown, I will always know that this beautiful woman crouched before me, tears streaming down her swollen cheeks, will be the love of my life. She will forever be my one. Nothing could change that. I take a deep breath and do what I need to do. I push aside memories of our lovemaking. I bury deep the warming feelings I feel for Roni and I grow up. I swallow the lump in my throat and accept it all, every shitty bit of it.

'Choose me.' Roni's voice is small, almost non-existent. Her pleading makes another part inside of me wither to dust.

I don't speak; I know what I will say, which won't help either of us. Given the choice of Roni and Louisa, Roni and any woman, in fact, I would pick Roni every time. But I can't think so selfishly anymore. This doesn't just affect us. Her strength, the emotion she reserves for use when faced with liars and cheats, the backbone of her resolve, is now set in place as her eyes go wide at my lack of response, her need to survive walling up a concrete divide in her chest quicker than I expected. Her tears are now dry, her stare complacent, aversion soaking her expression. I die inside as I watch her love for me fade to nothing, my soul a sharp, tortured mess, like a broken China mug sitting in discarded pieces on the floor at her feet, silently begging her to put me back together, because she's the only one that can.

'You, you... you.' She can't release the words on the tip of her tongue, her heartbreak morphing into anger again. Although she is speechless, the tone of that one word is enough proof to convey exactly how deeply the situation has cut her.

'I am not and will never again be someone you can play with on a whim. I'm not a quick fix when you are horny or when you realise you have made a mistake here. I am broken, Aiden. Used and discarded in the worst possible way, and you did that to me. I loved you, and you crushed me, stole something that should never have been yours, and I won't ever be able to get that back,' she says decidedly, her voice never faltering as she locks her eyes bravely with mine, holding the tears at bay. A vice-like grip squeezes my heart in response to her admission, my hands shaking as I bear witness to the devastation I've caused. Loving Roni is the easiest thing I will ever do, and in the space of five minutes, I have ruined it all. I can't find the words to make it right. My brain is desperate to soothe her, but I'm rendered speechless. My lack of fight only makes her angrier, and before I know what's happening, she gets to her feet, making me stumble back, and crashes into the kitchen to face Louisa—wiping furiously at her cheeks as she goes. Her sorrow ignites a sense of strength in her broken soul.

'It doesn't matter how many babies you give him. That jumper is mine!' Roni cries out, fury alight in her red-rimmed baby blues. She holds her hand out expectantly to Louisa, who is still clutching my jumper to her chest. She doesn't want it, but the idea of having yet another thing Roni doesn't makes her tighten her grip. Knowing Roni and being familiar with the crazed look now etched on her face, I can tell she is willing Louisa to defy her. I watch the scene unfold as Roni flexes her fist by her side, barely resisting the urge to punch Louisa in the face. Pregnant or not, Louisa has pushed Roni to a whole new level. Right now, that jumper is the decider whether a bare-knuckle boxing match is about to take over this kitchen.

RONI

There is no way in hell I am leaving this kitchen without that jumper in my possession. I'm not violent, but Louisa is pushing all the right buttons to warrant a slap to the face if she continues to goad me. I don't know why it means so much to me, but I know I can't possibly live without it. I stare at her as she evaluates the situation, trying to read the severity of my statement. Sensing danger, she wisely hands over the grey bulk of screwed-up material that retains so many happy memories for me. Just holding it against my chest like a comfort blanket, my anger softens, a weight lifting from my shoulders, my fist relaxing. Glancing down at her belly, I can see flashes of my brilliant, handsome best friend caring for a mini version of himself. Louisa will never be his world, of that I'm sure, but that baby will be. Convinced of that truth, I know I can never make him choose. I need to push Aiden as far away from me as possible. Magically removing myself to a different plane of existence would be preferable but most likely not a possibility, so Plan B it is.

The room grows colder as I stand between two people I don't want to be around. I clutch Aiden's jumper to my chest, ignoring the impulse to breathe in his scent from it. Against my better judgement, I glance up and lock eyes with my friend once more before the sadness riddled in his expression threatens to send me over the edge once again. Aiden doesn't know that he is the reason my heart beats. I don't think he even realises how much he truly means to me. He will always be my best friend and my family, but does he know how in love with him I am? How perfect he is for me? He is the only person who knows the real me, a promise of forever unspoken all those years ago when we shared that first kiss. He accepts the sometimes moody, the most of the time reckless and the always sarcastic sides of my personality without question. He knows my every flaw and celebrates them. He was my biggest advocate, and now he feels like a stranger. Through no fault of his own, he has severed the link between us. A slicing ache reverberates in my chest at the realisation, and it has me running from the room. I don't slow down, taking the stairs two at a time until I reach my room, determined to create space between us, to tear myself away so I don't have to watch the man that I love, walk away from me with another woman by his side.

What I had said to Aiden in the hallway plays out on a loop in my head, every hate fuelled word necessary to protect my shattering heart. It didn't work, though, and now I'm left alone, a buzzing mess of tears, regret, and unfiltered emotions. I bury my face in his sweater, breathing in a lungful of his scent even though I know it will only make all this hurt that much more. The broken parts of me that yearned to be put back together downstairs in the hallway are quiet now, an emptiness filling me as my cries morph into noiseless sobs—a heaviness tugging at my heart. Battered or not, I know it will only ever beat this way for him.

I can't even be mad enough at him to hate him because I know I love him more than I could ever put into words. I could hate myself, though, and the need to externalise my pain causes my sense of self-loathing to triple. I hate myself for the choices I have made, for the warnings I have ignored, and for allowing myself to take that last step with Aiden. To completely open myself up to him. It doesn't matter how much I wanted it. I pull frantically at the clothes hanging in my wardrobe, discarding them around my room—a colourful waterfall of rage blanketing the floor around my feet. My fingers still, and my wrath calms when I come to his t-shirt he had put on me all those years ago at his sister's house, the morning after my attack. It feels wrong to destroy it, but my fury still isn't satisfied. I move from my wardrobe, grabbing and throwing anything that isn't heavy or glued down around me to push away the sadness raging inside me like a monster possessed. I had hoped that the chaos around me would settle the chaos in my soul.

No such luck. I drop to my knees, every breath laboured, a pink throw pillow clutched in my shaking hands, my knuckles white, my bottom lip trembling.

I wanted him to choose me. I wanted him to stare Louisa down and think up any other outcome than the one she presented. I cry for the longest time, gut-harrowing sobs muffled by the damp pillow I hold to my chest. With my eyes blurry, red, and raw, I watch as the sun sets behind the rooftops, swathing my room in a ruby-red blanket that should warm me but doesn't. My teeth chatter; my body is drained as I lay there motionless and cold on my bedroom floor. Although it's been hours since I had stumbled into the kitchen, giddy with the prospect of what the day would bring, I swear the scent of cooked bacon still lingers in the air. Yet another reminder of how quickly the tides can change. My cheeks are now dry and sore from fallen tears, and my belly is grumbling. Although my body protests, I reach for my phone on the bedside table, scrolling through my previous WhatsApp messages until Casey's name shows up.

RONI

She's pregnant!

9:02 PM

CASEY

With the spawn of Satan?

9:03 PM

RONI

It's not funny.

9:03 PM

CASEY

I'm not laughing. I'm just not entirely sure whether a human being could even grow inside a demon like her.

9:04 PM

RONI

He's walking away from me.

9:04 PM

CASEY

And you will be strong and let
it happen. I know you better than
you know yourself, Roni.

9:05 PM

She isn't wrong; she has always known the inner workings of my frazzled brain before I even comprehended what mess it was trying to resolve. Her foresight has been the concrete foundation of our friendship. My inability to curb my brutal honesty is what I brought to the table. Fuck if that little gem is going to help me with this one.

CASEY

It may not seem like it now,
but you will get through this.

9:06

RONI

I can feel my heard breaking.

9:06 PM

I type at the keyboard on my phone as more falling tears blur the screen's surface, auto-correcting *heart* with *heard*. I tap away and correct my mistake, but she responds before I can hit the send button.

CASEY

heart

It will heal, eventually. I promise.

9:07 PM

She knows that this moment, this situation, having this obstacle between Aiden and me, is my kryptonite. Fighting for Aiden, inevitably driving a wedge between him and his unborn child, is a low I will never allow myself to stoop to. The thought alone is too toxic to even consider. Casey senses my need for strength rather than pity, even through the exchange of text messages, and I'm grateful for it.

CASEY

Cry as hard as you want and as furiously as you need,

Roni, but make sure when you stop

crying, you never cry for the same reason again.

If Aiden is meant to be yours, it will happen.

No one has control over your fate.

9:08 PM

RONI

So, you think you are *Oprah fucking Winfrey* now?

9:08 PM

I can't seem to stop the tears, and knowing my message will make her chuckle, I ugly-laugh between sobs.

CASEY

Did I lie?

9.09 PM

RONI

As always, you are a legend.

Thanks for always having my back.

9:10 PM

CASEY

Forever and always shit-face.

YOU WILL SURVIVE THIS.

9:11 PM

PS - Do you need Tequila?

I can deliver.

9.12 PM

SEPTEMBER 9TH 2019

20 HOURS LATER

RONI

I think I'm dying,' I groan, lifting my head from my pillow to find an empty packet of cigarette papers stuck to my cheek. I peel it from my skin and throw it at Casey. She doesn't even flinch. 'What genius brings two bottles of tequila to a pity party?' I guffaw, knowing full well that I would have been more than willing to consume a vat of petrol last night if she had offered it to me—anything to drown out the reminders of his sullen face in that hallway.

'A legend, of course. A far less superior friend would have brought wine. Tequila practically seeps into your veins within minutes. The most important question, Miss Roni, is, do you still feel sad?' Casey retorts as she makes no effort to sit up or even move an inch, drinking the cloudy remnants of what's left of the tequila from the bottle tucked under her arm, her tongue darting out and fighting to get the straw to fall into her mouth.

'Casey, I can't even feel my face. Let alone emotions.'

'My work here is done, and you're welcome.' She extends her arm into the air, gesturing her acceptance of my non-thanks with a thumbs up. Her other hand strokes Doris, the cat, who has wrapped herself around Casey's neck as she slept, her elongated torso reminiscent of a fur stole. With yesterday's makeup still caked around her eyes, the unmissable aroma of day-old intoxication hovering in the air, the half-smoked joint hanging from her mouth, and Doris, as a wrap-around accessory, it is about as regal as this scene is ever going to get. 'I think I have a gift, a sense for people, a calling, you know?' The joint still stuck to Casey's lip does nothing to help sell her moment of higher power clarity.

'Quieten down, *Obi-Wan*,' I say whilst trying to find a pair of sunglasses on my bedside table, accidentally knocking to the floor whatever has the bad fortune of resting on top. I only have one eye open, making it that much harder to focus. But the searing pain behind the left one renders it useless, so the one-eyed pirate look is my only option to keep out the light. Rummaging around, I find some condoms, a half-eaten packet of chewing gum, and a sticky bottle of lube that makes me inwardly cringe. I know there is a pair of sunglasses in my wardrobe, but I can't be sure that I can even walk that far without face-planting the ground, and I'm not about to test my theory. I groan again as I turn my head a little too sharply. The incessant *thump, thump* against my frontal lobe intensifies the further I get from my sleeping state. The familiar dull ache of a hangover is waiting to attack, the liquor's reminder of my piss-poor life choices. The intrusion of daylight creeping through the partially open red tartan curtains makes me squint with my good eye. Even a movement as small as this one has me swaying on the spot. Unsteady legs do nothing to support me as I get to my feet and stumble into the dresser. My twenty-four-year-old body feels more like an eighty-three-year-old one as my joints creak and I struggle to manoeuvre around the small room.

'I think I'm dying,' Casey moans, repeating my earlier statement whilst sucking on the unlit joint between her lips out of habit. Although broken, the slight tug of a smile never seems to leave her lips. I fall back down onto the bed next to her.

Fuck it. Standing's overrated.

'I feel like the ensemble cast from river dance is performing a celebratory number in my head. Don't be so dramatic,' I scorn with a smile, knowing my cheekiness is the push she needs to sit upright. She is up and out of her slump a little too quickly, though. I recognise only too well her taut expression. She sways uneasily as all the blood in her head circulates its familiar path around her tingling limbs.

'Rookie mistake,' she berates herself as she tries to right her failing body, her fingernails gripping onto the edge of my king-size mattress. Doris whimpers with frustration as her human hot water bottle deserts her. Casey's voice is croaky and small, and she coughs to clear her throat. A build-up left behind from the box of tobacco she worked her way through last night, the misty remnants of which are still clouding my ornately moulded ceiling. Once we had downed our twelfth shot of tequila, we stopped bothering to even hang out of the window to smoke, the ashtray on my side table overflowing with cigarette butts proof of that.

You hit a whole new level of low when you disgust yourself.

'I need liquids and preferably something consisting of eighty per cent grease to soak up all this alcohol,' Casey states flatly, her tummy audibly rumbling, voicing the fact that she is teetering on the brink of starvation. She may be small, but she can pack it away when she wants to.

'How can you even think about food?' I grimace, vitriol rising in my throat in response to the thought of letting any solid food pass my cracked lips. I scoot down the bed, wanting nothing more than to collapse back onto my pillow and sleep for the foreseeable future, drowning out all thoughts of Aiden and everything that has happened between us over the past seventy-two hours. But I refuse to wallow and curl up into an unresponsive ball as my brain pleads for hydration. Left alone with my wandering thoughts is the last thing I need.

'Suck it up, buttercup. As I am the guest, you should be the one to provide the refreshments,' Casey says sweetly as she cradles what I hope is two paracetamols in her hand. MDMA at 9 AM has never been a good look for anyone.

'You've slept in my bed more times than I can count. You are no longer considered a guest. You're practically part of the furniture in this place,' I state, even though I know it's pointless. I already know I'll be getting the water. She smiles as she reads my mind, nudging my legs off the bed with her index finger, a meek attempt at encouragement. She repeatedly taps her thumb and forefinger together once my feet hit the floor, the smallest congratulation she can muster. Luckily, I revel in this lady's sarcasm. I turn my head to face her, hitting her with a glare strong enough to level a city, but I'm met with soft hazel eyes imploring me to purchase bacon.

'As I said, beautiful lady, guest,' she coos, dipping back into her pillow with a gruff groan. I spray a fuchsia-scented deodorant in the air to mask the ashy aroma of tobacco. Casey practically coughs up a lung as the scent of lilies and coconut fills the space. Every second away from the warm comforts of my duvet, a little more life floods my body. I shuffle over to my wardrobe, kicking away anything in my path from yesterday's freakout and grab a hoodie off a hanger, dragging it over my head lazily without a second thought to my bottom half. Thankfully, the sweatshirt is long enough to cover my flowery print pyjama shorts. Just the idea of bending at the waist to retrieve some trousers off the floor has me questioning life, my confidence to follow through with the simplest of tasks weighing heavy on my frazzled brain. The choice to keep the shorts on is made for me. Gravity is not my friend right now. Gathering up the last shreds of my dignity, I stroll towards the door. *Stroll* is the wrong word; I navigate haphazardly around yet more objects on the floor and finally reach the door unscathed. That is the truth of it.

'If you find a medium rare garlic butter steak and some peri peri chips coated in mayo on your travels down to the kitchen, I won't say no. Just saying,' Casey utters hopefully, even though she knows it's impossible. I have a three-day-old egg spread and week-old kebab meat to offer her, and she knows it.

'Sorry, the chef isn't working today, mam.' I yawn, opening the door that whines at its hinges and barrelling out into the hallway. Walking backwards as I watch Casey's face disappear behind the closing door. My feet move a little quicker than I had expected them to as I amble down the hall. I slam into something rock solid, all the blood rushing from my face as I realise who it is standing behind me. I apprehensively turn on my heels, the fight-or-flight urge to run back into my room making my fists clench and my jaw tick.

I could turn around and face Genghis Khan right now, and it would be less uncomfortable. No such luck. I'm sad, not stupid.

You have to face him at some point, that tiny voice in my head notes. Her choice of an upper-class east Londoner accent has me standing tall, although that other voice, the frightened little one still trying to process the shit show that is my life right now, screams at me to hurry back into my bed with Casey. To shut out the world and pray that the apocalypse hits—anything to get me out of this. With the impending doom of an all-out war on the planet my only credible idea, I give in and turn to face him. A bubble of a gasp hitches in my throat and betrays my contrived composure as our eyes lock. The pain and torture from yesterday hits me like a train again as I am transfixed, boneless under his steely blue-grey gaze. Fuck my lady bits for pooling with heat, my folds glistening with the need for this man standing before me. *Traitors.*

'And some orange juice, please,' Casey yells from my bed, her voice raspy and low, muffled by the closed door between us. I note that she almost sounds like a man. Aiden's wide eyes soften and fill with what I want to believe is disappointment at hearing the voice resonating from my bedroom, which leads me to believe that he, too, thinks Casey is some random guy I have invited over to replace his scent from my skin. *He's hurt*. That small voice in my head adds hopefully. The idea that he thinks of me at all sparks a smidgen of optimism to swell low down in my belly, a few cracks in my heart mending as a sense of courage replaces the crippling fear.

Fuck me for being human. Fuck my urges for stealing every plausible excuse for my reaction to his presence from my lips.

I don't allow myself to dwell on the thought, though, as that smidgen of hopefulness throws itself against the wall in a bid for social suicide when his bedroom door swings open behind him. Heat billows across his shoulders, fanning my hair, like one of those reveal scenes in some rom-com movie where the art department has been gifted a leaf blower and told to make it work as their budget doesn't allow for much else. This isn't a feel-sorry-for-me moment, I assure you. It is, however, a learn-from-my-mistakes moment. Sage advice from a woman who will inevitably die old and alone playing *Guess Who* with her gay bestie surrounded by cats, our fourth spliff of the day, making us regret not ordering a takeaway—conversations of *what if* haunting me even then.

I digress.

Louisa loops her arms around Aiden's bare chest, her fingers tracing light circles over his tattooed flesh. Blinded by his apologetic stare, I'm yet to realise he is standing before me in only a pair of grey sweatpants. Her hands caress the taut lines of his body, and I can't silence the need to rip them away and remind him of what my hands can do. I snap my eyes closed, banishing the memory of our entangled bodies before they can fester. The silence between us is smothering. My need for water makes me gulp air rather than breathe it in as fire licks at the pink fleshy linings of my throat.

Louisa is the first one to speak. At first, I'm grateful for her interruption, but as is with everything regarding her, I regret my lack of judgement in the next breath. 'Isn't that Aiden's?' She points a perfectly manicured talon at me, motioning to the oversized sweatshirt drenched with his aroma that I'm wearing. Aiden and I look down at the offending article of clothing donning my now trembling body. She was correct, and with no more words uttered between us, I bound back into my room and slam the door behind me. Leaning against it for a moment, I slowly slide down the wood, falling to the ground as my legs turn to jelly and the last remnants of my spirit crumble into dust.

Laying it on a little thick there, no?

Fuck Louisa, and fuck the little voice in my head.

'Have it dry cleaned,' Louisa barks nastily from the hallway, making me wince. I hear Aiden's muffled voice as he scolds her, pulling her back into his room, the door snapping shut a moment later.

'Juice?' Casey whines expectantly as she pops her head out from under my duvet. I catch only one hazel eye and the telltale signs of a smirk in the gap between the duvet and the mattress, but it's enough to satiate my looming panic attack, coaxing that killjoy away for when I might feel a little less vulnerable. Self-reflection has no place in this moment.

'I'd rather fight a grizzly bear draped in raw salmon than go down to that kitchen. So my vote is for dragging on sweatpants and an oversized sweatshirt that doesn't reek of forbidden affections, finding some sunglasses and hitting the town.' It is a demand disguised as a suggestion. Reading me perfectly, Casey pushes the duvet onto the floor.

'*Wetherspoons* serves a full English with a beer for £5.95.' Casey adds, already jumping into her bootleg jeans at the mere mention of going in search of food. She bends and whispers sweet nothings into Doris' ear, fussing with the fur around her neck. Then she fixes her once disjointed façade, rolling her shoulders with her arms extended as she greets the day through my open window. That half smoked spliff, still tucked between her lips.

With a new sense of purpose and the promise of breakfast, the woman, who only moments ago was laid up in my bed, professing she was so near death she couldn't move, has shaken off the restraints of her hangover, the paracetamol or MDMA, whatever they were, finally kicking in. Casey re-emerges from her cocoon like a beautiful butterfly. My transformation is far less remarkable. Swapping out Aiden's blue hoodie for an orange one I'm sure is mine and jumping into a pair of torn jeans, I drape a floor-length heavy wool coat over my shoulders and push the sunglasses up my nose into place.

'I'm as ready as I'll ever be. Let's do this,' I say as my belly grumbles, supporting my decision. She offers me her hand, and I take it. Chancing a look outside into the hallway, I tiptoe towards the stairs. I am now ravenous, and although the idea of more alcohol only five minutes ago would have sent me running for the toilet to throw up, it is now the only option my exhausted brain will consider. Other than a grip on my sanity, I need greasy food and the hair of the dog above all else. I must be out of this house and away from the happy couple, shacking up in the room next to mine. There is a chance that homicidal is the next option on my roulette wheel of emotions, and that won't benefit anyone. It may settle some of my stress, but I refuse to do hard prison time for that conniving bitch.

SEPTEMBER 9TH 2019

RONI

The bar is heaving with bodies, some still scantily dressed in clothes they wore out last night and slept in, most of the others, myself and Casey included, sporting outfits described best as homeless shabby chic. Even at 10 AM, with the glorious scent of heavily fried meat lingering in the air, the beer is still flowing. I slump down into my high-backed wooden chair, fighting the need to cry out my frustrations as images of Aiden roam unwelcome in my head, that familiar pinch of unease choking my heart in a vice-like grip. The usually delicious ache in my thighs and the trickle of light purple bruises where he had dug his fingers into my skin to hold me in place, are unsolicited reminders that I neither need nor want. My greedy core, obviously not on the same wavelength, traitorously stirs to life as thoughts of Aiden smiling wickedly down at me as he worships my body hit me.

Fuck my life.

Casey doesn't need me to voice my thoughts, recognising my expression as she raises her hand to get the server's attention as he flits between tables, clearing plates and silverware. 'We need alcohol,' she says sweetly to a young guy wearing a pressed white shirt and a navy apron around his waist. He has to be nineteen at most, the telltale signs of teenage acne still marring his skin in places. He steps forward, eager to please and parts his lips, ready to ask a question, but Casey gets in there first.

'Two beers, whatever you have closest on tap is fine, and a full English each, please,' Casey says, rubbing her hand up my arm as misery and self-pity bleed out of me. 'Oh, also, coffee, not tea, and toast, not bread, please,' she adds, mouth-watering as a waiter with food piled onto a tray rushes past her. Our server glances my way, his nervous gaze flitting around so he doesn't have to make eye contact with the sad girl chewing on the sleeve of her jumper like a child. I know he is waiting to see if I have anything to add to the order. Apparently, he doesn't even need to know my predicament because it's impossible to miss as sympathy floods his chocolate-brown eyes. Even our bloody server knows I've been ditched. 'Ooh, and one of everything here,' Casey adds excitedly, running her index finger down an entire page of the small menu, oblivious to our wordless exchange.

'One of…' He begins, and Casey rolls her eyes.

'Everything. Yes, you heard me correctly.' She smiles as I notice him glance down at her minute frame. Instead of asking more questions, he nods and hastily makes his way to the bar to start our drinks order. Even behind the dark tint of my sunglasses, I am sure he could see the unshed tears pooling in my eyes. My misery feels big enough to be considered a third person at this table.

'Argh,' I exhale through gritted teeth, my fingertips tingling as I recall the sensation of running them across Aiden's stubbled jaw. As the alcohol haze lifts and the brain fog clears, it only makes room for more thoughts of him to bombard me. I lower my head to rest it on my folded arms on the tabletop, for a second praying to whatever one of my questionable guardian angels on duty to rewind my life at least seventy-two hours. Fuck it, let's make it a clean seven days. Our waiter places the beers down in front of us, and I don't hesitate to gulp down the cool malty offering, hoping the alcohol will dull the ache in my chest and make everything a little less in focus.

'She'll have another,' Casey says to the waiter as he watches me finish the beer without coming up for air. I slam the glass down onto the table and gasp, welcoming the lick of pain in my overworked lungs. As, for a short while at least, it swallows my sadness. I wipe the sleeve of my jumper across my mouth. The server doesn't waste any time and heads back to the bar, a glint of fear in his wide brown eyes.

'Screw this,' I state, slamming both palms down onto the battered teak. 'I was this close to having him.' I hold up my fingers so they are an inch apart, waving them at Casey to drive home my point.

'It could be worse, Roni. That could have been the size of his dick,' she soothes, gesturing towards my fingers.

'Here we go, ladies,' a young guy announces as he puts the plates in front of us, pretending he didn't just hear Casey's remark. My belly moans as I get a whiff of the processed meats and saturated fats piled high on my plate.

Just what the doctor ordered.

'On a scale of one to ten, how much did you want to deck the bitch?' Casey remarks as she greedily tucks into the sausage suspended from her fork.

'*Rocky Balboa,*' I grouse with a frown, both loving and hating the familiarity of this game. Casey has no idea this is how Aiden and I would usually answer such a question, so I'm met with pinched brows and a lopsided smile. Although answering her has my stomach bottoming out, I feel compelled to say it anyway. I recover the best I can and knock my fork against the edge of my plate, hoping the noise will distract her from trying to pry further.

'I could never hit a pregnant woman,' I retort, idly nibbling at a slice of buttery toast I have dipped into the entire tin of baked beans smothering my plate.

'That wasn't what I asked you,' she says slowly with a sly smile, popping a mushroom between her lips.

'It's an easy twenty, and you know it.' I chuckle. 'But can we leave the game of question time till after I've ingested my bacon and eggs, please?'

If I'm being honest, I'm not even really interested in my food anymore. Still, as the sick feeling slowly ebbs away with every mouthful, I know that eating is the only distraction that will chase away the alcohol still singing in my veins.

'I know not to fuck with a hungry Roni,' Casey chides with her hands held up in a show of defeat.

I beam, turning my appreciative gaze to the auburn-haired teenage waitress struggling beneath the tray adorned with a plethora of snack items from the menu that Casey insisted she just had to try. She may be small, but boy, can she pack it away.

'Do you think you've ordered enough food?' I chuckle as the waitress tries to find space on the small table for the extra plates. Giving up, she drags an empty table and pushes it up against ours, using that surface to empty her tray of goodies.

'There is no such thing as too much food. Ever,' Casey retorts, throwing an entire cheese bite into her mouth and chewing noisily. Her appreciative hums fill the air between us as her belly moans its thanks.

I welcome the calm satisfaction that eating away my sadness offers me. The beer, of course, also helps. The wreckage that is my life can be assessed at some other time. Now I want to think about anything but Aiden and the carnival act that waits for me at home. The mere thought of him makes my heart flutter lazily in my chest, my body betraying me at every turn. I snap my head to the side, trying and failing to dispel the image of his chiselled face, his grey blues alight with desire, his broad bare chest rippling beneath my fingers, his impressive length between my legs working me up into a frenzy, the high too addictive to come down from.

Damn it!

'Fuck men!' I shout a little louder than I had intended, slamming my palm down onto the table as a foreign bloom of heat courses through me.

'Here, here!' Casey cheers jovially, her hand extended proudly in the air, her other hand moving to cover her mouth full of egg. I ignore the disapproving glares from the other patrons settled at the surrounding tables. I have enough to worry about without internalising the judgemental glares of London's high society. One lady clutches her designer handbag to her chest. Another sips on her mimosa as she moves the ingredients of her eggs benedict around her plate, not even a crumb passing her inflated lips. I want to remind them that their snobby asses *chose* to eat in a *Wetherspoons,* but I don't have the energy right now to reel off some political speech about the working-class masses.

Casey raises her fresh pint of beer courtesy of our waiter, and, either out of solidarity or shock, other patrons, all women, of course, follow her lead, toasting my outburst with their drinks held high in the air. Little miss prissy 1 & 2 unsurprisingly keep their mouths shut as they shift in their seats, turning their backs to us. I sheepishly raise my glass and smile behind the rim at Casey. The hoppy bubbles tickle my nose as I gulp down a mouthful. Starting the day with beers and a protest isn't what I had expected when I rolled out of bed this morning, but it is a change in pace I welcome.

'Thanks,' I say, my voice meek. Casey is my only anchor in the Titanic mess of a world where I have placed myself, and I am grateful to have her by my side. If I had to drown in sadness with anyone, I'm glad it's her. Casey nods toward a table where two young girls in their early twenties chomp furiously into their sausages as though they are phallic symbols of girl power, their heartache at the hands of some man almost a visible green mist flitting between them. I recognise it only too well.

NOVEMBER 4TH 2019

TWO MONTHS LATER

AIDEN

It's been two months, and I haven't heard a word from Roni. As well as her day job at the office, she has taken up some evening work, to keep the distance between us I suspect. I'm only privy to that nugget of information because Paulie let it slip Roni had asked him for a reference last week. Roni is a lot of things but skilled in serving drinks is not one of them. I bet she's hating every minute of it. I rarely hear her in her room anymore. We exist like ships in the night. The house we share is now where she has a shower and sleeps. Our interactions reduced to an accidental encounter here and there when I catch her making her morning coffee or taking the bins out to the kerb. I make it a point to stay at Louisa's as much as possible, so if they did cross paths, it wouldn't make Roni feel worse, but I don't know how much longer I can keep up the façade. I don't want to be away from Roni, and the truth is getting harder to hide as the days pass.

I miss you.

Please talk to me.

Roni, I hate this.

I have written message after message since that day in our kitchen when I found out that I was going to be a father, the morning after the best night of my life. But she has ignored every single one of them, and I can't blame her. I'm a dick, not delusional.

I even tried asking about Doris, hoping that would soften her, but nothing seemed to work. I knew every side of Roni, and the grief contorting her features as I watched her heart break that day because of me, will forever be ingrained in my mind. I took a piece of her I hadn't earned, sliced from her soul with a rusty blade. Professing my love for Roni is as easy as breathing, but the fear of facing Louisa's wrath holds me tethered to the dark place where I've convinced myself I can live without Roni, that's if I ignore all the signs that assure me I am being a fool.

I have allowed each change that Louisa has imposed since her revelation. Fighting memories of Roni beneath me, my hands tugging at her waist, my length buried inside her as I worked her up into a frenzy, her bottom lip secured between her teeth as she fought to hide her need for me. I shudder at the vision, my fingers tingling, my body feeling more alive than it has in weeks. It's difficult to concentrate on anything other than her most days.

'I'm yours, Roni. I always have been. Always will be. If soulmates really exist, you're mine. Now take off your underwear like a good girl. I want to feast on what's mine while you scream my name.' I have replayed these words repeatedly in my mind these past two months. Time away

from her morphs and distorts them, so they are almost a wish rather than a promise. I'm unsure now whether I even said them out loud. She deserved to hear those words from me. I immediately hate that maybe I will never get to tell her how I feel. Like everything else lately, I push down what I'm feeling to the pit of my stomach and instead concentrate on a tangible memory that softens my whole body. Her serene face, lost to sleep as she burrows into my bare chest, waves of her chocolate-brown hair splaying across my torso, the curve of her full lips as she dreams, hopefully, of me.

Although I can't have her in my arms right now, holding her in my heart will have to do. It's the only lifeline I have until we can be together again. If it is the last thing I do, I will make it happen for us.

'Daddy's here,' Louisa squeals excitedly, dropping her spoon into her bowl of fruit and yoghurt. She tugs my arm, pulling me from my reverie. I watch out the window as an obscenely expensive Land Rover pulls up noisily onto the cobble driveway, almost totalling a weathered gnome as the bumper kisses the garage door. I lack the same enthusiasm at her parents' arrival, so Louisa drops my arm and, satisfied that I'm now standing, she moves to cross the room. I follow close behind as she totters down the hallway, her high heels clicking against the wood flooring. She practically runs down the path towards her father to greet him as he enters through the front gate. Paying little mind to her mother, who is by his side.

Once they've exchanged hugs and Louisa's feet are again planted on the uneven brick path, I take a step forward to approach her father. 'Mr Rinstein,' I say politely, holding my hand out to greet the man. He looks at it as though it's covered in shit; his lip curling up with repugnance. Instead of taking it, he eyes me warily as though I'm something gross he's just scrapped off his shoe. I'm here because Louisa wants me, that's evident, and as much as her father loathes the ground I walk on, he would never dream of saying no to his princess.

Louisa loops her arm around her father's, and they make their way up the path into my house, chatting enthusiastically about what ivy league school my unborn child would attend to make a statement on their social circle. The word *cult* springs to mind.

You can do this, Aiden, I tell myself as I inhale a steadying breath. I slap a genial smile on my face and hold out my arm locked at the elbow, gesturing for Louisa's meek mother to cross the threshold before me. She nods in thanks, her preened blonde bob swaying with the motion but doesn't say a word. The points to note are these. Louisa's father, a short, stocky man with a receding grey hairline, a protruding midriff, more money than sense, and less morals than the devil, doesn't much like me, and he has zero qualms about making me aware of his feelings. Things have only got worse since the news of the baby dropped. He knows for sure now that I had been regularly fucking his princess, although that can't be said for the past two months, much to her dismay. The thought of annoying Louisa's father, although it shouldn't, makes me smile.

Louisa's mother, who is considerably younger than her husband, is slim and tanned, an older version of her daughter as every inch of her is preened to perfection. A shell of a woman, she's likely been conditioned not to show any emotion unless her husband expressed a desire to see it. I can see where Louisa gets her tenacity to rule over every situation. As we sit around the dining table discussing what everyone but me thinks of my future life plans, I am steadily aware that my thoughts on the matter are of no consequence. I can put up or shut up, and there is no third option. If I am going to be a part of their family, if I wanted to play a role in my child's life, I would work for her father and endeavour to make his little girl happy. I resent my lack of fight, that I've convinced myself that staying quiet to keep the peace is my only choice. I am left suspended in a weakened state—any power or authority over my own life seemingly stripped from me. As Louisa and her father chat, I zone out. Roni's beautiful beaming face flashes in my mind, a random memory from years ago of us sitting in our wardrobe space, sharing bacon sandwiches and laughing about something inane. I'm up and out of my chair before my brain can catch up.

Fuck this! I bolster up what little courage I have left and say my goodbyes, making a point to shake Louisa's father's hand tighter than I normally would have. Which I'm pleased to say shocks him a little. I'll class it as a win. Louisa is stunned, her eyes wide with surprise as a slice of Victoria sponge slides off the serving knife in her hand onto her father's plate with a splat, decorating the old-lady lace-trim table cover with icing. Before Louisa can open her mouth to criticise me, I kiss her on the cheek and grab my jacket from the back of my chair, seizing my car keys from the bowl on the side table beside the front door as I pass.

If this is to be my future, I need my best friend by my side, that's if she will still have me.

NOVEMBER 6TH 2019

2 PM

TWO DAYS LATER

RONI

I'm standing in the fresh-fish aisle of my local supermarket, the fingers of one hand digging into the plastic wrap of a salmon fillet for one, reminding me it's plenty big enough to feed my sad single self. My other hand grips my mobile, which is vibrating. I fight to centre myself as a carousel of nerves has my foot tapping nervously against the scuffed linoleum as his name fills the screen, the contact image a picture of us mid laugh with drawn on moustaches that we would soon discover would take at least three days to remove. The metal swoosh of battered trolly wheels and the yells of mothers telling their kids to put back whatever chocolate goodies they swiped off the shelves fade. My brain can only process the phone that is still ringing. I drop the plastic-wrapped fish into the trolley and abandon the entire thing without a second thought, rushing towards the boujee pop-up café with the oversized alternative art covering every inch of free wall space tucked away near the shop's entrance. I ignore the glances of horror from other shoppers as I weave between the queues of people not currently staving off a panic attack. If anyone should ask, I didn't mean to launch that bag of spinach at that woman. I was testing her reflexes. They sucked – she should see someone about that.

Far from being considered hipster cool in any way, shape or form, I find thirty pairs of eyes trained on me as I barrel through the arched walkway to early 90's rock tunes pouring out of every floor-to-ceiling speaker circling the room. My phone stops ringing, and my raging heart rate settles. I tug at the waistband of the black sweatpants that are practically glued to my body. Wearing them for three days straight has the usually soft material stiff in places due to caked-in dirt, debris, and God only knows what else. I paw at the hem of a greying, old-band tee of Aiden's that used to be black before hundreds of cycles in the washing machine. I tug at the front panels of Casey's black and white houndstooth-patterned overcoat I stole from her wardrobe this morning, wrapping it around my body to generate some warmth. Even with the Air conditioner cranked up and the mass of bodies around me, the only semblance of heat to note is the familiar unfurling trickle of yearning that hits me without warning when my mind wanders to thoughts of him.

I slump into a dimly lit corner booth at the back of the room, away from prying eyes and judgemental glares. I have a sneaking suspicion my fur-lined boots and leather accessories aren't helping my case. If you could describe a place as being vegan, this would be it. Sweeping vines cascade from the metal pipework above, futons made of recycled materials dotted around the main eating area as alternative seating, and framed posters detailing the horrific nature of animal testing prettied up with floral borders line the wrap-around bar in the centre. Perusing the menu made of hemp, I find every variation of a vegetable grain concoction and decide I'm not that hungry. Thankfully, scrawled at the bottom is the section reserved for coffee. A sigh of relief rumbles from my throat.

As I take in my surroundings, revelling in the upbeat atmosphere of the café, I make eye contact with a young lady at the table beside me. Her short blue hair sweeps over her pixie features as she angrily chomps down on a piece of broccoli. The quintessentially British tight-lipped smile pinching at my lips does nothing to settle her expression. I don't know what I could have done to make this woman so mad, but every fraction of common sense I have screams for me to break eye contact. As though if I allow my gaze to linger there for too long, I might inadvertently join up to whatever faction this woman is likely a member of.

I stare back at the black screen of my mobile, nibbling my fingernails anxiously, trying to ignore the fact that *Carly Manson* at the table next to me is still glowering my way. I don't know whether I'm happy or sad that Aiden seems to have given up trying to contact me, but even as my heart ceases its tirade against my ribs, I'm left with the imprint of his touch across my skin. The calm doesn't last long as the storm stirs back to life when my phone buzzes with the fourth call from Aiden. I shuffle out of Casey's coat, rubbing my hands together as I stare down at the lit screen.

My finger hovers over the green accept button, but my need to bury my head in the sand and swipe across the screen with the red option has this little situation that, in retrospect, should be an easy one, feel more like a *Sophies Choice* sort of predicament.

Slightly dramatic. The little voice in my head larks.

I wrangle the urge to launch my phone into the copper industrial coffee machine, spewing out its latest order as though it is struggling to catch its breath. However small that voice may be, more often than not, it isn't wrong. I silence the phone, but I don't cut it off completely.

Why is this so hard? I tap at the screen, light enough that I'm not committing to a decision, heavy enough that my black-painted nails rap on the thin layer of Perspex protecting the screen.

Fucking your best friend, then watching another girl call him Daddy. Yeah, that has a way of messing with your head. Two for two, my conscience is on a roll today.

I don't know how much longer I can keep ignoring him. Even locked in my little bubble, forced to listen to hipsters discuss the new accent walls in their new townhouses. The scent of freshly ground coffee beans in the air making me desperate for a cup of sweet tea. And even overhearing how the word quinoa is pronounced, I still can't distract myself enough to completely wipe Aiden from my thoughts.

I'd be lying if I said I didn't miss him. Rehashing every moment of our night together does nothing to quell the flapping butterflies filling my belly that tell me I'm a fool in love, hope urging them on to keep up their frantic pace. The world spins beneath my feet as I weigh my options. It feels like I'm constantly trawling through my memories, trying and failing to find a moment from that night that hadn't felt right. It's like exploring a dirty *Where's Wally* picture book in my head where Aiden buries himself in me like I'm his reason to breathe, powering forward as if his life depends on it, each thrust a promise, each brush of his lips my ruination.

What sort of kids' books have you been reading? The little voice in my head snorts, and I lose focus for a second. The phone continues to vibrate against my palm. Before I can go back to torturing myself with the pros and cons of accepting Aiden's phone call, I hear what will forever be known as the voice of judgement pipe up, yet again—unhelpfully, as always. *Pervert.* Not even her comedic interlude can chase away thoughts of him, though.

'Mine.' The husky timbre of his voice is heavy with a smoky heat. Even as a daydream, that one word has goosebumps prickling my skin as

though it is a fluid promise dancing across the soft pink flesh of my exposed lower belly. My heart fumbles, each irregular beat the only proof I'm not yet lost to my new reality without him. Just the thought of hearing his voice again on the other end of the line is my undoing. *'I'm yours, Roni.'* I clamp my legs together, my knickers already sodden with my spent arousal, as excitement lights a flame that waltzes up towards the apex of my thighs. Although my body clearly wants what it can't have, every sane thought in my head assures me that seeing him will intensify the pain inside me. But I can't possibly go on like this forever. Tequila showdowns at *Casa Casey* will never be a wise go-to for healing. How long can anyone dodge the inevitable, though? I don't want to face the truth, but this isn't some fairy tale where I get to write the rules. We share a house; we are best friends, or at least, I hope we still are.

The inappropriate choice of ringtone that Aiden had selected for himself has me accepting the call before everyone in the vicinity gets an earful of *Jack Black* as he artistically hits the melodic strums of his guitar with a couple of strategically placed *fucks*. I suck in a crucial breath through pinched lips to steady my nerves, choosing the path of green and lifting the phone to my ear, hiding behind a mask of contrived composure even though he can't see my face.

'Hey, baby,' Aiden can't hide the surprise in his voice. He clearly thought I wouldn't answer his call. The awkward calm that follows as the familiar name he reserves for me tumbles from his lips doesn't go unnoticed. I make no move to talk. 'Sorry. Hey, Roni,' he says gently, correcting himself. The breath I hoped would steady me fails massively as I fight to hold back the tears teetering in the corners of my eyes.

'Hi,' I reply with little conviction. If I wasn't 100% sure before, I certainly am now. This phone call is going to be anything but easy.

'I miss you.' His words are soft, barely audible. Now it is my turn to be shocked. Has he just said that? Does he really miss me? Even though I can't see him, I know he is fretfully tugging at the hair at the nape of his neck. He has thought about this call as much as I have, but now it is happening, we are both at a loss for words. Expertly dodging what *needs* to be said seems the only thing our minds can agree on.

'I miss you too,' my tiny voice is soft, an almost pliable entity that I don't recognise as my own.

Don't cry, Roni. Don't cry!

I'm bombarded with everything I want to say to him, everything I need him to know. But the moment feels too small for that, as though my loud thoughts could do more harm than good if I don't keep them at bay, leashed to my soul and frothing at the mouth, ready to break free and swallow down whatever pain will come my way.

A thorny silence fills the line, and we collectively draw in a sharp breath, but our exchange doesn't feel as onerous as it had when I first accepted his call. My shoulders droop as the tension I'm carrying dissipates, my body thrumming with energy, desperate for his voice to bring me back to life in a way that only he can.

'I...' we both say in unison. I crumple on the inside; I hate that this is how we are now. Aiden clears his throat, and I imagine him standing a little taller. His broad shoulders flexed as he regains his confidence, metaphorically grabbing the bull by the horns as he is likely pacing across the shaggy carpet of his bedroom.

'Look, I hate not speaking to you. Can we get past this so I can have my friend back?' His words mix into a melody of vowels and consonants as he forgets to take a breath. His question is a gooey mess as it falls from his lips. My frantic thumping heart settles as I sigh, finally able to relax a little, grateful that he spoke first.

'Sounds like a plan. What you up to?' I ask, relief saturating my voice. I need to let this go and try to salvage whatever I can of our friendship. The fog between us begins to clear, and we're on the same page for the first time in what feels like forever. Just like that, our worlds collide, and it feels like it did before that night we shared in his bedroom. Once again, he feels like home. I ignore the thrum of unease that coils in my chest, sidestepping the reality that I would inevitably pay for not airing this out properly, but if I'm honest, for now at least, I need us to be what we were before my life turned upside down.

'Louisa's dad has me buried under a mountain of paperwork. I think he only gave me the job, so he didn't have to do the work himself,' he mutters. 'I also think Louisa likes that he can keep an eye on me. I don't know what she thinks I will get up to.'

So, Aiden is working for her father. She really has got everything she could ever want now. Next will be Aiden down on one knee, a little cottage by a river and blonde-haired grey-blue-eyed babies galore. The warranted thought spears me. I fight back the unshed tears stinging my eyes, thankful I have a phone to hide behind so that he can't see the devastation on my face.

'No more working at Paulie's then?' I quip. Jenny had mentioned he had taken some time off after I left, but I had no idea he had quit. He loves his bar job. It affords him enough time to work creatively on his art and music. Plus, he is a people person. It almost didn't feel like work to him. Imagining him stuck behind a desk in a suit and tie saddens me. The little voice of judgement in my head, however, notes how delicious Aiden would look suited and booted in a crisp white shirt, sleeves rolled up to his elbows, and dark slacks hugging every prominent line of his lower half. I chastise her opinion immediately as my toes dip into the dangerous territory that is visions of Aiden ready and waiting for me to strip him down to nothing. I shy away from the familiar pang of longing humming at my core that I'd shunned these past two months. This is hard enough as it is. I don't need the idea of kinky fuckery with my best friend fuelling this inferno.

'Nope, I've hung up the shot belt. Apparently, a father-to-be has no place half naked in a bar with intoxicated women.' In ten seconds flat, Aiden has offloaded the crux of his unhappiness, and I know who is to blame for this big shift in him. Louisa has been trying to get Aiden to work for her dad since they began dating, and the baby's impending arrival has secured that for her. I would never utter the declaration out loud, but to say I am jealous of Louisa is an understatement. It feels as though she is living the life with Aiden I had imagined for myself, not the him being unhappy in a job he hates part, of course, but all the relationship stuff in between.

'That sucks,' is all I can say. I don't want him to know exactly what I think of his controlling bitch of a girlfriend, so I keep my opinions to myself for now. He needs my support and nothing else.

'I'm supposed to complete some online course tonight, but my laptop stopped working,' he casually adds. To anyone else, this would be a mundane conversation filler, but I know differently. There is a question he wants to ask but can't verbalise.

'The keyboard is hanging on by a piece of wire. I'm not surprised. Ten years is an adequate amount of time to invest in a new laptop, dipshit,' I jibe, and the hearty laugh that rumbles down the line fills me with joy. Aiden was never one to spend money unnecessarily. He pays his rent, covers his bills, and always has food in the fridge. He is smart with money. He doesn't splurge or buy superfluous luxuries, which is why his being with someone like Louisa surprised me so much in the beginning.

'How about I come and see you for a bit?' I can hear the hope in his voice, and before I can think better of it, I agree. I want to see him. I could never lie about that.

'Okay,' I squeak, knowing that we probably shouldn't meet up, but agreeing for all the reasons I know why we should. I have to face him sometime.

'Paulie said you went and got yourself a new bar job,' he says and I realise a lot has changed in our time apart.

'It's Cable Road, Paddy's Bar and Grill,' I state flatly, my nerves at seeing him now getting the best of me. 'Will Louisa be joining you?' I add, chewing my bottom lip as I wait for him to answer. I know Louisa would never give up a chance to rub her happiness in my face, but I can barely contemplate seeing Aiden, let alone her aswel. I don't know how far my patience will stretch, and I'm not ready to test it.

'Just me for tonight. Her girlfriends planned some impromptu baby shower thing, and it's strictly no men allowed. I hear gifts are involved, so I'm keeping my fingers crossed for the latest *MacBook Pro* with all the bells and whistles. Babies need one of those, right?' He chuckles, the light-hearted sound music to my ears. My chest swells in response, and I'm grateful he can't see my reaction. 'She'll stay at her mother's after. She's been doing that a lot recently. Me working through all my free time means she needs the company.' His lacklustre chortle this time is devoid of feeling. The difference is night and day when he speaks about the baby and when he speaks about her. We arrange for him to pop by later in the evening when my shift ends so we can have a beer and an overdue catch-up. I decide to try to enjoy the wave of delight that the thought of seeing him sparks in my chest. I am equal parts sated and damaged, and it isn't a mix of emotions I would wish on anyone.

NOVEMBER 7TH 2019

12.38 AM

RONI

I wipe down my last table and take the empties into the back kitchen, stowing them under the side, ready for the dishwasher. Monica is taking over the late shift, and she has a thing for the kitchen liaison, so she is always grateful for an excuse to be back here. I haven't got a change of clothes at work, so I attempt to clean myself up. I pull my ponytail free from the hairband, running my fingers through the length and trying to settle the unruly curls. My hair drapes over my shoulders, the scent of steak and beer filling my nose. Arranging a side parting, I tuck one side behind my ear and assess my reflection in the fogged-up staff toilet mirrors as steam from the kitchens waft into the small room. With A fresh layer of coconut balm on my lips and another coating of mascara across my lashes, I'm as ready as I am ever going to be. I pinch my cheeks to draw some colour to the surface and grab my jean jacket and handbag hooked on the back of the door. As I exit the back room into the bustling main area of the bar, a voice grabs my attention. Even over the many conversations and general thumping hum of the background music, that voice from behind me pulls me in and tethers me to the spot, my legs refusing to move. Her cackles fade as she retreats, oblivious to my presence. I fight my better judgement and my brain's instructions to leave well enough alone and follow her out into the foyer.

'Louisa?' I don't know why I call her name, but I can't seem to stop myself. The gaggle of women stop dead in their tracks at the sound of someone summoning their leader. I wait for them to turn around, not knowing what I will say. She is front and centre with her hands on her hips, her minions falling back a step, flanking either side of her protectively, all draped in glitter, gold and animal print. Not one of them is able to outshine Louisa as she stands tall oozing confidence.

'Girls, this is Veronica,' Louisa spits, my name rolling uncomfortably off her tongue as it always did, sounding like a one-word curse. The other women assess me, my name obviously piquing their interest as though they had heard it before. I suddenly feel small, pulling at the fraying hem of my shabby white work shirt nervously. These ladies all wear couture, each item probably costing more than my monthly wage. My ripped black jeans and studded biker boots are the polar opposite of their diamante-drenched cocktail dresses and skyscraper heels. Although it shouldn't, it makes me feel like this is a perfect example of why Aiden doesn't consider me girlfriend material. Even pregnant, Louisa looks like she has just stepped out of a supermodel cover shoot. Thanks to my bout of self-doubt, it takes me a second or two, but something occurs to me as she animatedly regales her friends with embarrassing stories about me. Once she finishes, she moves towards me, breaking away from her pack, a twisted grin on her heavily made-up face.

'This is her dressing up,' she bellows to the women behind, her stare still fixed on me as she speaks. 'You wonder why he chose me,' she adds in a whisper, her nasty words for my ears only as she tugs at the collar of my denim jacket. My belly flips uncomfortably at her proximity.

'I know Hobo's with better taste,' Louisa-clone number one retorts, bringing her glass to her lips. Louisa follows suit and takes a swig of her drink. The intense flowery scent of her perfume is cloying as it clings to the back of my throat making me want to gag. She's close enough that the fizzing bubbles from her champagne flute are the only thing I can hear clearly. As heat rises in my chest, my expression must change because Louisa warily takes a step back away from me. She is clearly smarter than I gave her credit for.

'Should you be drinking?' I ask, glancing between Louisa's glass and her belly, ignoring her friends entirely. Louisa's words may hurt me, but I'm not about to listen to the cackling insults from a group of women who collectively decided a bar was a suitable place to hold a baby shower.

'One doesn't hurt,' Louisa declares, taking another long sip whilst palming her belly. I note the ringless finger of her left hand, and a slight smile pulls at my lips.

'I bet the bottle didn't help,' Louisa-clone number three mutters under her breath with a snort. Clone number two smacks her on the back, urging her with fierce wide eyes to shut her mouth as though she had just spilt a secret. Clone number two clearly outranks number three because she shies away like a berated puppy who has just been caught urinating on the floor.

'But the baby, why are you drinking at all?' I press. Louisa's lazy stare and the fact that she stumbles on her skyscraper heels means it's likely she has been indulging in alcohol for quite a while. I can't believe I didn't see this before. The tell-tale red-rimmed eyes, and the subtle sway of her body as she leans in closer towards me. I move to speak but she raises her hand, her palm in my face to shush me.

'Poor, lonely, sad Veronica.' She retorts with a disinterested nod, the smirk on her face taut. A flurry of insults are just begging to pass her lips as she eyes me critically from top to toe. Even unspoken I can sense the hate in them as she mulls over what to say to me next, choosing carefully from her prepared list of insults until she can find the one sure to hurt me the most. She doesn't seem fazed by my question regarding the baby and instead tips back her glass and finishes her drink, huffing in my face as though she is now bored with our little interaction, and the feeling is mutual. Turning on her heels, she flicks the length of her long blonde hair over her shoulder as she saunters back to stand with her inebriated friends. This baby shower is looking more like a Hen do by the minute, all we're missing are L-plates and various cock shaped accessories.

'What baby?' clone number three pipes up before hiccupping, then breaking out with a laugh, unable to contain herself. The glares the other women throw her way are almost palpable. The black-haired, big-chested minion in the cheetah print jumpsuit does as she is silently instructed and steps back in line ruefully to join the others.

My mouth is agape as I ponder what the trashy woman has just said.

Everything was a lie. Realising that I am not as stupid as she thought I was, Louisa stares intently at me, a flash of dread veiling her pristine face as a sheen of sweat starts to appear around her collarbone. My eyes meet hers, and it's as though everything else around us melts into the background. I open my mouth to speak, but she gets there first.

'The relationship between you two was always so juvenile. I had to make him a man. He needed to grow the hell up. I've helped him with that.' She taps a finger at her belly as though it strengthens her argument. Where once I saw my friend's destiny, I now see only her destruction.

'You're lying, aren't you? You were lying to him all along,' I accuse, stepping closer to her, filling the space between us, bravery stirring up inside me like a suit of armour shifting into place. Fighting for him always had come so naturally to me.

'You could hit her if she isn't pregnant,' the little voice in my head announces with glee.

'What's a little white lie here and there?' She giggles. The bitch actually has the audacity to fucking giggle. I'm beyond shocked by her admission, her nonchalance, and the fact that she refuses to see how messed up this is. Although I believe I now know the truth, I realise she hasn't explicitly admitted it.

'I will tell him the truth,' I protest, knowing it is the sincerest statement I have ever made. Whether or not Aiden wants me, he doesn't deserve to be catfished by her.

'And who do you think he will believe? His soon-to-be fiancé who is carrying his child, or you, the whore who sleeps with anything and everything that doesn't move fast enough and hasn't returned his calls for months?' she barks, that artificial innocent little laugh of hers now scratching at my skin like cheese wire. Following suit, her disciples laugh heartily behind her at my expense. 'I wasn't about to let you get your hooks into him. I had to move quickly,' she adds. 'I thought I was done for when Marie called me the next morning, telling me how close my boyfriend and some little tart were getting in Paulie's bar, in front of everyone, no less.' Her eyes are alight with irritation as she recalls the memory. A round woman with a tight top knot of auburn hair, wearing bright red lipstick and an obscenely short pleather dress of the same colour, steps out from behind Louisa and smirks wickedly at me. Marie, I assume. 'So, I made it my business to pop over and take him back. How was it playing with what's mine, Veronica, tasting someone who didn't belong to you? He's not half bad, is he?' She larks maliciously, running her finger along my jawline. My fists clench, and I fight back the emotions in my chest. 'He's very talented in that department. I'll give him that.' She sneers as though it is an afterthought. I have to admit, it's quite refreshing to see the bitch tell the truth for once. I think lying comes a little too naturally to her. As though her mask has finally slipped out of place, I realise this is the real Louisa, conniving and cruel at her core. 'He was always going to be mine, whether he wanted it or not.'

I recoil at her words, the slicing of pain reverberating through my chest as I pity my best friend and the life that he is now stuck in.

'He's going to notice when you don't give birth,' I press, begging the tears not to fall down my cheeks as she beams back at me with excitement. Even with my tears tucked away, she knows the effect her cruel words have on me, and she is relishing in it. She surprises me, though, as she cries on cue, an actual tear rolling down her face, her lips trembling, her arms swathing her belly. I suck in a gasp and swallow the sound, unwilling to give her the reaction she desires.

'I can't... I... We've lost the baby,' she whispers with a strangled breath, her voice distraught, easily the best piece of acting I have ever seen from her. Louisa has everything covered. She dragged Aiden into her world. He will never leave the woman who has just lost his baby, and she knows it. She has been playing him from day one.

'When I lose this baby, it will only bring us closer, and I will get that ring that he owes me. I'm doing him a favour. He has no balls to do it himself. He will see that I'm right... eventually.'

'Why would you do this to him?' My heart swells at how devastated Aiden will be when he finds out he isn't going to be a dad. Before I can ponder the thought further, Louisa shocks me again.

'It's not the first time we've *lost one.*' Her use of air quotes here makes me want to throw up and kick her in the face concurrently. 'He'll get over it, and then we can go back to our life,' she mutters with a smile, a sick sense of pride weighing heavily in her tone. The *'we've been through things'* reasoning Aiden had previously mentioned when I had asked him why he was with Louisa is suddenly becoming clearer. This isn't the first fictitious baby she has lied about. She has found my friend's weakness and used it to her advantage. 'He wanted to leave me. ME,' she howls, her tiara tipping as her face contorts into a grimace, smoothing out her hair and straightening her back when she realises I've noticed the change in her behaviour. 'So one dummy pregnancy test later, he was back in my corner. I knew he wouldn't leave me that first time. Losing a child can scar a woman.' She pouts, another fake tear rolling down her cheek on cue. I bite back the need to strangle Louisa as the mock empathy on her face switches from sad to conniving in a third of a second, as though she can turn her emotions from caring to crazy with ease.

'You don't deserve him; you know that don't you?' I holler, uncaring that I am shouting in the middle of a busy lobby, sounding like a jilted ex. I've clearly underestimated this sad excuse of a woman.

'Oh, what and you do?' she hoots, spearing my resolve. I know immediately that she can sense my unease. Like a hound dog, she has recognised the scent of fear. 'Oh my God, you love him, don't you?' She cackles condescendingly. 'How did I not see this? I knew you had a little infatuation, but love. You really are just as sad as I thought you were, Veronica. Pining for a man you could never have. Tell me, how lonely is it in that big house by yourself whilst I am at home straddling Aiden, running my hands through his hair as he thrusts up into me?' Her words hit me hard. Harder than I thought they ever could. I resist the urge to slap her. Pregnant or not, hitting her won't help anything. She'd probably use it to make Aiden hate me, and I can't have that. If Louisa has even an ounce of humanity, I will try to appeal to it.

'You can't treat him this way. He deserves to be happy. He is so excited to be a dad,' I almost beg, realising quickly that this woman is heartless. I had the name right; I am practically pleading with the Devil. I hope my words will knock her off balance enough to make her see sense, but it is clear she doesn't care if he is happy. A silent instruction from Louisa has the ladies dutifully lining up behind their master, turning in unison to walk away from me in fits of giggles, their glasses clinking together as they celebrate their win. With

one final triumphant smirk, Louisa turns to follow them. I am done giving this woman anything more than the loathing that she deserves. Something out of the corner of my eye catches my attention, and I march forward, pulling on Louisa's hair so she has no other option but to turn and face me.

'So you've been lying this whole time? You aren't pregnant. You never were?' I yell in her face. I need to hear her outright admit the truth I already know. I need to hear her say it. The clones gasp at my audacity. Little do they know I have reached my limit and have zero fucks left to give. Louisa continues to grab at my hand, trying to free herself. Her intoxication works to my advantage as she hangs there like a flaying fish out of water. Although I know I should stop this; I don't.

'Tell me,' I order her. Regretting the words as they leave my lips. Against my better judgement, I stoop to my lowest level as I let her speak her truth.

'Never have been pregnant, never will be pregnant, but then I'll still have him, and you never will,' she shrieks at me, venom in her words and a flash of sick satisfaction in her muddy green eyes. I let go of her hair and take a step back. My head falls as I expel a painful rush of air from my lungs. I know deep down I am wrong for letting this go on. I know just by looking into his hazy, tear-filled blue-grey eyes that he is broken. I know that as the fog clears and my better judgement steadies itself, I will regret this moment.

I don't know how long he has been standing there, but I know he heard Louisa's final admission. I made certain of that. Clone number one coughs, lightly silencing everyone and making Louisa turn to her. I glance up again for the briefest moment, and his red-rimmed eyes meet mine. I snap my gaze away, unable to look at him, guilt rumbling in my hollow chest as my heart breaks anew for him. The beer glass in his hand falls to the floor and smashes upon impact. That effectively brings the entire room to a standstill. At least a hundred sets of eyes are now trained on Aiden. He tugs at the hair at the nape of his neck, his bottom lip secured between his teeth as he bites back his emotions. He shouldn't have found out this way. He deserves so much more than this public torture display. My insides liquify as I watch on in horror at the destruction of my best friend. Louisa is by his side instantly, stringing together whatever web of lies she has concocted on the spot to placate him. He turns to leave without uttering a word, Louisa tottering off behind him submissively, struggling in her heels to catch up with him. Holding the pretend baby in her swollen belly out of habit rather than comfort. I want to run to him, hold him, and ease his suffering, but my legs refuse to move. So, I watch him leave, regret heavy on my shoulders.

My heart recognises the muffled stabs of loss as he pushes through the crowd and barrels out of the bar into the darkness, Louisa now hot on his heels as the women she's left behind gossip animatedly between themselves.

NOVEMBER 15th 2019

ONE WEEK LATER

RONI

'So how is he?' Casey chimes in, knowing that Aiden is on my mind. She watches me with concern as I tear a fraying beer coaster into pieces. My need to busy my hands does nothing to ease the barrage of thoughts I've had to deal with for the past seven days.

'As you would expect, he's utterly lost. He isn't the same person right now, Casey.'

'Because he lost her?'

'No, because he lost the baby that never existed. He wants nothing more than to be a dad, and she's ripped that from him. Twice. He gave up his job and assimilated into her life. She changed everything about him with a promise she had no intention of fulfilling. He thought he had finally got what he wanted most in the world. There's nothing I can say to him to fill that void.'

'You could be enough for him. I know how much he loves you,' she squeaks, gripping my forearm to comfort me, her small hands soft and warm. I lean into her slight frame, and she doesn't miss a beat, wrapping her arms around my shoulders, the scent of her lavender body oil filling my nose. Silently letting me know I can break in her embrace if I need to as she strokes my hair from my face.

'She's taken something from him I don't think anyone can replace. She has lied to him for months.'

'Good riddance.'

'She may be out of his life, but she has taken a part of Aiden that I don't know if I can repair. No matter how much I want to.' I hate how much I believe my own words. The knot in my belly tightens, and I feel helpless. Casey must be able to read my slight movements because she stiffens, pulling me closer into her embrace, trying to relieve me of some of the weight of my burden.

'He will come out of this,' Casey declares, her voice unwavering.

'You can't—' I interrupt before her finger flies to my mouth to silence me. She pushes me back in my chair, holding my shoulders at arm's length, dipping her head and imploring me with wide hazel eyes to look at her.

'I can tell you that because I know it's true. He needs to be by himself and lick his wounds, and then this will all be in the past. He will come back to you, Roni,' she hums, her beautiful full lips curving up at the edges. I smile broadly at my friend as she comforts me. I have been so concerned about Aiden and what he is going through that I haven't even thought about how I feel. We made love that night, and the baby was the only reason we couldn't be together.

Is it different now? My brain is exhausted. Every thought flies around in my head at breakneck speed, each fighting to be heard above the rest. I rub my fingers in slow circles at my temples, wordlessly pleading with the little voices in my head to cease their attack.

'Shot?' Casey sings, breaking my focus. I let out a breathy little laugh. I'm grateful for the interruption and the small glass filled with crystal clear liquid that Casey sets on the table in front of me. I pull it up to my lips, the aniseed aroma filling my nose. I knock it back with little hesitation, tapping the table to signal my desire for another. I don't have to ask her twice. Casey tips the bottle and fills my glass again. I know I'll pay for it later, but I don't care. Having a hangover is worth it if I can escape the torrent of mental torture that I'm currently living through.

'The relationship between you two is on a whole other level, Roni. When you roast him, that's some low-key love language. Everyone who spends time with you two can see it as plain as the nose on your face,' Casey says, bopping me cutely on the tip of my nose like my grandfather used to. With a shot of *Sambuca* hovering over her lips, Casey pushes a freshly filled shot glass my way. We don't hesitate to down the alcohol together.

An hour later, I realise just how grateful I am that Casey and I had bypassed the coffee shop and come straight to a bar. It may only be five in the afternoon, but it is party time somewhere in the world, and caffeine just wouldn't cut it. I need hard liquor, questionable advice, and low-quality strip lighting that masks my sadness.

'You're doing it again, aren't you?' she queries with a raised brow, downing her third shot. The vile liquid with the bitter aftertaste is sharp and intrusive as it flows down her throat. Her face screws up into a grimace, her lips puckering. I swallow my shot of the same liquid, refusing to react like Casey. My gag reflex steps aside to let the alcohol pass without protest as my determination to get as drunk as is humanly possible is now in the driving seat.

'I can't help thinking about him. Damn it!' I holler, my words slightly slurred, alerting me of my arrival to the point of no return in my quest for total inebriation. It doesn't seem to matter how much I ingest. I still can't seem to push Aiden from my thoughts.

A guy slinks towards us, a smarmy grin on his pencil-thin lips, his muddied honey-coloured eyes filling me with disgust. His structured beard is cropped short on his face, accentuating a firm jaw and defined cheekbones. 'The rapey vibe is strong with this one,' I bark at Casey, gesturing at the guy heading towards our table. As he stands at our side, we both look up at him expectantly, wondering but not caring what he has to say.

'Hey, ladies. Looking good, Roni,' he croons, tracing the index finger of his free hand up my tattooed forearm. I shudder as my body reacts unfavourably to the contact. He doesn't seem to care, though. It certainly doesn't make him vacate my personal space. Tipping his head back, he swallows a mouthful of his beer, using the back of his hand to remove the froth coating his top lip.

'I may have just thrown up a little in my mouth,' I whisper shout to Casey. Honestly, I'm taken aback by the audacity of this man practically gyrating in my lap as he sways his hips to a song that, from this day forward, I know I'll hate.

But Roni, he's quite cute. But Roni, he's clearly interested. But Roni, you are single. I have heard every excuse going why I should give men like this the time of day. Reasons why it's apparently okay for them to touch me without permission. Well, today is not the day. The staff here refer to this ding dong as *Dirty Dave*. He may be a regular at the bar, but I have zero fucks left in my arsenal, and this douchebag is about to feel my rage.

'*Fred West,* is it?' I ask curtly, my voice almost too sweet. The bravery needed to call out this guy warms my chest. The desire to feel something other than gnawing guilt and regret for just a flicker of a moment spurs me on. My opening line has thrown him, his smarmy smile disappearing, panic colouring his expression as his cheeks heat. In no setting does anyone want to be referred to as a sadistic rapist—not even actual rapists like being called that.

'What was your plan? Approach a drunk woman, ply her with yet more booze, and take her home where you plan on fucking her with your tiny cock, leaving her unfulfilled and swimming in remorse as she has to remember for the rest of her life that you were inside her?' I pointedly ask him, waiting wide-eyed for a response I know will never come. I can't blame him. I wouldn't go head-to-head with a crazy woman fuelled by crippling heartache and too much Sambuca, either. Dirty Dave isn't bad looking by any means. His personality, however, leaves a lot to be desired. He uses his handsome features for evil and feels no shame in exploiting women. I mean, what other reason can there be for him to pedal this little act of his in the same bar every night? 'You can leave,' I add flatly, shooing the pervert away. It's no fun when they don't fight back. True to form, he shuffles away and approaches another woman nursing a Long Island Iced Tea a few tables over from us. 'Not far enough, shithead!' I bellow over the music from the jukebox at the creep without even looking at him. I can tell by Casey's illuminated wide eyes that he has abruptly ceased hitting on the poor woman and ventured further down into the bar out of view. Casey applauds me slowly, baring a wide, toothy grin.

'Well, damn girl. You laid that guy out.' She chuckles, pride alight in her warm, fawn gaze.

A rush of air spills from my taut lips, the sound of my quickening pulse pounding in my ears, my chest heaving. 'I will not lie. It felt good.' I laugh, adrenaline spiking in my veins. The thrill of it all warms my blood. Dirty Dave, *little Dave* to any woman unfortunate enough to have been pinned beneath him, is a serial con artist who toys with his prey, able to identify when a woman is at her weakest. You've got to have supercar money to get away with his meagre three inches, and Dave here has wheelbarrow money at best. For the briefest of seconds, though, I feel bad for him. I didn't hold back on my public verbal assault on him. The second of regret flutters away quickly when I remind myself that he had given Jenny an STI last Christmas. *The womaniser deserves it,* I say to myself. Finally, at peace with my outburst, I face Casey again.

'Although I am in awe of the all-new and powerful you, and you know usually I'm the first one to suggest bar hopping as a suitable daytime activity, drinking isn't going to solve this, Roni. In the long run, you will have to face the music and air everything out with Aiden.' A flash of instant sobriety hits me in the face as thoughts of Aiden bombard me.

'If he wanted me, he never would have chosen her,' I mumble and grab the bottle of sambuca, desperate to feel that hum of dizziness filling my head only moments ago.

'He didn't choose her, and you know it. He chose the baby, he would have found a way to have you both, eventually,' she reasons, running her thumb over my hand. Even intoxicated, my friend is wise beyond her years.

'What if I can't be what he needs? What if he can't get over this?' Fear grips my soul in a chokehold as I fight to suppress my truth, just waiting to break free.

'Whether you want to admit it or not, you love him, and he loves you,' she coos, tucking a curl behind my ear. She tips up my chin so she can make eye contact with me.

'You don't get it; I can't give him what he wants most. I can never give him the baby that he deserves.' Tears build in my eyes, and I tug my chin from Casey's fingers. I hate that she can now see the vulnerability I always try to disguise.

'You can't know that for sure. You have no idea what is in your future, Roni.' She chuckles, concern stealing away her small smile as she tries to read my expression.

'Oh, but I do know.' My bottom lip trembles as I try to swallow the lump forming in my throat. I have never spoken to anyone but Aiden about the first night we met. Even he doesn't know the complete account of the aftermath of what happened to me the night my world collided with Lucas Tremay. Casey frowns, knowing that whatever I'm holding back has been eating away at me. The chink in my armour is exposed to the light of day for the first time in years. Every dent, tear and slash illuminated and bared to the world.

'Roni, you can talk to me,' she reassures me, sliding out of her chair and pulling it around the table so she can sit as close to me as she can without taking up residence in my lap. I glance around the bar, and once I am satisfied that no one is listening to our conversation, I clear my throat, wiping a stray tear from my cheek. I down another shot of the aniseed-flavoured liquor and grimace as it hits the back of my throat.

'Aiden and I met in 2011 at a party thrown by some of his classmates. I was only sixteen and tagged along with a friend. Her older brother was friends with the guy whose house it was. They played on the same cricket team or something equally cliché.'

'I thought you and Aiden met at university?' she asks, confused but intrigued, nodding at me to continue.

'I didn't know his first name then, and I had no idea we would meet again. He was my first kiss, and it was extraordinary. Not remotely sloppy like my friends said it would be.' I beam, remembering young Aiden with his shaggy mess of brown curls and his captivating baby blue-grey eyes. His soft lips. He was a natural even then. I run my fingers over my lips, curved in a small smile at the happy memory. But it doesn't last long as the ghosts of my past steal this from me, too. 'But that wasn't my only first that night.'

Fuck it. What's the point in delaying the inevitable? Let's rip off the band-aid.

'You had sex?' she whispers, beaming at me and bouncing on the spot excitedly.

'Not with Aiden.' I remark sadly as I fiddle with the pieces of the torn beer mat discarded on the table. Her enthusiasm dwindles as she leans her elbow on the table, her face closer to mine now, rightly sensing the air of sadness marring my tone. I can't stop the tears from rolling down my cheeks as the memory of that night hits me afresh.

If only it had been him that I had shared my first time with. Aiden would never have treated me like Lucas had. I would never have turned into this broken shell of a person who cowers behind the brutal reality of her damaged past—lost to the version of myself that couldn't fight for herself when she most needed it.

Everything could have been so different.

'Then who? Having sex at sixteen isn't all bad. At least you got it out of the way. First times suck anyway,' she says chipperly, trying to console me, completely sidestepping the revelation I am trying to convey to her in a roundabout way. She doesn't want to see me that way, lost and weak, and I can't blame her.

'What that guy did to me wasn't sex. It was painful and degrading. He stole something that wasn't his to take.' I sob, reliving the torture as the image of his face, which has been seared into my brain, hovering above me, resurfaces. Everything inside me is set ablaze as I struggle to clear my mind of him. But I've gone too far. The cat's out of the bag, and I cannot put it back. There's no getting out of this now.

Casey's hand flies up to cover her mouth, stifling the gasp that fights to break free, her eyes filling with tears for me as the penny drops. I continue with my story, hoping that sharing this with her will magically fix something inside me. I have said too much to stop now. And, if I'm honest, it feels good offloading to someone besides Aiden. I know he blames himself for not finding me sooner that night. The recall of what he had witnessed was just too much for him.

'Aiden found me and took me somewhere safe,' I state, my tear-soaked lips baring a fake smile. I gloss over all the depravity of my rape because voicing that aloud will crush me. Not even Aiden knows everything that Lucas did to me in that room. Bruises and cigarette burns that hid beneath the waistband of my knickers, the remaining scars almost invisible white marks. Broken fingers from my trying to push him off me—proof of my determination to protect myself, and the clumps of hair he ripped from my scalp to hold me in place that had taken months to grow back. I sense Casey knows I'm not revealing everything, but the reassuring smile creeping across her face tells me she understands why. She patiently waits for me to continue at my own pace, and I've never loved her more. It's the push I need to finish my story, to share the darkest part of myself with the woman I trust most in my life.

'I thought I was safe with him using a condom. Even with the drugs in my system, I remembered him using one. But fate had other ideas. I found out I was pregnant, cursed to live with what he had done to me forever. I was sixteen and knocked up. The problem was I couldn't tell my mum; I couldn't confide in anyone, and the hospital would have bought her in if I had gone there. I lived with the pain for six days. By the seventh day, though, I couldn't stand it anymore. I had a friend, Colby. I say, friend. She once lent me her science notes. Her dad was a doctor with morals compromised by alcohol and gambling. His predilection for hookers was the icing on the cake that led to her parents' messy divorce. There were rumours around school he had assisted a classmate of ours who found herself in the same predicament as me. Initially, I went hoping to get some advice. I was optimistic I could use that rumour to convince him to give me some pills or something. I was not schooled in the art of blackmail, but hopelessness pushes you to do things you never thought you would. It seems I didn't need the rumour as leverage, though. I caught him watching some videos, and the idea seemed to form from there. Drink, debt, and ladies of the night weren't his only vices. Dr Nasty liked to watch kiddy porn. But who would believe a pregnant sixteen-year-old's word against a renowned doctor celebrated in the community? He said it was the first time and professed his innocence, as any pervert would in that situation. I was desperate, so I cashed in on the threat. It's easy to convince a paedophile to give you a botched abortion when you had pull that could ruin his life. I didn't know that he had already necked a bottle of *Jack Daniels* before I had arrived or even what the procedure would entail. The pain was unbearable. I just needed it to stop.' Casey rubs my hand reassuringly but remains silent, urging me to lay every bit of my dirty secret on the table between us. 'He removed it whilst I lay there on the workbench in his garage, dirt and wood shavings covering every surface around me. He cleaned me up, took me home, and told my mother I had collapsed at his house, and after checking me over, he prescribed me some antibiotics and painkillers. My mother didn't bat an eyelid and took him at his word. You can always trust a doctor, right? It took about three weeks to recover fully, and over time, it became a little easier to push the memories of the whole shitty mess to the back of my mind. I knew I could never truly forget it, but I had to try to put it behind me. After I sent an anonymous tip to the police about Dr Nasty and his questionable inclinations, he was arrested, and I swore to myself that would be the end of the entire ordeal. But then girls started to come forward. Girls with stories just like mine.'

'Aiden has no idea about all this?' she queries, concern morphing her usually carefree expression.

'He knows what happened that night, not the rape but the attack. Beyond that, I didn't see him again for years. He was just the young man who saved me when I most needed it. I don't know what would have happened to me had he not burst into that room when he did.'

'But you healed. You can still offer Aiden everything. All he wants is you, Roni,' she lulls, trying to show me the light at the end of the tunnel. But my tunnel runs deeper than most to a place where no light can ever shine. I choose to continue with my story rather than address her remark.

'I was eighteen when I found out I more than likely could never have kids of my own. There was just too much damage from the procedure. Too much blood loss, too many unnecessary slices carved into my womb,' I mumble, trying to hide my grief, and failing. Casey doesn't hesitate to wrap her arms around me, her fingers desperate to embrace all of me. Instantly knowing that I am in a safe space, sixteen-year-old me lets rip. I bury my face in her shoulder, accepting her offer of support, and my tears soak through her button-down grey dress. We stay like this for a few minutes as I cry through the pain, eating away at my heart, each sob hollow and weak, my revelation changing something between us. She feels closer to me somehow.

'So you can't give him kids. Who the fuck cares? Maybe giving him you is enough for him. You'll never know if you don't tell him how you truly feel,' Casey states with an air of finality, almost like there is an order of action beneath her words. Knowing my truth makes her want to fight for me even harder.

'I want more than anything to give him what he wants. I've never wanted anything so desperately in my life,' I whine. The need to make my horrible history magically disappear so I can give my all to Aiden makes me tremble.

'But,' Casey finishes for me as unspoken words linger on my lips.

'But I can't watch him forgo being a father because of me. He will end up despising me, Casey,' I bite back the sob that settles in my throat and wipe at my flushed cheeks, stained pink, removing the streaks of sadness from my face with the back of my hand. Sucking in a steadying lungful of air, I pour myself another shot of *Sambuca* and watch as Casey strolls to the bar to order more drinks. In a moment of reprieve, I allow myself to drift to thoughts of my happy place, images that will conjure that familiar sense of contentment, memories that have the power to push what happened to me out of sight to the furthest part of my brain. *Aiden*. I think of him and only him, and my heart swells. He's my someone. He's my happy place. Aiden will forever be the light that holds the power to banish the dark, and, at this moment, I can't think of a single reason why I shouldn't tell him exactly that.

NEW YEARS EVE 2019

A LITTLE OVER A MONTH LATER

RONI

Louisa has spent the past month inundating Aiden with calls, texts, and gifts and having guys knocking at our front door at all hours dressed as cupid with telegrams, singing *'Everybody hurts'* and *'Sorry Seems to be the Hardest Word.'* They're nothing, if not creative, with their song selections. Although the rendition of *'Where Did My Baby Go'* seemed like a particularly poor choice considering the situation. I don't know if she has a voucher with their company or whether her daddy has invested money and got some freebies, but six visits are six too many, in my opinion. I make my way downstairs towards the living room, shuffling along in Aiden's grey hoodie, a pair of sleep shorts older than my past five relationships, and some chunky knit socks lovingly crafted by my Nana. The socks have me slipping and sliding on the worn wooden flooring like a new-born doe trying to find her footing. With an alcohol-fuelled headache that has me feeling like I have just gone ten rounds with *Mike Tyson,* I slump down onto the sofa with a groan. Nights out with Casey have become a regular occurrence of late, things are slowly getting back to normal between Aiden and I, but it was touch and go for a while. Aiden spent most of his nights on his sister Paige's couch for those first couple of weeks after that night in the bar. He assured me that his need for a change in scenery was in case Louisa made an impromptu visit, but a part of me knows that he needed space from me too. The fact that I knew he was standing there that night, witnessing it all unfold as everything he thought he knew was torn to pieces, made me complicit in his pain—whether or not he would admit it. I pushed Louisa to reveal that God-awful secret for all the world to hear, watching my best friend's heart split in two, his blue-grey eyes black almost, as if a part of his soul had died. Another sharp pain jolts behind my eye, making me wince. Although small on the karmic scale, I decide I deserve the discomfort. I could promise myself I would never drink again, but that would be a lie. Drowning out my misery is something I need in order to function these days. Unfortunately, the one thing the alcohol never seems to drown out is my effervescent desire to straddle my best friend whilst he hungrily devours me. That little imaginary play-by-play is stronger than any top-shelf liquor.

'Hey baby, feeling a little sensitive?' Aiden teases as he passes my prone body awkwardly splayed out on the sofa. I mumble a groan in response, my interest piqued, and my headache miraculously gone as I track every seemingly inconsequential move he makes, unable to drag my eyes from the six-foot-three godly creature sauntering across the room. I sit up in the chair, swiftly pulling Aiden's jumper off over my head. Tugging at the baggy neck of my t-shirt underneath so I have a little shoulder exposed. This is about as sexy as I'm getting. Hungover Roni isn't exactly going to win any awards, but I'm anything if not tenacious. Aiden is swathed in sunlight, his tanned skin warm and inviting. His broad shoulders fill the small space as he leans against the windowsill, his holey band tee doing nothing to dampen his sex appeal. If anything, it just adds a rough edge to his sweetness. If he notices me staring at him, he doesn't let on. His eyes meet mine, and I shift in my seat.

Just do it. You know you want to. I can't argue with my brain; she has a good point. Ruffling my curls, I unapologetically explore every inch of Aiden as he reaches for his coffee mug on the fireplace. A slave to my daydream, ideas of exactly what I would do to my best friend given half a chance have a taut whimper falling from my mouth. Even the thought of his touch makes my core throb. With my jaw slack and my knickers now wet, I watch as Aiden runs one hand through his mess of shaggy brown hair, tipping the cup up against his full bottom lip with the other. I'd love nothing more than to nibble on that lip.

We're practically ready to combust. Why are we not climbing this man like a tree?

Lost in thoughts of what I would give to have him lay me out and ruin me, I have no control over the words that barrel out of my mouth next.

'Fuck yes.' I breathe, and his head whips around to face me. I bite my lip, wishing I could take it back—no such luck. Our high-ceilinged living room suddenly feels too small, and I'm sweating.

Shiny and panicky—not the best of looks.

'Fuck what, Roni? I can see that mind of yours working overtime from here.' I can't regulate my breathing as his gaze falls to my lips. A knowing smile and a smug side glance only make my body react more as chills flicker at the base of my spine. We haven't spoken about whether we would ever have a repeat of the night in his bedroom, but he implies it every time he looks at me this way. I don't even need to touch him to know how good it would feel. Mr Aiden O'Shea was a gifted lover with talents that far surpass any partner I've ever had before, and if the flash of heat that warms his eyes is anything to go by, he knows exactly where my mind has taken me. This fucker knows what he does to me, and just because he can, he purposely stretches his arms up above his head, his jaw clenching as every muscle in his body flexes and rolls.

Fuuccckkk. I'm grateful for the mental intrusion as I clench my thighs together.

'Come here; I want to show you something,' he lulls sternly with his arm outstretched.

Please be cock. I giggle girlishly as the little voice in my head pipes up with interest. I do as I'm told, faking nonchalance as I glide across the carpet, knowing all I want to do is run to him and jump into his arms. But I won't do that. The dull thump of my headache returns the closer I get to the window, sunlight searing my retinas as my poor brain reminds me I consumed my weight in booze last night, leaving me a little worse for wear. I shut my eyes, my fingers rubbing concentric circles at my temples to ease the building tension.

'Open your eyes, *Daredevil*. Here.' He snickers enthusiastically, chucking a pair of sunglasses at me from the sideboard. I put them on and immediately feel better, not 100 per cent but a good 40 per cent, at least. Right now, I am in no position to debate the legitimacy of these statistics. I'll take the relief where I can get it.

Pulling the blinds apart like a peeping Tom, Aiden gestures for me to look. Rising onto my tippy toes and resting my chin on his shoulder from behind, I squint to focus on the street beyond the window. Not so discreetly inhaling the scent of him. I hold back the sigh threatening to breach my lips at his proximity. The sunglasses colour the outside world a tawny sepia. When my calf muscles can't take the stretch anymore, I give in to their protests and buckle, swooping under his arm to gain a better view of the street. Consider me intrigued.

'By all means, push in, little one.' He chuckles, his warm, minty breath fanning my cheek as he dips his head to resume his assessment of the street from my eye level. I know it's dangerous, allowing myself to be this close to him, but I can't help it. My body gravitates to his, that invisible teether that pulses between us the closer we get, just too addictive to ignore.

Without looking at me, he hands me a steaming mug of fresh coffee from the windowsill. I accept it with a meek smile, nudging the sunglasses up my nose as they slip out of place. The heavenly redolence of rich earthy beans brewed to perfection fills my nose.

'Thanks,' I mutter before taking a sip. Caffeine gets us up to an even 50 per cent. 'What are we looking at exactly?' I ask as I mentally note that the front garden needs mowing.

'If you wait a moment, you'll see a piece of shit in a black metal box appear in the driveway. Like magic.' I gaze at him for a little longer than I should, enjoying the playful burst of amusement that has pockets of amber swamping his usually cool grey blues. The sound of tyres screeching in the distance makes him smirk as I follow his lead and turn to watch the road again. His grin widens as though he can distinguish this set of wheels from all the others that have careened past our house in the last ten minutes. 'And in 3, 2, 1.' He holds his hand out as though presenting me with the piece of shit he had promised. There is Louisa, scowling as she climbs out of her matt black sports car. She slams the door behind her and storms up the front steps in her skyscraper heels with purpose etched across her pinched brows—or as much purpose as possible with the amount of Botox holding her usually expressionless face together. I laugh a little too hard, and coffee spurts out of my nose.

Sixty per cent.

I can't help but beam up at my best friend, knowing this is the last step in his journey to gain full closure. All thoughts of curling up into a ball and dying on the sofa today are officially off the table, as intrigue completely obliterates my migraine.

'Wish me luck,' he breathes, running his fingers across my chin before he turns to leave. My body stumbles forward, aching for him to touch me again.

'Luck,' I squeak, but it's a pitiful sound. Although his touch was fleeting, the warmth left behind remains on my skin. The addictive trickle of sensations that has me desperately wanting him to do it again cries out to be silenced before I can make an even bigger fool of myself. I need to strap down the hussy living inside me, greedy for all things Aiden. Our guy needs to heal, and my adding anything other than my support right now will undoubtedly do more damage than good. I ignore the snap of unwelcome misery at the thought of keeping my distance from him that unfurls in my belly.

Thank fuck for Ann Summers' winter sale, I think as I take another long sip of my coffee. A pounding on the front door alerts me to Louisa's arrival, and I shudder in response, my hackles rising as she sweetly regards Aiden.

After forty-five minutes of Louisa yelling, sobbing, and apologising, the thump of the front door slamming shut notifies me of her departure. My body sags. Figuring the coast is clear, I join Aiden in the kitchen.

'How did you finally get rid of her?' I laugh, refilling my coffee cup. I hold out the pot to Aiden, but he shakes his head and gestures to the full mug in his hands.

'I told her I was dying,' he retorts with a smile.

'Very funny. Just thought that up on the spot, hey?' I chuckle, grabbing an apple from the fruit basket and taking a bite. I spit it back out when my harassed stomach screams at me in protest, and bile builds in my throat.

Just Coffee it is, then.

'No, the doctors confirmed further treatment last Monday,' he says casually as a stunned Louisa passes by our front kitchen window. Her face is aghast, and each step laboured as he waves happily, saying his last goodbye to the Bitch that has been trying to train him like a show pony for the past two years. 'I'm not that inventive. You know that.' He chortles as I stand there stoic, my jaw practically on the floor. My neck heats, my lower lip bobbing there. I can't find the words as I note zero sadness or fear on his face. Mine, however, is a sight of abject horror as I try to understand what he has just told me—searching for the lie in his grey-blue gaze, hating that all I find is the truth.

'Apparently, she had no desire to look after me on my deathbed. The big C is an inconvenience she hadn't weaved into her life plan, it would seem. Never thought I'd be grateful to have Cancer as a get-out clause.' He glances at me, but only for a moment, turning back to watch the retreating form that is now officially his ex-girlfriend. I struggle to comprehend his revelation, and the fact that he won't look at me tells me he knows it. My brows pinch together, and my breathing is heavy as my heart thumps wildly in my chest.

'I can tell by your face that you're shocked, Roni. Me too,' he jibes, and I flinch as though his insouciance has speared me in my chest. My brain refuses to acknowledge the big terminal disease sitting between us. 'I know how you feel. I thought she was the next Mother Teresa.' He snickers light-heartedly as though he hasn't just told me the most devastating news. He continues sipping his coffee like nothing has even happened. I'm surprised by the confusion bubbling inside me, completely obliterating the heartache as my body fights to make sense of it all.

'You lied to me.'

'I didn't lie. I'd never lie to you.'

'You kept it from me. That's the same thing.'

'I know you're hurt, Roni.' He moves to close the distance between us, but I mirror his move, my hands braced out as if to ward him off. My back connects with the door, and he has me boxed in. I'm grateful he doesn't take the last step towards me. I don't know what will happen if he touches me right now. I know he doesn't miss the wreckage of my soul, painting my face a pale grey as my heart beats lazily in my chest, every breath arduous.

'Wh—when did you find out?' I splutter, trying and failing to hide the raw devastation in my voice as a breath catches in my throat. I struggle to hold back the tears threatening to fall in waves from my eyes, too scared that if my vision blurs, Aiden might disappear altogether. Fear niggles in my belly when he doesn't answer me immediately. I eye him warily, silently pleading with him to take back his statement, to tell me he was only playing and that it isn't true. But the words never come. Aiden shuffles on the spot and again moves to take a step toward me.

'No. Just no. Tell me. When did you find out you were sick, Aiden?' I demand an answer, my tone dripping with a strength I didn't know I possessed, even though inside, I'm falling apart.

'Doc called the morning you ran out of here, the night after we were.... um... together. I didn't have the heart to tell you. What good would it have done?' I can tell by his wide blue-grey eyes he is struggling with his own emotions but is trying to make it easier—for me.

'Three months. You've known for three months, and you let me stay away. I would have been there for you,' I squeak. My voice is small, my heart shattering into a million pieces as liquid ice explodes in my chest, eradicating the flames of infatuation that usually burn there when I find myself this close to Aiden. I wring out my hands to stop them from shaking, willing my body to relax as I try to process the truth I had never expected to hear fall from his full lips. He doesn't look sick, and although I know that means shit regarding the roulette wheel of adverse reactions to having Cancer, it is still the only thing that runs on a loop in my brain.

He can't be sick if he doesn't look sick. My reasoning is flawed, of course, but ignorance is the only feeling strong enough to settle the thrum of unease that is rocketing around my body. So for a moment or two, I'm grateful for my naivety. I welcome the comfort of that little voice in my head that tries to convince me I have heard him wrong, that something got lost in translation along the way. Before I can sort through my muddled thoughts, Aiden moves back into my line of sight, dragging me from a place of blind serenity that my heart has constructed to stave off the harsh reality staring me in the face.

'I had hurt you; I didn't want to make that worse. What I did was awful. I should never have let you walk away from me that morning. I should have fought harder to keep you. You didn't deserve a guilt trip on top of that,' Aiden soothes as he runs his thumb across my jawline, his fingers tangling in my hair behind my ear. I move into his touch and close my eyes. That familiar sense of tranquillity that he sparks in me washes over my body until the fear is pushed down, the dull throb masked by the warmth of his touch. But then I snap my eyes open, refusing to bow to the dreamlike state that has me seeing this as anything but what it is.

'For future reference, this is the exact thing that would be okay to drag me out of my selfish moping. You were never really mine, and I took you anyway. I was as much in the wrong as you were.' I pull away from him, and his hands fall limply to his sides. All thoughts of my hangover, the possibility of a fumble with Aiden in my bed, and my hatred for Louisa are gone. In their place, it's just him and the heart-breaking truth he's just shared that lingers around me like an outspoken drunk auntie around the Christmas dinner table. I let my head fall, running my palms into my hair and down my face, rubbing the flesh at my temples as I sigh with frustration. Frustration at not noticing a change in him sooner, at wasting the past few months when I felt I couldn't face him, and at realising he hadn't told me his truth. Pulling my hands from my face, he wraps his fingers around my wrists. His silent plea is almost palpable. I know he needs me to look at him, so I do exactly that, expelling the breath I hadn't realised had been lodged uncomfortably in my throat.

'I was always yours, Roni. I just never allowed myself to see it. I was so scared it would ruin our friendship that I tried to ignore how I felt. When Louisa said she was pregnant, I thought that was my sign. I trusted the universe knew what I should do, and I blindly followed suit, ignoring what my heart screamed at me—not to disregard what I wanted. As time went on, I thought she would take care of me and have our baby, and I could leave you relatively unscathed to carry on with your life,' he lulls. I step away from him again, shaking my head voicelessly, the motion enough to lay bare my protests. I fight back the urge to slap his face, reminding myself that playing the Cancer card also allowed for some majorly shitty life choices. I realise I don't need to hit him; my body language conveys my thoughts well enough.

'You are my life, stupid,' I retort, shoving him in the shoulder, so he stumbles back a step.

'Hindsight is an amazing thing,' he says sweetly, closing the space between us and running his thumb over my cheek to release the scowl pinching at my features. If he holds me, I will crumple. I know it. Until now, I have held back the tears, but as the seconds pass, I know it won't be long before the dam breaks. He ignores my hesitancy and pulls me into his bulky arms, tucking a curl behind my ear, his palm lingering near my neck as he tries to fight off the tears pooling at the corners of his eyes. 'You deserved a fresh start,' he states, his eyes twinkling, his bottom lip pulled between his teeth as he tries to read my face. I almost succumb to thoughts of that night, his hands exploring my body, his length teasing at my core, the scent of his woodsy aftershave pulling me back in time. But suddenly, that little voice in my head snaps into play, and I come back to reality hard as if I have just taken a baseball bat to the head.

'But that way, I don't get you. I don't get to spend this time helping you fight this, supporting you. What would ever make you think I wanted that? Why do you get to decide that for me?' The feeling bubbling in my belly now is not sadness, lust, or need for this man. It is pure, unfiltered anger. Tugging myself free of his embrace, I stroll past him, desperate to take a breath not perfumed by his scent. I wrap my arms around my chest, gripping onto my shoulders. It's nothing like having his arms around me, but I need comfort. I don't need my heart to gloss over the pain of his truth with my need for him. However difficult, it's essential I feel everything all at once. If I push this away, it will forever break me. 'Why, Aiden? Why didn't you tell me?' I plead, already knowing I will not like his answer.

'I didn't think that far ahead, Roni. The look on your face when you left here broke me in a way I didn't think was possible. I couldn't give you another reason to hate me. I couldn't be the reason you stopped believing in us.'

'So dying and leaving me behind without an explanation was what you went with?' I baulk, the humourless laugh I can't hold back bursting free, accompanied by a torrent of tears running down my cheeks. I am being insensitive. I know that, but I can't stop myself from blurting it all out. If Louisa hadn't turned out to be a liar, the baby had been real, and he hadn't reached out to meet me, would he have ever told me the truth? The fact that I don't know the answer to that question fuels my rage as I pace, tugging my hair at the roots until pain flares in my scalp.

'I would have left a letter, or at the very least, I would have personalised the lyrics to a *Tenacious D* song, just for you.' He smiles, and I calm. Even in the darkest of moments, he can find my off switch. I laugh lightly through my tears, dropping my hand and tugging at my shaking bottom lip as I wipe my face with the other. As always, this beautiful man has broken through my sorrow and fury and made me smile in a way that only he can. My wrath dissipates like sugar in hot water, but the imprint of despair it leaves me with makes me wish it would return. I feel helpless and lost. At least with the anger, a sense of determination fills me.

'Cancer boy – has a uplifting posthumous ring to it,' I add, and he smirks brightly, the genuine curve of his lips making my heart flutter.

'I like it. Sounds folky,' he quips. There is suddenly too much air between us, and my fingers tingle at the need to touch him. I run at him without warning, bounding into the man I love, resolved never to let him go again. His powerful arms encase me and lift me so I can wrap my legs around his waist; it feels like coming home.

'I'm here.' I breathe a sob into his ear and feel his taut body relax. A sigh of relief flitters from his full parted lips as he hardens his hold of me, locking his hands behind my back so I can feel his rampant heartbeat thrashing against his ribs. I lean back away from the safety of his embrace, but I don't move to get down. I trace my fingers over his features, committing them to memory as though it is now a necessity rather than a luxury. Another tear breaks free and runs down my cheek as Aiden watches me intently, trying to read my thoughts. The tear stalls on my bottom lip, and he moves to wipe it away, the calloused pad of his thumb lingering for the briefest of moments as though he is considering something. Before I can think about it anymore, he lands a bruising kiss on my lips, stealing the sadness from me as though his kisses can make everything okay. I melt into his hold as our tongues battle, heated pants of hurried breaths splashing against my harassed lips as he pulls away to stare down into my eyes. His need for approval from me is evident in his glassy grey-blue eyes, flecks of amber darkening as arousal swamps his gaze. I instinctually push my hips forward so my core rubs against his muscled belly. The toothy grin tugging at his lips can't be contained as he tucks a strand of hair behind my ear. He leans into me, keeping our bodies close. Warmth radiates through my extremities. The world is dreary and dull compared to the bubble of high-definition colour cocooning us in this moment, marked for a forever memory.

'I will always choose you. For however much longer we have, I choose you, Roni. I'm sorry I didn't see you when it mattered most. I'm sorry I didn't fight for you when I should have. I'm sorry, Roni, for all the things I had the power to make right but didn't,' he whispers into my ear, a sense of hope clouded in melancholy, making his voice shaky. I move to meet his gaze, each fleck of colour there entrancing. Apprehension swamps his features as he waits for me to respond. I run my hands around Aiden's neck, tugging him forward as my fingers snake into his hair at the nape and pull his forehead to mine.

'It has always been you, Aiden.' I beam. The sentiment carries far too much emotion for such a few words. 'I will love you for always, in this lifetime and the next, for however long you will have me,' I state, knowing no truer words than these have ever left my lips. I move to push the hair from his face and affectionately stroke his cheek. He dips his head, kissing my palm, gripping my hip a little tighter.

'Ditto, Baby. I'm all in for an always with you.' He lulls, wiping under my eyes with his thumb, sucking in a breath to compose himself as I hang from his body. Desire and need smother the unsettling heaviness I felt in my chest at Aiden's earlier revelation. I push thoughts of his illness to the back of my mind and tighten my hold of him. I'm afraid that if I let go, he might fade into nothingness and out of my reach as I realise that this moment is merely a dream, my best friend a figment of my already damaged psyche. Knowing me better than I know myself, Aiden grips my chin, tipping my head back to meet his gaze, refusing to watch me spiral down into the dark place where I store my pity party for one invite.

'We do this as a team. I want to know everything going on up here,' he states, tapping his finger on my temple. I nod meekly my promise to share the messed up musings in my head whilst running my fingers through the hair at the nape of his neck. Readjusting myself in his hold, his cock twitches in response when my breasts push up and out with the movement, and he eyes them wickedly. I bite at my swollen, harassed lips, suddenly needing more of him, desperate for him to make his mark on my mind, body, and soul, so even death can't take him from me.

'I'm here, Roni, and until the powers that be force me to, I won't leave your side.'

'Promise?' I mewl, running my thumb over his bottom lip.

'Pinkie promise,' he affirms, holding his little finger to me. I nod in response with a tiny grin playing on my lips, the only reassurance my tired body can offer my best friend, and I hold out my pinkie finger, wrapping it around his, solidifying our pledge to one another.

I will fight for him, even when he can't fight for himself.

NEW YEARS EVE 2019

RONI

So ignoring my body's claims of being too emotionally exhausted to do anything other than sleep and grieve, I spend the rest of my day under Aiden. Well, under probably isn't specific enough to describe our day. Straddling him on the marble island made me rethink my décor choice of the pots and pans that hung from hooks above us. His ploughing roughly into me against the fridge had almost been thwarted when the delivery guy knocked on the kitchen window, as he usually would. Aiden had grabbed a tea towel to cover his modesty as I crouched behind his stocky frame in fits of giggles, as naked as the day I was born. Taking me on all fours on the stairs was an interesting choice. We fumbled to *remove each other's clothing, our lips locked, and our hands grappling at one another as we failed to make it up to my bedroom. The carpet burns on my knees will be a funny conversation starter with Casey when we catch up, I'm sure. That was how our whole day had played out, with water breaks and cold leftover pizza to recharge our batteries—making love and laughing with my best friend until the sun settled. Wisps of purple and red smothered the soft blues as the moon climbed higher in the starry sky. We certainly made up for lost time, and although the truth of his revelation was still there, hiding in the back of my mind like the coward it was, I allowed our collective happiness to drown out its frustrations at being locked away. All I wanted was to be with him, to get lost in those mesmerising grey blues flecked with amber as he drank in my naked body with appreciation. I wanted to fully accept the safety I felt whilst trussed up in his broad armed embrace, to give myself over to him fully as I fed my core with what it needed, to quench the yearnings this beautiful man could detonate in my body with a mere smile. I didn't want to be anywhere but in the moment with him. So that is what I did.*

~~~~

Huddled in our wardrobe space, music and the hum of excited chit-chat from the neighbours' New Year's Eve Garden party filtering in through the open backdoors, Aiden and I sit cross-legged opposite one another. The rails above us in the high-ceilinged closet hold various coats, jumpers and other outerwear. I prop myself against a box of wellies as I watch my friend jovially sing along with the other partygoers. The *Queen* track is guaranteed to get Aiden moving even though our wardrobe space isn't big enough to swing a cat, let alone commit to a dance number as flamboyant as a *Queen* one. As the track dies and we hear voices calling for more tunes, Aiden pulls down a pink
~~~~

feathered cowboy hat from the shelf above, miming along to *Girls Just Want to Have Fun* by *Cyndi Lauper*. The familiar song blares from the stereo speakers followed by the cheers and whistles from the partgoers next door when the chorus kicks in.

'Suits you,' I quip, chuckling at Aiden sitting in just his grey sweatpants and that hat, his broad chest and feet bare. I lick my bottom lip as I watch the corded muscles in his torso tighten and flex as he moves. Will I ever get enough of this man?

No, the answer is no. All of Aiden, all the time, sounds like perfection.

'Want to play a game?' he teases around the rim of his plastic beaker. My body betrays me, his smooth voice making my core twinge for what feels like the thousandth time today. I move my head in a circle, stretching the muscles in my neck, eliciting a needy grunt from his lips. I smile, loving that I have this effect on him.

Calm the fuck down, Roni. Twelve orgasms are more than enough for one day. I laugh at the little voice in my head, knowing that it doesn't matter how tired my body gets. I would accept anything and everything this man offers me.

Fifteen sounds like a nice round number. I counter.

'You're on. What's the game?' I shrewdly ask with an eyebrow raised, knowing I am totally poker-facing him. I would play strip hopscotch whilst covered in honey if he asked me to.

'Truth or dare,' he asserts rather than asking, as he fills our cups with alcohol in preparation.

'Truth,' I quickly reply as he hands me a full cup with a cheeky smile.

'Why do you never settle on a guy?' He blanches. I don't expect the question, so my face hasn't had time to catch up with my brain. 'I figure now is the time to ask the questions we haven't addressed, and I've always wanted to know,' he presses. I purse my lips, debating my answer to what we would usually consider a pretty straightforward question. My handsome, whatever he is now, has played the *'I'm sick card'* to get information out of me. I don't fight it. I take a deep breath and answer his question with a question of my own.

'Would you have really wanted me to?' I blanch, already knowing the answer.

'No, but that is besides the point. You are beautiful, intelligent, and funny. You are a fucking rockstar in the bedroom.' He pauses for a moment, a nod of appreciation as he thinks back over our day of fun. 'And the fridge, the island and the stairs,' he chuckles, and I swat at his arm playfully as I revel in his words.

'You want to know the truth?' I laugh, pink flushing my cheeks.

'Stop evading the question, baby,' he coos, knocking back the last of his whiskey and cola and refilling it. I can't ignore the hum of arousal that spikes at the apex of my thighs when he calls me baby, my body greedy for his touch now that I have feasted on him properly. Aiden has the strength to overpower me, even mentally, and I don't like to lose, so keeping my cards close to my chest is a must. However, my brain has other ideas. Soaked with the remnants of my world rocking orgasms, heartfelt platitudes and images of Aiden's gorgeous naked body, I can't exactly blame it for letting my answer slip.

'They weren't you,' I say decidedly, my brain refusing to hold back what I know to be true. Aiden continues to overpour his whiskey as he gazes at me, shock alight in his eyes. I choose not to let him speak as I reach out to stop him from pouring more tawny liquid into his cup. Before I can question my sanity, everything I've ever wanted to say to this man falls from my mouth like a promise, refusing to stay hidden away any longer. 'I've always loved you, Aiden. I've always wanted you. Whether it was fate or timing, we could never seem to get our shit together. I chose those men because I could never feel about someone else like I feel for you. They were excuses, distractions to keep the longing at bay.' I blurt out whilst fiddling with the rim of my cup, watching as the amber liquid sloshes around in the beaker. When I decide to look at him, Aiden is beaming from ear to ear, that familiar hint of desire to lay me out and worship me swimming in his heated gaze.

'Come here, baby,' he says, setting down his cup and gesturing with his open hands for me to take them. I do it without question and move as he guides me onto his lap. Resting my face against his tattooed bare chest, running my fingers through the dark hair running predominantly up the centre of his torso, I breathe in the intoxicating scent of him. I've dabbled in both drink and drugs, but I have never experienced a high as body rocking as this current addiction. Aiden has stolen my senses, and there isn't a speck of me that can be mad about it. 'Words can never convey just how much you mean to me, Roni. I could never do my feelings justice, but I want you to know that my heart has been and always will be yours. There is no doubt in my mind, and I am sick of trying to convince myself otherwise. This feels too right,' he lulls, placing his large palm over my back where my heart is thumping beneath the surface, guiding my body closer to his. He doesn't have to tell me twice.

'I love you too, big boy,' I tease, edging up his lap, adjusting myself so my backside rubs suggestively over his crotch. I'm momentarily surprised by how easily the L word falls from my lips. But it only lasts for the briefest moment, as though it had been teetering on a precipice between us since we met for the first time that night all those years ago. The guttural groan forced from his lips is the on-switch my body needs to rev back up into sixth gear. My core is throbbing, my wetness already soaking the lacy material of my thong and onto Aiden's grey sweatpants beneath me. I grab the plate of sandwiches and deposit them on the floor next to us. 'Eat. We can't have you exercising on an empty stomach now, can we?' Before I begrudgingly shuffle out of his hold to stave off starvation, the little voice in my head protests that surviving on sex alone wouldn't be the worst way to go. I plant a chaste kiss on his lips and rest on my haunches. The space between us allows my brain the respite it needs, and my empty belly growls appreciatively.

'Are you scared?' I ask meekly before taking a large bite of the now-cold bacon sandwich sitting on the plate we're sharing. My throat is desert dry with the change in mood my question awakens. I don't want to dampen the spirit, but the issue has been fighting to get free since his revelation—my fears of existence without him, nudging the question forward into the light. I wrestle away the urge to look at Aiden as I notice him picking at the crust of his half of the sandwich. I instantly regret that I have more than likely upset him. Taking a swig of my drink to help the chunk of food move down my gullet, I am grateful that Aiden's spirit-to-mixer ratio is reminiscent of an all-inclusive package holiday bar. I welcome the sting of the whiskey as it sets my throat ablaze with warmth.

'Not anymore,' he lulls with a toothy grin as he places a finger under my chin to tip my face to meet his. I melt on the spot as he caresses my cheek with his thumb. I hadn't realised I had let loose a tear; my vision is hazy as I fight to contain the others pooling in my eyes. It feels like all I do is cry. My body's ultimate betrayal where this man is concerned. 'I'm okay, baby. The scans look good. We're going in the right direction,' he cajoles, pushing aside the bottle of whiskey and the bacon sandwiches and scooting across the floor of our special wardrobe place so that our raised knees touch. I don't allow myself to breathe a sigh of relief as he attempts to soothe me. I know how unpredictable his illness can be, and I will hide my fears from him if I can. Miracles, although possible, have never been a stand I would hang my hat on. I will take each day loving him with everything I have. I will no longer hold back or deviate from what we both want. If the only miracle I get in this lifetime is to know Aiden, that is enough for me. I can never control the outcome of our forever, but I can control our right now, which is what's important. I jump into his arms, making him fall backwards, his head banging against the now-open wooden door, so he is half in the wardrobe and half in the hallway. Resting on top of him, I run my fingers through his mass of messy brown waves, tracing a line over his eyebrow and down his cheek. A breath hitches in his throat, and his length jumps in his sweats against my thigh as I eye him hungrily—ready to collect on the three orgasms he doesn't know he still owes me.

'What did I do to deserve you, Aiden O-Shea?' Honesty drips from my question as I run the pad of my thumb across his bottom lip, sharing my gaze between it and his eyes as heat shocks a wash of amber to filter in around his blown pupils. He secures a tight grip around the back of my neck, his other hand holding my hip so he can reposition me over his now tenting length. He roughly pulls my face down to meet his, and a squeak of playful amusement rumbles from behind my pinched lips, making him beam boyishly at me. Remnants of a plan so solid I can see them like the pages of a play-by-play picture book contort his features with an unspoken fascination.

'I'm yours, Roni—always have been, always will be. If soulmates exist, you're mine.' I nip at his lips but move back to assess his expression when he doesn't kiss me back like I expect him to. 'Now take off your underwear like a good girl before I rip them in two and feast on what's mine whilst you scream out my name,' he snarls. His voice, although barely a whisper, is powerful enough to have my body dipping closer into his in response as I fight to steady the thrumming between my legs at his gruff statement. He isn't wrong. Everything I have to give from this point forward will be his, even my screams of pleasure. They are his and only his.

Glutton for punishment springs to mind as the next unfiltered question of the night leaves my mouth. Still holding me tightly in his embrace, he moves his face from mine but keeps my body close, refusing to allow any unnecessary space between us.

'Do you miss it – the thought of being a dad?' I know I shouldn't ask him the question, but I have answered his question candidly, and now it is my time to know this truth finally. As always, my mouth has run away with itself before my brain can protest the legalities of what such a question would bring to the surface. Our gazes meet, and I know instantly that we are on the same page. Aiden needed to know why I had never settled down with the rotation of unsuitable frogs that delved between my sheets. He got his answer in full. Now it is my turn. I need to know whether this is a deal breaker for him. I need to know if I'm enough.

'I had to give up the best thing in my life to become a father, Roni—something I swore I would never turn my back on. She manipulated the situation and made me choose. That should answer your question,' he declares, his honey-rimmed cool water gaze never leaving mine.

'What did she want you to give up?'

'You, baby. She asked me to give up you, and I hate myself for following suit,' he says softly, dropping his head, shame flushing his face with sadness.

'Just so you know, being a dad is the only reason I would ever have accepted you walking away from me, Aiden. You would have made an amazing father. You deserved that happiness; you deserved it all and more,' I press, fighting back the emotions that threaten to betray my resolve. I never wanted him to leave me, but I would have sided exactly how he had if it was a choice between his child and me. Aiden needed to be a father; he had earned the right to know that love, regardless of what woman was privileged enough to give it to him.

'But there is no baby, and that's okay,' he lulls, dragging me back to the here and now. Child-free and half-naked suits my best friend just fine, and I am happy to be along for the ride, but even though he thinks he is masking that sliver of regret at losing a child that never even existed, I can still see it lingering. The blinding light of his unspoken wish blends into his expression, but when he realises I am assessing his face a little too intently, it's extinguished, flittering away like leaves in the wind, only love and awe left in its wake. I trace my index finger down the centre of his ripped torso, the barely there touch enough to warrant an elicit gasp to stutter from my lips. Aiden rocks his hips forward, his body silently begging for more. Every other thought lands like melted marshmallows across a hot windscreen as I try to track back and gain some of my lost self-control.

Fuck it. We're past the point of no return. You've passed go, collect that £200, and screw him already. The familiar little voice barks hungrily, and I bite my bottom lip to stifle the laugh creeping forward.

'You want to play, Roni?' He grins wickedly, coiling a length of my hair around his finger before wrapping it around his fist, tugging ever so lightly and pulling my face closer to his. I can't help but bob on his lap, a heavy emptiness warming my core, desperate to be filled.

I have never been, and will never be, the girl that expects a happily ever after, but I will take all of this with Aiden with a skip in my step and a smile on my face. Whatever this is, I am all in for it.

FEBRUARY 9TH 2020

4 WEEKS LATER

RONI

I indulged in my naivety, spending the past few weeks lost in Aiden, never allowing my thoughts enough room to address Aiden's illness and what it means for our future. I'd play blind for however long I could to hold on to our current reality. It is a dream-like bubble of an existence we have created within the walls of this house, although to some it would probably be interpreted as an unhealthy way of life where I use sex and humour to gloss over every discussion Aiden tries to have with me regarding the big C. But there's no dodging the bullet today; today, the pristine bubble pops, whether I like it or not.

I can see the unease on Aiden's face when he opens the brown envelope whilst we sit at the kitchen island, eating our bacon and eggs. My appetite disappears completely as his thick fingers deftly prise the letter open. I smile at him reassuringly as he tries to cover the word 'urgent' scrawled in red marker from me. Smoothing down the rose-detailed material of my baby blue wrap dress, I observe him as his eyes run frantically over the words typed on the page, trying to gain an insight into what they might say by reading the changing expressions on his face. When what has felt like ten minutes has passed, he folds the paper and lets out a brutal sigh that could move mountains.

'What does it say?' I ask softly, twiddling my fingers anxiously, hating the sound of dread edging my tone. But no matter how hard I try, I can't hide the fear gnawing relentlessly at my insides.

'On a scale of 1-10, how much do you like my hair?' He queries, his broad smile wavering slightly as he masks his emotions. The need to break down blooms in his gaze as he tugs at the hair at the nape of his neck. I want to confront his concerns, but something in me bites back my protests.

'Sandra Bullock,' I reply automatically. My natural response to most of the vague questions he asks me makes him smile gratefully at me, genuine appreciation washing away the tension as his shoulders relax.

'The dates set. I'm officially going to start chemo on March 1st.' He sighs, waving the letter at me, his slight grin filled with sorrow. He tugs at the hair at the nape of his neck again as though saying goodbye to it. I climb across the island without a second thought, the desperate need to touch and comfort him the loudest thought in my head. Pushing aside our plates, I drop onto his lap, placing my hand over his, pulling it from his hair and bringing it to my lips. He heaves in a steadying breath and doesn't fight his need to pull me into his body, but his eyes still don't meet mine, and the need to soothe him, to chase away the stress lines marring his forehead, hits me with the jolt of optimism that I need.

'That's good. Well, not good, but you know what I mean.' I chuckle, nuzzling into his neck and planting a kiss under his ear, knowing that only light-heartedness will suffice. I can't let him see how worried I am. He needs me to be his rock. 'It's certainly no *Hogwarts* acceptance letter.' I snort as I slap playfully at his shoulder. I clear my throat and decide that this moment is as perfect as any to share *my* news with him.

'So, you'll be free in June then?' I ask as I rise from his lap, moving to the laundry room, busying myself with folding the washing from the tumble dryer into neat piles on the dining table. Nerves tickle my senses as I fill my lungs, my hands shaking around a pair of knotted socks as the secret I've held so tightly for the past twenty-four hours threatens to burst from my lips.

'As long as the big C doesn't get me, I'm sure I can make time for you in June, baby,' he quips, beaming broadly across at me as he stabs at his egg. 'Will hair be required at this June thing?' He chuckles, trying to lighten the mood. I ignore his implication that the chemo might not cure him and concentrate on his wide, playful grin, the understandable smidgen of fear that never leaves him hidden behind it. My heart sinks for my man. He leans across the worktop separating us and strokes my face tenderly, his thumb running over my lips to dispel the forming frown. 'Enough of the sadness. What's happening in June?' he asks, physically shaking away any thoughts of his plight from his mind as he drops his fork and gets up from his seat, moving to put his plate in the sink.

'I'll be giving birth and thought you might want to be there,' I say nonchalantly as though I am merely telling him what I plan to cook for dinner. Dipping my hand into the drawer to my left, I grab one of five positive pregnancy tests and whip it out, watching as he turns slowly on his heels to face me. His beautiful grey-blue eyes widen with shock. I have stunned him into silence, and a giggle escapes me as I watch him try but fail to push syllables out of his mouth, like a guppy fish fresh out of water trying to catch its breath. I recognise the effort because it mirrors my reaction exactly when my doctor told me the news yesterday morning. I had planned on some grand revelation, but I couldn't hold it in for another minute. I'm sure he will still be happy enough to devour the giant cookie in the fridge with the words 'Hey Dipshit, you knocked me up!' piped in frosting. Aiden's never one to turn down a sweet treat.

'Really?' he breathes, looking between me and the test, a mixture of disbelief and sheer wonderment colouring his pale face, his jaw slack. His feet rooted in place. He takes in a lungful of air. I can practically hear his heartbeat from where I stand across the kitchen as adrenaline courses impatiently through his veins.

'Either that or the handful of pregnancy tests I just took are faulty,' I retort.

He barrels towards me, knocking the neat piles of clean washing onto the floor, scooping me up in one fluid motion into his broad arms. Hugging me tightly and biting back the urge to squeal with excitement as I hang here in my favourite place, the woodsy scent of his aftershave enveloping me. My head falls back as he dots ardent kisses up my throat, each one a promise of its own. When he pulls back to admire my harassed, needy state, I lift my head and languidly bring my gaze to his, revelling in the heat pooling low in my belly that burns bright when he worships me with his mouth like this.

'But how?' he asks, his broad smile still stretched across his face. All the worry that had been there only minutes before my revelation melted away.

'Well, when a man and a woman have sex,' I begin dead pan.

'You are hilarious,' he quips, squeezing me tighter, peppering featherlight nips and kisses over my face, spinning me around in his hold excitedly as though I weigh nothing at all.

'So, you're happy?' I ask tenderly, struggling to hold back the swell of emotion building in my chest. Aiden and I had discussed that I couldn't have children without a miracle, and we had both come to terms with it. Although acceptance never took away the hope that bounced between us every time he finished inside me. With everything that had happened since that night in his room when we made love, Louisa's pregnancy announcement, her turning out to be a bare-faced liar, and their breakup, I hadn't even had the forethought to consider a missed period or two. I had been spotting here and there, and any early morning sickness I had, I put down to a mixture of nerves, a hangover, and the flu. The idea of it being down to the baby currently housed in my uterus hadn't even popped into the mix of possibilities. The nurse had informed me I was five months pregnant with no visible indicators, and a healthy baby was growing nicely inside me. Those crazy *I didn't even know I was pregnant* birth stories suddenly seemed more plausible. I opted not to find out the sex of the baby, instead purchasing probably ten or more of the grainy ultrasound pictures for our own little game of guess who. Even with proof in spades, I still find myself witlessly re-checking that there is a baby in them whenever the dream seems too good to be true.

'Happy doesn't cover it.' Joyful tears roll down the face of the man I love, his smile broad, refusing to settle even when the corners pinch at his cheeks for too long. His lips crash against mine, and I wrap my legs around his waist, my arms looping around his neck, the pregnancy test still secured in my hand. All is not lost; my body hasn't betrayed me when it matters most, and I will give this man what he has always wanted. The miracle of life that is growing inside me also offers me hope. I want to demolish the wall of unease I've built around me like armour these past few weeks. That familiar little voice hollering with everything she had, determined for me to believe that Aiden *could* get better, that the cancer *could* be eradicated, and that he *could* fight against the odds set to defeat him.

APRIL 28TH 2020

TWO MONTHS LATER

RONI

As I hover over the toilet bowl, the scent of bleach and bile filling my nose, my earlier comment to Aiden regarding my miraculous gift of *missing all that morning sickness* that I proudly joked about the day I revealed to him I was pregnant has come back to bite me in the arse—like a ten-tonne sledgehammer, chipping away at my resolve. I am not exaggerating when I say if anything other than crackers and tepid lemon water passes my lips, I am set for a date with the toilet. My knees dig into the cold linoleum as my fingers grip the porcelain until my knuckles are white. It feels like I am about ready to throw up a lung, each rock of my body making the baby kick and squirm.

'I'm sorry, am I inconveniencing your nap time?' I quip to my considerably larger belly as I rub over the material of my oversized t-shirt, soothing our little bundle of joy the only way I can. It is as though by finding out the truth about the baby, my body has gone into panic mode, catching up on lost time and throwing every pregnancy attribute in the book at me with no pre-warning—five months of harbouring a little fugitive condensed into a matter of weeks. Swollen ankles, engorged breasts, core twinges of the uncomfortable kind—If it's been documented, I've had it. At seven months pregnant, my moods are tired, hungry, and horny predominantly, and not necessarily in that order. I want nothing more than to nap intermittently whilst also licking squeezy cheese off Aiden's bare chest as his impressive length wears me as a hat.

'Oh, cheese.' I groan. *I miss cheese*. I can't keep up with this pregnancy's ever-changing loop of madness. It certainly proves to keep me on my toes, and once baby O'Shea makes their appearance, I will have everything cheese for breakfast, lunch and dinner until I can't stand the sight of it. Sadly, the mere thought of all that cheese has me dry-heaving over the toilet again as my empty belly fights to expel air.

'Hey, bathroom buddy,' Aiden squeals as he rushes past me and empties the contents of his stomach into the sink. A sheen of sweat coats his back as his muscles contract under the movement. He only has a few weeks left of chemo, and out of the two months, this last leg of his journey seems to take the most from him. We brush our teeth in unison, each fixing ourselves up in the two circular mirrors attached to the bathroom wall. His and hers with a two bucket sink; surprisingly, mine is the messier side. I mime the words along to *Letters to Cleo's* version of *Cruel to be kind* that's playing downstairs in the kitchen. Shaking my hips from side to side as the minty freshness eradicates the stale stench of sickness from my mouth, my protruding belly following suit in time to the beat, making Aiden chuckle. He spits out the toothpaste collecting in his mouth and turns to me.

'I love you, baby.' His sentiment is heavier than I think he had intended, and I note the sadness marring his brow line. He doesn't let it linger, more for my benefit than his own.

'Ditto, dipshit.' I profess with a grin, stroking his freshly shaved head. Aiden had jumped to the hair clippers about a month ago before the chemo took away his ability to choose the fate of his hair. I miss tugging the curls at the nape of his neck, but he has a whole action man/rugged *Jason Statham* thing going on, so I'm not about to complain. Aiden can pull off pretty much anything. I rinse my mouth with cool water as a memory of Aiden dressed as Lara Croft for some fresher's week mayhem back in university hits me. My libido is shaken awake. *Horny,* my current mood, is battling for supremacy. Strangely, even thoughts of Aiden wearing a tank top and camo shorts with guns strapped to his legs are enough inspiration to stir to life the needy bitch that has my core now throbbing restlessly for attention.

'It will grow back,' he assures me, and my face falls, all humour, and thoughts of him railing me into next week until I scream his name gone. I never want him to think I'm not attracted to him because that couldn't be further from the truth.

'I couldn't care less if it didn't,' I state firmly, pulling his face closer to me to eradicate the space between us. I girlishly squeal as he lifts me onto the side in one quick motion, his fingers digging into the soft skin of my hips. He manoeuvres around my swollen midriff and positions himself between my legs that dangle there, leaning in to plant a chaste kiss on my lips. It's not enough. I groan with hunger for him, and his body jolts as he recognises the wicked glint flashing in my big blue eyes. I hadn't considered how much shaving his head would affect Aiden; it is as though that change made everything else real for him. He is by no means vain, but besides his lack of hair, his outward appearance hasn't changed. The minimal weight loss is to be expected, and his skin's slight paleness is only noticeable if you are intently looking at him, which I often am.

~~~

I sit at the kitchen table, one hand resting affectionally over my bump, the other secured around a mug of decaf tea. I yearn for the moment I can reintroduce caffeine back into my life. Aiden busies himself as he gets ready to leave for his chemo appointment. He grabs a navy baseball cap out of his coat pocket and pulls it onto his head before he leans down to kiss me on the cheek, his broad frame enveloping me as he leans across me to stroke my belly tenderly. I note the straightness in his lips, but I don't comment on it.

'You ready for the midwife?' he asks, refusing to move from my belly as he kisses over the broadest part of my bump, pulling up my t-shirt to gain better access.

'Ready as I'll ever be. Little junior here won't let me eat anything right now, so hopefully, there is some magic she can pull out of her arse because I am running on empty. If I have to look at one more cracker, I might kill someone.'

'Not long now, baby,' he mumbles affectionately, his voice masked as he moves to lay another kiss on my lips. I watch him leave; the tentative grip of emotion that stirs me as he walks out the front door is way too familiar now. Heartburn pulses at my sternum, making every organ in my body feel crowded, and I search for some tablets. Lack of hair isn't a problem for our little one if the old wives' tales about heartburn are to be believed. I waddle into the living room, trying to ignore my body's demand that the hundredth toilet break of the morning is necessary. Getting up off the toilet at this stage in the pregnancy game feels like cardio. I pull out the crap drawer where things go to be forgotten for the backup heartburn relief tablets. My fingers skim over a pile of photos tied with string pushed to the back under a chipped crystal paperweight. I pull them free, my heart stilling as I realise what they are. Photo after photo is of Aiden, pre-diagnosis,
~~~

pre-haircut, pre-chemo. I take a moment and glance around the living room, only now noticing that he has swapped out the photos in nearly every frame that hung on the walls or perched on a shelf. I can't fight the frustration I feel at myself for not noticing, for not being aware of his spiralling mood. In the frames now are images that make Aiden happy. Sonogram pictures of our baby, pictures of me dancing around the kitchen, a snapshot of me right after I told him I was pregnant. Before I know what I am doing, I pull the photos from the frames. All of them except our sonogram picture, and refill them with the images of us together that Aiden removed. I need him to know I love him in every way, regardless of how much hair he does or doesn't have. He could decide to wear a monkey suit for the rest of his life, and I would still stand proudly by his side, questioning his sanity as any supportive girlfriend should.

~~~~

I drive up to the hospital's outpatient centre and mull over the morning's events, trying but failing to ignore the rumble of unease currently attacking my stomach as the tuna mayo sandwich I had grabbed after leaving my midwife appointment, threatens to make a reappearance. The Baby is growing nicely and hitting every percentile it needs to; the heartbeat is strong. Even though the midwife could tell me the sex of the baby, I fought to divert my gaze away from the ultrasound screen. Aiden wants the surprise, and I'm not strong enough to discover the truth and not inadvertently spill it. Secret keeper is not a part of my skill set. As I turn off the engine, I slip the black and grey snapshots of our baby into the front pocket of my bag. With so much to be happy about, I still have to quieten my fears and school my expression for Aiden. With the raging pregnancy hormones riled up by my ever-changing body and the mixed emotions about
~~~~

Aiden's health battle, it is hard to get on an even footing most days. I am happy that he is so determined to have our home a cancer-free space, but I also don't want him stressing about the inevitability of his health changing the dynamics sometimes. Every day without fail, he is determined to get us back to our normal before his diagnosis, whereas I have accepted this as a bump in our road to our happily ever after. For Aiden, it runs to the darkest depths of his psyche, and although I want to help and support him, I can't see the internal battle he is fighting against himself. It is only every so often that my grief for my beautiful man surfaces. Every time it has, something in Aiden breaks, a small piece of him chips away, and a light extinguishes in a field of positive affirmations that threatens to set Aiden back a step. As the months have passed, I have got better at hiding my concerns from him, concentrating on how I can pull him from his head long enough to remind him of all the brightness in our lives that cancer can't touch. Hitting the lock feature on the key fob and pulling up my raincoat's hood to shield me from the rain, I attempt my version of running across the carpark. My baby bump wobbles from side to side with the motion, pushing me off balance when I hit speeds greater than a determined stroll.

A for effort.

Ambling into the hospital, I readjust the hefty bag over my shoulder, trying to hold on to the boombox secured in my other hand while gripping the crocheted blanket under my arm. For a pregnant woman, I'm not ready to concede to the fact that I probably should take it a little easier than I am. The fact that I am loaded up like the buckaroo donkey as I shuffle along in my beaten-up converse is a testament to the fact that I hate to conform, the fifteen-year-old punk in me rising to the surface for a peak at grownup life. Pushing through the double doors into the ward, I let go of everything I am holding so that it slumps messily onto a rocking chair to my side.

Grey faces deprived of energy look up lazily at me. Six people sit hooked up to tubes and wires as the machines track their vitals. The repetitive clunk clunk of vials lazily spinning in the equipment above them is an all too familiar sound of late that I won't miss when Aiden is finally free from this place. I can't help but smile at him as he sits huddled in the corner, his baseball cap firmly on his head as he drums his fingers on his knees, his legs jumping as they always do when he's in a situation he doesn't like. All movements cease when I pull the hood of my raincoat down, and anyone that wasn't already looking my way, the nurses included, fixes their wide-eyed stares on me. Aiden guffaws as he fights to contain the surprise in his voice. I have a habit of shocking him lately.

'What the hell have you done?' Aiden laughs heartily, a pink warmth returning to his cheeks.

'I know you said leggings were a no-go, but I'm having a bloated day,' I say sweetly, rubbing my bump affectionately, tugging at the uncomfortable waistband of the trousers he knows I hate.

'Yeah, the leggings. That's the surprise I am referring to, Veronica.' He laughs, throwing his head back, hoping that using my full name will inspire me to take the situation seriously for a few brief moments. The cheeky grin that can inspire any love song spreads across his face, assuring me he is enjoying my little performance. 'Okay, so next topic of conversation, baby, where's your hair gone?' He beams, running his thumb and forefinger over his bottom lip as he looks me over. Holding out his arms, he beckons me forward, and I do exactly that with a skip in my step, making sure to wave hi to Andrea, a sixty-eight-year-old mum of three who treats Aiden like her fourth child, hooked up to a machine beside him.

Between finding the photos Aiden had hidden in the drawer at home and meeting up with my OBGYN at the offices, I had made the bold choice to shave my head. Being impulsive isn't a new add-on for my pregnancy, but this is beyond anything I have committed to before.

Aiden's soft expression lets me know he knows why I am now sporting a new and unexpected hairstyle.

'Do you like it?' I ask, running my palm over my head first, then removing his baseball cap and doing the same to him.

'I love it, *Sinead O'Connor* vibes, baby,' he coos. 'You'll be growing a beard next,' he quips, running his finger around my ear like he usually would when moving my hair from my face.

'Whatever floats your boat, I guess,' I beam. I lightly kiss his cold lips before scooting to my feet, a little less majestically than I had planned, and moving to retrieve the boombox.

'Now let me play you a 90's classic to soothe your inner torment as we did back in the good old days,' I say, hitting the play button and crooning along to *R.E.M's Everybody Hurts* as I pull a bacon sandwich wrapped in foil with the new ultrasound photo of the baby from my bag. I sway my hips and rub my freshly shaved head as I move towards Aiden. The other patients join in and sway along to the music, for a moment forgetting where they are.

'Should this be turning me on?' He chuckles as I reach him. 'Because it is,' he affirms, and I can't stop the bark of laughter rumbling up my throat. Placing a hand on either side of my swollen belly and laying his lips on the material of my leggings, I can feel his lips moving beside my belly button. The baby kicks in response as Aiden talks, his voice too low and the music too loud for me to hear what he is saying exactly. Before the song can reach the chorus, Aiden pulls me into his lap, swathing me in his embrace. My lips part, desperate to have his on mine. Reading me perfectly in that way that only he can, he doesn't make me wait a moment longer, and his mouth crashes against mine to whoops and cheers from the other patients around us. Our tongues battle as I melt into my happy place, secure in his strong arms, the world around us like paint in water as everything but him disappears from my view. My lungs scream for air as he pulls his face from mine, my heart thumping in my chest as that flicker of sadness that I have become accustomed to seeing in his face flitters out of view, the honey tones of contentment lighting his eyes now.

'What did I ever do to deserve you, baby?' he asks, his face filled with adoration as he runs his hand over my shaved head. His smile is broad, his gaze set on mine, and in a split-second, sadness fills his expression again as he tugs at my neck, pulling my forehead to meet his as though my closeness is what he needs to breathe. He feels weak during his treatment, and although he tries, it is harder for him to hide his pain from me in moments like this. Moments where his resolve is stripped bare beneath the weight of everything life has thrown at him, everything his sickness has taken from him. He doesn't need an answer from me. His question is more for himself than for me. The jolt of electricity pulsing between our bodies is enough to convey my opinion, and he knows it. I can't be angry at his illness anymore. To have him in my life and by my side is where my attention lies, the brightness peaking through the darkness, an appreciation for everything I have right now. Hesitation flits across his face as he opens his mouth to speak. I shuffle around in his lap, rubbing his tense jaw as he fights the words desperately needing to break free. I don't hesitate to fill the silence.

'Why did you take them down?' I squeak softly, failing to disguise the broken flick of trepidation in my voice. Fiddling with the hem of my sleeve, I instantly regret my question as I watch the light in his eyes dim—a beat or two passes as he seems to consider his answer. My heart lodged uncomfortably in my throat.

'I thought it would be easier if I pulled down the pictures. For you and the baby,' he whispers. Pain tightens its hold on my heart. I know where this conversation is leading, and I have zero desire to see it through. His pulling away from me will never make any of this hurt any less. I have to make him see that.

'When I go, I...' he begins, but I refuse to let him finish. I can't hear these words from him. I can fight this with him and be his champion if he needs me to be, but one thing I can't do is watch the determination to believe in himself dwindle from his eyes.

'Please,' I say tenderly, pressing my finger to his full lips. My single-worded plea is more like a prayer to God himself. It is enough to still him, and instead of finishing his sentence, he hugs me a little tighter into his body, pulling up the crochet shawl across his legs so he is bundling all three of us in his warm embrace. I bite back my sorrow, our wriggling baby, the reminder of what he is fighting for, making me grip onto him a little tighter.

'Now smile for me. However sad this journey is, it is a part of our story, and I want to remember every damn second of it.' I beam, licking at the tear that has escaped as it roams across my trembling lips. He wipes away the streak left down my cheek, and his thumb settles on my bottom lip.

'Definitely a story to remember,' he states with a smile, nodding. His determination is unwavering as he spears me with his intense gaze. In one swift movement, he pulls his phone out of his jacket pocket and preps it for a selfie. I curl into his side, resting my head in the crook of his neck as he snaps away. Alternating our positions and features only slightly with every click, the storyboard collection of this moment is only one chapter to our fairy tale. I have probably sixteen varying shots of us together. I plan to get at least four of them up on the wall before the weekend is over. Hashtag bald club is now locked into the memory bank whether he likes it or not. I refuse to let the fear of dying stop us from living.

JUNE 21ST 2020

ALMOST TWO MONTHS LATER

RONI

'Honey, I'm home,' Aiden yells jovially like a fifties husband home after a hard day at the office. I hear him whistling whatever song is blaring out of his headphones as he hangs up his coat in the wardrobe space by the front door, kicking his converse into the back and completely bypassing the shoe rack beside him. *Old habits die hard.*

'You took your fucking time,' I roar out from the kitchen, and sensing my tone, he comes barrelling in through the door in a panic, almost slipping onto his arse as he crosses the threshold.

'The baby?' he questions, his brows raised, eyes wide.

'Give the man a diplo—' I don't finish my sentence as pain slices through my abdomen, bending me in half, the crack of my spine reminiscent of a snapped glow stick. The only glow about me is the sweat dampening my chocolate brown pixie haircut, gluing the strands to my forehead. Without warning, a loud pop penetrates the air between us. You would have thought shots of unfriendly fire had rained down on our small kitchen as Aiden visibly shuffles on the spot as he panics. The warm liquid runs from under my orange summer dress and down my thighs, pooling around my battered pumps that are two sizes too big, thanks to the swelling in my feet. I writhe against the incessant jolt of stinging pain that hums uncomfortably between my thighs. We are officially a rocket ship ride past the dull ache the books warned us about.

'Someone's happy to see me.' Aiden chuckles awkwardly as my waters gush down my inner thighs. 'How much does it hurt on a scale of 1-10?' he asks hurriedly, as though he has lost control of his faculties. I eye him suspiciously, glaring at the beautiful man I now want to slap some sense into with the heaviest frying pan we own.

'On the scale of I will gut you like a pig if we are not in a car and on our way to the hospital in under five minutes.' I grimace, tensing my jaw as the tail end of the contraction pulls at my belly muscles to where I feel like I am going to be split in two. I groan, not recognising my own hoarse voice as I grip Aiden's arm, snarling through the pain like a woman possessed. I double over, unable to hold my weight, my knees hitting the shaggy blue rug beneath me before Aiden can grab and support me fully.

'Kill me. Kill me now,' I beg, swaying as I try to disperse the pain between my clenched thighs. It's no use as the vibrations of the contraction, although easing, still thrums there.

'Why didn't you call me? Why didn't you tell me sooner, baby? I would have taken you to the hospital this morning.' He panics, tugging at the short hairs that had grown back at the nape of his neck in the way he used to do when anxiety wracked him about something.

'I thought they were just those Hoxton hick things the midwife was telling us about,' I whine, gripping the edge of the cooker as the pain distorts the last syllable out of my mouth.

'Braxton Hicks, baby,' Aiden corrects, and I scowl at him as though my glare alone can banish him and his smart mouth to the depths of Hell. 'Not the time,' he adds with a small smile that I know he hopes has the power to placate me. It doesn't. The reverberating sting, which is like a knife slicing against my skin, remains in my lower belly as the baby's weight pushes down. Suddenly best friends with gravity, it would seem, as my knees threaten to give way again. Unbridled concern is the only expression on Aiden's face now as my battered *converse* squelches on the sodden rug beneath us, my ankles shake as a cool rush of panic sweeps through my extremities.

'Preparation. preparation. Preparation,' he reiterates, moving around the kitchen and pulling open drawers and cupboards. I hold out my already packed hospital bag to him, the one he had packed and re-packed himself at least twenty times after devouring every new parent guidebook he could find online.

'Whiskey, Aiden, really?' I splutter, exasperated, trying to remember the lamas lady's teachings and counting out loud to three, remembering not to push as it was a keynote of literally every class we had attended. With a multipack bag of *Wotsits* under his arm, an old pack of cigarettes left here by someone from our last house party in one hand, and a half-drunk bottle of *Jack Daniels* in the other, the love of my life is panicking to epic proportions the midwife hadn't pre-warned me about.

'Surprisingly, I'm not in the party mood, Aiden. Although I won't say no to an epidural if you have that in your little party package.' As I say the words, another contraction slices through me. Instincts have Aiden rushing to my side, the contents of his hands now spread across the floor. Helping me over the broken glass of the bottle, seeping amber liquid all over the floorboards, he grabs my car keys from out of the bowl by the front door as we pass. Pushing my hospital bag up his arm and over his shoulder whilst he moves to lift me, cradling me in his arms marriage style, he runs down the stone steps to the driveway, the front door left wide open behind us as I cry out.

'Four and a half minutes apart. Shit just got real, baby,' he coos as he glances at his watch whilst strapping me into the passenger seat, his eyes never leaving mine. 'Do I have time to run back for the alcohol?' He laughs, and I scowl in response, my heart fluttering at his cuteness, even though labour is stealing all humour from my body as a human the size of a large watermelon prepares to exit my body unceremoniously. Sliding across the car's bonnet, *Starsky* style, Aiden fights to get into the vehicle at top speed. A fresh wave or fear induced tears from me fuels him to push himself harder to start the car and peel out of the driveway.

'AIDEN!' I scream out as we hit the motorway at speeds likely to get us pulled over by the police, hitting a speed bump that makes my body feel as though it's turning itself inside out. He pushes his sock-clad foot against the brake as we hit a hard curve. He had rushed me out of the house without putting his shoes back on, but I didn't have enough energy to protest. If I want baby O'Shea born in an actual hospital, time is of the essence. 'AIDEN, FUCK!' I scream as my shoulder hits the door panel with a thud as he takes another sharp turn towards our exit.

'You know what you do to me screaming my name like that, baby,' he teases as I grip his thigh, digging my nails in so I'm sure I leave crescent moon marks in his skin below his light denim jeans.

'So not the time,' I admonish as I dig my fingers in a little tighter for good measure.

He steps on the gas; the smile falling from his face as he notes my distress.

~~~~

People in blue scrubs rush around the small mint green painted room, the rough starched sheets scratching my bare legs secured into metal stirrups, making me feel like an animal in a vet's office. The hum of the air conditioning unit buzzes so loudly in the corner of the room that it briefly distracts me as more people playing doctor gather around me. I could have the resident hospital cleaner in here, and I wouldn't have a clue. 'Okay, I don't want to do this anymore,' I screech as another excruciating contraction rips through me. My legs are useless as my body fights against the pounding fullness at my core, my face burying into the pillow beside me, the metallic, medicinal scent of the sheets making me want to throw up.

Natural birth, they said. It's too late for pain meds, they advised.

Fuck all this shit. I'm about ready to give up. I plead with the nurses to let me go home, even though I know it is a crazy idea that no sane medical professional would ever consider. Aiden is by my side, pulling my sweaty face between his palms, desperate to break through the onslaught of pain that flushes my face a beetroot red as I puff out my cheeks.

'You got this, baby! Nothing can beat you. It won't be long, and you will bring our baby into this world like the legend you are. This cannot beat you; nothing can beat *my* Veronica,' he states with an air of finality as he stands tall with his broad shoulders squared, his formidable body language commanding me to take stock of his words.

'Don't call me Veronica!' I howl, followed by a muted growl of
~~~~

frustration as my little inner voice demands for freedom behind my clenched jaw. Although my body and tone say otherwise, he calms a little at my admonishing him for using my full name—seeing anything other than pain on my face is clearly a relief of sorts. I see the nurse mouth the word *push* out of the corner of my eye, and something in me snaps. Fighting against the burn between my legs, I do as she instructs without hesitation, bearing down with every molecule of energy that my tired body can muster as an almost unbearable heaviness slices through me. My spine throbs as it threatens to snap beneath the pressure as the *Rubix cube* that is my internal organs shift and slide to accommodate the space our baby needs.

'You are giving me the best gift anyone ever could. You are a mother fucking superstar, baby. You got this,' he protests, whispering ardently in my ear. As his warm breath fans my face, his words push me to find the little strength I have held back to see this through.

'She's ready,' the midwife says to the nurse from behind her mask, grappling for the towels stacked in her outstretched arms.

'It's show time, Veronica,' I hear someone say, but my vision is hazy. I don't have the time or energy to correct whoever it was with what I prefer to be called. Everything but the agony is a tedious afterthought.

'You got this,' Aiden affirms as he nods and grips my hand in his, squeezing it to where his knuckles are white. He pulls my hand up to his lips and takes a deep breath, planting a kiss on the back reverently as the bleeping on the monitor signals my next contraction. I brace myself, the fear of the inevitable making me shudder as the pain between my legs hits me like a freight train. The stretching, the pulling, I feel like a loosely wrapped burrito that has been left outside for too long in balmy September heat, my insides mushy and messy. Thankfully it doesn't seem that my body needs a fully functioning brain to get our baby out, with every morsel of energy it can find, my body fights to get us through this. A part of me, that terrified part, refuses to push. The pain is too much to bear. But a spark of reality has my brain kicking into gear; I'd guess mother nature is intent on doing her job.

The more you push, the quicker this is finished, and the baby will be here. With that hurried thought and everyone in the room encouraging me, I push, bearing down. I push with everything I have, even with that terrified part of me. Although monumentally harrowing and more than likely what's going to send me to therapy, becoming our unit of three feels as natural as breathing.

As my body works its magic, I scream an ethereal wisp of a plea. Our little girl takes her first breath as the nurse between my legs cradles her in her arms. I sag into Aiden's embrace as he kisses my sweat-drenched forehead hard. My thighs quiver as my brain recognises the shock to my system. His cries of praise and thanks melt into the background as I noiselessly thank a higher power for getting me through this. Thoughts of the heaviness, the tightness, the immense pressure, the soreness - they all fade into a collection of tolerable sensations as cold air slaps at my skin, everything is suddenly sensitive, and I don't just mean the car crash left behind between my legs. The intrusion of the light on my eyes, the lapping air across my skin, my engorged breasts that feel twice as heavy as they did before. Using the sleeve of his sweatshirt, Aiden wipes the sweat from my hairline, our collective heavy breathing the backing track to this incredible next chapter in our story.

'I can never thank you enough for this. You are my all,' Aiden lulls in my ear as a nurse places the loosely wrapped baby O'Shea on my bare chest. Her little broken cries are music to my ears. The tiny human in my arms compels every sense, a confusing mix of love, sadness, joy and fear taking hold of my heart as I try to fight against the chaos in my head. My conflicting emotions war for a voice, but the haze surrounding us is too strong. So instead, I cry, soul-wrenching tears falling down my cheeks as I lay trembling lips on our baby's cheek, her matted head of blonde hair finally answering my heartburn debate.

'Beatrice Cassandra O'Shea,' Aiden coos softly, tears of his own staining his cheeks as he bends down to kiss our little girl on her head, moving to plant a lingering kiss on my shaking lips next. Beatrice hadn't been my choice of name; it had been Aiden's favourite grandmother. I had opted for Lottie, my grandmother's name. But as we did with everything else in our lives, a good old-fashioned game of rock, paper, scissors had leaned heavily in Aiden's favour and chosen for us.

'Our beautiful little Bea,' I second with a giddy side glance at Aiden, knowing that the nickname will stick as he repeats my sentiment. His attention is squarely on our little miracle.

A little later, through the haze of a cocktail of pain meds, the names of which I probably couldn't even pronounce, I watch as Aiden sleeps soundly on the wooden rocking chair in the corner of the hospital room, the stark black night streaming into the room through the blinds on the window behind him. The soft glow of the light clipped above my bed bleeds out onto every surface of the quiet room. I fill my lungs with air as my heart swells with love at my view. Our daughter is lying on Aiden's bare chest, soft rumblings of slumber falling collectively from their lips, the similarities in their features even at this moment unmissable.

I would do it all again.

Even with the pain from today's events still fresh in my mind, I know it's true. I would go to the ends of the earth to give him this, to have her with us. I've been broken in the best kind of way, and just looking at her perfect little face dispels any memory of the pain immediately, like a magic trick mother nature has us all programmed with to keep humankind in rotation. My eyelids are heavy, my body succumbing to the slumber that so desperately wants to whisk me away, my vision filled with the two people who mean the most to me. Our content unit of three. Our future.

NEW YEARS EVE 2020

SIX MONTHS LATER

RONI

I dance around our kitchen wearing last night's pyjamas, my hair pulled up into a messy topknot. The sun streams in from the bay windows; a light breeze from the open backdoor is pleasantly warm against my bare legs. With Bea fast asleep secured in Aiden's arms, he bounces her along to the beat whilst seated on a stool at the island as he watches me sway my hips along to *T-Rex's 20th-Century Boy* blasting from the radio. I don't slow my movements as I stir the browning goat meat in the pan on the stove, intermittently using the spatula as a mic. I round the breakfast bar and sing along with the chorus, out of tune, of course. Singing isn't my thing, and although we both know it, he howls with encouragement anyway, jumping to his feet. All six foot three of my handsome man moves effortlessly to the beat. He grabs my hand and twirls me into his body, Bea still asleep in his embrace, as though her parents aren't attempting a full-on Glastonbury set around her. Extending his arm for the last time, he pulls me back into his broad frame. Our eyes lock, that familiar rumble of heated desire pooling low in my belly. I rise onto my tiptoes, wondering if I can ever get enough of this man, every inch of him moulded to perfection just for me. My lips hover over his, a breath hitching in my throat as he plants a featherlight kiss on my mouth. But it isn't enough contact to quieten the thrum of fluttering butterflies dancing wildly inside me. I drop the spatula and wrap an arm around his neck, pulling him into me, deepening our kiss to where my knees feel weak. Tugging at the curls of hair at the nape of his neck, I elicit a feral groan from him that speaks to my core, wordlessly ramping up the intensity of the flickers of electricity raging down my spine. He pulls away but holds me there, suspended in his taut arm. Nuzzling in my neck and nipping at the skin there, I cannot help but shudder, his warm breath making the areas he dotted kisses extra sensitive.

'God, you do things to me, Mr O'Shea,' I say, my statement breathy and laden with yearning.

'Given half the chance, baby,' he smiles cheekily, a brazen glint of fervour alight in his hazy blue greys. Although I had initially protested, he knows how much I love it when he calls me baby. The cheesiness alone has me swooning.

'That curry isn't going to finish itself,' I whisper, beaming up at him, never wanting to leave his hold but knowing that spice of the kind I want with Aiden right now isn't on the cards. Prolonging this little game of sexual back and forth will only leave me with a tender case of blue bean. Bea is due a feed; the dull ache in my engorged breasts is the best tell-tale sign of her snack time, and I can't ignore the smell of burning onions wafting over from the oven. I would happily butcher most meals but not curry goat. For some reason, that feels sacrilegious.

'I concede only for the sake of the curry. Otherwise, I would happily let it burn to ash,' he coos, planting a kiss on my forehead and releasing me. Grabbing for another wooden spoon, I tend to our dinner, removing any blackened onions and adding a little more cooking oil, moving the ingredients around in the pan to continue cooking the meat.

'Hey, sous-chef, can you pass me the chillies, please,' I ask him sweetly, gesturing towards the sideboard with the wooden spoon as I sprinkle some cumin seeds and coriander powder into the pot.

'Yes, boss,' he replies, handing it to me, making sure not to touch the diced chillies. 'You sure this isn't too much heat?' he questions.

'Casey always says when it comes to adding chilli, *make it right, not white*. Buckle up, big boy.' I chuckle, scraping off the contents of the chopping board into the pan and loving the sound of the intense sizzle. Bea mews and wriggles as she begins to wake, and I lovingly watch as Aiden rocks her, singing quietly in her ear as he shuffles back to the stool at the breakfast bar. This is what the books meant by happily ever after. I am sure of it. Although Aiden's illness is always present in our lives, he never lets it touch us. He refuses to let it dampen any of the moments we share, and because of this, I often forget about it. Call it ignorance or wishful thinking, but I enjoy these moments with as much happiness and clarity as I possibly can. He's told me the doctor is happy with his development, and there is no need for more chemo as his bloods are coming back all clear. So, I will take the win with a smile for the foreseeable future. I don't know what is going to happen five years down the road, no one does, but I refuse to let that uncertainty stop me from being here, lost in the moment, with him. I turn back to the food and close my eyes, pushing back the happy tears that threaten to fall from my eyes. The *Spotify* playlist Aiden has named in my honour shuffles to *You and I* by *Ingrid Michaelson,* and I am grateful for the change in pace. Moving the pan from the heat, I rinse my hands in the sink, wiping them dry with a tea towel hooked above the cooker. Reaching for the open bag of chocolates on the side, I pop two pieces into my mouth greedily.

'Will you marry me, Roni?' His question takes me off guard, and I stumble, almost swallowing the chocolate whole and choking as I momentarily forget how to chew. I stare at the wall as I decide whether I have heard him correctly, letting the chocolate fall from my mouth and into my hand before I dump it into the sink. As I turn slowly to face him, I find an empty room. Aiden clears his throat, and my gaze drops to see him on one knee at my feet. I cover my mouth to stifle the gasp. Holding back the happy tears is impossible now. With a smiling Bea tucked under one arm, he holds out a gummy *Haribo* ring with his free hand.

'What are you doing?' I chuckle, wiping my chocolatey palm down my pyjama shorts.

'I was waiting for the right time,' he states, nerves ticking in his jaw as he forces out an awkward toothy smile, tentatively waiting for me to respond.

'And midday on a Sunday whilst we dance around in our pyjamas mid-chocolate binge is the right time?' I chuckle, wiping at my eyes before I run my palm along his stubbled jawline, taking the gummy ring with my other hand and admiring it as though it is the most beautiful thing I have ever seen.

'The perfect time. This is everything I could ever have wished for,' he states resolutely, cupping his hand over mine on his face and leaning into it. Our collective stares dart to Bea, who beams at us as she yawns sleepily. 'We were never meant to do things by normal standards, Roni. You know that.'

I did know that. Our particular slice of unusual normal is my favourite, and I feel blessed it is something we share. Nothing about us has ever fit societal norms, and I love it. I ease the ring-shaped sweet down onto my finger and fall to my knees, pulling his face to mine as I kiss his lips, my fingers playing with the hair around his ears as I push my forehead against his.

'I love you more than I ever thought it was possible to love another person,' I whisper, my cheeks flush with adoration, my heart thumping wildly in my chest. 'Fuck yes, I'll marry you,' I squeal. He snakes his arm around my waist and hits me with a swoon-worthy kiss that knocks me for six and has me melting on the spot. Desire, need, and joy fuels our embrace. I take and give in equal measures as we show one another everything we feel. Each stroke of his tongue against mine propels me further into the abyss of us as I hug him to my body. My lips are harassed and full as I inch away from his face, allowing him to take a much-needed breath, his chest heaving as he fills his lungs.

'I don't know how much time we have left, but I want to spend however long it is with you as my wife.' His words are sobering, and a smidgen of sadness threatens to wash away my happiness, but I quickly school my features. I don't want him to see my unease. I want forever with him, but the reality is always there as a reminder that forever might not be as long as we would want, even more so in moments like this. Aiden has never looked sick. In the darkest moments of his treatment, he had lost weight, but since Bea came into our lives, he has looked like the old Aiden, building up his muscles again, the brightness restored in his features. It is why it is so easy to ignore the elephant in the room. His doctor is always quick to remind us it could come back, but all that proved to do was to remind us we have to live in the moment, and boy, is this one hell of a moment.

'I love you to the moon and back again, dipshit. An undecided forever is better than no forever at all. I want all of you for as long as I'm allowed.' I beam proudly up at him, sitting back on my haunches. 'So, is this a genuine diamond?' I chuckle, admiring my gummy ring.

'Of course,' he says, feigning mock offence.

'It's perfect,' I coo, reaching onto the breakfast bar to pull an identical sweet from the open packet. I run the pad of my finger over his full lips and move to push the gummy ring onto his finger, so we match. 'For always,' I say pointedly as though the word is enough to set the sentiment into stone.

'You better go get ready then,' he says, getting to his feet, handing me Bea as she suckles at her little fisted fingers, wriggling as the hunger for my breastmilk kicks in.

'Where are we going?' I ask, his statement drawing my attention away from Bea.

'To get married,' he states pointedly like it should be obvious. 'Time waits for no man. You've said yes. This is happening today.' He chuckles, dancing across the room to finish the curry with a Cheshire cat grin spread brightly across his face.

'We can't get married now. We need a marriage license, a priest, witnesses.'

'Done, done and done,' he replies cockily. My jaw drops as I eye him quizzically. 'I wanted to wait until your birthday to ask you, but this felt right. Everything is in place.'

'You never do things by halves, do you, Mr O'Shea?' I muse with a cocksure smile.

'Nope, I don't, soon-to-be Mrs O'Shea.' He beams, and his statement makes my heart swell.

'What will I wear?' I laugh, as though even the thought of getting an entire wedding prepared in under six hours isn't utterly insane. If there is ever a guy who could pull it off, it would be Aiden. Determination is practically his middle name.

'I think that little blue dress with the roses would do the job,' he suggests. I mentally flip through my wardrobe and wonder absently for a moment why he has selected that outfit. Reading me like he always does, he moves to my side. 'It was the dress you wore when you told me about Bea. That is my happiest memory of us before we became a team of three,' he whispers in my ear. 'All my other favourite moments of us, you were naked. So unless a naturist wedding is what you have always dreamt about, the blue dress it is,' he says, lowering to kiss me on the cheek. I bat at his arm playfully.

'What will you wear?'

'Your choice, baby. Whatever makes you smile.' For the first time in a long time, I am speechless as he ushers me out of the kitchen. 'You have until 6 pm, so chill with Bea upstairs and get yourself ready. I'll bring you some lunch when I've mastered this,' he lulls, gesturing to the iron pan.

'You're going to finish the curry?' I snigger, knowing that beans on toast is my hunky man's go-to meal to prepare. I'm not knocking it; he makes a mean beans on toast, but this curry is anything but easy to tackle for a novice.

'I have Casey on speed dial. I will be fine, and if in doubt, there's a tin of *Heinz* in the cupboard,' he teases, gifting me a wink. I leave the kitchen in a daze, trying to determine whether that has happened. Before I reach the stairs, I hear Casey's voice on loudspeaker, '*Make it right, not white,*' she orders Aiden, and I listen to him laugh heartily in response.

'Your daddy makes my heart sing, Bea,' I whisper to our little girl as I twist the little gummy engagement ring on my finger, admiring it, holding her close to my chest as I make my way upstairs in a giddy stupor.

NEW YEARS EVE 2020

6.22 PM

AIDEN

Seeing her dance around our kitchen without a care in the world as I held Bea in my arms was the moment, the perfect slice of heaven that had pushed me to get down on one knee without a second thought. I didn't want to wait anymore. I didn't want to spend another moment denying myself; I wanted her to know that although I couldn't promise her time, I could promise her everything that was within my power to give her, and I wanted nothing more than to make her my wife. I would declare that whatever time I had left belonged to her.

~~~~

I have spent the rest of the day pulling together the most impromptu wedding ever, and I have to admit, I am pretty damn proud of my efforts. It helps that I have been in love with my best friend since the moment we met all those years ago. Even though we were both either too idiotic or too blind to notice. I still at the thought; I hate that we could have spent all those years like this, and we hadn't, but hindsight is a bitch, and as it is something I can't change, I won't allow myself to dwell on it. The saying *life is too short* has never been as apt as it is in regards to our relationship.

The open French doors leading into the back garden are decorated with a wire archway filled with pink peonies and white roses. Trellises of the same flowers and lengths of faux vine leaves wrap around the wrought iron bannisters that flank either side of the stone steps that lead to the gravel path sprinkled with rose petals below. Six hours may have been a small window for pulling this off, but once I had told Casey of my plans, she was here within the hour to save the curry and help me prepare. Finding me hovering over the pan with an open sachet of artificial spice seasoning had her screaming at me huskily to walk away from the stove, and I was only too happy to oblige. Jenny was my next phone call, and she squealed when I proposed my plan, eager to help in any way she could. She has been amazing since Bea was born, and I know Roni would never forgive me if she wasn't here. The fairy-tale display of flower arranging is all thanks to Jenny. Prettying up anything is not my forte, and to make it perfect for Roni, I was happy to pass the torch and ask for help.

Putting the final touches to the wooden gazebo at the back of the garden, I wait tentatively for Roni to step out of the house. Casey throws me a thumbs up, which does nothing to settle my thumping heart as I crack my knuckles, shaking my hands and instantly calming as I hear Bea giggle in Jenny's arms. I purposefully kept the guests to the required two witnesses. I didn't want to have to share Roni with
~~~~

anyone else. We have never been ones for the fanfare, and, as with everything else in our lives, we would do this just the way we wanted, intimately promising to love one another for the rest of time.

'You've got this, my boy,' Paulie says gruffly from behind me as he stands stoically in place in a three-piece grey suit, looking like an overweight mobster rather than a man of the cloth. Along with the speech he downloaded from the internet in his pocket and the two cases of beer from the bar he gifted us, Paulie came prepared with the certificate proving he is now a fully-fledged, ordained wedding officiant. It's crazy the things you can get on the internet these days. Paulie is the closest thing I have to a father figure, and he jumped at the chance to be involved. Pride radiates from his chubby face as he lightly bonks me on the shoulder with his fist, a gesture that warms me as I blow out a steadying breath.

'Interesting choice of attire.' He chuckles, gesturing at my outfit. Like me, Roni had gone for one of her favourite memories, and I didn't decline because I had asked her to pick me something that made her smile. Standing, waiting proudly for my woman with the out-of-this-world sense of humour, I'm swathed in a pressed black shirt, a pair of dark denim jeans, black pointed boots, those infamous leather chaps and a black studded cowboy hat.

'If it makes her smile, it's worth it.' I guffaw. I would do practically anything to see the light blossom in her eyes.

Bea reaches out her stout little arms to me, flexing her fingers, urging me to take her. 'Dada,' she coos cutely. Before I can respond, a wave of blue in my peripheral pulls my attention away from my daughter, and my eyes go wide as I take in the beauty of my best friend, the woman soon to be my wife. Following my gaze, Bea settles and beams at her mother, standing on the concrete, admiring the flowers that frame her as she strolls down the stairs. Her lips tip up at the edges as fluttering harp music plays out of the speakers. 'Mama.' Bea coos. My heart skips in my chest as I try to work out when I got so bloody lucky to have this woman agree to be mine. She fights back the happy tears as she takes in her surroundings, waving excitedly at Casey and Jenny, her hands gripping the bouquet of white roses as she wanders down the pathway littered with petals. She tugs at the corners of the white lace veil so that it drapes over her shoulders, the gossamer material billowing in the wind as the spindly branches of the leafless trees above her seemingly dance along to the music. When I had told my mum of my plan to marry Roni, she didn't hesitate to send over the heirloom passed down to every woman in the O'Shea line going back four generations. If Paige ever decides to settle down, she'll be next in line. Roni's toothy grin is wide, her tear-filled eyes meeting mine as she mouths a *thank you*. I beam back at her, tears of my own threatening to fall as I drink in the glorious sight of her. The blue flowery dress hugs every curve of her body, her hips and boobs fuller since giving birth to Bea. I have to remind myself that we aren't alone as I clear my head of all the dirty things I want to do to this woman once she says *I do.* Throwing her over my shoulder caveman-style and taking her upstairs to ravish her will have to wait—for now.

When I catch sight of the white cowboy boots on her feet that I had brought her for her last birthday, I can't help but giggle as they crunch over the gravel. I don't need to read her mind to know she already misses the comfort of her *converse.* I search the lines on her face, needing to know if this is enough for her, to know if she would have preferred the big white wedding with all the bells and whistles. But all I see when I look at her is bliss, joy, and contentment. Screw normal standards. I love the crazy way we love each other. Soft chocolate curls fall down her back, one side pinned into place with an ornate pearl grip behind her ear, each tendril stroking against her bare skin that peeks through the cut-out in the dress that is hugging her curves. Rolling the twisted gold bangle on her wrist, Roni nods her thanks at Casey, who winks in return with a broad smile. She has everything she needs, her something old, my mother's veil—the hair slide from Paige, her something new. The bangle Casey has loaned her, her something borrowed, and the stunning dress that hugs her form that will forever hold my favourite memory, her something blue. It feels like an eternity has passed before she finally reaches me. My fingers itch to pull her into my body.

All I can see is her. It has always been just her.

The world around me melts away into a hazy blur of pink flowers, happy faces, and the twinkling white bulbs of the lights strung up in the tall trees as I lose myself in her gaze. The honey-ochre blanket of night warms her soft cheeks as dusk falls. The music stops, and Roni lets out a giggle, which pulls me from my reverie. I exhale for the first time in minutes as she lifts her palm to my cheek, holding it there, running her thumb over my skin and wiping away the tear that has escaped. 'Thank you,' she mumbles lovingly.

'Always my pleasure,' I say with conviction, my fingers twitching, desperate to grip her arms, pull her towards me and never let her go, to really show her in my own way how much she really means to me.

'You guys ready?' Paulie asks, stepping into place, breaking the moment, binding us and bringing us back to the present. Roni lowers her hand, taking mine in hers, and turns to face Paulie. Glancing over at me when she strategically tugs her bottom lip between her teeth. My head falls back as I try to calm the heat threatening to take my semi to a full on rocket ship ready for take off. She grins knowingly, pride brimming from her face when she steals a glance at my crotch.

'So, those crates of booze in the kitchen are your doing?' She chuckles, addressing Paulie. He merely nods with a crooked smile. I gulp down a knot of guilt at tying this woman to me without knowing the outcome of our future as a nervous breath hitches in her throat. But any speck of apprehension I might find in her expression doesn't last a moment longer as I take a step closer to her, my proximity calming her instantly as contentment tugs at her cheeks. This is what we need. Whatever we will face, we will conquer it together. As she pulls her bottom lip between her teeth again, this time without realising she's even doing it, I react, bouncing on my feet to cool the thrumming at my groin. I lean into her space so my mouth is inches from her face. I tuck a loose curl behind her ear, and her body shudders in response, her skin alight with a need for me as I let my fingers settle on her throat. A purr of satisfaction tumbles from her lips as the undercurrent of sexual tension feels heavy between us. She instinctively leans into my touch, and I have to keep at bay the rogue thoughts that could bring this wedding to a halt pretty fucking quickly if I don't shut them down now.

'Trying to seduce me is a dangerous play, Roni. I have no problems making everyone wait whilst I take you up them stairs and show you just how much it affects me when you bite that lip of yours,' I growl before taking a step back into position. With her eyes closed, Roni stumbles forward a little. A squeak of excitement bubbling up in her throat as she regains her composure. *Two can play at this game.*

I readjust my jeans and mentally berate myself for offering a visual of Roni bent over the banister wearing nothing but a smile because now I can't think of anything else. Roni moves to bite her lip again as she reads my heated expression, but she thinks better of it and smiles sweetly instead, stifling the chuckle fighting for freedom from her glossy full lips.

'Later, baby,' she promises with a wink, her craving for me filling her hooded electric blue gaze.

God, I love this woman.

Still not satisfied and, as always, greedy for more, I run my thumb over her cheek, eliciting a subdued groan from her lips that makes my cock twitch in my trousers. She doesn't miss the change in my heated expression, knowing me too well and recognising the point of no return.

'Down, boy,' I mumble quietly behind clenched teeth and clear my throat as Paulie turns to face us, a shabby brown leather notebook filled with illegible scribbles in his stubby hands. I hit Roni with a playful glare as she grins wickedly at me.

'We are gathered here today to *finally* celebrate the union between these two idiots who took their sweet old time, realising what everyone else around them already knew.'

'If I haven't said it before, Paulie, you have a magical way with words, man,' I quip, punching him in the arm in jest.

'Hey, you two are meant for each other. I knew it from the moment you both fell through the doors of my bar. How you feel about each other was as true then as it is now,' he states, his eyes watery as a thrum of emotion hits him. He sucks in a breath and collects himself, standing a little taller as he glances back down at the page.

'Roni.' Nodding in her direction, he prompts her to pull free the scrap of paper that I presume is her vows. Not a scrap, but a flyer from some event at the bar, Tequila Tuesday printed in a large text on the side facing me, a grainy black-and-white photo of me shirtless with the shot belt strapped to my chest below it.

'I like the inspiration,' I whisper.

'You shirtless has a multitude of uses,' she teases with a salacious grin. 'Now be quiet, Mr O'Shea. I have some nice things to say to you.'

'The floor is all yours, baby,' I croon, willing her to continue as I tighten my grip on her hand.

'Aiden, it has taken me far too long to realise just how much you mean to me. My only regret is the missed opportunities to have had what we do now earlier in our relationship. You make me whole on a level I didn't believe I deserved, and I might be partly to blame for that. You are the first person I think of when I wake up in the morning and the last face I see when I close my eyes at night. You are the centre of my world, the reason it continues to spin. I will forever be grateful that you chose me, that I was enough to be yours. You are an amazing father, partner and friend. Eternity isn't long enough, dipshit, but I'm thankful to be by your side for the journey, for always,' she lulls, wiping away the tear that has escaped as it rolls over her cheek.

'Only you could add dipshit to your vows and make it cute, baby.' I chortle, wiping away my own tears as my heart thumps wildly in my chest. I can't help falling in love with her all over again as she bares her heart to me.

'Aiden, can you top it?' Casey yells from her seat, pawing at her face with a tissue. I level her with my most charming grin and turn my gaze back to the woman who makes my soul sing. I pull my vows from a pocket, unfolding the paper so she can see how worn it is at each fold line. I have read and re-read it at least a hundred times. There are words crossed out with others in their place and scribbled notes in the margins where I ran out of space. But I still stuck with my original piece of paper, feeling like even with the mistakes, it was important to detail the thread of my thoughts, to show her how desperate I was to make sure it was perfect for her.

'Roni. There are not enough words in the world that will ever be able to express just how much you mean to me. My life doesn't make sense without you, baby.' I let out a rushed breath, covering it with a toothy smile as I try to dampen the piercing jolt of affection that feels like it has made my heart swell to twice its size in my chest. I will myself to pull it together and hold back the happy tears that threaten to spill from my eyes. I don't miss that Casey and Jenny grab their chests and sigh sweetly at my soppiness. I turn back to Roni and straighten to continue reading, looking down at the paper in my shaking hands even though I already know it word for word. 'You just being you is the greatest gift I could ever have hoped for, a gift I tried to ignore for so long. The thought of you not feeling the same forced me not to act on what I truly felt. All the wonderful memories I have are because of you, your light, your laughter, and your smile. I don't know what I did to deserve you, but I will not question it. Instead, I'll be thankful for it. I didn't think you could give me more than you, and then you gave me our beautiful Bea.' We turn in unison to beam at our little girl, who is excitedly clapping at us as she destroys her pink flowery dress tented with tulle with a half-eaten rusk biscuit in her hand. Moving closer to Roni, needing to feel her skin against mine, I cup her face.

'You are my everything, baby. I'll love you for always. I'll be with you for always. And when we're not together, I'll miss you for always,' I lull, my last sentence a whispered promise for her ears only as I run my finger over the temporary jelly ring on her finger.

My speech is her undoing as her body melts into my considerably larger frame. I snake my free arm around her waist, my fingers ruffling the material of her dress as my fingers dig into her hip. As though floating through the air in slow motion, I dip her back, her eyes lazily fluttering closed at the change in position. Holding onto her almost horizontal body with ease, I don't hesitate to take what's mine as my lips crash against hers for a bruising kiss. Her arms fly around my neck, her fingers delving into the hair at the nape of my neck and tugging, making me gasp into her mouth as she deepens the kiss and stokes the flames firing in my belly.

'I now pronounce you husband and wife. You may kiss the bride,' Pauli says quickly, although as I stand here suspended in the moment, lost in my woman, I barely even hear him. I pull my lips free from hers, appreciating her glossy blue gaze filled with lust as she hangs in my arms. I pull her into a standing position as she stumbles a little on her feet, grasping her waist to steady her as we turn to our guests.

'Let's get this fucking party started,' I holler, Paulie's cue to hit the play button on the remote for the sound system. *The Black-eyed Peas 'Let's Get it Started'* blares from the speakers flanking the other end of the pathway. As though I had planned it, rainbow bursts of fireworks whizz up through the air, colouring the now cloudless, faded navy sky with crackling rainbows. I watch on proudly as my stunning wife dances over to pick up our daughter, not caring that Bea's face and hands are coated in the remnants of one rusk too many. The love of my life, the woman who just agreed to be my wife, saunters back to me. We sway to the beat, our little world of three lost in bliss as I tip my head to the stars in thanks to whoever is watching over me.

Heart, body, or soul, whatever she wants from me, she can have it without contest. I'd raise hell and level the heavens for her, and I wouldn't need to think twice before doing it.

NEW YEARS EVE 2020

11.48 PM

RONI

Settled beneath my husband, I trace my finger over his lips, my thighs clenching as thoughts of him devouring me have me tugging at the collar of his shirt, my breasts now pressing against his chest. A familiar mix of his woodsy-scented aftershave, malty beer and desire linger in the air. The lit candles flickering on the windowsill cast shadows that dance across our skin and add a hint of jasmine to the unique mix of aromas. His silent pleas to open my legs to him make me shuffle a little in his hold. My jaw tightens as he lowers his face, languidly expelling a warm heavy breath along the column of my neck, teasingly just inches from my skin, goosebumps forming in its wake.

'What does my wife want?' he asks, but I don't need to respond. As always, he knows the answer to his question already. I think he likes how the word *wife* sounds, enjoying the taste of it on his tongue as it darts out to wet his lips.

'Please,' I beg, the breathy moan almost an unfinished word as my back arches, my skin desperate to have his lips worship me. He doesn't give in as he lifts his body away from mine. I mewl in response; my brows pinched in annoyance as the cold air licks at my exposed skin. His penetrating steel grey gaze finds mine, his sly grin wild with amusement. He is teasing me and enjoying every second of it as his length hardens between us. It seems I also don't need words to know what he wants. I bolster up an air of vulnerability that I know will crack him, pursing my lips playfully, my doe-eyes saucer-like as I commit to it, talking directly to the part of him that desires to give me everything I need exactly when I need it. I tug on the collar of his shirt again, more forcefully this time, pulling him towards me, fisting the material until I'm swathed in his scent. My full lips part and every little breath of mine mixes with his as he fights the pull, enjoying this little game of cat-and-mouse building between us.

'I love you, Mr O'Shea,' I cluck, my lungs emptying. I would happily drown in this moment with him, basking in the glow that his love gifts me until I'm raw and desperate for him to consume me. But I already have an orgasm waiting to be claimed, and as I buck up in his hold, I sense his composure slipping.

'I love you more, Mrs O'Shea.' His sentiment is a promise, not a promise of a forever, I note. He would never promise me something he couldn't be a hundred per cent sure he could give me, but it's a promise for right now, and that is good enough for me. I bite back the sadness lingering in my head—that little voice analysing the carefully worded promises Aiden had made in his vows. 'Mrs O'Shea suits you,' he beams, and one look at his chiselled face has me pushing away all the negativities threatening to ruin this moment. To have him submerged completely in the here and now with me is what I need, or what I need for now, at least.

Our promises don't need to look like everyone else's.

He tucks a curl of my hair behind my ear, his fingers lingering on my neck. He grins wildly, and in one swift motion, he has me straddling him, my knees digging into the comforter, his broad back pressing into the mattress, his legs slung over the edge of the bed. Even at this new angle, he holds all the cards. Tugging my thigh with one hand, the pads of his fingers dimpling my skin as he pulls it closer to his body. The palm of his other hand ghosts over the hollow of my throat, his fingers searching for a comfortable place to settle. Once happy with their new destination, his grip tightens, and my belly drops in response. Without realising it, I buck up in his hold, my back arching, daring him to squeeze harder. With his hands where they are, I am caged into his body, compressed, and held in place, unable to move backwards or forwards, much as I had been when lying beneath him. My inner siren wails her approval as warmth permeates my core, my stomach in knots. I'm a slave to the anticipation of what this man will do to me.

'Want to show me how much you love me?' I purr into his ear. I cover his body with mine and nip at his earlobe when his hold on my throat slackens slightly. His hand skates up my side and works deftly to unbutton the back of my baby blue summer dress. Locking my ankles in place with the underside of his knees on the edge of the bed, he begins to gradually widen the space between them, pushing out his thighs until my stretched muscles burn. I move without contest to accommodate his widening hips, just the more of him to appreciate. He shows no signs of stopping the delicious torture, and when I've reached my limit, my torso flies back, so I'm sitting up on him, my freshly painted fingernails digging into his skin through his shirt. I can sense him fighting the urge to rip the clothes from my body as he sees my breasts fighting to break free in my low-cut dress, but it has too much sentimental value to him. Each connection he makes with my exposed skin stirs that familiar lightning strike to hit at the apex of my thighs. I tilt my head as he moves to sit up and meet me, exposing my neck to his mouth, urging him to push our limits until I'm spent and fulfilled under his skilled touch. Pulling me down to lie on top of him, he snakes a hand down my torso, skimming past my belly button until his fingers reach the flimsy lace covering my wet folds. Even before he applies any pressure, the thought of him exploring me there has me panting, his lips dancing up my neck as I grip the pillow beneath his head. His hips rock up to meet mine lazily, a sweet, surprising gasp falling from my lips as he trails his finger over my centre, the rough denim of his jeans scraping against my bare thighs.

I groan into his mouth when his fingers glide over my sensitive bud of nerves, eliciting a feral hum of excitement from him. He works to unbutton my dress a little faster, his grey-blue stare wide with craving. They quickly dip to half-mast as I shift my body across his lap, taking what I want by force as I press myself against his hand between my legs. His fingers working apart the buttons on my dress, momentarily still in their journey down my spine as my move affects him. His taught length pushes against his jeans, annoyed that it hasn't already been invited to join our little friction party. His pupils dilate as my partially open dress falls down my front, exposing my pert breasts bundled up in a cream lace bustier.

'If this has buttons, I think I might cry.' He guffaws. I laugh in response to his adorably cute face as the need to have me naked has his brows raised. I pull my bottom lip between my teeth, eliciting a stifled moan from my husband, a throaty roar to follow as he raises his hips to meet my centre, the contact almost excruciating as the need to rip his clothes from his body hits me. I have zero issues tearing his shirt into scraps. The sentimental value is of no consequence to me; the desire to be sweaty beneath him is the only thought that rings out clearly in my head now.

'Excited Mr O'Shea?'

'Just a tad, Mrs O'Shea.' He bucks his taut hips forward, his cock rocking against the layers of material against my absurdly expensive lace underwear. Any thoughts of the if, buts or maybes of what our future may hold are finally in our rear-view mirror, every dirty moan a blissful soundtrack to our union. Aiden tugs down my dress, freeing my arms, and something between us shifts as his gaze darkens. All bets are off now. We are no longer playing nice; incessant beats of savage need ring like a clock tower bell beneath my husbands' expression, each thwack in time to his pounding heart. I couldn't stop him now, even if I wanted to. He tugs at my hair at the root, the slice of pain in my scalp egging on the thrum of electricity lazily beating low in my belly as his tongue darts out to taste my lips. My eyelashes flutter closed when his fingers skim the elastic of my thong settled high on my hips, tracing invisible circles into my skin, my body is practically levitating on his lap as it cries out for more. More pressure, more speed, I don't know what it needs exactly, but it for sure wants MORE of whatever it is.

He pulls his fingers away, and that is my undoing. I can't wait a moment longer. I rip at his clothing haphazardly, regardless of the damage. Buttons pinging in all directions. *Fuck it.* Laid out beneath me is my Adonis husband, half-naked, a levity illuminating his features as his eyes find mine. Completely transfixed, hypnotised by his beauty, I lose my balance, sliding off the bed and hitting the floor with a thump. I can't hold back the laughter as Aiden's cheeky face appears over the edge of the mattress, his hair a tousled mess, a roguish toothy smile gracing his lips, a brow cocked.

'Five-second rule.' He chuckles as he joins me on the floor, his words a roar of potential. Lifting the skirt of my dress currently bunched around my waist, he watches me intently as he lowers his head, splashes of his hot breath hitting my bare thighs between my legs, his mouth ghosts over my lacy underwear, even without contact he has stoked a thrumming pleasure to crackle at my core. Unable to hold back a moment longer as I writhe in his hold he nips and licks at the material, I howl in laughter, my thighs pinning his face as his hands run up and down my torso, rough hands splayed across my stomach to hold me in place when I buck away from his mouth. As he gets comfortable, my laughing stops. Every subtle touch his mouth makes against my skin is almost too much for my oversensitive body. He nips at the inside of my thigh, which has my breath hitching, my glassy blue eyes fighting to watch him—silently pleading with him to continue whilst begging him to stop. My head lolls back in response to the harsh laps of his tongue against the delicate fabric covering my opening. It's as though this is his reason for being as he feasts on every drop of my essence that he can work from my body. He locks his forearms around my thighs and yanks me to him, a small smile playing on his lips as he devours me. Before I can give in to the already blossoming orgasm, relishing as he pins me to the ground, he has me up and back onto the bed in one smooth movement. His angular jaw tense as he licks remnants of my pre-cum from his lips. Slapping my backside for good measure as I groan my displeasure at the sudden change in position.

'Aiden,' I whimper.

'All good things come to those who wait, baby,' His tone is dark and rough as his thighs nudge apart mine, an order I happily follow without a second thought. He could want me upside down with an apple in my mouth, and I wouldn't refuse him.

All good things come to those who wait, I repeat in my head, unable to quieten the spasms of pleasure as he rocks the heel of his hand between my legs.

God, this man is everything. Drunk with yearning, I rake my gaze greedily up and down his body, each muscle corded and defined as he supports himself on one arm, hovering over me.

'I need to be in you now,' he murmurs in my ear, moving to rid me of everything but my thong and stockings, my dress pulled up over my head, floating whimsically to the floor as the heat of arousal permeates the air between our bodies. He tears the corset from me without a second thought as he tugs frantically at the satin ribbon securing it to me. Aiden's blue-grey eyes lighten, sparkling flecks of amber surfacing as he gazes appreciatively down at my body. My choice of expensive white lace was obviously the right way to go. I am by no means virginal, but there is a sense of irony to wearing white that I knew he would appreciate.

'You like?' I coo playfully, securing my bottom lip between my teeth as he drinks me in. Knowing it will drive him crazy. He clears his throat, adjusting himself through his jeans, a glow of excitement heating his skin. It doesn't matter how often he has seen me this way, I never tire of seeing that faraway *'fuck I'm lucky'* glint in his gaze when he has me like this.

'You'll do, I guess,' he teases. Before I know what is happening, he pulls my thong aside and plunges two fingers into me without warning. Stretching the internal walls of my slick core, each thrust causing my back to arch as I writhe in response to his skilful touch. He expertly works my release from me, further heightening the languid pulse in my belly as he rubs his thumb over my sweet spot in determined circles. I scream his name as my legs shake, his free hand gripping tightly across my belly to keep me in place whilst he continues working into me softly, bringing me back down to earth. As the peak of my orgasm fades, I slump down onto the bed as flicks of electricity whizz up my spine, my orgasm refusing to settle completely as a hum of sensation still vibrates at the apex of my thighs. Those expert fingers that a moment ago were driving unremittingly inside me are now running over his lips and into his mouth. Aiden knows my body better than I do, and my hips roll, the dull ache at my core pulsing back to life as I watch him, my eyes hooded, my hands gripping onto his bare tattooed chest. I dig my fingernails into his shoulders as I gyrate my core against the bulge still confined to his trousers as he moves to cover my body with his.

'You want more, baby?'

'Always.' A hushed promise flickers between us as his tongue darts out to taste the remnants of me still coating his lips. He rolls us over, so my small frame sits on him again. Although considerably smaller than my husband, I love the power this position gives me. I rise on my knees, pushing forward up his body to plant a small kiss on the corner of his mouth teasingly, my gaze never leaving his. Once I'm sure his attention is fixed solidly on me, I roll back roughly against the bulge in his trousers, returning to my position, hovering over his body, my lips inches from his, the movement almost fluid. I crave everything this man does to me, the way he makes my soul sing. Aiden O'Shea is my addiction.

'I can help you with that,' I say sweetly, playfully, as I slam my body down onto him again. He rewards me with a flash of unbridled delight on his face, his taut jaw begging me to do it again. I do as he requests and provoke a gravelly moan from him that I have been hoping for as I repeat my move.

'I can't wait anymore,' he barks. Aiden lifts me onto the edge of the bed and flips me over onto my knees. He doesn't hesitate to pull my minuscule white lace thong down over my backside, skimming my creamy peach skin with his knuckles as he goes. He taps each stocking-clad thigh, and I raise each knee so he can remove the material already soaked in my release. His palm traces painfully slowly from my neck to the hollow at the base of my spine. My back arches into his touch, revelling as the pads of his fingers trace hidden lines across my skin, delicious tremors flooding my every sense as my body screams for more.

'Aiden!' I cry out, his name slightly muffled, as I push my face into the sheets. 'I need you.' I'm begging now, and he doesn't hesitate to give me what I want. I hear him lower the zipper of his jeans, and he jumps off the bed before smacking the still-pink flesh of my arse cheek with his palm again. I rock forward, enamoured as the sting of pain melts away, leaving carnal want in its wake. I don't dare move an inch, knowing that Aiden is stripping out of his clothes behind me. As he gets back into position, I feel the bed shift under his weight.

Lowering his full weight over my back, bracing his arms on either side of my head, his mouth dips down to my ear. 'Good girl.' I could come again with just those two words. This is my reward for staying in position whilst he undressed, and boy is it worth it. As he moves to resume his position, cold air splashes against my exposed back. I grip at the sheets until my knuckles are white, waiting for my husband to fill me to the hilt. He answers my wish and slams into me. Each thrust determined and unguarded as another orgasm awakens in me, thrumming beneath the surface, waiting for this beautiful man to draw it out. 'I – fucking - love – you.' Each syllable is a declaration of its own, every word matched to a hard thrust of his hips. With one hand angling my waist so he can enter me without restriction, he circles his hips on each drive forward, hitting the deepest part inside me. His other hand works its way up to my neck, pushing me down and holding me in place. Every plunge forward he makes delectably rampant, as he doesn't hold back. Feeling my pleasure tip the edge of no return, I reach my hand down, dragging my index finger down my centre as he continues to rock inside me. I massage my sweet spot, not as softly as he would, as my core pulses, my head swimming, everything around me other than him hazy.

'Roni, I need to see you.' He pulls himself out of me and flips me over, so my back is flush with the bed. I don't have time to miss him being inside me as he resumes the task and powers forward, his length hitting inside me even deeper in this position. His sweaty brow connects with mine as he dips down to my face, his eyes clenched shut as the fire of his release builds at the base of his spine, his lips thrash against mine, our tongues warring, a beautiful orchestra of nips, licks, and bruising kisses.

'You are my all,' I say as I grip his muscled shoulders for traction as he pushes me further up the bed with every unrelenting drive forward of his hips. 'Don't stop,' I cry out.

'Never, baby,' he soothes, his pace and power not altering an inch as he continues to plough on. My foggy brain is heavy. My head lolls and falls back onto the pillow. 'Look at me,' he barks, and he doesn't have to tell me twice. 'I want to see the fire light in your eyes when you tip over that edge. I want to see what I do to this beautiful body when you finally relent.' Sensing that we are both on the verge of exploding, I chew frantically on my bottom lip as my legs tense. Aiden, detecting how fast my orgasm is approaching, quickens his pace, and my walls grip him. The feeling of him climbing inside me, our bodies becoming one, makes me feel like I'm floating. I tug desperately at his hair, keeping his face glued to mine as we pant open-mouthed against one another, our expressions contorted as our bodies attempt to level themselves through the heady confusion of everything we are experiencing. I happily drown in this moment, appreciating Aiden's taut, stubbled jawline, his mess of curly brown hair falling over his brow, and the dimples donning his cheeks as he strains and pounds forward, searching for our collective release.

'Aiden,' I scream against his lips as white spots form in my eyes and a welcomed rush of pleasure sweeps through me.

'Baby,' he responds gruffly against my lips as though it is a command, his fingers gripping the flesh of my arse as he pulls me down to meet every rock of his hips, a sybaritic mixture of pleasure and pain making my head swim. He rockets into me three more times as we both give in to the pleasure, climaxing loudly as every nerve in my body sings, my heart beating frantically against my ribs. A fiery heat warms my blood, and I throw my head back, severing our kiss. My body caves to the sensations this man evokes in me. For what seems like the longest time, we linger in the moment without uttering a word, the noise of our satisfied ragged breaths the only thing between us. Dipping his head, he rubs his nose against mine, his fingers dancing over my features. Pure adulation, a welcomed expression on his handsome face, his taut angled jaw with a dusting of stubble rubbing against my cheek as he claims me, as much with his softness as he does with his passion. He drops beside me and pulls me into his arms as we try to settle. My hysterical heartbeat pounds in my ears as the room around me slips back into focus. Aiden dots feather light kisses over my face and mouth. I relish everything this man does to me: the strength and the gentleness, the powerhouse and the romantic, the sad and the happy. I mould into his body, wrapping an arm and leg across him, staking my claim, my face flush with his tattooed chest as our heartbeats fall in sync with each laboured breath.

When soft wisps of satedness fall from his full lips, his arms heavy around my waist, when I know he is finally asleep, I cry, shifting up his body, so we are face to face. I sob inaudibly, running my fingers through his short crop of brown curls. I gently push them off his face so as not to wake him to get a good look at him. I want to recall every line and dip of my best friend's face. I don't want to live without this man, and the nagging realisation that I don't have a say in the matter fills me with fear. Although he is here, living and breathing, his balmy tattooed skin beneath my palm, it is quiet moments like these, when I'm left unsupervised at the mercy of my mind, that I realise we could have forty years together like this. But we could also have only four years. I don't know our fate; I have no idea what is in store for us.

'I love you, Aiden, more than you will ever know. I promise to keep loving you, for always,' I whisper into the crook of his neck. The darkness is swallowing his form now as I fight back, yet more tears, haunted by thoughts of an existence without him. Tucked into his side, smothered with a settling warmth, I welcome sleep as my heavy lids finally succumb to my exhaustion.

JANUARY 14th 2021

14 DAYS LATER

RONI

'Hello, husband,' I fuss, running my fingers through his shaggy brown hair. He dips his head to kiss me as I sit at the kitchen table. The eggs benedict on the plate in his hand hits the table with a bang as I deepen the kiss with a lap or two of my tongue. An invisible symbiotic bond joins us as electricity fizzles in the air, taking him by surprise as he stumbles a little into my hold.

'Hey, hey, wife,' he answers breathily when I reluctantly pull my lips from his. I love how much I affect him. That almost live-wire jolt of fervour in his hooded gaze feeds my addiction. His body sways, and I giggle as I pull him down for another chaste kiss, each one magically feeling like the first.

'God, you do crazy things to me, baby,' he hums, his twitching length rubbing against my shoulder as he stands at my side. The feral need to clear the kitchen table until the contents are shattering on the floor around my feet and take him here and now is practically vibrating in my veins, but with little eyes in the room, it will have to wait.

'Rain check, dipshit,' I coo, cheekily rotating my shoulders against his trousers to tease him. A growl breaks free from his full lips, making me swoon, his fingers twitching as my body calls out to him.

'When is Bea's naptime again?' A roguish grin is on his face as he winds a curl of my hair around his fingers, tugging it so my head snaps back. I internalise the *fuck* that wants to barrel out of my mouth in response as he teases me with rubs and tugs against my scalp. He knows exactly what he is doing to me and grins wickedly. I don't fight it. I enjoy the sensations he pulls from my body too much, every inch of my being a slave to him in moments like these.

'Not soon enough,' I say softly, a guarantee of *later* hidden in my tone. His face is now inches from mine, the heat of his minty breath fanning my cheek. Inhaling the air feels arduous as my heart swells for him. He knows what he is doing to me, yet he doesn't move. Crossing my legs, I try to calm the thrum of excitement pulsing at my core, but all the move does is remind me of the sensitive bundle of nerves throbbing at the apex of my thighs. My skin itches to be swathed in only him.

'Adulting sucks,' he states with a cocky smile, pulling me closer for another kiss. It manages to sate the liquid fire pooling in my belly, but only briefly. When Bea gurgles her excitement as another light flashes pink above her on the rocker, the spell between her father and me breaks. I'm forced to put a pin in fantasies of having him pole-drive me without abandon into next week—until nap time. 'Okay, maybe it doesn't suck,' he beams as he watches Bea, all pent-up sexual tension gone, replaced with loving devotion for his daughter. This little miss will have her daddy wrapped around her finger one day. Who am I kidding? He's already smitten. He'd feed her ice cream for every meal if she asked. We will hit dangerous territory once she starts talking. She's already mastered the head tilt, doe-eye, lip tremble combo. That's how she is currently on her third rusk biscuit of the morning.

'I need you to sign this,' Aiden says whilst pushing clipped papers to my side on the tabletop as I cut into my breakfast. He sits down next to me, and it takes a couple of seconds for his words to register.

'Wanting me to sign my soul over to the devil so quickly after our wedding, Aiden. What did I do to deserve you?' I quip, shoving a forkful of food into my mouth and chewing hungrily as my belly grumbles at the offering. The multiple sex sessions last night with my husband roused a healthy appetite. 'What is it?' I question when he doesn't respond, a flicker of concern heavy in my voice.

'My will.' He holds his hands up to silence me, sensing I am ready to spit out my food and protest.

'Whatever way you look at it, we should do this. I will also sign. This is a joint policy. If anything happens to you or me, I want to know that Bea is safe and cared for,' he says with an air of finality, and although I want to argue, I can't contend with his reasoning. The news of the doctor giving Aiden the all-clear from the dreaded big C rings in my head, and it's enough to settle me. Whatever way I look at it, he is right. If our journey has taught us anything, life can be unexpected. I notice the two suggested guardians for Bea are Casey, whose interests are limited to seducing women over thirty and anime comics, and his sister Paige, whose interests are limited to men with facial hair who don't live with their mothers and cocktails with inappropriate names.

'They would offer an interesting upbringing.' He smirks. Chuckling to myself, I turn to the last page and scrawl my name with the pen I whipped from Aiden's fingers. If we are on the same page about who would care for our little girl when we are gone, then I'm sure we agree on everything else. Aiden knows me inside and out, and I trust his decisions wholeheartedly. I don't even need to read the rest of the document in front of me.

'Should we pre-warn Casey or Paige of our decision?' I ask lightly, knowing my husband enough to expect his answer.

'Fuck no. This way is more fun. Close your eyes and imagine them finding out.' I do as he has instructed and smile broadly at the thought of some social worker turning up on their doorstep with all the stuff needed to look after a baby. It may, on some level, be cruel to laugh about, morbid almost, but both women are more than capable, so I feel it is okay to find this scenario hilarious. Imagining how differently our little princess would grow up under the tutelage of each woman.

'So, how's the hip?' I ask, pushing another lump of food between my lips to mask my concern.

Even though his injury is thanks to a midnight fumble with our wardrobe, worry seems to follow me at every turn of late. Where Aiden's health is concerned, each dip or lull he comes across feels like a fresh punch to my gut, a bitter darkness looming over us until it passes. Which it does, but that doesn't settle me any. The poor guy can't even sneeze without me jumping into preservation mode armed with jugs of honey and lemon and demands of bedrest. I let the rumble of concern pass, resolute to enjoy such a beautiful morning, even with an uncertain future looming over us as it always did.

'Not great but bearable,' he lulls, clipped but almost poetic as he placates me, his face alight with positivity, his words dripping with happiness. He shakes a bottle of medication, depositing two painkillers into his palm. The rattle of the tablets against the plastic makes Bea squeal. This dosage has become a regular occurrence and although the choice between needing paracetamol and chemo is easy, that he *needs* anything to function doesn't settle well with me.

'We need that follow-up. You shouldn't be bruising that easily. If you won't call them, I will.' I'm careful not to sound imposing, pushing his plate towards him and urging him to at least attempt a bite or two. We had been told that lingering aftereffects of the intensive chemo treatment are likely, but it doesn't hurt to make sure, if for nothing other than my peace of mind.

'On it, baby.' His smile softens me almost immediately, as it usually does, his little superpower that makes my knees weak and my heart beat a little out of rhythm. Saluting me with two fingers on his forehead like I am his first in command, he kisses my head before moving to the sink for a glass of water. I don't miss the flinch as he moves, his hand gripping his side as he tries to silence the pain without me noticing. I'll never understand why men fight the need to talk to a health professional when they clearly need to.

'What have you been feeding this one?' Aiden laughs as he pulls Bea from her sea-creature-themed rocker. She fusses in his hold, desperate to get back to her mini light show, the whimsical styling of some old nursery rhyme a little morphed, signalling the need for new batteries. Aiden ignores her bird-like whines, planting little kisses along her cheek and calming her instantly. I am convinced he has a magic touch. The second their skin meets, it's as though a sense of calm blankets her, an unsung song he recites telepathically to her that has her cooing up at him as she paws affectionately at his stubbled face.

'The kid appreciates a boob.' I chuckle as my breasts ache in response, signalling Bea's next feed is due.

'Don't we all,' he quips cheekily, rubbing the tip of his nose on Bea's as she wriggles in his hold, her giggle hearty and full. It takes a moment for her to register the mention of the word boob, but when she does Bea grumbles hungrily and my body responds to her, milk soaking through my vest top.

'I'm going to post these, baby.' Aiden lowers Bea into my arms, planting a soft kiss on her forehead, dipping to worship my lips. When he breaks away from me, I let out a stifled sigh, dreamily remembering what those lips had done to me this morning as the light of dawn crept through our curtains, a knot of craving low in my belly makes me shudder, and Aiden doesn't miss my reaction. He lowers his mouth to hover near my ear, his warm breath caressing my neck.

'What are you thinking about, dirty bird?' He knows exactly what I am thinking about but plays coy, an air of slick satisfaction playing across his full lips. 'All in good time,' he promises, laying a kiss in the hollow below my ear. I fiddle with the curls at the nape of his neck, tugging at them and eliciting a groan, an insight of what's to come for him to ponder. I watch as he moves across the room to pull on his trainers, hating seeing him leave but enjoying the view of his backside all the same. His coat is already on his back as he trudges over to scoop up the stuffed envelope and his backpack from the table. He seizes an apple out of the fruit bowl and rubs it down the front of his sweater before taking a large bite. I eye him warily, a surge of that motherly instinct I have become so familiar with now squarely directed at my husband.

'Breakfast,' he states, holding out the fruit to me.

'Breakfast.' I tut in response, motioning towards his plate of untouched eggs.

'I'll grab something while I'm out.' And here is his magic again: that sing-song voice, that broad smile, and those penetrating warm blue-grey eyes immediately pacify me—these powers of his know no limits.

'You know that's unfair. How will I ever win an argument with you channelling your *inner Professor X*?' My heart squeezes as a boyish grin creeps across his face—the mere mention of superheroes stirring to life the nerdy fourteen-year-old Aiden persona obsessed with comics.

'Unfair maybe, but you love me regardless.' He takes another bite of the apple and moves towards the doorway, his smile unmoving.

'Can you pick up some date night essentials?' I ask sweetly whilst manoeuvring Bea into a comfortable position as she latches onto my nipple.

'Whiskey?'

'You got it.' I titter. He nods in response, and I blow him a kiss, which he catches theatrically and slaps against his cheek. A rumble of laughter barrels up my throat in response, making Bea laugh.

'See you soon, girls,' Aiden yells from the hallway before the front door slams shut behind him.

~~~~

The sun settles in the sky, a warm golden glow splaying through the back windows and painting every surface of our kitchen. Fresh from my soak in the bath, I shuffle into the room in a pair of silky sleep shorts and one of Aiden's oversized jumpers that drowns my slight frame. The room is quiet, almost too quiet, the soft chimes of one of Bea's toys echoing from the living room. Sundays have a set routine, one we never deviate from. I grab a pack of streaky bacon from the fridge and turn to heat a pan on the stove.

'Thank you, baby,' I yell affectionately to Aiden, coining his pet name for me when I see the stack of already cut and buttered bread on the side. Once the bacon is ready just the way we like it—burnt to a crisp, edges disintegrating to ash when I pull them from the pan—I pile the fatty pieces of meat and make four sandwiches. I coat each slice with more ketchup than is probably necessary and slice each sandwich in half, helping myself to any pieces of charred goodness that fall free from the bread. Sundays are my favourite day of the week when I can relish in the home comforts of Aiden and Bea with zero distractions,
~~~~

when life feels subdued and easy, and when we can enjoy ... time.

With his will posted, his prescription filled, and an online doctor's appointment arranged for early Tuesday morning, Aiden has fulfilled his chores. I ignore the larger dose of painkillers he swallows down at lunchtime and revel in his spritely mood as he spends the rest of the afternoon devouring my homemade vegetable soup and playing with Bea. There is not a modicum of pain in sight, and everything feels content as I lose myself in the beauty of our little unit of three.

Our date night playlist begins humming through the speakers, and I dance around as I return all the ingredients to their rightful place in the kitchen. Using my phone, I turn the music down a few notches as I see the sun sink out of view behind the rooftops, navy streaks smothering out the fading orange glow in a matter of seconds as the night descends. If she isn't already, Bea will surely be asleep soon, and the chime of the grandfather clock in the hallway affirms my assumptions. Bea likes a routine, boob, bath, book, and bed.

Shimmying to the fridge with the butter in hand, I sing along quietly to the indie track playing, miming each high soprano note with only half of my usual enthusiasm, my inner diva holding back her potential. Attempting to challenge my already limited range isn't worth waking a sleeping Bea. If her routine is interrupted, little miss grumpy sunshine will inevitably fight sleep into the wee hours, and Aiden and I have a date night to get to. Even though Bea is always asleep during our date nights, Aiden insists we settle her in the hallway just outside the wardrobe room. He wants her to be a part of each one; it is a tradition he told me we would pass down to her, and the idea of creating memories for her felt almost essential with everything we have been through. I push against the fridge door with my sock-clad foot to close it. I can't help but chuckle. Scrawled on the whiteboard is a message from Aiden.

I don't know what I did in a previous life to deserve you, baby. P.S.

Hurry up with that bacon. He finishes his little love note with a smiley face, leaving enough space below for me to write a response as he always does. Notes are our thing, and I treasure them. Snapping a photo of each one he leaves so I will never forget them. Sometimes they are silly, sometimes sexy, and sometimes downright hilarious; a *yo momma* joke going a long way to lighten our dark days.

Clearly, something amazing, you lucky boy! Love you, Dipshit. I finish my note with a little love heart and, happy with my response, I replace the marker and move back towards the cooker. On the chopping board to my side, I find the two plastic beakers filled with two shots of whiskey with a splash of ginger ale, Aiden's signature date night drink. My eyebrows pinch together when I notice the ice has melted, as the liquor is paler than usual. I add another splash of the whiskey to each, load them and the sandwiches onto the round metal tray, and make my way to our wardrobe space.

I stand at the entrance to our special place, admiring a peaceful Bea as she sleeps in her car seat at the threshold as soft angelic wisps of slumber fall from her tiny lips. Her long lashes flutter against her full apple cheeks as she wanders around dreamland without a care in the world.

'Baby, where's your phone?' I whisper to Aiden behind me, the tray teetering on one arm as I outstretch the other to him. The urge to document every moment of cuteness with Bea has my phone's memory dwindling, but I can't say it isn't worth it. My womb jolts as broodiness smothers my senses, my belly in knots, that familiar hum of need to take our unit of three to a team of four, an idea Aiden and I have been toying with, practising for it is certainly a fun way to pass the time. I glance at my husband, laid out on the floorboards, his arm slung over his eyes, his chest bare, wearing only a pair of basketball shorts. I snort, knowing he hasn't played a basketball game in his life, reasoning that Rugby was more his thing. I haven't realised yet that my brain has started a banal conversation with itself as a means of protection—a distraction of sorts, the inner ramblings a tell-tale sign that my fight-or-flight mode has been activated.

'Aiden.' I chuckle his name, although it lacks all humour. I gently swipe my foot against his but get no response. His leg is limp. I shuffle a little further into the space, putting the tray down and grabbing for a pillow from off the rack above my head.

'There is no way anyone can be comfortable in that position, baby.' I sniff back the hot tears pricking my eyes, confusion making me laugh and cry in the same breath as a sickening wave of reality dawns on me.

JANUARY 28th 2021

<u>14 DAYS LATER</u>

RONI

Within fourteen days of the happiest day of my life, I had died, but no one knew it. No one knew it because I wasn't the one in the coffin. That darkness had been reserved for my husband.

Glancing down at Bea sleeping in her swing chair, I push myself to apply concealer under my eyes, attempting and failing to disguise the lack of sleep and continuous fits of blubbering that have left my face puffy and almost unrecognisable. The world feels like it has stilled. The stars no longer shine as bright, the grass is a muddy green, and the bird's morning tweets are hollow, haunting almost. A light rattling knock at the front door tears me from my thoughts, the bottle of liquid concealer upending on the rug as I jump to my feet. I make my way out into the hallway swiftly before the visitor can knock again and wake up Bea. The effort it takes just to reach the door has my legs aching and my calf muscles protesting at the rapid change in pace. Since Aiden died, I have done little other than sleep and cry; my inability to walk properly is the result of that.

But what is the point in it all, anyway? Why is it fair that I am here and he isn't?

'Delivery for Mrs O'Shea,' a young man, russet hair tucked beneath a bright orange cap, chirps softly. He wears a broad grin on his pimpled face and carries the package in question tucked under his arm as he ticks my name off his list on a clipboard. I wince at the use of my married name. Locking myself away and having Casey look after Bea means I haven't spoken to another living soul since Aiden's body was taken away. Ignoring any attempts at communication from the outside world.

'Delivery for Mrs O'Shea,' the young man repeats, concern heavy in his deep brown gaze as he tries to read my expression. Panic that he has got the wrong address, making his brows pinch as he rechecks *our* door number. *My* door number, I correct myself silently, pushing aside the twinge of pain that bubbles up my throat.

'Yes,' I croak finally. It is at this moment I realise not only had I not spoken to anyone for the past week, silently existing when I saw Casey and Bea, but I also haven't spoken aloud to myself. Instead, fighting silently with my torturous inner monologue of what ifs and maybes and shaming myself with blame. He hands me the package as dryness licks at my throat, and I nod as a way of thanks. Pushing my way back into the house, I shut the door before he's even reached the gate at the end of the stone pathway. Everything beyond my front door feels terrifying, as though leaving *our* space means leaving him behind, as if doing so will mean I will forget him.

My space. My brain reminds me unhelpfully. For an inner voice devoid of presence, it sure has a way of intruding when it wants to.

Sliding down the door, I fall in a heap on the mat, the rectangular parcel wrapped with string sitting in my lap. Noticing the handwriting of my name scribbled across the front and the little smiley face drawn in marker in the corner makes my heart swell uncomfortably. My stomach sinks with a thud as I brush yet another tear from my cheek. Using my teeth to untie the string, I pull frantically at the brown paper, careful not to tear the writing on the front. My hands fumble with the lid, and as I pull it free, it's suddenly impossible to stop the flood of tears. Its contents are my undoing.

Written in black biro on a white card is, *A pinkie promise is unbreakable, baby.* Before I can read the rest of the message, I launch the box across the hallway, folding my body in on itself, my malnourished frame unable to bring me the warmth or comfort I desperately need as I wrap my arms around my waist and quietly sob. I stay here on the cold tiles for what seems like forever, only stumbling to my feet when I hear the soft hungry cries of Bea coming from the living room. I drag myself on unsteady legs, my head pounding as I wipe furiously at my eyes, my skin so tender it feels like I'm tearing it. I stagger up the stairs with Bea cradled in my arms, desperate for the comfort of a duvet to swaddle us in, bypassing the spare room and heading for *our* main bedroom.

My main bedroom. My brain adds, and my heart sinks at the reminder.

I pull back the cover and slink down onto the mattress, Aiden's scent filling my lungs as I take in a long breath, welcoming the burn in my throat as I fight against the instinct to cease and breathe out. I want the world to stop, for everything to blur like oil on water as I forget my heartache, an almost heady high sating me briefly as the weight of my new life hits me. But having Bea's little body beside mine drags me from the edge of destruction. It's the main reason Casey insisted Bea come home. She knew I needed a part of him with me. As I have done every night since my true love left us, I cry myself to sleep, heart-wrenching sobs that never solve the problem but merely distract me from it. Cradled to my chest, our daughter's warmth and soapy scent light the wick of calm I need to resist the urge to burn it all to the ground and end my suffering. She will be the one to save me; she will be the one to pull me back from the darkness, to piece back together the broken parts of me. The house feels cold; the love and laughter that his presence kindled in its ashes are now gone forever. But with her, a part of him will remain, at least. The first thirty seconds or so when I wake every morning are the hardest to deal with. For that half a minute, my thoughts are cloudy with sleep, the weight of dreams and confusion blurring the lines between worlds; for that short time, he is still with me, and all is okay. I don't falter when caressing his hair or stroking his stubbled cheek; my slim legs wrap around his broad ones. Any offering of comfort is a moment I would happily steal and stow away. I both pray for and fear these moments, a mixture of happiness and sadness as I envisage his face resting on the pillow next to me. I fight the truth with everything I have, realising that what I have in retrospect is nothing.

Losing myself was hard. Losing him was harder.

FEBRUARY 4TH 2021

7 DAYS LATER

RONI

A *pinkie promise is unbreakable.* I chuckle around a sob as tears stream down my face. Every inhale laborious as a crushing weight settles on my chest. I no longer feel compelled to throw the parcel across the room and instead continue reading the note. *In this lifetime and the next baby, I am yours, for always. Aiden.* I toss my head back, beaming, clasping the card to my chest as though I can feel where he had touched it. Opening my eyes and wiping away the streaks of fallen tears, I rest the card against the turquoise stone embellished frame on the mantlepiece that holds a picture of Aiden, Bea and me from our wedding day. Running my finger along the weathered natural wood, I come to the last gift my husband gave me before he died. Our gummy rings he had proposed with that day in our kitchen sit in a multicoloured resin cube beside our photo, the date of his unconventional proposal scrawled in gold paint on the base. Casey walks through the living room door with Bea in her arms. The sombre black pencil dress that Casey wears doesn't suit her personality; the velvet black puffball dress with the white lace collar that Bea is wearing is just as unsettling. Even for a day like today, their outfits seem to snuff out their naturally bright auras in the worst of ways.

Clothes, Roni? You're thinking about that right now? I have to mentally regroup as my brain fights to busy itself with anything other than the real reason my daughter is wearing black and sporting a forlorn expression. Even at her age, *our* little empath can sense the sadness in the room. I'm grateful for Casey's interruption before my traitorous brain can attack my use of the word *our*.

'We ready?' Casey clucks, that pitying head tilt of hers doing nothing to lift my spirits. The realisation hits that it's something I should get used to, as I'm sure it won't be the last time I see it today. There is a whole church full of people waiting to console me, after all. Casey bounces a fussing Bea in her arms as she challenges against her hold, her little chubby arms outstretched towards me. The familiarity in her blue-grey gaze spears me in my chest, and although it is wrong of me, I know that taking her will be my downfall. I'm barely holding it together as it is. Do you know how hard it is to be happy that she is too young to one day remember this pain and equally sad that she is too young to one day remember her father? Every thought I have feels like a chore, my head throbbing beneath the pressure of trying to survive. Casey hugs Bea to her chest, tickling her to distract her as she senses my need to be left alone, shrouded in my desolation.

'As I'll ever be,' I state, stumbling on the last word, my nerves and unease betraying me. I run my hands down my clothes. Before today I would have said black was my colour, but now it only proves to remind me it is the colour of death. In a little over a month, I have gone from the happiest day of my life to the saddest. I am now the shell of a person. Roni of old is a distant memory forever tarnished by his absence. But today isn't about me; it is about him. This day is to lay my husband to rest; however much it hurts, I vow to make him proud.

'He certainly had a sense of humour,' Casey quips, gesturing towards my outfit.

'It would have been funnier if I had died first,' I snigger, not realising how my response would sound to anyone other than Aiden. Casey's mouth falls open, her hazel eyes wide with concern, and her perfectly plucked eyebrows raised. 'No, it's not what you think,' I cut in as she eyes me curiously. 'It's actually a happy memory, and I haven't experienced many of those lately. It feels ... nice.' I allow the slightest pinch of warmth to tug in my chest, silently pleading with my tears not to fall, my skin sensitive with how many tears I have shed since he died.

'So, tell me. Watching you smile right now makes this a little easier,' Casey practically sings, still bouncing Bea in her embrace, our shared contentment flowing into her little body as she giggles.

'Aiden and I made a bet. Whoever died first had to wear the fancy dress costume the other one wore at Smith's Halloween birthday bash, with subtle corrections, of course.' Her expression is blank as she cannot remember the party I'm referencing. 'That party where you did all kinds of dirty things to that woman dressed as Poison Ivy,' I prompt, and her eyes fizzle with recollection.

'That woman had legs for days,' she quips, snapping her fingers. 'And gonorrhoea,' she finishes after a beat of silence, and I can't contain my bark of laughter as I almost choke on my saliva in surprise. 'So, you're telling me Aiden would have had to dress up as *Jessica Rabbit* at your funeral?' She realises, snippets of that party coming back to her slowly as we reminisce.

'A pinky promise is unbreakable,' I lull with bated breath, my sentiment a hushed whisper, repeating the first line written on the card in the package that held the outfit I am currently wearing. Full-on fringe cowboy chaps, ornately stitched pointed boots, and a wide-brimmed leather hat wouldn't have been my first choice of attire, but, dead or alive, I can't break a promise I made to Aiden. Hashtag cowboy funeral is officially a theme. Just imagining the cocky smile on that man's charming face has stirred the confidence in me that I need to climb into the limo and make my way to the church to say my final goodbye.

~~~~

I pick at the hat's fabric in my lap, fiddling with the rope that decorates it nervously. With my forehead resting against the window, I watch as the world flies by outside, waves of greens, greys and blues almost soothing the mental torture banging around in my head. I shut out the conversation between Aiden's mother and sister next to me as I work Aiden's wedding ring, hanging from a string around my neck next to my father's, between my thumb and forefinger. My attention piques when Paige removes her seat belt, moves forward to the glass partition separating the driver and us, and murmurs something in his ear that I can't catch. As he turns up the radio's volume, Paige slides back into her seat next to me and snaps her belt back into place. I have nowhere to hide now; I can't blank out the memory the song reverberating through the car leaves me with. I put the hat on and pull the brim down to cover my eyes. Soft, silent sobs make my shoulders rise and fall as I try to fight off the intrusion of the memory that I am a slave to, the memory of his end that will forever haunt me for as long as I live.
~~~~

JANUARY 14th 2021

21 DAYS EARLIER

RONI

'Aiden.' I chuckle his name, although it lacks all humour. I gently swipe my foot against his but get no response. His leg is limp. I shuffle a little further into the space, putting the tray down and grabbing for a pillow from the rack above my head.

'There is no way anyone can be comfortable in that position, baby.' I sniff back the hot tears pricking my eyes, confusion making me laugh and cry in the same breath as a sickening wave of reality dawns on me. My senses are on high alert as I try to make sense of the scene playing out in slow motion in front of me. The buzz of the bare overhead bulb feels too bright as it swings on its plastic tethering, the melodic styling of some songstress blaring out from the kitchen, doing nothing to soothe me. I glance at Bea, content and still fast asleep in her car seat. The cuddly blue bunny Aiden had gifted her for Christmas gripped in her little-fisted hands. I drop to my knees in one fluid motion by his side.

The sane part of my panicking brain screams at me to grab my mobile in my bag on the floor beside Aiden. I fumble around inside, cursing myself for the pointless bullshit I have crammed in it that is only slowing down my search. My shaking fingers opt to grip the leather, turn it upside down, and empty the contents onto the floor. I beg my hands to stop trembling as I fight to type the three numbers on the screen. Before I can take control of my panic, Aiden grabs my wrist, tugging the phone from my grasp, pulling my hand to his cold, blue-tinged lips. It's impossible to contain the emotions as my heart plummets to my stomach, bile creeping up my throat.

'Baby.' The word feels too heavy as Aiden struggles to mask the rapid rise and fall of his bare tattooed chest with his splayed palm. His fists flex as he reaches out to take the phone from me, the biting pain attacking his body, almost an alive creature colouring his blue-grey eyes a murky slate. I welcome the wash of relief that courses through me. He *has his eyes open. He is still with us.* Whether or not I want to accept it, on some level, I know that the sense of calm stirring inside me will be short-lived.

'Please, baby, don't. Please.' I don't have long to consider his pleas before his back arches off the floor, jagged puffs of air escaping his clenched lips. He is gripping his side, pushing his fingers into the hollow of his hip in an attempt to subdue the pain, it doesn't matter how hard he tries to hide this from me though, I can see the truth in his wide eyes, fear contorting his strong features as his lips tremble. The fear I see on his face now is unlike any other I've seen before, unguarded for the first time since he told me that day in our kitchen that he was ill.

Stowing away his anguish, holding his girls at bay from the scary reality he has been hiding to protect us. I want to ask why. I want to yell that I would have supported him, that he didn't need to hide his pain from me. But then all the beautiful memories of the past fourteen days flash like a carousel of images in his hazy steel-grey gaze. He has gifted us the memory of him, a collection of memories unmarred by the torture I see on his face now. So, I don't protest or argue or question him; instead, I thank him for all the things he did for us when he was pretending to have strength, for all the moments we got to share because he wanted to protect us, for showing us our forever when he knew he more than likely only had days. Salty tears fall over my lips as they curve up at the edges. The slight sad smile is the only mask I can pull into place, thankfully it seems to warm Aiden as a small smile of his own has his dimples on show. It's gone far too quickly.

An ink blot just beneath the surface of his skin, a bruise-like mass, spreads across his torso like blue wisps of every shade, interconnected rivers that feast too quickly on his veins to keep track of. We sit here, huddled on the floor of our special space, my arms locked around him as I pull him to me, laying his head in my lap. Every breath he takes is heavy but short, as though a weight sits uncomfortably on his chest, his lungs fighting but failing to do what would usually come so naturally to them. I tenderly stroke the sweat-matted strands of hair from his forehead as though his pale skin is delicate porcelain. My voice is taut as I sing *Amazing Grace*, humming the lines I'm unfamiliar with, each word a prayer of its own—a small smile tugs at his lips as he recognises Bea's favourite tune. Time passes, and the pain eases a little as he's notably calmer. A tear runs down his cheek as he looks at our daughter thoughtfully, blinking away the mental agony of what this moment means. Before I grabbed my mobile to call an ambulance, he knew what was coming. Instinct kicks in, and I reach for my mobile again, but with what little energy he has left, Aiden stops me, gripping my hand until his knuckles are white.

'I want to finish it here, in our place, with my girls. I don't want to be anywhere else but by your side.' He squints as the bare bulb above us blinds him, and I don't hesitate to snuff out the light.

'No!' I bark brusquely with a strength I didn't even know I possessed, as though my words have the power to defy him and make it so.

'I will love you for always, baby.' He coughs, spluttering the sentiment as he grips his side again. Tears roll furiously over my sad smile at his words. I have so many things I want to say, but each word catches uncomfortably in my throat. After a few beats, I finally find my voice.

'They never gave you the all clear ... did they?' I accuse, knowing it is the truth even before the words have left my mouth. He doesn't answer me. Instead, he dips his head, confirming my claim.

'I was never getting better, Roni.' He stumbles on his words, biting back the urge to cry, desperate to be strong for me even now. 'If I had to spend this last month watching the light in those eyes fade, it only would have killed me quicker,' he whispers, tentatively running his thumb across my cheek, even though the movement costs him. I lean down into his palm, craving the contact, desperate for his familiar warmth.

'I'm okay,' he assures me, the lie lacking his usual soothing magic. I move to unstrap our sleeping Bea, knowing that nothing I say can stop the inevitable from happening but needing our unit of three to be close. This sad realisation is the emotion that hits me the hardest. It is the one I have zero control over, and there is nothing I can do or say to gloss over this. No matter how hard I wish I could, I can't save him. Pushing the contents of my handbag aside and placing Bea on Aiden's chest, I move to fit around them, encasing them both in my embrace as I wrap myself around Aiden, my cheek resting on his as I stroke his forehead, running my fingers through his hair to settle him. I don't know how much time has passed, but I notice that Aiden's chest is no longer rising and falling as it had been. The arm he had wrapped around Bea is now limp on the floor by his side.

'Aiden,' I grumble meekly through my sobs as I rise on one arm, my lips quivering. 'Aiden,' I repeat, fear choking me as I shake his shoulders tentatively. Everything goes dark, my sight hazy through the tears. I jump to my feet and get a still-sleeping Bea back into her car seat, moving her further into the hallway as Aiden's legs hang out over the threshold. I scramble back to Aiden's side, pushing my tear-stained curls from my face, trying to organise my frantic thoughts. The time for action is now.

'Don't leave me, please, Aiden, please don't leave me here alone,' I beg, my screams strangled. My throat is dry, the air from my lungs coming out in terrified bursts as I try to shake some life into his still form. I punch at his solid chest, panicking that my attempts at CPR are doing more damage than good as I apply more pressure, my considerably smaller body unable to do what he needs. Blowing breath into his mouth, I pinch at his nose, instructions from a year nine health and safety course jumping into the forefront of my mind and guiding me. My thumps on his chest slow as too much time passes, my palms gripping around the back of his neck. Straddling his torso, I pull my best friend up to meet me, fighting to hold him there as gravity pulls his considerably larger form back down to the ground. 'Please, please. Wake up, Aiden,' I plead, my voice almost non-existent. I hug him into my body, locking one arm around his waist, my other hand still secured around his neck and rock back and forth as I often did with Bea when she fought the urge to settle. I run my hands through his hair, keeping us cheek to cheek as I pray to the universe to give my love the second chance he deserves. We are alone, though. No one will save him; no one is here to grant my wish and return him to me.

'We've been gifted more miracles than most,' I say softly over his lips on a broken breath, turning to look at our daughter. Even during the commotion, she sleeps peacefully in her car seat as though her father and I have been locked in our own bubble of grief, all sound lost beyond the wooden closet door. When my fragile body, wracked with grief, can no longer hold him, I gently lay him down, scooting to rest against the wall of our special place, his head in my lap. 'I will love you for always,' I promise him, tears falling from my chin and splashing against his face. I sit for an age that way, his face serene and finally free of pain. I trace my fingers over his features, committing every inch of him to memory, for what I know will be the last time.

~~~~

Bea's crying pulls me from my stupor. My body is unhurried and confused as I take a second to work out where I am and what has happened. I blink away the daze in which I've been lost. I don't know how long she has been crying, but the neighbours are banging on the front door. My eyes are red and sore, my cheeks rough and battered from the streams of tears. I soon realise that Bea's hungry cry has pulled me from the darkness, so it must be at least four hours since she had fallen asleep. I carefully place Aiden's head down onto a crumpled jumper on the floor of our special place and head for our little miracle, scooping her up into my arms, blocking Aiden from her view. I hug her into my body, and she pulls at the neck of Aiden's oversized sweatshirt that I am wearing, impatient to feed. I don't hesitate to pull it over my head to grant her access, but I refuse to drop it, clutching the material in my hand as Bea tugs at my satin camisole, latching onto my painfully engorged breast quickly. Soft, whimsical coos from my little beauty soothe my battered soul a little. I placate the neighbours, apologising profusely and lying about teething or something just as absurd, trying to hold back the grief in my voice until I hear them descending the front steps. Left alone again with my torment, I move back to be with Aiden, sliding down the hardwood slated wall to sit beside him with Bea in one arm as she continues to take what she needs from me. I hold his hand and sit in the darkness for what feels like an eternity, stroking his face as the warmth seeps out of him.
~~~~

As the minutes tick by, the heaviness in my chest grows. It is a slow transition as the life drains from my husband, his soul the last thing to leave the space. I have never felt so alone as wisps of warm air flitter from my trembling lips in the now cold little room. With his hand clasped in mine, I notice the slight tightening of his extremities and the sallow grey hue of his skin. I tug my hand free from his, immediately hating the lack of contact and move shakily onto my knees. Fresh, salty tears hit his chest as I hover over him. Covering him with a blanket, I lay a bruising kiss on his parted full lips, knowing it would likely be for the last time. I shakily get to my feet, carefully edging around his body, bracing myself on the door frame as my legs threaten to give way. Stumbling towards the living room with Bea still gripped in the crook of my arm, my brain is fuzzy and uncooperative. I pick up the landline and call the necessary people, and from that point on, everything is a blur of lights, questions, and confusion. Casey comes over to help with Bea. Even at eight months old, her usually bright face is sad, and grey, her eyes wide as her little mind assesses the situation. Our team of three is now down to two, and we both feel the loss. A part of me wants to roll myself up into the foetal position in our special place until I starve to death, to stop the constant drum of heartache thrumming on a loop in my chest.

I don’t even know who I am without him.

FEBRUARY 4TH 2021

21 DAYS LATER

RONI

I married my husband on a Sunday,

I lost my husband on a Sunday,

I mourned my husband on a Sunday.

Rising to my feet, I make my way to the priest at the head of the church; the stain-glass depictions of the old-school bible teachings encircle him high on the sides of the stone building walls. The tear-tainted paper in my hand rustles as I clench my fist around it, hating that I must deliver my last words to my husband this way.

You can do this, baby.

His voice is clear and soothing in my head as I bite back the heartache constricting my throat. I smooth out the paper on the wooden ledge in front of me with shaking fingers. Closing my eyes, I swallow a calming breath, wanting nothing more than to run from the church, head home, and hide out in our special place. The need to completely block out everything since the day he died makes my heart beat uncomfortably against the ribs trying to contain it. Looking up into the red-rimmed eyes of Aiden's nearest and dearest as they choke back their emotions, their faces hidden behind tissues, I clear my throat and begin to read. I appreciate the comforting smile on Bea's face as my eyes catch on hers; those blue greys remind me of her father's. I smile at her, the familiar façade that slots into place when I'm ready to crumble, a gut reaction I realise I no longer have control over. My psyches' offering of protection does nothing to dispel the thrum of loss that feels like a whole other person trying to take over my body—consuming me, devouring me whole from the inside out, until I'm nothing more than a shell of a broken woman.

You can do this, baby.

I hold on to the words like a comfort blanket, warming my sallow skin just enough to stop my teeth from chattering.

'To the young boy intent on saving the girl, determined to put her needs before his selflessly. To the guy who would walk through fire to tell his friend that she mattered in this world, that she had a soul that could light the stars. To the man that became her protector, her saviour, her soulmate. To the husband who was always carefree, funny and loving, who would surprise her with breakfast in bed and hug her so tightly—his wordless promise to always be by her side.' I sniffle, faltering on every other word as my emotions get the better of me. 'To the father who was taken too early and never afforded the time to excel at something, he was so clearly gifted in. I have lost so many people: my caretaker, my conscience, my best friend, my lover, my secret keeper, my one true love, and the father of my child. But there is something that I haven't lost, something that I will take with me, something that means a little piece of him will always be with me. My memories of Aiden are a gift that I will share with our daughter. Knowing him was an honour, and I thank the heavens that I was blessed with the short time I had with him by my side. He inspired me to be a better person and encouraged me to love harder. He was my light, and although that light has been taken from me, my memories of him will never dull; they will never fade. He will live on through the stories I tell our little girl, and he will live on in my heart until it ceases to beat. I will never stop striving to be the woman that I saw in his eyes. This is not a goodbye, my love. It's a see you later, for always, your baby.' As the last sentiment leaves my lips, I inwardly wince. I know they will forever haunt me, as each one feels as though it's been carved into my flesh, marked on my skin like a tattoo, a constant reminder of my loss.

I begin to fold the piece of paper, wiping at my cheeks as tears stream down my face, an onslaught of memories of him hitting me, the gaping hole in my chest unable to hold them back any longer. I don't dare make eye contact with anyone in the crowd as I make my way to move from the platform. Before I can settle back down into my seat, the priest stops me. The low hum of interest from our friends and family as he places an envelope into my hand has my legs shaking as they threaten to give way. I recognise Aiden's handwriting instantly. The scrawled *Hey Baby* makes me chuckle through a sob. Never one content to let me have the last word; I should have anticipated this.

'He asked me to give you this once you had spoken,' the greying old man said tightly with a small smile. Holding out his robed arm, he ushers me back to the podium. I fight to see the words on the page. My eyesight blurs with tears as my already broken heart shatters a little more.

'Roni, my baby, my wife, my light.' I squeak out, fighting to continue as my hands shake. My forehead is now flush with the stand as I try to regulate my uneven breaths, my lungs struggling against the immense pressure in my chest. I stand up straight to continue reading, his voice in my head encouraging me as it always did. ***I can do this.***

'You are all those things and so much more, sadly more than I will ever get to thank you for. I will forever be grateful for everything you gave me and the happiness you brought into my life. Without you, I wouldn't have been half the man I was, and I want you to remember that when the days get dark or when you feel alone. I will always be with you and Bea, watching over you both. Remember me, miss me, mourn me, but not for too long, baby. Miracles happen; I promise you that. You were mine, after all, so I know it's true. I was the luckiest guy in the world to have had you and Bea in my life. To have been gifted the honour of calling you both mine. Now wipe away those tears, baby, and let's get this fucking party started.'

I will love you for always. Aiden

An audible groan falls from my lips, a part of me dying all over again as the weight of his words hits me anew. The unexpected chuckle that follows, bursting out of my mouth without warning, takes me and everyone else by surprise when the priest flips a switch, and the *Black-Eyed Peas ' Let's Get This Party Started'* blares out into the church. Snapshots of our wedding day fill my mind. Aiden twirling me around our garden, ropes of twinkling, lights warming us from above, his fingers caressing my cheek, his large body caging me in to the warmth of my favourite place, our souls finally offered the forever he had promised me—the forever that sadly could never be fulfilled. Bringing the letter to my lips, I silently thank my husband for his final gift. A gift that I know, with time, will help to heal the broken parts of me.

MARCH 12th 2021

JUST OVER ONE MONTH LATER

RONI

When he died, I hated him. I hated him for everything he hadn't said, for the years we missed out on, and for the memories we would never get the chance to make. He was my all, and then he was gone. When my best friend died, I hated him for all the things he didn't do, for all the things I didn't do. I hated him because I hated myself for not saving him. But what I hated most was that I never really hated him at all, not one bit. He left me here to remember and guard the memories of us, of everything we had created together. All those times his hand grazed mine, when his lips were mere inches from my face, and the times he made me laugh so hard I couldn't see straight. My heart was irreparably shattered into a million pieces the day he left me; the love of my life was gone. I was a new version of myself that was dark, damaged and devoid of hope, forced to watch as my best friend slipped through my fingers. There was too much information to process in those first few days that followed his death. The assurances of his remission had been a work of fiction, a lie he had kept to himself so as not to hurt me. But all he'd done was delay the inevitable. The cancer had returned, and aggressive was a lukewarm description in the grand scheme of the deterioration that had been happening in his body. Rebelling against the prognosis set for him by medical professionals was a testament to his fiery tenacity to proudly hold up a middle finger to anyone who set forth to tell him how he would live out his last days. Those final days about which I had no idea.

A shopping trip rouse Aiden had planned a week before Christmas hid his appointment with his doctor, his advisement to Aiden to get his affairs in order and to say his goodbyes falling on deaf ears as Aiden instead pushed to plan a wedding. He never uttered a word about that day at the hospital, instead choosing to gift Bea and me with a little under a month's worth of days wrapped up in our beautiful little world of three. A time unmarred by the ugly truth that would soon steal any modicum of happiness that once danced hopefully like fireflies between us. But they couldn't possibly thrive; trapped in a blacked-out box with no air, they tinkered crazily around the space as they fought to survive the loneliness and anguish that tore at my insides. It was as though Aiden had staved off his illness. Our wedding and Bea's first Christmas being the last additions on his bucket list, he could finally cave to the pressures that had been quietly attacking his body from the inside out for the past year. He had been holding it at bay, enjoying Bea and me to the fullest until his body couldn't stand it any longer—until the life drained out of him that night on the floor of our special place.

It was the small things I missed the most. Fighting over whose job it was to wash up after a house party, badgering him every Sunday morning to make the post-hangover coffee run to Starbucks. I spent the rest of that third day after we buried Aiden trying to think of something we hadn't done, an experience that he hadn't gifted me, but I couldn't come up with a single thing. A memory buried so deep I had almost forgotten about it presented itself. Wrapped up neatly in a big red bow as though it had been preparing for its revelation the whole time, waiting for the exact moment I would need it most.

The time – Three AM. The place – Parsons Green, London. Drinks – Stopped counting at Tequila shot number six. Song of the night – Shakira's Hips Don't Lie. Shoes – one, three if you count his; he was always good at ensuring he ended the night with two. For some reason, I liked to throw mine at pigeons in a drunken haze. Before the oohs and aahs. I'm not a monster; I never hit one; the challenge just unexpectedly became a tradition. I couldn't throw straight when I was sober, so intoxication would hardly have helped me. After way too many drinks, a packet of cigarettes I had found crumpled up at the bottom of my handbag, and a suspiciously greasy kebab takeaway, we were strolling through the park. The dimly lit Christmas lights were still high in the tree branches that flanked either side of the pebble pathway; their sparkle was still strong even after the festive season had officially been and gone. Even with only one shoe, a grease stain down the front of my blush pink racer dress and the breath of ten drunk sailors, it was still the most romantic encounter I would ever have before Aiden and I officially got together. Aiden had a way of seeing the bright side of pretty much any situation. He always said there was nothing a hot bag of chips, a hug and a Fawlty Towers marathon couldn't fix. Even then, before we had admitted to the feelings that bounced between us, he saw me for who I was. He was my safe place.

On the seventh day after we said goodbye to Aiden for the last time, my heart felt a little less broken. I realised it had been easier to feel angry than it had to feel sad. On day seven, I took Aiden's advice and tried to look on the bright side. I'd had him; however short it may have been, he had been mine, and I had been his completely. I was both scared and excited when that first Sunday since he passed rolled around, scared because I couldn't remember the last Sunday I had spent without him, excited because It was the first day I actually felt him with me, as though he couldn't possibly miss our Sunday dates, even in spirit. I propped my feet on the coffee table and pulled the cover over my legs. I pressed play on the remote, opened the paper-wrapped bacon sandwiches on my lap and watched as our beautiful daughter tottered into the room on unsteady feet, pulling herself up onto the sofa next to me and snuggling her little body into mine until she was comfortable. On the seventh day after Aiden's funeral, I started to live again, not as bright or as contented as I once had. Still, as I looked down to my left, I realised that Aiden had left behind the best part of himself, a gift I could cherish for always; our daughter would forever be our greatest accomplishment. She would remind me daily of how much I loved her father, of how much he loved us. She would be the part of that beautiful man with whom I got to share my life. On the seventh day of the next chapter in my life, the chapter without him, I cried a little less. The tormented voice of my heart ache softer. I had a lifetime to tell our little girl all the amazing things her father did, to let her know what a brilliant man he had been. She would know her father, and our story would continue. Aiden wasn't wrong when he said that miracles happen, though. He had one more in store for us—a parting gift of sorts.

Well, Aiden was always one for a surprise, after all.

AUGUST 23RD 2021

FIVE MONTHS LATER

RONI

I sit on the sofa in our living room, glancing around at the framed photos decorating the flower-papered wall to my left, admiring the bright and colourful history of our past that hangs there. I haven't changed a thing since Aiden's death. The overflow of plastic toys that belong to Bea, the noisiest ones now missing their batteries, crowding the far corner beside the black wrought iron fireplace, is the only difference to our surroundings. Before I can wallow in my sadness again, my emotions running rampant recently, the door clunks against the marble doorstop as Bea strolls into the room. Garbed in a blue princess dress adorned with plastic crystals, the tatty blue bunny teddy with chocolate splotched matted fur secured to her waist with a gauzy sash. The scent of Aiden's aftershave soaked into the stuffing as Bea refuses to let me wash it. Her hair is up in two uneven little bunches, except for the impromptu fringe falling over her face; she's oddly proud of the wonky chunk of hair she had cut herself with a pair of kiddie scissors. The pair of neon pink *my little pony* sunglasses she's wearing mask her big blue-grey eyes. An array of sparkly rings adorn every finger on one hand. Ever the drama queen, my daughter stills in the entryway with her hands on her hips as though addressing her avid followers.

'Well, hello, madam. I'm getting rockstar vibes,' I say, stifling the amused grin tugging at my lips. I am grateful she has pulled my focus from my despondency, my heart swelling as I appreciate her grandeur entrance. If there is a show to be made, Bea Cassandra O'Shea will forever be front and centre.

'Mama!' she exclaims excitedly, but her movements don't match her energy. Taking a few more tentative steps into the room, Bea pushes a plastic shopping cart filled with the paper bags containing our bacon sandwiches – the ones we consume every Sunday in honour of her father. Under the paper bags is an older, greyer Doris who meows her protests at being crammed into such a small uncomfortable space, all four legs up in the air. Old age stops her from moving as she sinks further into the cart. With her free hand, Bea holds a Peach *Ribena* carton, the straw secured between her lips as she takes a sip, comically sighing as she swallows the drink as though she is parched. I finally see myself in our little Bea for the first time since she was born. Although, I would have been rocking a porn star martini, wearing a pair of *Raybans* and in a dress far more fitted with less of the fanfare.

'Mama,' she coos again, making my heart swoon, the word a direct call to my soul. Pulling me out into the hallway, Bea directs me to the wardrobe space by the front door, the special place that her father and I had shared on so many occasions. I had fought to open the door every day since we buried Aiden, not wanting to air whatever ghosts lay dormant there. I can't fight it anymore, though, not if Bea had gone in search and felt drawn to it. I promised myself that I would hide no part of her father from her, drink, drugs and debauchery aside. I wanted her to know this place. Not everyone could say they fell in love cooped up in a 4-foot-4 walk-in closet, after all. I whine as I slide down the wooden slat wall of our special space, my spine creaking in protest, the ache in my knees throbbing, yet another reminder of my current condition. Memories of that night hit me, each flash of his face in the forefront of my mind threatening to break me with as much force as they had the night he had left us. But I clear my throat and fight through it. Bea deserves better than the broken woman I had been. She deserves all the happiness and light that the memories of my relationship with Aiden could ignite, and if it is the last thing I do, I will give that to her.

'Hello, baby. You there, baby?' Bea questions as she places her tiny hands around my swollen midriff. A little annoyance colours her tone as she still can't grasp why her brother, growing strong in my belly, doesn't answer her. After months of her little one-sided conversations, it still proves to make her snap. *Brothers and sisters love each other eventually, right?* I giggle at the thought. She is already a mini Mumma bear. Our little boy will indeed have his life planned out by Bea, whether he likes it or not.

'I have chocolate and toys, lots of toys,' she exclaims, stumbling a little on the word chocolate, selling her side of the bribery case well, if I'm honest. I don't have long before our little boy enters the world. I hadn't known about Aiden's final gift on our wedding night until three months after his funeral. That cocky bastard must be smiling up there, knowing that his little *'miracles do happen'* line had worked its way perfectly into our lives. I grip my chest as that familiar sadness at the memory of his roguish grin hits me like a sledgehammer. Although now it doesn't hurt; it merely reminds me to honour him and strive to be the strong independent woman he had said with conviction that I was. With our sandwiches consumed and the early nineties indie tunes blasting from the kitchen radio, my heart and head finally agree to settle on the same page. I caress Bea's soft pink cheek, my other hand running over my belly, determined to include our unborn son in the memory I am forming. I swallow a calming breath, making a silent promise to myself as I enjoy our time in my happy place. I will face the next chapter of my life with the memory of my best friend by my side. I don't even need to ask myself how he felt about us. I know without any doubt that he would love us for always, that he would be with us for always and that he would undoubtedly miss us for always ... as we would him, in this life and the next. Bea rests her head in the crook of my arm, snuggling into my body. I dip my head to kiss her forehead, inhaling her candyfloss and bubble bath scent. She stares up at me, a warm smile pinching her cheeks.

'Your daddy always gave the best presents,' I coo as I sweep her wonky fringe from her eyes, admiring the familiarity in her grey-blue gaze that reminds me so much of him as she stares up at me lovingly. The hope and wonder I so sorely need to survive settles there in her little impish face. It may not have been the happily ever after that I was expecting, but it was one that I would grip tightly to my chest with both hands.

My memories of him frozen in time won't fade, but the thoughts of him will. He will slowly transition from my first thought of every day, steadily becoming a daydream that will catch me off guard sometimes. But I vow to hold his love in my heart, sandwiched between the folds because Aiden O'Shea is the reason it beats and understands what love is.

Every love story has a journey; however crazy, messed up, and awesome it may have been, this was ours.

THE END

AUTHORS NOTE

Thankyou to everyone who has got to this point and read VERONICA. If it wasn't for my readers Roni and Aiden's story would never have been created. This story has been a labour of love filled with trauma, fear, fate and emotion that like every author finds, started out as an idea I was at first too scared to explore. Not every book is for every person and even knowing that there is a certain element of vulnerability that every author faces sharing their stories with the world. I'd like to thank every author of every book that has pushed me and inspired me to put my thoughts and ideas down on to paper, you don't know how much your words have touched my soul.

Roni and Aiden's story, although parts of my tortured soul live within the pages, I want it to resonate and hopefully touch my readers, possibly help them to understand, imagine or even overcome a theme they may relate with in my writing. My books are for you readers, they always have been, thank you for taking this journey with me.

If you would like to chat about the book, please feel free to find me online, I love to chat all things bookish on Facebook, Instagram and TikTok so follow the links and let's be book buddies.

Author Billie Jade Kermack | Facebook

https://www.instagram.com/billiejadekermackauthor/

Author Billie jade Kermack (@authorbilliejadekermack)

Goodreads – Billie Jade Kermack

Tiktok – Author Billie Jade Kermack

Facebook – Author Billie Jade Kermack

Instagram – billie jade Kermack author

There will be many more adventures to follow in the twisted fates series so if you enjoyed Roni and Aiden's story, please follow us on the socials for updates of new releases. More interest makes me write that little bit faster.

ACKNOWLEDGEMENTS

First and foremost is thanks to my other half, the man who has supported me without question since day one, funnelling me support, love, laptops and money to keep my dreams alive for more years than I can count. All that support and he isn't a reader, his eyes wide when I turn around and tell him I finished reading an entire novel in a day because I couldn't put it down. Not much else got done on those days but rather than ask where his work shirts are or what's for dinner instead he listens to me intently babble on about characters he will never know, in a world he will never experience with an interested gaze as he orders a takeaway on his phone. You my love will never know how much your support means to me, you will never know how much your understanding has allowed me to do a craft I love, to give other people stories they can adore.

To Caron Pescatore and Kia McMillian, I've never met women like you two, women intent to build a fellow author up, women determined to support someone they have never met in person, women that I consider my sisters, because without you both I don't think I would have got through the publishing of this book. I am in awe of the beauty and grace you both possess, and I will forever cherish the friendship you have extended to me. I am here for you both always.

To my kids, for keeping me current in the social world, although the youngest still believes the whole world was black and white when I was young, it hurts but the laughter helps the healing process. You three are my reason for living and I couldn't be prouder to call you mine.

To my dad, who passed away too soon. I may have been six and you only twenty-eight, but you live in the bones of everything I write. My emotional rock tethering me to my characters, to tell their stories with honesty and heart. You inspire me daily to fight for what I want, to enjoy everything I have and to never take anything for granted. You live on in my words, in my stories and in our memories.

To my family, if you have got this far, hey hey mutherfuckers, welcome to the party that is my imagination. It may be a shitshow sometimes but it's my shitshow and I love it. You guys rock for all the support you've shown me, letting me throw ideas at you even when you didn't ask for them, prepare for round two because I have plenty more ideas coming your way.

Lightning Source UK Ltd.
Milton Keynes UK
UKHW010734130123
415295UK00001B/20

9 781739 098735